RITA fina

"In modern romance, the described as 'that man of lo ble that no one writes him bett books are as dark and dangerous as

—Buried Unde

"Meredith Duran unceasingly delights and a master at understanding the elemen complex, genuine, and lovable characters."

"Incredible sensuality. . . . Crazy hot."

—Fiction Vix

"Spellbinding. . . . Meredith Duran's writing is polished and sophisticated."

—Books With Benefits

"Engrossing and unexpected, this may be Duran's finest novel yet."

—RT Book Reviews

THAT SCANDALOUS SUMMER
RT Book Reviews Top Pick

"Sophisticated, witty, smart romance."

—RT Book Reviews

"A powerful story with emotional punch. . . . A joy to read."

—The Romance Dish

"Charming and deliciously sensual from beginning to end."
—*Romantic Times*

"Witty, often hilarious, sensuous, and breathlessly paced."
—*Library Journal*

"Sexy, inventive, and riveting, it's hard to put down and a joy to read."
—*All About Romance*

"Rousing . . . delightful . . . heartwarming, with deeply affecting emotions."
—*Single Titles*

WRITTEN ON YOUR SKIN
**RT Book Reviews Top Pick and a *Romantic Times*
Best Historical Romance Adventure award nominee**

"Mesmerizing . . . a glorious, nonstop, action-packed battle-of-wills romance."

—*Romantic Times* (4½ stars)

"Wildly romantic."

—*Dear Author* (Grade: A+)

"Everything a great historical romance should be."

—*Romance Junkies*

BOUND BY YOUR TOUCH
**A Best Book of 2009 in *All About
Romance*'s Reviewer's Choice column**

"Sophisticated, beautifully written, and utterly romantic."

—*The Book Smugglers*

"A great love story. . . . I found new layers and meaning each time I read it."

—*Dear Author*

THE DUKE OF SHADOWS
**Finalist for the *Romantic Times*
Best Historical Debut award**

"Riveting . . . emotion-packed. . . . A guaranteed page-turner."

—*The Romance Reader* (4 stars)

"Without a doubt the best historical romance I have read this year."

—*Romance Reviews Today*

MEREDITH DURAN

LADY BE GOOD

POCKET BOOKS

New York   London   Toronto   Sydney   New Delhi

Pocket Books
An Imprint of Simon & Schuster, Inc.
1230 Avenue of the Americas
New York, NY 10020

This book is a work of fiction. Any references to historical events, real people, or real places are used fictitiously. Other names, characters, places, and events are products of the author's imagination, and any resemblance to actual events or places or persons, living or dead, is entirely coincidental.

First Pocket Books paperback edition August 2015

POCKET and colophon are registered trademarks of Simon & Schuster, Inc.

For information about special discounts for bulk purchases, please contact Simon & Schuster Special Sales at 1-866-506-1949 or business@simonandschuster.com.

The Simon & Schuster Speakers Bureau can bring authors to your live event. For more information or to book an event, contact the Simon & Schuster Speakers Bureau at 1-866-248-3049 or visit our website at www.simonspeakers.com.

Manufactured in the United States of America

10 9 8 7 6 5 4 3 2 1

ISBN 978-1-4767-4137-6
ISBN 978-1-4767-4140-6 (ebook)

For Estelle, Madeleine, Grace, and Sophia—
may all your stories end happily

ACKNOWLEDGMENTS

When one's acknowledgments continually generate a sense of déjà vu, it's an excellent sign that one's life is blessed with friends and family who deserve far more gratitude than a single page could contain. My thanks, as always, to the usuals: S. J. Kincaid, whose gift for encouragement is rivaled only by the inspiration her talent provides me; The Family Duran, of Oakland and Denver; Lady Rohlfs, Doctor of Law, Philosophy, and Unrivaled Weekends in St. Louis; Janine Ballard, Critique Partner for the Ages; Lauren McKenna and Elana Cohen, who make Pocket Books feel like home; and my husband, who keeps me fed, rested, encouraged, amused, optimistic, amazed, and impossibly happy. (Happy ever after, indeed.)

Kit's Charge

Who o'er yonder battlement, when enemy drums did pound,
Did shout the name of Britain, and vow to stand his ground;
Who for sake of Queen and Country, pressed forward unafraid,
As through the hills of Bekhole, he led the fateful raid—

What courage lifted him through that dark and bloody vale!
What brave emboldened heart, where ordinary man must pale!
Nary a flinch or falter, nor thought of turning back—
"Onward," he commanded, "to the ridge; attack!"

For him alone does England, which tenderly forged his mettle,
Await the end of battle, and the dreadful smoke to settle.
We pray God his soul to keep, his awful duty to acquit,
For our nation's pride rests soundly on our brave and noble Kit.

His mother's face so tearful, his father's lit with pride—
These visions linger with him at every desperate stride.
Our grateful praise and adulation, our applause so proudly won—
He hears nothing but the cannon, until the bloody war is done.

Together will we gather, on that destined glorious day,
To welcome home our hero, with garlands bright and gay
And cry out the name that rings in every patriot's soul:
Major John Christian Stratton, Hero of Bekhole!

PROLOGUE

London, March 1882

$\mathcal{S}$he was stuck between two buildings and she was going to die.

It took Lily a minute to reach this conclusion. How quickly a night went downhill! She'd not been prepared to do a job tonight. Uncle had assigned it to Fiona days ago. But then Fee had taken sick. *Don't worry,* Lily had told her. *I'll do the job.* Sisters looked out for each other, didn't they? *You just rest now.*

But overnight, Fee had grown feverish and weak. Barely able to explain the job. *Look in the drawer under the till,* she'd said. *He never keeps it locked.*

Lily had found the deed just where Fiona had told her, beneath the till in the unlocked drawer. But Fee hadn't warned her of the guards. They'd come barreling out of the back room and fired without a warning. Pigs! Decent men offered a girl the chance to surrender before they shot her.

You're all right. Just a flesh wound. So Uncle Nick would say. But the gunshot had deafened her, and it burned like the dickens. Disoriented, in pain, Lily had taken off running. No chance of sticking to the plan. She'd ducked down an alley she'd never used before.

Turned out this alley wasn't an alley, after all—only the space between two buildings that had pulled apart over time. The passage had kept narrowing, damp walls hugging tighter and tighter . . . until they pinned her.

She took a deep breath and tried to jam herself forward.

No luck.

This couldn't be happening. Tonight of all nights, she had to get free. Fee was bad off. Surgeon said it was an organ gone rotten. He meant to operate. Lily needed to be there, holding her sister's hand, not stuck in this bloody alley!

God, why was it so dark? The eaves above blocked out the stars. The cold damp air reeked of rot.

Fee didn't like doctors. She needed Lily there when the surgeon made his cut.

On a great agonizing effort, Lily pressed forward. The ringing in her ears was fading now. She heard her own wheeze, and voices from the street she'd fled. One of the guards. "I tell you, I saw her go in there," he said.

"Between the bleeding buildings? Ain't space enough for a rat."

"She squeezed in."

"Then she'll rot in there."

No, no, no. If only there were a bit of light! These buildings pressed tighter than a coffin—

Stay calm. She focused on the pain, her arm burning like live coal.

Fee felt worse, though. She'd looked so bad, earlier. Yellow-faced, muttering nonsense. Lily had tried to calm her. She'd recited that poem Fee loved, about the war hero. It chanted through her mind now, singsong:

> What courage lifted him through that dark and
>   bloody vale!
> What brave emboldened heart, where ordinary
>   man must pale!

She could do this. Clenching her jaw, she fought for another step. Like stone jaws, the walls clamped around her.

Oh, God. She swallowed the taste of blood. *Fee, forgive me.* She couldn't go farther.

"Lily."

She was so tired. If only she could lie down. But the press of the buildings wouldn't let her sit.

"Damn it, you stupid girl! Make a noise!"

"Uncle . . . ?"

"Yes. That's it. Follow my voice, now."

She squinted into the blackness. Uncle Nick's voice came from ahead, the far side. But the passage narrowed to a pin's width, first. She would never fit through. "I'm stuck."

"Then unstick yourself."

"Can't!"

"I say you can."

He was always bossing her. It was his fault she was stuck, didn't he see that? Fiona had told him they were done with thieving. Fee had grand plans; had found them both places at a typing school, with ambitions to go higher. They could be decent ladies, she'd told Lily. Earn a living as honest girls did.

But Nick wouldn't permit that. *You've got a duty to your family,* he'd said. *Do what you like, but as long as you're under my roof, you'll earn your keep here.*

"Come on, then, Lily." Nick crooned the words, like she was a stubborn baby. "Only another few steps."

This was *his* fault. "You happy now?" She panted the words. "Got your . . . deed. You'll have to . . . pull it out . . . with a hook." Along with her. "I'm done for."

"Move." His voice got hard. "Make yourself. *Push.*"

The crush of the walls—she couldn't bear it. In the dark, seeing nothing, not even stars . . . only rats died this way.

We deserve better, Fee had said. *An honest life, free of fear.*

"The surgery's done, Lily. But Fee's bad off still. She needs you now."

God above! Tears salted her mouth. "I *can't!*" Her voice sounded strange. Shrill and wheezy. "Help me!"

She heard a grunt. Nick was coming for her. Hope revived. Her uncle was bossy, sometimes cruel—but he'd never leave her to die here. She was family, after all. He'd get her out. She reached out a hand, praying fervently—only let his hand reach her; only let her feel his grip—

Her fist closed on empty air.

He spoke calmly. "All right, it's tight." She heard her death in those words. "But you're small. What's stopping you?"

What wasn't? "My shoulders—"

"Shoulders come out of their sockets," he said flatly. "Push forward. We'll set it after."

For a moment she didn't understand.

"Break your fucking shoulder," he bit out. "Do it, Lily! Or I *will* haul you out with a hook. Is that what you'd prefer?"

"I hate you," she whispered. If it weren't for him, for the job *he'd* wanted done tonight, she never would have run into those guards.

"Fiona's going to die." His voice seemed to come from far away. "Unless she sees you tonight. She needs her little sister."

A gasp slipped from her. To fail Fee now, the only time she'd ever needed Lily's help—

Her lungs wouldn't fill. No room for it. But Lily shoved herself forward. Ah, God, the passage was so tight. She made an inch of headway. Then another.

A horrible pressure bore down on her shoulder. A fist of stone and steel, it would snap her spine.

She drove into it.

A *cracking*, God in heaven, the worst agony, she could not hold back her cry. The walls fell away and she was on her knees in the dirt, her arm . . . Ah, it *hurt*.

An icy wind raked over her. Hands closed over her waist, pulling her up. She gaped helplessly into the dark shadow looming over her. *Never again.* The words rang through her brain. "We're done," she gasped. She and Fiona were *done*.

The hands held her roughly in place. Searched her body, pausing only briefly at the evidence of blood. She felt her uncle locate the deed. He tucked it away with one hand, holding her up with the other.

"Come on," he said roughly, turning her toward the road. "We'll take you to Malloy, get you stitched up."

Malloy? No. There was a real doctor waiting. The surgeon with her sister. "Fee," she managed.

A hesitation. "I'm sorry, Lily."

She blinked and tried to bring him into focus. But with the streetlamps guttering and the clouds blocking the moon, his face was lost in shadow. "What?"

His grip tightened around her waist. "He gave his best. I made sure of it. But Fiona passed. She's gone."

Northwest Frontier Province, India

"The Hero of Bekhole. How many more will die at your hands?"

The sneering words came to Christian through a haze of agony. Every inch of his body burned. He remembered the explosion, fire billowing toward him like a sheet. *I am going to die*, he had thought. And then . . . what?

He forced his eyes open. It felt as though a hot poker had been jammed into his leg in place of the bone. The darkness resolved into a low stone ceiling above him, rough rock. A cave?

Somehow he was alive.

Groaning, he pushed himself upright. He lay on a rudimentary cot. His vision focused on the flames of a candelabrum sitting on the earthen floor.

He was hallucinating. The candelabrum was ornately molded from gem-encrusted gold, marred by a single dent. Rubies, sapphires, emeralds reflected the shimmering light.

"I asked you a question, Major Stratton."

The voice was male. Heavily accented. *Russian.* Christian would have flinched had he had the strength. Instead he squinted into the depths of the cave. "I am an officer of Her Majesty's Army. By the rights accorded . . ."

Something was wrong with his throat. His voice sounded threadbare, ragged. It felt like a razor in his throat.

The silence extended so long that he began to wonder if he'd dreamed the voice. *Turn, look around you, get up. Get moving.* His men would be searching for him— if any had survived.

He waited for the strength to do it. So dizzy. He wanted only to lie back again. To lie still and surrender to the mercy of unconsciousness.

"What rights," said the voice, "did you accord to the woman and children you murdered?"

"What?" He paused to catch his breath. His lungs were shot. "I don't . . ."

Memory flickered, like lightning in a far-off field. It drew closer. It broke over him, showing what he'd forgotten. The moments after the explosion.

A man leaning over him, white-bearded, wild eyes reflecting the flames around him. He had raved in a language that Christian did not speak. And then he had spoken in English: *My seed. My seed! You have murdered my seed!*

"Bolkhov," he whispered. The mad Russian general. That was who had him.

Bolkhov was infamous. A lunatic who had refused to accept the end of the war. Repudiated by their own army, his rogue troops had wreaked havoc across the southern territories of Afghanistan, moving at last into the Northwest Frontier of India. They obeyed no codes of decency. They slaughtered entire villages, framing the British for their atrocities. They slit throats like butchers on market day.

He waited to be afraid. But the pain left no room for other feelings. What could Bolkhov do to him? Slit his throat, too. End this misery. It would be a mercy.

The cowardice of that thought registered. It goaded him to try to sit up again. To stand.

But his leg was a red-hot blade. Sparks hazed his vision as he collapsed onto the cot.

The laughter began sharply, then faded into a dream. Christian dreamed of green fields, Susseby, his family embracing him . . .

Bolkhov's voice called him back. "What business has God with you? You, the murderer of innocents."

There had been no innocents in that fortress.

"You have slaughtered his children. You have murdered his handmaidens."

The fortress should not have exploded. The battery of cannons should have destroyed the ramparts to enable a direct assault.

"You mined them," Christian realized. "The . . . fort walls."

"You will place this sin on me?" The enraged roar came very close now. From the darkness emerged Bolkhov, his face a mask of soot, his white beard stained with blood. "You are the murderer of my seed. My line is dead!" His eyes filled with the dancing light of candle flame. "Women and children. God's lambs."

Insanity's own face loomed over Christian. There had been no children in that fortress. It stood in the deep, cold reaches of the Hindu Kush. No one had occupied it for centuries—until Bolkhov's men had seized it for their base of operations. "What children?"

Bolkhov leaned low, baring teeth stained pink. The

teeth of some wild predator who had drunk blood. "*My*
children."

A cold clarity briefly muted the pain. There had been
rumors . . . bizarre rumors, that Bolkhov stole women
from the nearby villages. That he also carried with him
three Afghan women, abducted at the start of the late
war, all of whom he called wives.

But those were only rumors. Christian and his men
had reconnoitered the fortress for weeks. They had
never seen any sign of civilians.

"My line is dead," Bolkhov said. "And in return, I
will end yours. Everyone whom you love."

Something glittered—a blade. Bolkhov laid it against
Christian's cheek, pressing until the blade bit. Christian
did not move. Did not allow himself to blink. He would
meet his death with eyes open.

A thousand memories rushed through him: the green
rolling parkland of Susseby; the softness of his mother's
palm on his brow; the joy in his sister's face every time
he returned home; his father's gruff nods. His brother's
grin.

Everything in the world that mattered to him. *Home.*

"I would take out your eyes," Bolkhov said softly.
"But they are my gift to you, so you may watch. Watch
as I slaughter your beloveds, as you have slaughtered
mine." He lifted something. A ring. Christian's ring,
which his father had given him. *Go with my blessing.
Never forget that I am proud of you.* "I will start by returning this to them."

"No." The word slipped from him, inadvertently
driving the blade deeper. Hot blood slipped down his
cheek.

"Oh yes." Bolkhov lifted away the blade. "We will

make sure you are in good health to witness these deaths. My men will take care of you. And while you recover . . ." He smiled. "I will pay my respects. In England, I will call on Viscount Palmer, proud sire of the Hero of Bekhole."

Christ God. Fear finally penetrated. Those goddamned journalists had made a hero of Christian. They had advertised his biography to the world. This lunatic would know precisely where to find his family.

On a great roaring effort, Christian lunged to his feet. His hands closed around the candelabrum. He turned.

The knife caught him in the belly. He staggered. A great weight struck his skull.

He knew no more.

CHAPTER ONE

April 1886

There was room for only one thief in this ballroom. Yet a newcomer had slipped past the guards and was attempting to pickpocket the crowd.

Lilah watched with increasing dismay. Dukes and princes vied for invitations to the annual ball at Everleigh's Auction Rooms. It seemed impossible that a ragamuffin could infiltrate their company. Yet this urchin did not belong. She was pale, underfed, and poorly dressed. The sleeves of her gown flapped around her elbows.

Worse, she had hands like hams. Her mark felt her brush against him, then politely sidestepped before she could take his watch.

Lilah winced. In a second, some well-heeled guest would cry for the police. That would ruin everything, for Lilah could not afford police on the premises tonight.

Tonight, for the last time, *Lilah* must be the thief in this ballroom.

"What do you say, Lil?"

Forcing a smile, Lilah turned back to her friends. Like her, Susie and Lavender were Everleigh Girls, professional hostesses paid to flatter and cosset potential clients of the auction house. Their evening's task was straightforward: to direct the guests' attention and curiosity toward the salons adjoining the ballroom, which contained various collections bound for auction this season.

But while each of the girls had been given a list of guests to focus upon, Susie and Lavender had wasted the last five minutes locked in argument about somebody else—a celebrity important enough to be attended by Miss Everleigh rather than the hostesses.

They stared at Lilah, waiting for her to settle the debate.

But she had no opinion about Viscount Palmer. "I can see both perspectives," she said.

Susie flushed. "What? Nonsense! Everybody knows he was tortured in the war. Where else did he get that scar?" She shoved a dark curl back under her feathered headpiece, the gesture aggressive. "You can't imagine the Russians are *merciful* to their enemies."

Lavender, to whom this challenge was directed, lifted her shoulder in an elegant shrug. "Not all Russians are savages. Count Obolensky, for instance, seems very gentlemanly. Oh dear—weren't you supposed to corner him, Sue?"

Susie gasped, then cast a wild look around the room. "Drat it! He was the last on my list—I was meant to show him the samovars. I'll be dead if I've lost him!"

Lavender gave Lilah a smug look. "Never let them go until they've seen the goods," she said. "I finished with *my* list before supper was laid. And now . . ." She idly flipped through her dance cards, then wrinkled her nose. "Pah! That dratted German has claimed all my waltzes. Quick, who has a pencil? I'm scratching him out."

"Forget your German!" Susie turned full circle, her plum silk train knocking into Lilah's. "Help me find Obolensky. Do you see him?"

Lilah saw worse: the thief had grown bolder. She had abandoned the wall and was making a dash toward the exhibits. "I'll check the salons," she said. "Susie, you look by the punch table; Vinnie, try the hall."

Before they could reply, Lilah slipped into the crowd. As she cut across the dance floor, she spotted Miss Everleigh dancing with the object of the girls' argument.

The scar across Viscount Palmer's cheek was generally accounted to be dashing. Certainly it did not hurt his looks. He was the picture of virile, laughing health: tall and broad shouldered, with thick gold hair and eyes to match. In Whitechapel, the girls would have called him a goer.

In fact, they *had* called him a goer. Her sister, Fiona, had clipped his likeness from the newspapers, and eagerly followed tales of his wartime bravery. *A true gentleman,* she'd called him. *This is the kind of lad we deserve, Lily.*

Had she lived, she would have been disappointed by the stiff competition for him. Now that he'd inherited the viscountcy, he was catnip for wealthy debutantes. One of the most eligible bachelors in the country— so Lilah had overheard Mr. Everleigh telling his sister recently.

He's a useless flirt, Miss Everleigh had replied coldly.

As Lilah passed, she caught sight of Palmer's dimpled smile—undoubtedly flirtatious—and Miss Everleigh's grimacing reply.

Ha! The viscount would dash himself against *those* rocks until his bones broke. Gents called Miss Everleigh the "Ice Queen" for a reason. She had no interest in pretty smiles, or human beings, for that matter; art was all she cared for.

Lilah returned her attention to her quarry. Some animal instinct caused the thief to glance up. Their eyes met. The thief ducked into a salon.

Drat it! Lilah dashed after her. By a statue of Catherine the Great, she caught the girl's elbow, then ducked a slash of nails. "Enough!" She shoved the girl by the shoulders through a set of curtains into a shallow alcove.

The girl punched Lilah in the belly—or tried; there was no muscle to her. Lilah caught her fist and twisted it hard behind the girl's back, jamming it between her scrawny shoulder blades. One good shove slammed the girl against the wall, where she squirmed and hissed like a cat.

"Quiet," Lilah said. "Bleeding fool! Or I'll yell for the police."

The girl's eyes opened wide. "'Oo are you? Yer no nob!"

Lilah snorted. A common mistake, expecting to find easy marks in a ballroom. Without ceremony, she groped down the girl's skirts—then made a warning sound as the girl tried to jerk free.

The hidden pocket was poorly disguised. Lilah pulled out a bracelet, a glimmering skein of black pearls and Whitby jet that made her stomach sink. She knew to whom this belonged.

Her expression must have reflected her feelings, for when she glanced up, the urchin went pale. "Please," the girl stammered, "I . . ." She bit her lip and ducked her head, bracing for a blow.

Lilah narrowed her eyes. The girl's freckled cheeks still had the soft fullness of childhood. She could be no older than fifteen, sixteen at the most.

Lilah knew that youth carried no special innocence. At sixteen, a girl could be as wicked as a witch. *She* had been.

But she reached into her own pocket, regardless.

The girl tensed. What did she anticipate? A knife? Lilah might have shown her one. Old habits died hard; she always went armed.

Instead, she plucked out a coin. "Now listen close," she said. "You've no talent. Hands like hams and a bad instinct for marks."

The girl squinted, her expression doubtful.

"Your life's worth more. Do you hear me? If you're smart, you'll buy a place in a factory. You . . ." She paused, battling the urge to preach onward.

It would do no good. She knew that, too. Sighing, she said, "The choice is yours. Leave now, or get caught." She pressed the coin into the girl's hand. "In five seconds, I call the guards." She turned on her heel and swept out of the alcove, pretending not to notice when the girl dashed by.

At the threshold to the ballroom, Lilah paused. The merry hubbub, the noise and the heat, felt like a solid wall blocking her path. The bracelet in her pocket weighed like an anchor, threatening to drag her down—another unforeseen complication on a night that could not bear any.

Lilah took a deep breath. She stood attired in silk and lace, looking over a crowd of princes and politicians. Some of these rich folk knew her name. They smiled at her when she passed. She had earned her position and finery by honest means.

Look at us now, Fee. So she always thought in such moments. Sometimes she felt—she hoped—that her sister was watching from above, cheering her on. That this triumph was a triumph for them both.

But tonight the sound of the thief's voice was too fresh in her head. *Yer no nob.* The girl had seen it in an instant. Lilah didn't truly belong here. If this crowd of fine folks learned whose niece she was—and what she'd once done to earn her keep—they would call for her head.

Her uncle would enjoy that. He'd said as much. *So you'll do me this small service, Lily—or I'll be glad to tell the Everleighs your true name and family. The choice is yours.*

She would do him the service, all right. For two weeks she'd thought of nothing else but how to accomplish it. Tonight was her chance.

But first she had to slip this bracelet back onto Miss Everleigh's wrist. Pasting a smile on her lips, she stepped back into the ballroom.

The old ache was throbbing through his leg. It did not help that Catherine Everleigh danced like a wood-jointed puppet. Christian could feel her resistance at every step. Had circumstances allowed it, he might have felt sorry for her, so clearly did she wish to be elsewhere. Instead, he registered her reluctance as a minor irritation, easily overcome by brute strength. He pulled her closer on the next turn, ignoring her grimace.

Meanwhile, from the sidelines, her brother, Peter Everleigh, watched with open delight. He was envisioning wedding bells, no doubt, and the subsequent boost to his business.

"The Russian enamels are extraordinary," Christian said. Catherine had shown him through the collection earlier.

Violet eyes lifted to stare coldly into his. "Was it the enamels that caught your interest? You seemed more taken with the metalwork."

Yes, he'd spent several minutes staring at a particular piece—a distinctively dented, jewel-encrusted candelabrum more familiar to him from his nightmares.

Bolkhov had come out of the woodwork again. But he'd finally made a mistake. This demented taunt was a clue that might be used to hunt him down.

Amusing to recall: once upon a time, Christian had envisioned a pleasantly ordinary life for himself. A fat military pension. Some rosy, cheerful girl to wed and bed and make children with.

Now his greatest hopes circled on butchering a madman. He lulled himself to sleep at night with fantasies of blood. "Oh, all of the collections intrigue me," he said to the icy girl in his arms. "But yes, the metalwork is striking. Am I to understand that you had a direct hand in the acquisition?" How well did she know the lunatic who owned that candelabrum? Was she aware that she'd become a pawn in his game?

Somebody squealed nearby. As Catherine glanced toward the merriment, candlelight rippled over her honey-blonde hair. Her elegant profile belonged on a cameo. Whatever she saw did not alter her bored expression. "Is it so remarkable?" she asked. "I am, after all, joint proprietor of these auction rooms."

"Much to my good fortune." For until Catherine had sent him the catalog for the upcoming auction, with the candelabrum featured in laboriously painted detail, he'd had no notion of where to look for Bolkhov. His contacts in the War Office had suggested that Bolkhov was dead. That he had never made it to England at all.

That Christian's brother had died of bad luck, rather than murder.

One could dwell on such matters only so long before rage and terror collapsed into something colder and darker. Christian would dance with this girl all night, and make very pleasant conversation, and even marry her if that was what it took to bring Bolkhov's throat under his blade. For he stood to lose everything, otherwise. Everyone.

"Indeed," he said, "I never thanked you properly for my invitation tonight. How did you guess at my interest in the Russian collection?"

"I do not make guesses," she said crisply. "Everleigh's operates on referral."

"Someone referred me, then?"

She sighed, clearly impatient with the need for small talk. "One of the contributors to the upcoming auction."

"Who," he asked, "is this mysterious contributor?"

"He prefers to remain anonymous."

Christian bared his teeth and hoped it passed for a smile. "How inconvenient." Inconveniences abounded of late. The morning after he'd received the catalog, he had forced his mother and sister to cancel their plans for the season. They waited now in Southampton; on Sunday they would embark on an extended tour abroad—New York, Boston, Philadelphia. They would not return until this was over, and Bolkhov was dead. "I don't suppose I can ask you to pass along a note to him?"

"To what end?"

So I can follow you while you deliver it. The vision was vivid. *So you can stand by as I slaughter the bastard.* "To convey my thanks," he said.

A line appeared between her pale brows. Unlike every other woman in this country, she seemed to find him irritating. "I shall do so in person, then. I cannot be bothered to keep track of notes."

He began to understand why men rarely spoke of Catherine Everleigh's beauty. Astonishing though it was, her charmless nature quite overshadowed it. "Then do tell him how greatly I appreciate it. I hope he plans to attend the auction in June. If so, we'll meet there."

"I'm glad the invitation was welcome to you," she said. "It occurred to me that you might still be in mourning." Her glance flickered down his evening suit, pausing pointedly on the flower pinned to his lapel. One of the hostesses employed by the auction house had been handing them out at the door. "I can't imagine," she said, staring at the festively beribboned tulip, "how deeply you still grieve. Ten months, has it been?"

The implication being that he had not observed the proper mourning period for his brother. "Fourteen, in fact." Long enough for the pain to dull from a lancing agony to a dull, bone-deep anguish.

But it had sharpened again as he'd stood before that candelabrum tonight. His fury had formed a litany of silent accusation.

You grew careless. You believed that his threats were empty. You thought you were safe.

Geoff is dead because of you.

He forced his thoughts away from that black endless plummet, back to the girl in his arms. She must have seen something that he did not intend to reveal; her frown had taken on a puzzled quality now. "You loved him," she said.

"Of course I loved him." Was she quite right in the head? "He was my brother."

Her mouth twisted. "As if blood were enough to guarantee love."

He took a hard breath, reminding himself of his task here. Catherine Everleigh had no friends. Reticent and withdrawn, she spent her days in dusty attics, poring over other people's treasures. She showed no interest in gentlemen, much less potential confidants.

But she must know Bolkhov, for she was coordinating the sale of that candelabrum. Evidently she anticipated seeing him again. And so Christian's strategy was clear. He must ensure she did not leave his sight. Ideally, he must win her trust and affection, God help him.

The waltz slowed to a conclusion. He stepped back from her, sketching a formal bow before offering his escort off the dance floor. "I suppose I will not see you again until we meet at Buckley Hall."

She paused, a feline quality to her unblinking regard. "Then we will not see each other. My brother has decided to appraise your estate himself. Did you not know?"

"No, I did not." *Damn it.* That must be what Peter Everleigh wished to speak to him about later. "How curious. I'd understood that he handles the sales, and you, the appraisals."

"Indeed." Her smile looked sour. "That is the typical arrangement. In this case, however, I believe your reputation has won his particular interest. You are, after all, the Hero of Bekhole."

This would not do. Christian had contracted the auction house to handle the sale only because it would give him a chance to keep Catherine in sight. "Would he reconsider his decision?"

Her pause was guarded. "Certainly, if you spoke to him, he might do. I daresay he—" She grabbed his arm for balance as a passerby, a raven-haired woman in a pink gown, stumbled into her.

"Forgive me, Miss Everleigh!" The woman's husky tone and quick curtsy struck Christian as oddly servile. As she straightened, her glance brushed his, giving him a start. Her eyes belonged to a medieval Madonna. They were round and heavy-lidded, a deep oceanic blue.

"I do hope you are not intoxicated," Catherine Everleigh said coldly to her.

"No, ma'am." This time, the woman's abashed smile was shared with Christian as well. "Only clumsy," she purred. After bobbing another curtsy, she moved away.

"One of our hostesses," Catherine said.

"I see." It occurred to him that an Everleigh Girl, by virtue of her duties, might have cause to know a good deal about Catherine.

"These girls are more trouble than they're worth," Catherine went on. "But my brother insists on them." She paused. "Do you mean to speak with him tonight?"

Christian caught the urgency buried in her question. She wished very much to manage the valuation of his estate. How convenient. "I will find him at once."

A faint smile escaped her. "Excellent." She offered a

handshake, the gesture businesslike. As she drew away, he noticed something.

"That's a very fine bracelet you wear," he said.

"It was my mother's."

"Do you always remove it while you dance?"

The small degree of warmth that had crept into her manner now vanished. "I never remove it."

Then somebody had done so for her—only to put it back again. How peculiar. He looked across the crowd for the dark-haired hostess, eyes narrowing as he found her slipping out the door.

No, not slipping. *Sneaking.*

CHAPTER TWO

Once more, then never again. After tonight, Lilah would be good for the rest of her life. She'd be a perfect lady. She vowed it.

As she walked, the sounds of merriment receded. She passed the great stairway that led up to the auction rooms, marble steps marching into darkness. Anybody could be standing above, spying on her from the shadows. The silence felt like the hush before a scream—or a crash. If she was caught tonight, she would be ruined.

For four years she had worked to break free of her fate. After Fiona's death, Nick had finally let her go. She'd put her sister's plan into action with ruthless self-discipline. Endless hours poring over etiquette manuals. Then, volumes of art and history. For the first two years at Everleigh's, all her savings had gone to a tutor of elocution. She'd not spoken without first rehearsing each word in her head, focusing on those wretched vowels and consonants that no Whitechapel girl knew to pronounce.

Only recently had the tutor declared there was no more to learn. Only now did she sleep soundly through the nights, confident that Fee would be proud of her. *You didn't die in vain. We made it out.* She'd opened a savings account, and at last dared to revise her sister's dreams, aiming now for something so extraordinary that even Fiona had never thought of it: a respectable retirement fund, perhaps a little house of her own. Imagine it: growing old in peace, free of the fear of the law—or her uncle!

Yet now, as she crept down the hall, she stood to lose everything. She could all but feel Fiona beside her, panicked and fearful. *You never see it coming,* Fee had said shakily one night, having returned from a job gone bad. One of Nick's men had died. *In a blink, you're done for. It happens so fast.*

She gritted her teeth. *Focus.*

Near the end stood the door to Peter Everleigh's study. Lilah reached into her chignon, feeling past the crystal-tipped pins for the prick of the pick she'd tucked into a curl.

She expected her fingers to tremble, for she'd had no practice in years. But as she fitted the pick into the lock, her hands were steady. It took only one touch, one twist, before the door swung open.

She bit her lip, strangely dismayed. Did it come back so easily? Four years felt like a century to her, an age in which she had transformed. But if she remembered the way of it so well, then perhaps she was no different, after all.

Frowning, she forced aside that thought. *No distractions. Think later.* As she stepped into the room, the thick carpet absorbed her footfall. She groped her way around the furnishings toward the oak desk, then felt down the drawers.

One would do better not to keep one's private documents in a desk. For that matter, if one did use a desk, better to lock every drawer in it. By locking only the topmost, Peter Everleigh announced where he kept his loot.

This lock was trickier than the other one. As she fumbled—once, and then a second time—anxiety breathed a cold, creepy whisper down her nape. The pick slipped out of her hand; she heard herself whisper a curse that she'd banished from her vocabulary long ago. Biting her lip, she felt across the carpet for the tool.

It hadn't fallen far. Now her fingers *did* shake as she fitted the pick into the lock. But the lock changed its mind about her; it suddenly yielded.

She still had the talent, even now, years out of practice!

After a moment, her pride struck her as shameful. Frowning, she reached into her sleeve and plucked out a stub of candle. From her bodice, she pulled a match. The wick lit, shedding a small, unsteady light. She riffled through the contents of the drawer.

Opera glasses. Theatrical programs. Crumpled telegrams. Gambling markers. A mess of letters.

She riffled quickly through the pages, finding no order to them. The brisk, slashing penmanship of a business correspondent pressed side by side with the curlicues of some wealthy widow with poor taste in men. Amorous phrases leapt out: *your bed last night . . . the feel of your mouth . . .* Grimacing, Lilah flipped faster. Her uncle had mentioned three names, none of which she'd recognized, though the society columns were required reading for Everleigh Girls.

But it seemed these men weren't part of high society.

She plucked out three letters, all of them concerning matters of construction and sanitation. The men must be members of the Municipal Board of Works; Peter Everleigh served on it, too. Puzzled, she folded up the letters and slipped them into a hidden pocket in her skirts, then shut the drawer on a long breath.

As she stood, a wave of dizziness rocked her. Mr. Everleigh had recently decreed that the Everleigh Girls' waists must be seventeen inches at most. Lilah hadn't eaten since breakfast; otherwise, her laces would never tighten so far.

Yet even with her lungs crushed by whalebone, she could outwit Pete's defenses. All it took was a single pick.

Smiling now, she hurried toward the door. Her hand had just found the latch when she heard her doom: masculine voices approaching in the hall.

She recoiled, but there was nowhere to flee.

Frantic, Lilah groped her way back toward the desk. *No, no, no; this can't be happening.* In her mind's eye she saw the room's sparse furnishings. There was nowhere to hide but beneath the desk—a terrible concealment, too easily discovered.

She yanked up her skirts, dropped to her knees, and clambered into the space.

It made for a tight fit, curled up like this. The boning in her corset jabbed into her ribs. She gritted her teeth and resisted the steel grip of the stays, which wanted to force her spine to straighten.

The room brightened as the door opened.

"—discuss this privately," came Peter Everleigh's voice, "it being a matter of some delicacy."

Young Pete, the older girls called him, for they had known his father before him, and could not think of

him, they said, as a worthy heir to the title of "Mr. Everleigh." But he had always struck Lilah as perfectly suited
to his position, smooth-spoken and assured around rich
men.

Now, though, he sounded hesitant. Apologetic, even.
"I do hope you understand," he said.

"I confess I don't." The reply came in a low drawl that
could cut glass. Lilah had learned to recognize such an
accent. Her tutor said it couldn't be taught, only bred—
but Lilah suspected money and a fancy education had
something to do with it, too. "I believe your sister would
do a splendid job at Buckley Hall," said the blue blood.

Lilah found a crack in a wooden join and squinted
through it. All she could see were legs. The men had
paused by the chiffonier, with no apparent intention of
moving deeper into the room. A miracle that they didn't
hear her heart drumming.

"Your faith is gratifying," said Young Pete. "However,
my sister would be the first to tell you that she lacks
experience in such appraisals."

"Would she?"

The gentleman's obvious skepticism made Lilah bite
back a brief smile. Whoever he was, this client knew
Miss Everleigh well enough to doubt claims about her
modesty.

Pete gave a knowing laugh. "Well, I'm certain she'd
be glad to try her hand at it. But I would not dream of
asking you to indulge her. I will gladly handle the estate
myself. Indeed, I look forward to—"

"I would not like to disappoint her."

The smooth remark held a buried edge, not quite
sharp enough to be aggression. But the message was
clear all the same.

When Pete replied, the smile in his voice confused Lilah. "Naturally, we both wish to see my sister happy. But you must see . . ."

A pair of legs turned, strode out of view. She recognized them as Pete's, and swallowed hard, panic all but throttling her.

Beneath the protective layer of carpet, the floorboards squeaked. Slate-gray trouser legs paused two feet away from her. As she shrank back, her corset squeezed her ribs harder yet. *Damn it all!* If she so much as twitched, she was done for.

"A drink?" asked Pete.

"Why not?"

Glass clinked. Liquid sloshed. "To be frank," said Pete, "it wouldn't *look* right. That is, a bachelor's house . . . without chaperonage. She is, you know, a most eligible young lady."

Now the other man's shoes came into view. "Very eligible," he said pleasantly.

Lilah panted silently against the pain. *Think of something else.* She focused on the client's patent leather shoes, which were polished to such a high gloss that she could see her skirts in them.

Stars above—she could see worse. Peeking out from beneath the client's heel was a pink bow identical to those sewn all over her gown.

"She did have a companion for a time," Pete said.

Lilah stared at her doom, disbelieving. Pete insisted on approving the girls' gowns before a party. He would recognize that ribbon in an instant.

"Quite the dragon," Pete went on. "Catherine claimed that she got in the way of the work. I suspect what that means is that Mrs. Ogilvie insisted on the observance of proprieties. At any rate, Catherine grew skilled in losing the poor woman."

Holding her breath, Lilah shifted onto her knees and eased forward. She would snatch up that bow.

The client shifted, exposing the ribbon fully. Something in his bodily posture suggested a moment of surprise. He began to kneel.

Her thoughts scrambled. No choice but to run for it. She could explode out from under the desk, make a dash for the service stair—

The client's hand closed on the ribbon. He ducked a little, bringing his face into view.

Great ghosts. It was Viscount Palmer!

He regarded her without any sign of surprise. His eyes were an impossible color, the shade of whisky held to the light.

He gave her a fleeting, ironical smile. Then he plucked up the ribbon and lifted himself out of sight.

"How embarrassing," she heard him say. "To be caught carrying lovers' tokens, like a schoolboy. I expect you recognize your sister's hair ribbon."

For a dumb moment, the lie made no sense. She was waiting only for the addendum: *By the way, you've a woman beneath your desk.*

But then Young Pete said, "Of course"—his overly jovial tone betraying that he was not quite comfortable with Palmer carrying tokens from his sister.

Palmer continued, "As for the question at hand—we can't force your sister to tolerate a chaperone. But the solution seems simple: supply her with company that doesn't interfere. An assistant, say, to help with her work."

"I don't think—"

"Yes, it's a splendid solution. One of the Everleigh Girls, perhaps? And may I say, I'm so glad that we had the chance to speak privately. As you've certainly gathered, it is my hope that by coming to know her better, I might also persuade Miss Everleigh to look upon me more . . . tenderly."

Pete exhaled. "Yes! Yes, indeed. That is my hope as well." Their footsteps moved away. "An assistant will serve," Pete decided.

The door shut.

For a moment longer, Lilah remained frozen. For what possible reason would a stranger—much less *Viscount Palmer*—protect her?

She crawled out from under the desk. Her legs shook so violently that it required both hands on the desktop to pull herself to her feet. She stared at the door, which—miracle of miracles—remained shut. Palmer had not yet told Pete about her.

Her relief felt fragile, tainted by confusion. Or foreboding. She hobbled toward the door, wincing at the hundred small complaints of her knees and hips, and the giant, throbbing complaint from the vicinity of her rib cage. With one hand on the doorknob, she pressed her ear to the keyhole and listened.

No voices.

She opened the door and stepped into the hallway. It was empty.

Did she truly owe her escape to Christian Stratton? Kit of "Kit's Charge," the famous poem that commemorated British bravery overseas? How Fiona would have squealed!

A hysterical giggle bubbled up. One hand over her mouth, she started down the hall. With each step, the unlikely seemed more credible. She'd gotten away with it. She'd been saved by a war hero. Better not to ask the reason. The music was growing louder; the letters were tucked safely in her pocket. *She was safe.*

Her relief made her giddy. She allowed herself a laugh, a short and exultant sound that broke into a gasp as a hand caught her elbow.

Lord Palmer stepped out from between two statues. "How awkward," he said pleasantly. "I forgot to ask your name."

The thief had marvelous composure. The first second, her panic showed plainly. It drained the blood from her face, exposing the artful blending of rouge that had lent her cheeks such fresh color. Her new pallor revealed freckles—a great many of them, long faded.

In the next moment, as though a switch had been flipped, roses bloomed again in her cheeks. She called up a lovely smile, which turned her blue eyes into cheerful half-moons. "Lord Palmer! Why, I hadn't dreamed to be noticed by you. You are quite the most popular gentleman in the ballroom!"

"Lucky that we're not in the ballroom, then." He spoke the words absently, surprised anew by the husky pitch of her voice. She was of average height and size; her voice, however, promised the ability to boom. It was rich enough to belong to a giantess in metal breastplate, with Viking horns atop her head. "I confess, I did not notice you there, Miss . . ."

"But of course you didn't," she said warmly. "It's my good luck to catch you alone. But how selfish it would be to hoard you!" As she started past him, she nodded toward the direction of the ballroom, her fleeting touch along his arm—and her quick, flirtatious glance—suggesting her great desire that he follow.

She was clever. He captured her hand before it could slip away. Without hesitation, she twirled around to face him, her train hissing in a broad arc across the marble floor. Her wide smile had not budged a fraction. "Yes, Lord Palmer?"

He matched her light tone. "And once again, I feel my disadvantage. Must I beg your name from Mr. Everleigh?"

Mention of her employer, whose study she had so recently infiltrated, made her flinch. She had not expected him to segue so quickly to threats.

She glanced over her shoulder. The hallway was empty, of course, the strains of a waltz dim but distinct. Nobody would leave the ballroom until the next set.

Seeing her plight—alone, quite alone—she redoubled the brilliance of her smile, then surprised him by stepping closer. "It's terribly awkward." What a magnificent voice she had! And how well she used it. Her hushed tone conjured intimacy, inviting him into a sweet little conspiracy. "I do hope that I can rely on your discretion."

He gave her a lopsided smile. "Well. You know what they say."

She looked up at him through thick dark lashes. He could no longer imagine how he'd mistaken her, however briefly, as servile. Between her voice and her oceanic eyes and her unflappable charm, she was a siren.

Her measuring look also suggested a shrewd mind. She was not yet sure how much trouble she was in. He might simply be a blundering idiot. Or he might be a cad, who meant to press his advantage. She was still making up her mind.

So was he. Blackmail was a precarious art, as likely to go wrong as to aid him. But her composure seemed promising. Only a trustworthy tool would serve his purposes.

"No," she said. "I don't know what they say. Will you tell me?"

He extended his elbow in an offer of escort. Her hand fluttered down, landing on his sleeve as lightly as a butterfly. "They say a man is only as good as his word," he told her as they fell into step. "And I've been told by several sources that mine is irredeemably rotten."

Her laughter held a carefree lilt, very convincing. "But that's nonsense," she said. "You're a great hero, Lord Palmer. Everyone has heard of your feats abroad."

Ah yes. His bloody, much-celebrated bravery.

To prove her point, she began to recite the damned poem. "'Who o'er yonder battlement, when enemy drums did pound—'"

"Yes," he interrupted. "I believe I've heard that one before." Five thousand times or so. It did not improve with repetition.

She was gazing at him brightly. "So then my point is proved: who would dare call you rotten?"

Nobody called him rotten, of course. They begged for autographs instead. "Perhaps you will."

He felt the slight, nervous dance of her fingertips on his forearm. "I can't imagine why."

They had been making very slow progress toward the ballroom. But now Christian drew her to a stop by the darkened stairwell. "Tell me," he said. "I knew Everleigh was a man of particular tastes. Does he often require you to wait beneath the desk for him?"

The skin tightened at the corners of her eyes. "I wish you wouldn't mention it," she said.

He almost laughed. How odd that he should find this pickpocket diverting. But for a woman who'd gotten herself into a great deal of trouble tonight—removing and replacing her mistress's bracelet, breaking into her master's locked study, hiding beneath his desk to eavesdrop, and perhaps worse (for a pickpocket, surely, did not break into studies *only* to eavesdrop?)—for all these redoubtable sins, she nevertheless did a brilliant job of playing the breathy naïf.

He admired a good performance. After all, he played the hero on regular occasion.

"A gentleman wouldn't mention it," he said. "Alas, I already warned you. I'm a rogue."

This time, she believed him. He sensed her reassessment, her subtle change of posture and tone. "Lord Palmer," she purred. "I don't expect your approval, of course. But Mr. Everleigh and I . . . That is, you must know that I'm one of the hostesses here, what they call an 'Everleigh Girl'—"

She was still trying to cozen him. Make him believe he'd interrupted her plan to surprise her lover. To disconcert her—for clearly he hadn't managed it yet—he lifted his hand to cup her cheek. "Indeed. I believe I've seen your face before." He stroked her jaw. "An advertisement for Pearson's soap, was it?"

She went still. Her skin was satin-smooth, warm, almost feverish to the touch. She smelled, he realized, like a garden in hot weather, climbing roses and jasmine and honeysuckle warmed by a noonday sun.

Their eyes locked. She blushed, then looked away. "That was Miss Ames in the advertisements," she said. "I am not one of the girls who wins such honors."

He studied her—the casual grace of one spiraling

black ringlet; the faint trace of freckles on the crest of her round cheek. "I can't imagine why."

That was empty flattery, of course. He knew why the advertisers favored other girls. This woman before him had no special beauty, apart from the angelic magic of her eyes—and a certain sensual grace in the way she held herself, slim and erect—and the softness and warmth and scent of her skin.

None of which would translate in photographs.

He retreated a step. "I still don't know your name." Not a creative remark. But his brain felt oddly unfocused, as though he had just taken a few fingers of whisky.

"Ah." She turned back to him, and he was oddly relieved when their eyes met and she looked, once again, quite ordinary to him. "You see that it's hardly worth knowing, though. Miss Ames models for Pearson's. You will find Miss Snow on the boxes of Ruben's Toothpowder, and Miss Lowell and Miss Rousseau smiling on bottles of Mr. Munson's Tonic. I am the lowest in our ranks—I know it very well. But if you imagine this would protect me from jealousy, you're mistaken. Should the girls come to know of my . . . special friendship with Mr. Everleigh, I assure you they would make my life a misery." She paused here, slightly breathless— a state that drew his attention, no doubt deliberately, to the snowy rise of her modest but excellently formed décolletage.

It felt wrong to be so riveted by her performance. He had far more important tasks than parrying words with a woman who made her living batting her lashes at the wealthy. Yet . . . what harm in admiring her? She was as cool under pressure as a professional soldier, but her talents clearly ran toward charm and coercion. She would fit his purpose splendidly. A fine spy.

"Such a peculiarly impassioned plea," he said, "when all I ask is your name."

"I . . ." Her face briefly went blank, as she groped for a new script to guide her.

He decided to help. The most predictable narrative was also the most credible. Grasping her by the waist, he eased her deeper into the shadows. Unwittingly, she helped by backing into the wall.

It was no hardship to place his face so close to hers that he could breathe the perfume of her hair. "It isn't Pearson's soap you use," he murmured.

Without hesitation, she murmured back, "I see no need to support my competition."

He hid his smile by turning his face into her throat. After a night spent in humorless company, she rather felt like balm on a wound. His lips brushed the tender spot beneath her ear as he spoke. "Perhaps you should adjust your aim." But not her soap. Whatever she used was perfection. "I can think of many areas in which you would have no competition."

"Oh?" The syllable was more like a croak. She cleared her throat. "Do tell."

There was no call to keep touching her. She was clearly disconcerted. Yet the scent of her skin . . .

With the very tip of his tongue, he tasted her.

Salt. Flesh. Sweetness. How peculiar and perverse, after so many months of deadness, to feel desire stir now.

But why not? The ferocity of desire was only a shade away from bloodlust, and she would make a very good weapon for him. A fine advantage in the battle to come.

As he breathed against her, her hand briefly tightened at his waist. He understood that the gesture was not meant to encourage him. Nor was it a protest. She touched him merely by way of acknowledgment. He had intentions; she understood that; she would not object.

Had he nursed any doubt about her guilt, this moment would have killed it. Her passivity answered the question he'd yet to ask. *What were you doing in that office?* Nothing innocent. Otherwise, she would have protested by now.

How far would she go to avoid explaining herself? His curiosity on the matter was as pragmatic, he supposed, as her willingness to distract him. After all, the first rule of war was to know the constraints and potentials of the weaponry at hand.

Taking hold of her chin, he lifted her face. She did not flinch from his regard. Her blue eyes were wide and bright as robins' eggs.

"Perhaps you're right," she said lightly. "You're rather rotten, after all."

How refreshing to be viewed so honestly. He offered her a faint smile. In reply, her own lips curved the slightest degree, the angle defiant.

Defiance did not suit him. He leaned forward and kissed the smile from her lips.

Flirt, evade, parry, giggle, flatter . . . The moment his mouth touched hers, these desperate tactics fell away like so much irrelevant fluff.

Kiss.

He tasted like champagne. His lips were warm and soft. He sucked on her lower lip, leisurely, testing, and

God help her but the pit of her stomach dropped away. She realized her arms were around him. Only to placate him, of course—and to test a theory.

His suit was not padded. This broad, hard muscle was all his by effort and training. *A soldier.* Well, she should have known. Not a gentleman after all, with apologies to Fiona. He had not saved her as an act of chivalry. He meant to press his advantage.

He pressed it now as he stepped into her fully, and she felt the size of him, his height and the muscled brawn of his thighs and the . . . distinct protuberance hardening against her skirts. Large, everywhere. *Think.* A brute. A bully, to catch her in this hall and harass her. She knew how to handle a bully. She—

He opened her mouth with his own. Ah, God, his tongue was clever; the kiss was skillful and gentle in the way that a spider was gentle; as he teased her, as he tasted her tongue and lured it, he wove a snare to trap her. And her body liked it. A delicious heat curled through her; she sagged back and his arm tightened around her waist to hold her against him, keeping her compliant to the ministrations of his clever, clever mouth.

A dozen gentlemen had kissed her. She knew how to handle this. Keep his interest at bay, accept the kiss and then break free, with every show of flustered flattery—

He angled his head. Oh yes, he was clever. *Go deeper.*

Appalled at herself, she turned her face aside. What was wrong with her?

He made some noise in his throat, a growling sound like approval. Like she'd done something wonderful. He kissed the corner of her mouth, then kissed his way down her jaw. He nuzzled her throat—ah, he smelled of some brand far rarer than Pearson's. He smelled expensively clean, like foreign spices and Christmas wreaths.

He bit her neck lightly. A sound escaped her. She opened her eyes, goggling at the empty hall over his shoulder. What was she doing?

Perhaps he sensed her distraction. His hand pressed harder at the small of her back, reminding her of the raw power of his large, hard body. Instincts like a predator. Ah, heaven help her, a man who knew how to read a woman's signals . . . How solidly his muscular thighs cradled her. She could intuit, as though her hand had already pressed against his belly, the hard planes of muscle that knit him together.

She had to stop this. She grasped his shoulder, ready to push him away. But the unyielding bulk fascinated her fingertips. She squeezed, amazed, as his hand slid down her arm, cupping the point of her elbow. His callused fingers stroked her, soothing and then gripping harder as they massaged her forearm, testing her strength as she tested his.

He kissed her mouth again. So sweetly. Had she ever been kissed like this? Pray God this would not be the last time—

"Wait." That wasn't the right thought. "I—"

"Shh." He looked into her eyes, his own the shade of tarnished gold, intent and sharp. He placed a fingertip very lightly against her lips.

She stared at him, ensorcelled.

"Someone will hear," he told her.

Yes, someone would hear. It made a very good reason to stand quietly, passively as he laid his thumb on the wing of her collarbone. His gaze dropped to follow the trailing stroke of his thumb. The backs of his knuckles brushed her breastbone. He seemed only curious. Harmless. Intent on following the slope of her breast.

She licked her dry lips. *Someone will hear.* She could call out—

The neckline of her gown conspired with him. The tightness with which she'd laced, to compress her waist that extra inch—it caused her bodice to gape, slightly. He reached beneath her neckline, beneath her corset and chemise. His thumb, it knew what it was doing. He found her nipple. Rubbed gently.

This throb between her legs . . .

His next kiss felt like approval, a reward. His tongue played with hers as he stroked her nipple. He was . . . dangerous.

"I don't think . . ." How dazed she sounded. Like a dash of ice water, it sobered her. She pushed him away.

He stepped back agreeably, one hand slipping into his jacket. Why?

He produced a handkerchief, offering it to her. Befuddled, she said, "No, thank you." And then, as he retreated another step, the full awareness of her idiocy broke over her, and she felt the blood drain from her face. God above! Everleigh Girls had been sacked for consorting with clients.

She peeked around the corner. The hall remained empty. Thank God!

She crossed her arms over her breasts, unhappily aware of how bereft they felt, before she turned back. He was watching her, those chiseled lips quirked in a faint smile.

Her dazzled agitation died instantly. How satisfied he looked with himself! As though he imagined he had been seducing her, instead of using his discovery earlier—her hiding place beneath a desk—to coerce her into a kiss.

Oh, bloody hell. He hadn't coerced her. She *had* been seduced. Absurd!

She reached for her composure. Squared her shoulders and straightened to her full height. "But I'm still waiting," she said, and was proud that her voice did not tremble.

He cleared his throat. "Waiting for what?"

His voice was not so steady, either. That bolstered her. "Waiting to hear the areas in which I might excel."

He gave a soft laugh. "Apart from the obvious?" His gaze dropped briefly to her mouth. "I'll gladly tell you, if you tell me your name. Or must I beg?"

She edged away from him before remembering to flutter her lashes. "I imagine you do so very hand-somely."

He laughed again. "I think you've seen precisely how I do it."

She blushed, then wanted to kick herself for it. It was not her way to fall in with the competition. Every other woman in England pined after this man. She counted on herself to remain at least *somewhat* immune to his charms. "I'm Lilah Marshall. And the rumors are true: you, Lord Palmer, are a flirt."

"Lilah. A very pretty name." His smile was dimpled, that long scar as pale as silver.

"Now," she said, "your reply."

He shrugged and glanced down the hall. "I'm sure, Miss Marshall, that there are many fields in which you are unmatched. Certainly, for instance, the field of lock picking."

She could not have heard him right. "I beg your pardon?"

When he smiled again, she felt her heart skip a beat.

Only now, for the first time, did she notice that his smile did not reach his eyes. His smile was easy and charming; his golden eyes were watchful and dispassionate. His gaze belonged to a sharpshooter in battle.

"I liked you better flushed and sighing," he said. "Alas, frankness will serve us better. Where you don't excel is keeping hold of what you've stolen."

What on earth? Her hand flew to her hidden pocket. The letters were gone!

Why, this cad had not been seducing her—he'd been distracting her in order to pickpocket her!

Palmer bowed and started past her. She grabbed his hand, and he pivoted. "Not here," he said, and nodded down the hall.

The set had ended. Guests were filtering into the corridor to enjoy the cooler air.

Desperation made her reckless. "I don't care! You—"

His hand twisted in hers, took control of the grip. His palm was much larger, hardened and callused. She tried to yank free. His grip tightened—not to the point of pain, but certainly to the point of clarity. He was far stronger. He could hold her against her will without breaking a sweat.

She looked up, startled, and found herself pinned in his sharp, steady gaze. Silently he waited for her to acknowledge the truth: *she* was the one who was caught.

A chill ran through her. She took in the size of him, his brawny, strapping build. The gentlemanly polish—his dimples, his clean-cut good looks, his title and fame—had fooled her before. But now she saw the man behind that charming mask. His cool-eyed composure, and the power of his carefully gauged restraint, caused her instincts to sound an alarm.

Danger.

She made her hand go limp in his. Without hesitation, he bowed over it. "Good evening, Miss Marshall." As though they had just concluded a dance.

Frozen, she watched him walk away, tall and straight-shouldered. Faintest suggestion of a limp—or was that her imagination?

Guests caught sight of him. Merry greetings rang out. He lifted his hand to them. Never once did he look back.

A war hero! Pah! A thief, a rogue—what did he mean to do with those letters?

She cupped her hands over her mouth as the disaster registered. Why, he could have her imprisoned. Those notes were solid proof that she'd gone into Young Pete's study to steal.

Worse yet—without them, she could not keep her bargain with her uncle.

Panic robbed her of strength. She sagged against the wall. No matter what Palmer did now, he had already ruined her.

CHAPTER THREE

At eight o'clock the next morning, Lilah stepped off an omnibus and made her way down the high street to church. Inside the damp and sour-smelling hall, she searched the crowd, hoping to find her cousin Sally.

The front pew was always reserved for Uncle Nick's family. As she worked her way toward it, men leapt to their feet to greet her, asking after her health. Women came into the aisle to deliver compliments she didn't deserve. She was exhausted from a sleepless night, with bags beneath her eyes. Even old Mrs. Reilly, half-blind from cataracts, could see she wasn't "fresh as a daisy."

Once upon a time, her fellow parishioners had been a comfort. In the dark days after Fiona's death, they had mourned with her. But times had changed. They no longer saw her as their dear old Lily. Now she was the niece of Nicholas O'Shea, whom they idolized and feared as the ruler of these parts. In Nick's absence, they paid court to her.

On good days, the groveling embarrassed her. On bad days—like this one—it shamed her. Her smiles were curt as she dodged questions about her uncle: where he was, how he fared, if he had plans for the abandoned building on the corner, if he would consider taking the tanner's son beneath his wing.

"I don't know; I can't say"—she repeated these words with a tired, grimacing smile, as all the while her thoughts gnawed on the disaster last night. What had happened in that hallway? A rich nob had gotten the best of her. Had kissed her senseless, and stolen her only chance at keeping her uncle happy.

She was furious with herself . . . and frightened. Nick didn't tolerate failures.

In the front pew, Cousin Sally was already seated, her little boy, Daniel, by her side. No sign of Sally's husband, Thomas, who no doubt was lying drunk in a gutter somewhere. But Sally herself looked hale, even plump, and her dark hair was glossy, prettily done up in rolls atop her head.

"Here's a surprise," said Sally, and drew Daniel onto her lap to make room for Lilah.

"Hello there, Danny!" As Lilah sat, she held out her arms. But Danny turned his face into his mother's bosom.

That small rejection felt like a poisoned dart through Lilah's throat. She tucked her hands under her skirts. "How are you?" she asked Sally. Then, because it was polite, she added, "And how's Tom?"

Bouncing her knee to boost Daniel upright, Sally gathered him closer. "Can't blame Danny," she said briefly. "You haven't been by in months; you're all but a stranger to him. As for Tom, I've no idea where he is. Hasn't been home in days."

"I'm sorry," Lilah said softly.

"Don't be. It's Nick's doing. Told Tom he's not to appear drunk around me or Danny again. Scared the living wits from him, I tell you." Sally flashed a small, hard, satisfied smile.

Lilah hesitated. "Is Nick coming today?"

"I've no notion." Sally's blue eyes narrowed. "Have need of him, do you? I should have known. We'll not see you, otherwise."

Lilah sighed. They had never been close, she and Sally—the twelve years that separated them made too large a gap for friendship.

But blood guaranteed Sally's loyalty, if not her affection. "Is something awry?" she asked Lilah grudgingly. "Toffs giving you trouble at work?"

Here was another reason they'd never been close: Sally thought Nick could do no wrong, never mind that *he* was younger than Sally, too. As long as his power kept people bowing and scraping to her, she'd sing his praises and nothing else. If Lilah was troubled, it must be somebody else's fault.

"Nothing's wrong," Lilah said. "Just felt in need of a blessing." She paused, sensing a fierce scrutiny from behind her. A quick glance found Deirdre Mahoney glaring at her. She and Lilah had been bosom friends as children.

Lilah made herself smile. In reply, Deirdre flashed a quick, false smile of her own. Then she bent her head to the girl beside her. Above the din of a dozen conversations came the verdict, in Deirdre's high voice: "Thinks herself too good for us now."

Lilah faced front again, face burning. Would the service never start? Through the cracked door that opened into the alley, she spied the priest loitering over his pipe.

"Don't pay them no mind," Sally said. "Silly tarts."

"I don't." For they were right. Bettering herself was the whole point of her efforts. It was Fee who had first put it into words: *dodging the coppers for our uncle, risking our necks—this is no life for us.* She'd known her looks would win her a place at Everleigh's, if only she could talk and move like a lady. *You'll see,* she'd told Lilah. *I'll make enough money for us both. We'll have a nice little flat, and gentleman callers who prefer tea to gin.*

But Fee had been undone by an enemy she couldn't fight, and Lilah hadn't been able to save her. All she could do was take Fee's dream and make it her own. *Yes,* she aimed to better herself. It was the last loving thing she could do for her sister.

Only one thing she'd never anticipated when she'd set out on this course: her old friends felt slighted by her desire to change. They no longer spoke to her. They sneered at her in church.

When she'd lost Fee, she'd lost everything. But she'd found new friends and a new life. And then she'd let a toff kiss her. All her hard work, undone by a handsome mouth. She laid her head on the pew and stifled a groan.

"Megrims?" asked Sally.

"Or she wants to show off her pretty hairpins," said a familiar voice from above. "Move aside, Lady Drama." Nick nudged her roughly on the shoulder.

Peculiar how relief and anxiety could well up together. She scooted over, catching sight as she did of Deirdre pinching her cheeks and smoothing down her hair.

God above. Lilah looked narrowly at her uncle. He'd always been a pretty one. Indeed, placed side by side with Viscount Palmer, Nick would draw a woman's eye faster. He had the dramatic coloring of a Celt—hair as glossy and black as a crow's wing, and eyes like gray ice.

But she knew what lay behind that perfectly chiseled face. His beauty must be the devil's particular gift to him, to keep people fooled.

"You look very well today," Sally said to him.

It was true—his jacket was buttoned properly, his jaw stripped of stubble. Shaved clean, he looked younger. Barely thirty, he'd ruled the East End for twelve years now. One oft forgot his tender age.

She caught his glance toward the pew behind them, where Deirdre sat. Pray God he hadn't taken up with her—Deirdre would be unbearable, given a share of his power.

Sally's thoughts strayed down the same path. She leaned across Lilah to whisper to him. "Say you're not sweet on the Mahoney girl."

"I'd reckon it's none of your business who I'm sweet on." Nick slouched into the pew, his attention trained on the priest, who had finally finished his pipe and come inside to start the Mass.

"You can do better than her, surely!"

"I can do just about anyone I please, Sally darling."

Sally made a choked noise. "We are in the Lord's house."

"It's my house," he said calmly. "The Lord only has it on lease."

Sally paled. Casting Lilah a wide-eyed look, she gathered up Danny and inched toward the far side of the pew, no doubt fearing a lightning strike.

Lilah restrained the urge to follow her. "Nick," she said in a low tone, "I've got to speak with you."

He ignored that remark. "Have a look at your cousin,

why don't you. I might as well be wearing horns and a tail."

She was immune to his charm. "It's about the job," she said. "Something went—"

He gave her a quick, hard look. "Later." He hooked his kneeling cushion with the toe of his boot, kicking it up into his grip. "It's the Lord's day." He winked at her as he knelt. "And it appears I'm in sore need of his favor."

It took two hours after the service to get her uncle alone. First, Lilah had to stand by as parishioners lined up to pay their respects, while a brawny stranger kept a lookout in the doorway, barring newcomers from entry.

Nick had never kept guards before. For that matter, this pomp and circumstance was new as well. Nick looked less like a criminal than a politician campaigning for office, kissing babies and bowing over old ladies' hands.

As the last petitioners dispersed, the sun clouded over, dulling the stained-glass windows and sinking the church into darkness. Lilah walked out to the road with Nick, conscious of the burly man trailing them.

"So," Nick said. "Trouble in paradise, is it?"

The guard was all but stepping on her heels. "You tell me," she said. "Why the hired lad? Don't you trust our own boys? Or did the Shaughnessys and McCoys fail to lick your boots to your liking?"

A moment of stone-cold silence. Then Nick's lips twitched. "Fierce little Lily." Placing a broad palm on her back, he urged her on down the lane. "Just like your ma. I forget, sometimes."

And she forgot how hard he was to anger. It took a great deal to make him drop that easy, smiling mask and show the truth of his temper. But wise men knew not to cross him. After the McGowan gang had slain her father, Nick had stepped into Da's shoes so quickly it was as though he'd already sized up the fit. A month later, the McGowans were finished—dead or fled, to a man.

The night he'd killed the last of them, Nick had collected Lily and Fee from Sally's. *Your da is avenged. You'll stay with me now.*

Da had run a ring of thieves that stretched from East End to West. But he'd never involved his daughters in the business. Nick had felt differently. *Nothing you don't do for family,* he'd told them, time and again. *We stick together, in work as well as play.*

Nick guided her around a puddle. "I'm bound for the pub," he said. "Come, if you like. Been too long since you've tried Neddie's oysters."

"I've got to get back to the auction rooms," she lied.

He came to a stop, a look of amusement stamped on his handsome features. After Fee's death, he'd finally released her to do as she pleased. But he still thought her a fool for aiming higher. "Very well," he said. "Then tell me here in the road—bearing in mind our audience, of course. Johnson has got sharp ears."

His new guard wasn't Irish? She found that very strange. Nick liked blood ties, the better to bind a man into his sticky web of loyalties.

But the reasons for his new arrangement were not her business. She laced her hands together, staring hard at her knuckles. "I had a problem last night," she said. "Somebody caught me."

"Is that so? Yet here you stand, free as a bird."

"He wasn't in the mood to call the police."

A pause. "Look at me," said Nick.

Resentfully she glanced up. His cool gray eyes rested on her face, skeptical, assessing. He had the devil's talent for reading minds. She focused on the bridge of his nose, forbidding her thoughts to wander from that spot.

But somehow, a memory seeped out anyway, spreading through her like heat, making her flush. Palmer kissed very well, damn him.

"I see," Nick said softly. "Persuaded him, did you?"

She gave a jerky shrug. Gentlemen had kissed her before. They mistook the hostesses for loose women. One grew skilled in permitting a small liberty, to avoid giving a larger one. Men were easy to manipulate when lustful.

Usually their kisses were inoffensive. Rarely, Lilah found them pleasant. But never, ever had she allowed a man to distract her from her duty.

Never before had a kiss made her hair stand on end.

"More to the point," she said tersely, "he took the letters."

Nick's expression was unreadable. "Who was this?"

"Lord Palmer."

"Don't know the name."

"Christian Stratton." When Nick still looked blank, she said, "Kit Stratton, of—"

Nick interrupted her with a startled sputter—something between a laugh and a snort. "The bloke from the war? The one who made all the headlines. *Kit's Charge?*"

"Yes, that's him."

He laid a hand over his mouth to cover his grin. Cloudy light glittered on the rings he wore—trophies from the McGowans, little children liked to say.

For all Lilah knew, that stupid tale might be true. But

Nick had not worn all those rings when she'd known him best. He'd been a different man then. Less certain of his power. Blunter in wielding it.

"You got caught." He sounded as though this was the best joke he'd heard all week. "*You*. By a toff!"

She felt stung. "You've no idea. He isn't what you think. He's . . ." *Different,* she wanted to say. But how? In appearance, Palmer was as sleek and idle as the rest of his lot.

It was in the full force of his physical presence that she sensed the difference. Finding herself the focus of his attention, she had suddenly believed the wild tales about his heroism, the bloody charge that had decimated a stronghold of enemies. A simmering energy crackled around him.

And for some dreadful reason, it took her breath away.

"Well, then." Nick dropped his hand to show her a predatory smile. "I see he meets your approval. *Miss Marshall.*"

He never lost an opportunity to jibe at her for the name she'd adopted. As if an Irish girl named Monroe would have any chance of working at Everleigh's! "He's not stupid, is what he is."

"That's bad news for you." With a shrug, Nick resumed his stroll.

"Wait! I . . ." He looked over his shoulder. "What will you do?"

"*I* do?" He lifted his brows as he turned back. "'Tisn't me who has the problem, Lily."

Fear kicked through her stomach. She crossed her arms, hugging herself. "I can't get the letters for you. He took them."

"Aye, it's a proper conundrum. But I'm certain you'll find a solution for it. You do have a knack for pleasing those toffs."

"Nick." She dug her fingers into her sides. "Please. Do you really mean to tell them about me?"

"Stupid question." His voice snapped like a whip. "Try another one."

It wasn't right that he should sabotage her like this! "I'll be done for if you tell them! Don't you have any care for your own niece?"

"Care?" He stepped toward her, his gaze hard as a bludgeon. "That's ripe, Lily. 'Twas *you* who turned your back on your kin. Shook off your family like dirt from your shoes, and rubbed out your true name like a stain from your skirts. And for what, I ask? To grovel for swells who wouldn't spit on you to put out a fire. And now you come asking if I *care*?"

"I never turned my back." Did he think she enjoyed bowing and scraping? It was only a means to an end— one that would take her a sight further than bowing in Whitechapel to *him*! "I only wanted to make a future for myself! Can't you see—"

"Aye, I've heard that speech," he said grimly. "You wanted *better*. And I let you make a choice. But now you'll live with it, Lily. You won't come calling me Uncle and begging for mercy, just because it serves to remember your family today. For tomorrow, we both know you'd forget me again, and look away if we passed in the street."

"That isn't fair." The words came out in a whisper, for this was an old argument, and she stood no hope of winning it. But why did he always refuse to see it from her view? "All I wanted was a life where I'd never suffer from trouble. *This* kind of trouble." Suddenly she was angry again. "Family, you say? Some family, that threatens and blackmails and harasses me—"

He made a contemptuous noise, a sharp puff of air. "Aye, yours is a sad story, no doubt. But if it weren't for your rotting bastard of an uncle, ask yourself where you'd be now. Who gave you the fees for that typing course? Who paid for that fine gown with which you interviewed at the auction rooms?"

This was his trump card. She gritted her teeth and glared past him down the road. Onlookers who'd paused to eavesdrop made a quick retreat to avoid her notice. Always a spectacle, in these parts.

"No reply to that," he said. "You know you'd be plucking cat fur in some garret, praying the week's pay would cover your rent."

"So I'm forever to be indebted to you," she said bitterly. "Forever to answer to your call when you need me."

He offered her a beautiful smile. "Take heart. It's a rare occasion when I do. And bound to grow rarer, now you've lost your talent and been swindled by a nob."

Despair leached through her. "What shall I do, then?"

"Find a way to get those notes back," he said with a shrug. "I'll be needing them by the last week of June. No later. Otherwise those toffs will have the truth from me."

"You'll enjoy that," she said dully.

He snorted. "Won't be my doing when they sack you. But no doubt it will make a fine lesson, to learn how your *betters* care for a girl named Lily Monroe."

*   *   *

"Please lower your voice. And stop that pacing! For heaven's sake, Kit. Melanie is right; you're not yourself lately."

Christian pivoted. Across the broad span of the foyer's checked tiles, his mother stood, one hand perched dramatically at her brow, her face a mask of bewildered hurt.

"I was not yelling." He was certain of it. But he had not arrived with the intent of charming and delighting her, either. There was the rub. It had always fallen to his brother—and their father before him—to be the serious ones. Christian's purpose was to entertain and amuse.

But his mother's telegram this morning had left him in no mood to entertain her. She had decided not to board the ship to New York. Instead, she and Melanie had turned back for Susseby, the seat of the viscountcy. The whole country knew where to find them now.

Astonishment washed over him anew. "I thought you understood. You cannot remain here."

"Yes, yes." She cast an impatient look toward the front door. "Quigley, at least take his hat and gloves. Let him lecture me in comfort."

He held up a hand, halting the butler in his tracks. Taking her elbow, he led her out of the servant's earshot, into the nearby morning room.

Inside, she drew away to yank the bell pull. "Watch the carpet," she said. "You've mud on your boots."

Indeed, God forbid. He took a long breath. This was not the first time he'd had cause to restrain his temper in this room. She worried far more for the carpets than herself. "I am rebooking your passage," he said. "I will personally escort you onto the ship."

The door opened. "Tea," his mother instructed

the footman. "And perhaps a heartier repast for Lord Palmer."

The man bowed and shut the door again.

"Poor dear," she continued, "you do look famished. Did you ride straight through the rain? How awful the roads are. It must have taken the whole morning!" She lowered herself to the settee, readjusting her fine jemadar shawl about her shoulders. "I *am* sorry," she added with a bright smile. "I would have enjoyed New York, but your sister has a point. At Melanie's age, one must be marriage-minded. Missing a season in town means risking her chance at—"

His patience snapped. "There will be no marriage if she's killed."

"Kit!" On a sharp breath, his mother reached for the jet cross at her throat.

She still wore half-mourning for Geoff. The dark wool did not suit her blond coloring, but he knew that part of her pallor, at least, was owed to him. No doubt his words were cruel. But if she did not wish to enter full mourning again, she had no choice but to listen.

He took the seat beside her. How would Geoff have conducted this conversation? Somberly, brooking no opposition. "I do not like to say it. But you must face facts. Geoff's death was no accident."

"Stop it." She turned her face away, showing the elegance of her profile, the high cheekbones and swanlike neck that by all accounts had struck men dumb in her youth. "I won't listen to this again."

Christian's brother had not believed in involving her in unpleasant business. But there was no choice for it. Ignorance would only endanger her. "Be angry with me, if you must. Had I not crossed paths with a madman,

Geoff would still be alive." The words tasted foul, unbearably bitter. Had he been a shade less *brave* at Bekhole, the entire world would not have read the details of his life—and his family. Bolkhov would not have found them so easily. "His blood is on my—"

"Don't be a fool." She swung a blazing look on him. "Life is unjust. Accidents happen all the time. Why . . ." Her lips pressed together, whitening. "Just look at your father. Always reckless on a horse. I warned him against such jumps, didn't I? But he always said he knew what he was doing. The finest horseman in five counties, they called him."

"I'm speaking of Geoff now," Christian said gently.

"I know," she snapped. "That's my very point, Kit. Even when one sees the danger . . . I always told your father, I said he would break his neck and leave me a widow. But did he listen?" She pressed a hand to her mouth. "And when it finally happened, it had nothing to do with his skill, only bad . . ." She swallowed. "Bad luck. It happens, you know, all the time."

Christian nodded. He had no grounds on which to argue it. On his return to England—dazed, ragged from fever—the tidings of his father's death had seemed like a piece of black luck to him as well.

But he had proof of foul play in Geoff's case. "I've been working with a friend in government," he said slowly. This was not a piece of information he'd meant to share. "The fire that killed Geoff. It was arson."

She closed her eyes as though to shut out the news. "The war has left you troubled. These delusions . . . the vicar says they arise from an unquiet mind."

Christ God. Had Geoff given her such news, she never would have consulted the vicar about his sanity. "Do you require proof? I can arrange for it."

For a moment, her face seemed to sink in on itself. He saw then how she would look at ninety, sunken-faced and frail, and the vision triggered a rush of terrible emotion.

The feeling hardened his resolve. She *would* live to be ninety. She would be ancient and gray before she passed away in her sleep. That was what he meant to ensure.

As she opened her eyes, a single tear slipped down her cheek. "If the government is involved, then let them solve this," she said unsteadily. "Let them—let them protect us while they hunt this Russian! But to pull me away from my friends, Kit—and to ask Melanie to go among strangers, when she's only now begun to recover her spirits—"

"You would rather be under lock and key here?" He rose. "That can be arranged."

She frowned up at him. "What do you mean?"

"I mean you will remain at Susseby, under guard at all hours."

"No!" She scowled. "That, I won't tolerate. Melanie will have her season."

"Neither you nor Melanie has a choice in it," he bit out. "*I* am the head of this family now."

She stared at him, struck mute. A rare sight, indeed. Enough to trigger a fleeting lick of black humor. *Obey.* That was the line he should have taken from the start.

Obey your brother, she'd always told him as a boy. No matter the nature of his quarrels with Geoff, or Geoff's share of the blame, it had been Christian's role to make peace. *One day he will be the head of the family,* she had lectured him time and again. *All this—Susseby, the estates in the north, the fortune and title—all of it will be his. So respect him, Kit. Obey him, for one day* he *will be your authority, as much as your father.*

He had chafed at that instruction. Sorely resented Geoff for never having to apologize. Resented his mother, too, for turning a blind eye to Geoff's flaws.

But he had never coveted his brother's place. In his bones, he knew they'd been born in the proper order. He'd never wanted the burdensome duties of the title. Never wanted . . . *this.*

Yet here it was. "New York or Susseby," he said with the same brutal bluntness that he might have used on a wayward troop. "Make your choice, madam."

"Here," she said faintly. "Susseby."

The door opened without warning. Two maids carried in silver trays reeking of chop.

His mother hastily wiped her eyes. "Lay them down at the table," she said. "Lord Palmer will require—"

"I am not staying."

Her mouth flattened. "At least pay your respects before you go."

That she imagined he needed a reminder was the harshest punishment she could have dealt him. Perhaps she realized it, for her face softened as she held out her hands. He took them and kissed her cheek. "This will be over soon," he said gruffly.

"Oh, Christian." Her fingers tightened around his. "Promise me you will pray for guidance."

"Of course." He prayed nightly for guidance, on how best to kill a monster.

A winding path led from the house through the terraced gardens, past a stand of trees to the small graveyard where generations of Strattons lay buried.

In the rainy light, Christian paused by his father's

grave to bow his head. But it was by Geoff's marker that he knelt. With damp earth soaking his trousers, he watched the wind ruffle the wet boughs overheard, scattering droplets that darkened the grass.

It was a tired cliché that a second son should find his true home in the military. But the military had not only offered him brotherhood, it had also instilled discipline. Through harsh experience, it had taught him that courage and denial were often the same. Over the course of countless battles, Christian had learned to ignore his inward emotions. He'd grown expert at denying his fear, his anxiety, and his doubt.

With the help of that practice, he rarely permitted himself to think on Geoff. Otherwise, the weight of his guilt would have crushed him into the earth.

Geoff had invited him on that ill-fated trip to York. But on the eve of departure, they had quarreled. Christian could no longer remember the name of the girl— some opera dancer whom Geoff had brought to a late dinner at Café Royal. So unlike him. He'd always been painfully sober—devoted, often to a pompous degree, to the great duties fated by his birth.

But that night at Café Royal, Geoff had seemed a different man. He'd arrived beaming and disheveled, eager to show off the woman on his arm. Christian, who had gone to confer with a waiter about an unsatisfactory cabernet, had turned in time to see this unlikely scene: his brother removing the opera dancer's cloak as reverently as though he were unveiling a queen.

Then the opera dancer had caught sight of Christian.

It's that bloody poem, he'd told Geoff later that night, by way of apology, as they'd driven home. *It's everywhere now.*

The dancer had been dispatched by then. Geoff's interest in her had died a sudden, cold death when she'd thrown herself into Christian's lap and begged for a kiss.

The poem? Geoff had asked in a slur. *Are you certain it's not the medals? Or your pictures in all the newspapers? Or that ball the Queen held for you last month?*

Christian had never seen him drunk. Unnerved, he'd helped Geoff out of the coach, into the house. But in the lobby, Geoff had pushed him away. *Just once,* he'd said, swaying. *Just once, Kit, I'd like to know how it is to have it so deuced easy.*

Christian had been astonished. *You imagine it was easy?*

Don't start on that again, Geoff had said. *The mad Slav in the cave. Nobody believes you! Boy who cried wolf. You've always been one for wild tales.*

Yes, all his wild tales. He'd always been the entertainer. Not the sharpest at studies, but very good for a laugh. *You think it was easy to grow up in your shadow? The firstborn, the genius, the one who could do no wrong?*

The next morning, he'd woken with a savage hangover and a remorseful recollection of how angrily he'd stumbled to bed. He had gone downstairs prepared to apologize. Geoff was the head of the family, after all. *Respect him.*

But Geoff had already left for York.

A day later, when the note had arrived for Christian—a single line, in nearly illiterate scrawl, which the authorities had dismissed as a prank—he'd dispatched a telegram to Geoff's hotel and boarded the next train in a frantic blur he still could not wholly piece together.

But it had been too late. Geoff had been dead, the hotel in flames.

Not a faulty gas line, after all. But it had taken months to persuade the government to mount an investigation, and even longer to determine that the evidence pointed to arson—although the scrawled note had been unequivocal: *Now it begins.*

He laid his hand atop the wet earth over Geoff's grave. Once this soil had been freshly turned. Now the grass had healed over the scar, making a smooth bright cover. He sank his fingers into it, severing the grass at its roots.

"I will avenge you," he whispered. *But not replace you.* The one who could do no wrong—that had never been Christian.

But he would do this right, or die trying. "I will keep them safe. On your life and Father's, I swear it."

A drop of rain hit his nose. Then came another, ice cold, cleansing. He closed his eyes and lifted his face into the light of the oncoming storm. He had killed men in battle, of course. But he had never murdered. God save him, but he dreamed of nothing else now.

CHAPTER FOUR

The town house was huge. Lit top to bottom. A party was under way. Lilah stood on the curb, staring up in indecision. It had taken a full day to build her courage to come here. Now she wondered if the cabman had delivered her to the wrong address.

Movement caught her attention. Across the road, a slim figure huddled in the shadows of the trees, features concealed by a voluminous shawl.

Lilah called out. "Is this the Viscount Palmer's residence, do you know?"

The figure made some abortive movement—a gesture at flight, arrested. After a moment's hesitation, hands emerged, drawing away the shawl. A young girl, perhaps seventeen, nodded tentatively at Lilah.

"Yes, that's right," the girl said. "Do you . . . do you know him?"

That was a very fine strand of diamonds at her throat. Lilah looked beyond her and saw nobody else in the park.

The rules were different in Mayfair, of course. But

Lilah had the suspicion that this girl was not supposed to be prowling outside after dark without a chaperone. She looked the age of a debutante, and wore the jewelry to match.

"I do know him," she said.

The girl gasped. Then she scuttled across the road to Lilah's side. "Can you give him this?"

So close, Lilah could catch the subtle scent of the girl's perfume—something exotic and expensive. The girl's skin was flawless, as though the sun had never touched her.

Lilah felt her resolve faltering. She'd reconciled herself to a trade: her body for the letters. What choice did she have? Remaining chaste was well and good, as long as one's circumstances remained decent enough to give chastity its proper meaning.

But once Nick told the Everleighs about her, she'd be hard-pressed to find any respectable position. The Everleighs would feel obliged to warn everyone of their deceitful former hostess. Her virtue would do her no good then. Her body would be all she had to sell.

Better to sell it when the price was still high. But would Palmer even be inclined to make the purchase? Not if his taste ran toward this girl's bland, delicate beauty.

"I'll give it to him," she said, taking the note before the girl could change her mind. "Or maybe I won't."

"Oh!" The girl's eyes widened in outrage. "Then give it back!"

Lilah shoved the note down her bodice. "Don't be stupid. Men who force you to scurry about in the dark, writing love letters you daren't post, mean nothing good for you."

The girl covered her mouth, smothering an unsteady laugh. "No, you have it all wrong." She lifted her face to the house, and the light spilling through the open windows caught on her eyes. They were a golden shade, like whisky held to the light.

"He's my brother," the girl said. "And he won't . . ." Tears shone, threatened to spill over her lashes. "He won't even see me. He's denied me a season and refused to explain himself, and I—I won't have it!"

Lilah looked her over. The girl was wearing a traveling cloak, wrinkled from much use. "Did you run away?" she asked. "Does anybody know you're here?"

"I came to visit a friend. Mother made me promise not to go to town. She said it would upset him. But look—he's having a party," the girl said bitterly. "While the two of us rot away, with nothing to do but sulk and sit about, as though our mourning will never end. As though for the rest of our lives, all we must do is think of . . . of Geoff . . . and Father!"

Suddenly she sobbed. Alarmed, Lilah glanced again to the shadowy park. Mayfair was the safest area of London, but criminals found opportunities here as well. A weeping girl in fine diamonds would make easy pickings. "Where is this friend? Is her house nearby? Shall I walk you there?"

The girl dashed away her tears. "No! I'm not alone. My maid is waiting in the park."

A very worthless maid. "And she let you come over on her own, did she?" Something in her own voice gave her pause. That scolding note . . . Fiona had liked to berate her so when she was rash. "I'll have a word with her," she said more stiffly. She owed this girl nothing. "Or perhaps it's your friend's parents I should speak with."

By this threat, she meant to compel compliance. The girl flew into a panic. "No! Please, I beg you—the walk isn't far. And my maid—Mother would sack her if she found out we came out at night. Please, Loulou is the only true friend I have at Susseby—"

"Fine," Lilah said quickly, for it occurred to her that if somebody came along and spotted this scene, neither of them would benefit. "Run along to Loulou now, and I'll see that Palmer gets your note."

"Oh, thank you!" Beaming, the girl made a flying retreat into the park. Sure enough, another figure emerged from the darkness to meet her. The two huddled together for a moment, then waved to Lilah before slipping from view.

Inside, someone hooted, and a great chorus of masculine laughter followed. Lilah stepped out of the lamplight, frowning.

A week ago, it would not have surprised her to learn that Viscount Palmer threw wild parties. The wealthy were a breed apart, easily bored, prone to strange amusements. She had long since learned not to try to understand them.

But now that she had spoken with Palmer . . . now that she had learned, to her detriment, of his agile wit, and his skill at picking a girl's pocket—she could not square him with the usual aristocratic nonsense.

They say I'm rotten.

Perhaps so will you.

Best to know as much as possible about the lion before she entered his den. She opened the note, reading quickly.

How can you do this to me, Kit? Do you think you're the only one who has suffered? Or worse, the only one who should get to enjoy life, after such a long horrible period of grieving?

Well, I shan't go to New York—and I shan't be locked up, either! WHY should I submit to such treatment? Am I to be punished forever? You know I loved our brother with all my heart. I weep for him nightly! But what my sore heart requires to heal is <u>diversion</u>! I am twenty—other girls are married and widowed by that age! I should be making my debut at Lady Southerton's ball as I write this! Why, the love of my life might even now be dancing with some other girl. What if I never meet him? What if I go to New York and marry some dreadful American and end up alone in some uncivilized wilderness only to be eaten by bears? That will be YOUR fault! ALL of it!

But what do you care? You are cold and unfeeling and I'm through with it. You can lock me up as many times as you like—I shall only break free and come back! I will stand outside your house and HOWL AT THE MOON if I must! But I promise you, if you do not give me permission to stay in town, you will regret it!

Your loving sister,
Melanie

Amused, Lilah refolded the note, then tucked it into her bodice. Had she ever been so young?

Above, the door opened. A man lurched down the steps, drunk as blazes. Something clattered onto the pavement ahead of him. He cursed and came to a standstill on the last step, gripping the iron rail as he wobbled indecisively.

His left leg ended in a wooden stump. It was a cane

that he'd dropped. Surprise drew Lilah from her hiding place. As she picked up the cane, he cursed again. "Where in 'ell did you come from?" he demanded.

"Around the corner." She handed the cane to him, but got no word of thanks for it. He hobbled past her and took a lurching turn toward the high road, his patched coat billowing out behind him.

How peculiar! On a deep breath, she marched up to the knocker.

The butler did not even ask Lilah's name before admitting her. With a bow, he took her cloak and directed her upstairs. "You will find his lordship at the end of the hall, through the last door on the left."

As she crested the stairs, she saw that this was no party after all—not the kind favored in Mayfair, at least. The male assembly wore rough-spun cotton and ragged jackets, and carried plates of plain chicken and potatoes. The group nearest her drank from tankards that smelled of ale, and they made conversation in a variety of unschooled accents. "This was afore that mess at Kabul, y'ken—"

"Aye, I kent it fine. Right sorry affair, that. Bloody Fred Roberts—"

She could spy the far hall, but the crush afforded no easy way to reach it. She sidled into the crowd, sidestepping elbows and carelessly handled tankards.

Evidence of injury was everywhere. Eye patches. Slings. These were military veterans, she suspected. As they took note of her presence, news traveled in a silent wave of nudges and nods. A path cleared, conversations pausing as she passed; with startled glances, men com-passed her figure, then quickly and respectfully looked away.

The crowd thinned as she passed into the hall. To the left, a door stood open to a handsome salon, velvet-flocked walls and gilt molding, furniture upholstered in silk. Men in scarred boots and threadbare trousers sprawled across the sofas, playing chess and smoking pipes.

The third door stood ajar, only a sliver of light escaping. After a brief hesitation, Lilah nudged it open.

It was a very masculine kind of morning room, with the requisite writing desk, scattered stands of potted ferns, and a cluster of chairs drawn close to the fire. By tall windows that stood open to the night air, she located the host of the motley crew outside. He was sitting alone, his attention fixed on the street below.

Belatedly she rapped her knuckles against the door. He did not look over. "Go ahead," he said quietly. "Shut the door behind you."

She lingered at the edge of the carpet, strangely nervous. The first rule of any job was simple, and also, on rare occasions, impossibly complex: *Know your mark.*

She had spent the day reading old newspapers, reacquainting herself with Palmer's celebrity. His charge at Bekhole was considered an act of inspired lunacy. From that, she gathered he was a man who liked risks. He had continued his military service after the war's conclusion, rebuffing the prize of a diplomatic position for the mundane task of cleaning up the war-torn border. When an injury had brought him home, everyone had predicted a political career for him. But the glamor of power did not lure him. A year after his assumption of his late brother's title, he had yet to take his seat in the House of Lords.

What did he want, then? *I am eager to reacquaint my-self with the pleasures of peacetime,* he'd told a journalist. But that had hardly prepared her to find him brooding alone in the darkness, while an assembly of rough veterans caroused through his public rooms.

Her silence finally won his attention. He turned to look at her. "What did she want?"

This was decidedly not the best start to the conversation she hoped to have with him. "Whom do you mean?"

He rose. "The girl in the street."

From an animal perspective, he'd been fashioned for power: tall and long legged, with powerful shoulders and thighs. She remembered the breadth of his upper arms, which she had gripped during their kiss. Soldiering had shaped his body, laid layers of hard muscle over his large, solid frame. He would have made a fine brute, were he in the market to work for her uncle.

She cleared her throat. "She wanted to know if this was your house."

The darkness of the room veiled his expression from her. But she had made a study of him at Everleigh's. She found the spot where that wicked scar carved a curving arc from the corner of his right eye to the middle of his cheek.

The war had made him a hero. Perhaps it had also done other things to him—difficult things that sharpened one's instincts. She should not treat him as an ordinary mark.

"She knew very well whose house this was," he said impassively. "What did she want? The truth, Miss Marshall."

The note was her only advantage. She had not intended to surrender it until it promised to bring good value. But his fierce gaze made her feel transparent.

Unnerved, she reached into her bodice and drew out the letter. "She asked me to give you this. She intends to stay in town."

He took it and put it aside unread. "Was that all?"

Lilah hesitated, puzzled. There was a starkness to his face, a stripped-down quality, quite at odds with his quicksilver charm that night at Everleigh's. It was a strange mood, for a man throwing a party.

"Why are you in here all alone?" she asked.

One brow edged upward. "My guests do not require a host. Merely an excuse to gather, and eat a square meal."

And he had given that to them. Why? "I am glad one cannot say the same of the crowds at Everleigh's." With humor she tried to lighten the atmosphere, for in this state, he would shoot down her proposition in an instant. "I would be out of a job."

"I feel certain you would land on your feet," he said.

That might have been a compliment. But feline imagery so rarely was used to compliment a woman. Why was that? Cats, in Lilah's view, were tremendously admirable creatures—self-sufficient, but very skilled at being charming, when they wished to be.

Perhaps that was the reason, though. What man did not fear a self-sufficient woman?

"I expected to see you yesterday," he said. As he turned up a lamp, the strengthening light painted his hair gold and laid shadows in the hollows of his cheeks. He had good, strong bones: a hawkish nose, a broad, square jaw. Solidly hewn, in every regard.

"I pay no calls on Sunday," she said absently. His lips riveted her. She had seen handsomer mouths with fuller lips, but his were finely molded, his upper lip so sharply bowed that it lent his slight smile a wicked cast. She still didn't understand how he had managed to scatter her wits. A kiss should not have done it, no matter the mouth.

"Ah. Sunday." He settled his weight against the writing desk. "The Lord's day. I suppose you spent it in church, praying for forgiveness."

"I did go to church. But it wasn't forgiveness I prayed for."

He drummed his fingers on the desktop. "Do you think God takes much interest in the prayers of a thief?"

"You'll have to hope he does," she said. "For I believe you became one Saturday."

That startled him. He laughed, flashing white teeth. One of his incisors was slightly crooked. A relief, to spot that imperfection. "You're quick-witted," he said. "But surprisingly easy to distract. How long would it have taken you to notice the papers were gone, had I not told you?"

"About two minutes," she said. "Or maybe longer. I confess, you did distract me. I'm not usually so easily confounded."

His head tipped. "And now you turn to flattery," he said softly. His gaze ran down her, pausing with unnerving accuracy at each point of her toilette that she had chosen with him in mind: the glass pearls at her throat, to conjure demureness. The delicate gold chain at her waist, to suggest its opposite.

Her neckline, a shade lower than fashion demanded.

When he met her eyes again, the air between them seemed to snap.

"You want them back," he said.

"Of course."

"Do you make a habit of stealing from your employer?"

"No." She said no more. Defending or explaining herself would be pointless. He had no cause to believe her.

And yet he asked, anyway. "What could you possibly want with those letters? Debates on a proposal before the Municipal Board of Works—a suit to condemn some buildings in Islington. I can't imagine how it concerns you."

She had asked herself the same question. Her brief scan of the letters had suggested nothing to do with the East End, and Nick did not care what happened outside that area. "I took them for someone else. I don't know his purpose for them."

"Who?"

She shrugged.

He rose to his full height, the movement as leisurely as the stretch of a cat. A lion: he had the coloring for it. "This conversation will go better if you're honest."

"Be that as it may, I will not worsen my situation by betraying his confidence." She grimaced. "Believe me, it is from no desire to protect him—only myself."

"So you were tasked to steal these letters by a gentleman." He paused, his keen eyes catching something in her expression. "A man," he amended. "Not a gentleman, in your view."

She crossed her arms, then thought better of the posture. This was meant to be a seduction. Defiance was not the proper attitude.

On a quick breath, she made herself relax and stroll toward him. The roll of her hips, she borrowed from

Susie, whose charms were conspicuous. The quick flick of her glance through her lashes was Lavender's. Vinnie was a mistress of subtlety. "Forget the more tedious questions," she said. "Perhaps you should ask what I'll do to get them back."

He let her approach, the faint smile on his mouth suggesting a willingness to be amused. But once she came within reach, he did not pounce or straighten off the desk to close the distance. Instead, very slowly, he reached out and caught hold of a strand of her hair, a loose ringlet that he lifted from her shoulder.

He rubbed the lock, and that slight tension on her scalp sent a startling shiver through her. "You manage to be lovelier than your looks," he murmured. "The total effect transcends the sum of your parts. Is that a trick they teach at Everleigh's, or did you master it yourself?"

"That is not quite a compliment." Another surprise: standing so close to the warmth of his body, she felt breathless. As though he touched her in places that were clothed.

"I don't believe compliments are required in this case." He laid his thumb against her collarbone, as he had that night in the hall. "This is not a courtship. It is a . . ." He dragged his thumb down to the hollow of her throat, rolling it over the coolness of the glass pearls. "What would you call it, Miss Marshall?"

She licked her lips. "A discussion," she said. "Possibly a . . . trade."

"Ah." He nudged her chin to lift her face. They stared at each other. "Is this the kind of trade you make often?"

A proper lady would have taken offense to that question. But given the circumstances, she could not be indignant. What did he know of her, but that she was a thief who offered her body in exchange for stolen goods?

"No," she said. "A pity, that. With some experience, I probably would have managed to seduce you already."

His hand fell away, leaving her oddly cold. "Shall I give you a piece of advice? There is nothing more deadly to seduction than honesty."

She exhaled, disliking the butterflies in her stomach. Her inexperience in these matters had never before seemed like an inconvenience. But had she accepted some other man's proposition, perhaps the prospect of physical intimacy would not have left her so nervous now. "I am not innocent in mind. But I am in body." A privilege of being Nick O'Shea's niece: there was no man in Whitechapel fool enough to touch her. "That's a piece of honesty that I understand a gentleman might appreciate. You would be the first. Is that worth three letters that would otherwise prove useless to you?"

"Let me think on it." Once again he settled against the desk. "Stretch out your arms and turn around."

Her nervousness died. A cad, she could handle. She had dealt with so many of them. "Certainly," she said coolly. She lifted her arms, slowly twirling.

When she faced him again, he gave her a slight smile. "Very nice," he said. "Your figure is very pretty. But there are greater beauties in London. "

Her stomach sank. It was very clear that he had no interest in her, after all. "Well." She took a deep breath, hoping he saw nothing—*nothing*—of her despair.

There was always another way. She was inside his house! If he were . . . temporarily incapacitated . . . she could find those letters. From the corner of her eye, she saw a few potential weapons. A bronze bust. Fire irons.

But hurting someone had never been her way. And to do so would bring the police down on her, regardless—if the veterans outside didn't get her first.

She would plot some new course once alone. The key now was to exit gracefully. "You'll forgive me for intruding, I hope." She curtseyed and turned to go.

"No call for despair." His words halted her. "I have a different trade in mind, Miss Marshall. Less pleasant, I'll admit. But of more benefit to you."

Warily she turned. He waved her to a nearby sofa.

What in God's name could he want of her? Mustering a stiff smile, she took a seat. "Do tell."

"I find myself in possession of an estate that requires auction." He crossed to a sideboard, filling two glasses with amber liquid. Her hands were steady as she took the proffered glass, but never had whisky tasted more necessary.

He settled in the oversized wing chair opposite, his smile blandly pleasant. She felt slightly disoriented. Two nights ago, as he'd played the villain, his eyes had looked cold as bullets. Now, with the wing chair disguising the strapping muscularity of his frame, he might have been the idealized model of an English gentleman, blond and blandly smiling. It was as though he'd never kissed her. Never thumbed her nipple and made her whimper.

"The estate belonged to a cousin," he said amiably. "Recently passed away."

"I'm sorry to hear it." She was out of her depths.

He shrugged. "I scarcely knew him. He was a lifelong bachelor, bit of a curmudgeon. But he greatly admired the military. In return for my services, he bequeathed me Buckley Hall." He took a sip of his drink. She allowed herself another, and felt a burning warmth start to brew in her chest—a warning not to indulge further.

"I suppose," she said, carefully setting the glass away from her, "it must be delightful, being left such a gift." She could not begin to imagine it. One inherited clothing, books, beds—not entire houses.

"Oh, it's a ramshackle pile, I assure you. The first thing to go will be the rubbish he collected. The house is chockablock with antiquities. Everleigh's will handle the sale."

She nodded. The hostesses had no hand in such matters. Their sole purpose was to advertise the collections that had been cataloged and appraised and were ready for auction.

"Catherine Everleigh intends to manage the sale." He spoke more slowly now, rolling the glass in his long, tanned fingers. "But propriety forbids her to poke about the house on her own—and as you know, she does not tolerate the interference of chaperones."

In truth, Lilah knew very little about Catherine Everleigh. She looked down on the hostesses. "She is very independent minded, they say."

"But your assistance would be a great boon to her."

She frowned. "Are you proposing that I . . . chaperone Miss Everleigh?" Was he mad?

"You're far too young to make a proper chaperone," he said. "But an assistant—why not?"

She suddenly remembered Palmer's conversation with Peter Everleigh. He had proposed this very scheme to Peter. "Have you been planning this the whole time?"

He looked puzzled. "What do you mean?"

Yes, what did she mean? He could not have known that she was beneath that desk when he'd proposed his solution.

Still, something did not sit right. "To assist her would be a step up in the world."

"Yes. I'm glad you see that."

"Miss Everleigh would never offer that position to a hostess."

"She will."

He sounded very confident. Her puzzlement grew. "Then . . . why on earth should you wish *me* for it?"

"Do you mean, why should I wish to have a thief on my property?"

"Yes," she said bluntly.

He gave her a wolfish smile. "Because I will require that Catherine's assistant answer to *me*."

They were coming to it now. "For what reason?"

"To facilitate my courtship of her. Imagine the hints you might offer me, as you come to know her better."

She mulled this absurd proposition. "And in return, you won't go to the police about me?"

He leaned forward. "In return, I'll give you back those letters."

Her heart tripped. The bargain sounded very simple. Advantageous, too. Assisting Miss Everleigh would make a very fine credential for her.

Why, it could mean everything. A true step upward! Other auction houses had female associates—society matrons, mostly, but there was a precedent. With this opportunity to learn and educate herself, Lilah might have a real chance at such endeavors.

For a moment, the happy fantasy unspooled in her brain. A cluttered attic. Miss Everleigh's dismissal of the rubbish therein. An overlooked treasure, which Lilah discovered and presented, thereby winning Miss Everleigh's respect and support. And then . . . why, a position of a different kind. A raise in salary, to fatten her savings. An office of her own, with a cunning little card that announced her new title: *Lilah Marshall, Appraiser, Everleigh's Auction Rooms.*

And yet . . . She gave a pull of her mouth. Miracles only happened in fairy tales. Miss Everleigh would never esteem a hostess to that degree.

And in the real world, gentlemen like Palmer did not need thieves to facilitate their romances.

"I don't believe you," she said quietly. It felt cruel of him to taunt her in this way. He could not guess how cruel it was to appeal to her ambitions, but that did not prevent her from thinking him rotten for it. "You need no help in wooing women."

"What a fine compliment." Setting down his glass, he came to sit beside her on the sofa. "I'll put another name to it, then, shall I?"

His warmth reached her, the displaced air carrying a trace of the spice of his skin. His jacket brushed softly against her bare arm. She realized she was holding her breath. "Go ahead," she whispered.

Gently he cupped her cheek. His fingers pressed as lightly as a breath. Rough fingertips. He placed his thumb on her lower lip. "You are to be my spy." His gaze dipped, following his thumb as he traced the shape of her mouth. "You will befriend her. See whom she writes. If she meets anyone—goes anywhere—you follow." As his thumb reached the corner of her mouth, he paused. The silence between them vibrated. His gaze lifted, and goose bumps broke over her skin. Hawk's eyes, lambent gold. "And then you will report all of it to me."

Her mouth was dry. A pulse seemed to thrum in it. "And where does your touching me enter this picture?"

He leaned down. Their lips brushed. His were warm and smooth. She was not going to open her mouth. This time, she would not lose her head.

His tongue traced the seam of her lips. Coaxed them apart. Her stomach seemed to fall. She could not catch her indrawn breath. His tongue followed into her mouth, taking a slow, leisurely taste before he pulled back.

"It's not a requirement," he said huskily. "But you seem to enjoy it. As do I."

She folded her lips together, bit down on them. He was right, of course. To deny the obvious would make her look like a fool. She took a hard breath through her nose.

His eyes narrowed. She saw his intent to kiss her again. Heart tripping, she eased away from him. "But it's not required." Her voice was unsteady. "To be clear on the matter."

"Not required," he said. "But an option, regardless."

She nodded. After another fraught second, he moved back to his wing chair. Only then did the air seem to cool around her so she could breathe properly again. "I help you woo her." She cleared her throat. "Or spy, as it were. And in return, you'll give me the papers."

"The moment she accepts my proposal, they are yours." He paused. "But you really haven't much choice in the matter, have you?"

There was the rub. "I need those letters by the last week of June. No later."

He shrugged. "Then you must do a quick job of befriending her."

Lilah could not imagine working beside her, much

less winning her trust. But he was right. What choice did she have?

"What happens," he asked, "in the last week of June?"

She pressed her lips together. "Nothing." And then, with a shrug: "The devil will have his due."

"Sweet girl." He held out his hand to help her rise. "I have good news. From now on, the only devil you need fear is me."

From the front door of his town house, Christian watched his new conspirator make her way down the pavement toward the high street. She'd declined to be driven home by his coachman. *Hostesses cannot be seen to consort with clients,* she'd said coolly. *There's an omnibus that runs directly to my boardinghouse. I expect no trouble.*

Indeed. He pitied the man who thought to test her. Quick-witted, confident, and clearly experienced in unsavory pastimes, Lilah Marshall was more likely to make trouble, he'd wager, than suffer from it.

She reminded him faintly of someone . . . He could not place it. Certainly he'd never met a woman precisely like her. What a fine asset she'd make. And how astonished she would be to learn that he felt grateful to her. God, but he could have spent an hour watching her turn in circles for him. The narrowness of her waist, the swell of her hips . . . Her shape, her voice, the intentions that had brought her here, were now burned into his brain. It made a rare and welcome distraction from his other preoccupations.

He pulled shut the door. A cleared throat drew his attention. Howe, his butler, was lurking by a potted plant, making a conspicuous study of the floor.

Christian had found the man—and most of his servants—through a charity for veteran relief. From a long line of butlers and valets, Howe had wished to follow the family tradition, but his limp had barred him from service until Christian made an offer.

"Any sign?" Christian asked. His open-door policy on these nights was well publicized. Bolkhov must know that if he presented himself, he would be admitted without hesitation.

"No, my lord." Howe touched his waistcoat, where—like all the men in Christian's unusual staff—he carried a small firearm. "But the staff is prepared. And Lord Ashmore has arrived. He waits in your study."

"Excellent." Christian took the stairs two by two. At the first landing, one of his former troops cried out a greeting, and the hubbub paused briefly. He lifted his hand in acknowledgment and continued to climb.

These gatherings had started shortly after his return to England. For so long he'd dreamed of homecoming. But he'd returned to a world transformed—his father dead, his family in seclusion. He'd come late to mourning; Geoff had already thrown himself into plans to improve Susseby, fervently pursuing his duty to the Stratton legacy. But that legacy was not Christian's to uphold. At Susseby, he was loved, but not needed. Meanwhile, crowds threw flowers and applauded him—for what purpose? After a time, even adulation grew tedious.

His men needed him. In the field, they had entrusted him with their lives. Now, cast adrift in a country that neglected its veterans, they came to his table half starving, rattled and uncertain. He fed them. He used his celebrity to find them lodging and employment. He made loans that he never expected to be repaid. He was of use.

He was not, however, at home. Campfire camaraderie did not survive in a drawing room. His men welcomed him, but their conversations grew muted in his company. They watched their language around him now. Major Stratton had made a home for himself in the military, but Lord Palmer could not.

On the second floor, in a small room that overlooked the street, he found Phineas Granville, Earl of Ashmore, waiting with a book under one arm, his admiring attention on the collection of scimitars atop the mantel. "Where are your goddamned men?" Christian asked as he stepped inside. "My sister paid a midnight call."

Ashmore turned. He was a tall, dark-featured man in his early thirties, with piercing black eyes and a certain innate gravitas that made him a powerful speechmaker in Parliament. But it was a rare occasion that saw Ashmore airing his interests so publicly. Secrets collected to him like moths to a light. "Good evening to you as well," he said calmly.

If anything ever fractured that calm, Christian had yet to discover it. They had first met in Afghanistan, where Ashmore's cool head had come in handy at the bloodiest and most dangerous hours. Whatever his involvement in that war—for he'd worked for the government in some secret capacity, appearing and disappearing at will—it had obviously required a man of unshakable composure.

But Melanie had slipped past him today, regardless. "Were your friends sleeping?" Christian asked. Those "friends" were a deadly assembly, mercenaries trained to operate in the shadows. Certainly they should be equipped to handle a girl of twenty.

"Check your post," said Ashmore. "I sent word when she lit out from Susseby this afternoon."

"They should have stopped her before she boarded the bloody train!"

"That would have required a very uncomfortable discussion with the policemen on the platform." Ashmore turned, retrieving a glass from Christian's desk. "Drink?" He took a leisurely sip, then lifted one dark brow in appreciation. "Very fine collection of port in that cabinet. Your brother's, I take it? You always preferred rotgut."

That liquor cabinet had been locked, last time Christian had checked, and he'd not yet managed to locate the key. He spared a brief, wry smile. "A soldier drinks what he can get. Any other discoveries worth noting? How fare my finances? Find any skeletons in the walls?"

"Come now. I never pry into friends' affairs."

Christian snorted. "Certainly. Why bother, when you'd rather manage them entirely?" When Ashmore had insisted on helping with this manhunt, Christian had hesitated before assenting; he'd known it would turn into a circus of spies.

But he'd never expected incompetence. "Melanie was wandering the park with only a maid at her heels."

"My men were ten paces behind."

"Not that I saw."

"Well." Ashmore swirled the liquid in his glass, then bolted it. "That's something to their credit, at least. I've replaced the crew who let her slip by," he added. "Get her back to Susseby. She won't get out again."

With a curt nod, Christian said, "Then come with me, please." He turned on his heel, leading Ashmore down the hall and through a servant's stair into the basement.

"Dare I hope you're taking me on a tour of the wine cellar?" Ashmore asked as they emerged into a low-ceilinged hall. "If the port was so fine . . ."

Christian drew up outside a door outfitted with several locks. The keychain weighed as much as a small child.

Ashmore lifted dark brows. "I stand corrected: it seems you have a dungeon."

"More useful than a cellar, to be sure." He opened the last lock, then swung open the door. A single gas lamp lit the small, stone-walled chamber. A chair sat on the bare floorboards. The man tied to it emitted a groan—or perhaps a garbled word. The gag did a fine job of muffling him.

"Christ!" Ashmore put down the book and ran a hand through his hair. "What in God's name, Kit?"

So he could be startled. How gratifying. "Not a guest, you may gather." The overfed ginger was dressed in black, head to toe. Christian walked up to him. "No biting this time," he warned, then pulled out his dagger and sliced through the gag.

"Bloody lunatic! Eejit maniac—" The round vowels of a Welshman echoed off the walls.

"Bolkhov's?" Ashmore asked.

The redhead shook his head. "No, no—"

"He persuaded me otherwise," Christian said. "But he has yet to account for why he was skulking in the park across the road."

"A poor choice on his part," Ashmore said dryly. "Did anyone see you take him?"

"No!" the redhead burst out. "Not a soul, and I've been here for hours!"

Ashmore squinted toward the door, as though mentally conjuring the park. "That's a good distance," he said, sounding grudgingly impressed.

"God save you," the redhead panted. "Please, sir, I beg you! This madman—"

Christian spoke over him. "He carried an interesting item on his person." He reached into his pocket, pulling out the slim steel bar. The man's blubbering got louder. He laid the edge of the bar to the man's cheek, which shut him up.

Ashmore cleared his throat. "May I?"

Christian handed over the bar. Ashmore was a man of multifarious talents. Very good at secrecy. Even better at killing. There was no weapon that he did not recognize.

"A thief's tool," Ashmore decided. He squatted to look in the man's eyes. "A common burglar?" he asked gently. "Is that it?"

The man hesitated.

"Come, now. If you don't answer honestly, I'll leave you here with him."

"Fine! Yes! I was casing the houses in the square—"

Ashmore rose so quickly that the redhead cringed. He had always been remarkably light on his feet. In Afghanistan, troops had taken to calling him the Black Cat, for his knack at slipping past the men on watch. Too, his mysterious visits had always signaled bad luck ahead: a hazardous raid; a battle with losing odds. Certainly he'd never appeared to celebrate a victory. "You want me to deliver him to the police?" he asked Christian.

"Fine. But first—" Christian nodded toward the door. "A word."

"Of course." Ashmore bent to pick up his book.

"Don't go!" the man cried. "Sir, please, take me to the police. Don't leave me with—"

Christian shut the door on his cries.

"I recall an argument outside Kabul, long ago." Ashmore leaned against the wall, an odd look on his face. "A young lieutenant, castigating me for claiming that torture had its uses."

Christian allowed himself a faint smile. "You dismissed him as a useless idealist."

Ashmore gave a quick, wry tug of his mouth. "I'd only just met him. I quickly revised my opinion." He paused. "But I admired his idealism from the start."

"Have no fear. Barring the burglar's removal from the park, I never laid a hand on him."

"Indeed? Only words?" When he nodded, Ashmore looked struck. "A good thing you didn't discover that talent in Afghanistan. They might have reassigned you, put you to work with me."

"A pity they didn't. I could have used the experience." It would have prepared him better to face an enemy like Bolkhov, who aimed at innocents and struck from the shadows.

"No," Ashmore said. "You're not a man who would thrive in that line. And I mean that as a compliment to you."

"One does as one must." Christian recited the words flatly. "Your words to me once."

"Spoken in wartime. But Bolkhov is a common criminal, and this territory is yours. Never forget that you have the advantage here. You're home now."

Home, was he? Christian bit his cheek to stop a bitter smile. He felt no sense of homecoming, not even at Susseby. All he sensed was his brother's ghost at his heels, demanding justice . . . and accusing him.

This is not your life. None of this was meant to be yours.

These ruminations were pointless. As long as Bolkhov lived, regret and doubt would hold no interest for him. He turned toward business instead. "I'm leaving London at week's end. Catherine Everleigh will be traveling to Buckley Hall, and I mean to join her for the duration of her visit."

Ashmore's narrow, unblinking gaze probably proved very useful in his own interrogations. "The Russian collection goes to auction in June, yes? That's eight, ten weeks."

Christian nodded. "In the meantime, I'll make a show of courting Catherine. If that doesn't lure Bolkhov out, the auction will do it."

"And if it doesn't?"

The prospect of this nightmare extending indefinitely . . . "He's putting that candelabrum to auction for a reason. It was a message to me; he's done with waiting."

"I do hope so." Ashmore turned his book in his hands, his signet ring gleaming as he rubbed his thumb across the gilt-stamped spine. "Bolkhov deserves a bullet, of course—for his crimes in the war, as much as for your brother. But . . . once it's over, Kit. Have you thought on what awaits you?"

"My conscience won't trouble me, if that's what you mean."

"Indeed. I'm not one to lecture on that, am I?" A grim cast came over Ashmore's face; his brief silence felt fraught, clouded by what he'd never plainly admitted. But Christian had pieced the truth together, over the years. Before Ashmore had inherited his title, he'd traveled the globe for the government, but he'd never done so as a proper soldier.

Assassin. An ugly word. No honor in it.

Ashmore continued, a rare hesitance slowing his speech. "I will help you in whatever manner you allow. And you're probably right to say you must take a direct hand in it; that he won't emerge from his hidey-hole unless you offer the bait. But I can't like it, Kit. This isn't the role you're meant for."

Wasn't it? Christian glanced toward the bolted door, the medieval-looking padlocks. He'd made a prison in his own home, and another one for his family at Susseby. Each night, he prayed to shed a man's blood.

No wonder that he no longer slept well.

"What role do you recommend, then?" he asked. "Am I more suited to signing autographs and donning medals, while a lunatic plots to murder my family?"

"Of course not," Ashmore said sharply. "But don't mock the man who won those medals. God knows he earned them—not just at Bekhole, but every day of that bloody war. I saw that with my own eyes. And I hope to see him again, soon enough. For his scope and promise are far larger than this passing lunacy with Bolkhov. And I won't allow you to forget that."

Christian recognized kindness when he heard it. But it felt wasted. "Once I kill him," he said. "We'll revisit this discussion."

"Fine." Ashmore loosed a long breath, then pulled the book from under his arm. "I've been carrying this all day. A gift for you, fresh from New York."

Christian glanced at the spine, then startled himself with a genuine laugh. Sun Tzu: *The Art of War*. "From you? No—from Mina, am I right?" Ashmore's wife was an American *bon vivant*, petite and pretty as a doll, and dangerously sharp. She had once told Christian that etiquette manuals were a sham; all a woman needed to succeed, she claimed, was a copy of Machiavelli's advice for tyrants.

"Her newest inspiration, yes. I advise you to read it thoroughly." Ashmore added dryly, "She'll probably quiz you on it when next we meet."

An intuition brushed through Christian. Here was why Lilah Marshall sometimes seemed so familiar to him. She and Mina shared the same brand of brazen self-possession, a winking awareness of their own charm and wit. "Cover to cover, then," he said, and tucked it under his arm before taking his leave of Ashmore.

Once upstairs, however, he left the book unopened in his sitting room. Ashmore was right in one regard: Bolkhov had claimed too many pieces of his inward reserve. For months he had fantasized about nothing but blood. But tonight, he would push aside all thoughts of warfare, and dream of more pleasant villainies.

With God's grace, he would dream only of what he wished to do to Lilah.

CHAPTER FIVE

Tu n'es pas qualifié pour être mon assistante."

Lilah had been staring out the window at rolling fields. Startled, she looked up. "I beg your pardon?"

Miss Everleigh sat across from her, swaddled to the chin in a most unattractive, but no doubt extremely expensive, coat of fine-twilled puce-colored cashmere. "I said, *Tu n'es pas qualifié pour être mon assistante.*"

Lilah recognized the language as French. There, her knowledge ended. "Yes," she said. "Indeed."

Miss Everleigh narrowed her eyes, which Lilah knew could shine a striking violet, but which today—thanks to the coat—more closely resembled the color of a mud-clogged puddle. For all Lilah knew, that was the very reason Miss Everleigh had chosen such an unflattering color. If the past two hours of stony silence had demonstrated anything, it was the lady's ability to make everything—even Lilah's first trip into the country—deeply unappealing.

"You have just admitted that you're thoroughly unqualified to be my assistant," Miss Everleigh told her.

"Either you do not understand French, or you are un-usually honest."

Charming! They were bantering now, only a hop and a skip away from becoming bosom friends. "I would like to think myself honest," Lilah said. It *would* be nice to be Lilah Marshall in truth, the daughter of a respectable clerk. "Alas, my French is very poor."

Catherine sniffed. "Why am I not surprised?"

"Because you're a woman of great insight," Lilah said smoothly.

From Catherine's sour look, it was clear that flattery would not work. "This is a mad arrangement. You will only get in my way." She straightened her muff—was she really so cold that she required all that outerwear?—and returned to staring fixedly out the window.

How could someone so pretty, so fortunate in her circumstances, and so widely admired by handsome young gentlemen in need of a fortune, be so unpleasant? In her shoes, Lilah would never have stopped smiling. Every door in the world stood open to Catherine Everleigh. She only needed pick which one she felt like exploring, as the mood took her.

Instead, she buried herself in business. Nothing else seemed to bring her joy.

Her gloom was a subject of some speculation among the Everleigh Girls. "See if you can crack her," Vinnie had advised Lilah, in an uncanny echo of Palmer's instruction. "They say she had a lover once, but he was too proud to marry a woman whose family was in trade. I'm sure that's what left her so shriveled inside."

Vinnie, Lilah feared, was a secret romantic. The truth was probably much less interesting: Miss Everleigh had been cursed by a fairy at birth, to be as ugly in her disposition as she was beautiful in looks.

But all this was irrelevant. She could be an actual monster, for all it mattered. Lilah would still win her over—and get her betrothed to the viscount by the last week of June.

"I'm a very quick learner," she offered. "And very motivated, miss, to learn as much as I can from your admirable example." For instance, she'd not known that ladies never handled money. For a brief, happy moment, she'd imagined that the coin purse Miss Everleigh had thrust at her on the platform at Paddington was for *her*.

But, no. Apparently it was her job to tip everyone, sparing Miss Everleigh's delicate hands from the touch of filthy lucre.

"I'm sure you're very shrewd," Miss Everleigh said, in a tone that suggested shrewdness was the province of lepers. "But my task at Buckley Hall is not to play tutor to the ignorant."

"Naturally," Lilah murmured. In the concealment of her skirts, she made a fist so tight that her knuckles throbbed. "I shan't impede your duties, I promise you."

"Of course not. I would not let you." And with that pronouncement, Miss Everleigh pulled out a book and began to read.

Had Lilah wished earlier for a spot of conversation? She now sank most gratefully back into silence. The sights of a country road offered ample diversion. She had only been outside London three or four times in her life, always to Margate. That was where the common folk went on their holidays, to take the sea air and clear their lungs of soot.

But coastal Kent looked nothing like its verdant interior. Here, the soil must be rich and fertile, for oaks grew in abundance alongside the road, and in the openings through the trees, Lilah spied endless rolling fields of green and yellow, bushy crops she could not name, which waved in the unseen breeze.

The carriage took a fast turn, causing them both to gasp and reach for their straps. "This coachman!" Miss Everleigh snapped, and banged the ceiling. The vehicle instantly slowed, the driver already having been chastened thrice for his speeding.

Lilah had no sympathy for him. Once at their destination, *he* would get to leave.

The coach crested a gentle slope, and suddenly the vista opened up. In the distance, at the top of a green grassy knoll, perched a house of . . . terrible proportions.

Lilah must have made a noise—a gasp of horror, she didn't doubt. Miss Everleigh laid down her book and leaned forward to take the view. "Oh," she said quietly. "Buckley Hall."

The building was long and squat, no more than two stories, built patchwork in red brick and pink wash, with long, narrow windows that stretched from ground to roof. Above these windows, strange turrets were capped by copper-topped cupolas, which stretched like taffy into fantastical points.

Lilah had never seen anything like it before. Would they find skeletons in the cellar? And Egyptian mummies in the attic? A delicious shiver coursed through her. "How awful," she said with relish.

"Awful!" Miss Everleigh cast her a blazing look of dislike. "Buckley Hall is a marvel. One of the premier examples of the Tudor Gothic style." She frowned. "Remodeled through the course of several generations, naturally." Sitting back, she opened her book again, saying sharply to the page: "It is a national treasure."

"Oh, quite." Lilah battled temptation and lost. "You must tell Lord Palmer so. He will be very glad to hear it, I think. He called it a 'ramshackle pile.'"

"Did he?" Miss Everleigh peered up, scowling. "When did you speak with him?"

Lilah wanted to kick herself. "I overheard him, the night of the ball."

Miss Everleigh remained staring, her suspicion plain. Not a dumb woman, more was the pity. "You make it a habit to eavesdrop on our guests?"

The charge was ridiculous. "No, miss. But Mr. Everleigh instructs us to attend closely to their conversations, so we might better know their tastes and preferences."

Miss Everleigh wrinkled her nose. "Yes, of course he does. *Some* auction houses trust in the quality of their curation to entice clientele. But my brother insists on cheap flattery and pandering." Here she paused, obviously waiting to see if Lilah would take the bait and make the mistake of agreeing—and thereby insult her own employer.

Lilah offered a shy, bashful smile.

With a snort, Miss Everleigh snapped shut the book. "Quality," she said, "and beauty are not solely the functions of the physical object itself—be it a vase, a painting, or a house. *Provenance,* Miss Marshall, is a key constituent of value. Is that word too French for you to grasp? History, then, is what I mean. The richer an object's history, the more value it possesses. And this house"—she tipped her head toward the window, and the view it offered of the monstrous squat palace drawing nearer—"is rich in history, indeed."

It seemed Lilah would be tutored, after all. "Yes, miss. I'm certain you're right."

"You need not take my word for it," Miss Everleigh said crisply. "The Barons Hughley were descended directly from a member of the Conqueror's court. They survived the War of the Roses, and the depredations of Henry Tudor. They saw Queen Elizabeth crowned. This house was built by one of her favored courtiers. Eustace de Hughley was his name."

Her lifted brows suggested this name should mean something. Lilah wracked her brain, but try as she might, she could not recall reading of Eustace de Hughley during her visits to the library at Everleigh's.

Catherine Everleigh sighed. "The astronomer."

"The telescope!" Lilah's exclamation made her new mistress twitch.

"Many telescopes," Miss Everleigh said coldly.

"But surely one of the finest examples of his scientific acumen was the telescope auctioned at Everleigh's as part of the Houston estate," Lilah rejoined instantly. "Why, many scholars believe that that very specimen provided a crucial inspiration to Galileo."

Her reward for this recitation—which she had repeated almost verbatim from the catalog for the Houston auction—was a slow blink from the woman opposite.

"Yes," Miss Everleigh finally allowed. Before this triumph could register, she quickly continued, "Of course, it's the women of the family who are most notable." Her pause felt challenging.

Lilah could think of no satisfactory reply. She nodded.

"The Hughley women were visionaries," Miss Everleigh said. "In every recorded generation, one finds evidence of spirited, noble, freethinking lady scholars. This house and its many alterations are almost solely the work of the Hughley women."

Was that how Miss Everleigh saw herself? As spirited, noble, and freethinking? Fine euphemisms, Lilah thought darkly, for *rude* and *unfeeling*.

She checked herself. If she meant to win the woman's trust, she could not afford to think this way. She must cultivate a sympathetic, interested, and transparently grateful air. "How lovely," she said. "It's so rare to hear of a noble family distinguished by its womenfolk."

"Ladies," Miss Everleigh said through her teeth.

Evidently *womenfolk* was one of those words that unwittingly betrayed Lilah's origins. She made a note to strike it from her vocabulary. "I would be most grateful to learn more of the family's history."

"Indeed." Miss Everleigh leaned forward again to gaze at the house, which was very nearly upon them now. "It will be an honor to walk in their footsteps," she said more softly. "They managed so well to blend their scholarly pursuits with familial duty."

Lilah's instincts pricked. Was that a pensive note in Miss Everleigh's voice? Very cautiously, she said, "They were great ladies."

"And even greater matriarchs. All the Hughleys of note had several children. Happy families, by most accounts." Miss Everleigh seemed now to have forgotten to whom she spoke, for she no longer sounded stiff in the least, only . . .

Wistful.

Miss Everleigh wanted a family of her own. She wanted to be a scholar and a . . . matriarch!

Had the heavens opened and angels announced they

were on Lilah's side, she could not have felt more relieved. For if Miss Everleigh wished her noble scholarship to be accommodated within a fecund marriage, there was hope after all.

Lilah would have her *wed* to Palmer before the last week of June!

"Of course, it came to nothing in the end." Having remembered herself, Miss Everleigh sat back, subsiding into her typical gloom. "The line has ended. The barony has been retired."

"But not the house," Lilah said, trying hard to conceal her happiness. "Nor their legacy, Miss Everleigh. You'll make sure of that."

Wonder of wonders, the look Miss Everleigh cut her was only half-suspicious. The other half, Lilah felt sure, was hopeful.

Rupert Hughley had been rich in land and dusty souvenirs, and sadly short of cash. What minimal staff he'd employed, Christian had kept on. Perhaps that had been a mistake. The house looked very ill-kept, a thick layer of dust mantling every exposed surface. Furthermore, the housekeeper—already a suspect figure, for obvious reasons—did not seem to know her way around.

"This wing's never been used," she grumbled as she led him down the hall.

"The furniture would suggest otherwise," Christian said politely. Through the opened doors to left and right, he spied various objects swathed in white sheeting.

Mrs. Barnes shrugged. For a woman of advanced age, she had a great many iron-gray curls springing from her scalp. They formed the widest point of her body, for below them, she was as stringy and straight as a beanpole. "Baron Hughley—rest his soul!—did not like this wing. Two generations ago, p'raps, it was favored."

"The layer of dust would suggest longer yet." He rubbed a finger across his nose to forestall a sneeze.

Mrs. Barnes snorted. "Well, it's not for lack of my trying to keep it clean. But the silly girls that Lord Hughley—rest his soul," she muttered quickly, and crossed herself. "The girls what he insisted on employing, they won't set foot in this wing for fear."

"Fear of asthma?"

Mrs. Barnes impressed him by replying with a rusty laugh. "That, too," she said. "And don't think I hadn't suggested we sack them and start afresh. But no, Lord Hughley"—she crossed herself, and Christian, catching on now, chimed in with her:

"God rest his soul."

"Indeed." She gave him an approving look. "Churchgoing man, are you? And a proper hero to boot! Happy day for us, Lord Palmer. But I needn't tell you that. I expect the whole village turned out to greet you."

"Yes, they were very kind." A troop of schoolchildren had been marched into the road to shower his coach with flowers. The horses hadn't liked it. But the schoolchildren had seemed to enjoy the impromptu lesson in how a coachman cursed. Their parents and the mayor had looked . . . less pleased.

"At any rate . . ." Mrs. Barnes clicked her tongue. "Lord Hughley was too sympathetic to the maids, I think. Maybe the ghost scared him, too."

"The ghost!" He'd no idea that he'd inherited a spirit. "Very fearsome, is he? Rattle some chains now and then?"

"And occasionally knocks things off the shelves," she said. "A pity, I've often thought, that ghosts so rarely make themselves known by tidying a place. As to this one, I've not seen him myself. He likes to keep to the spots where the cleaning goes hardest."

He grinned. Questionable toilette aside, he rather liked his new housekeeper. "Well, Mrs. Barnes, I cannot claim any expertise in ghost hunting, but I will seize the authority to hire and fire staff. If you'd like to handle that business, I'll give you a free hand."

"Isn't the hand I'm lacking." She drew up outside a set of arched double doors, trussed in iron; they looked more appropriate for a medieval fortress than for a genteel country home. "It's the coin," she said. Not for the first time today, she ran an appraising look over Christian's figure.

Only now did he understand the cause for it. She was trying to judge the relative fullness of his pockets. Difficult, of course, when he still wore traveling clothes.

"Market rate, Mrs. Barnes," he said. "And not a penny more."

Her broad smile made her eyes sink into a hundred fine-lined creases. "Very good, my lord. Very good, indeed. I do think—"

Raised voices from within the room interrupted her.

"Put that *down*!"

"I didn't mean to—"

"Enough! Your incompetence beggars disbelief!"

"I'll be leaving you to it," Mrs. Barnes said hastily, and scurried off down the hall.

"How kind of you," Christian said dryly.

He opened the door. The scene within would have been remarkable even without its players: the two women faced each other across jumbled piles of books, in a vast room topped by a rib-vaulted ceiling straight from some Gothic cathedral. The light pouring through the stained-glass windows painted their scowls in shades of crimson and teal.

"Ladies," said Christian. "Good afternoon to you both."

With the instincts of a performer, Lilah Marshall immediately dropped her scowl for a smile, giving him a neat curtsy for accompaniment.

He really must remind her that it was not *he* who required charming. But God help him if he didn't have a soft spot for performers. She'd have made a fine hero; she knew how to beam on command.

Catherine Everleigh acknowledged him with a regal nod. "Lord Palmer," she said. "I trust your journey was pleasant?"

"The train was on schedule, so I cannot complain." He stepped through the maze of piled books, taking note of the bizarrely medieval flagstones and the bare shelves that lined the walls. This seemed an odd strategy on Catherine's part, not to mention an exhausting one. "I see you're hard at work," he said. "It must have taken all morning to remove these books from the shelves."

Lilah made some noise. It sounded like a warning.

Alas, it came too late. Catherine Everleigh huffed. "I certainly would not dream of removing books from their shelves for storage on a damp stone floor. This disorder you see was the work of some lunatical housemaid—though if any remain in the place, I've yet to see them. Why, last night I had to ring the housekeeper for fresh sheets on my bed!"

"It was very awful," Lilah said blandly. "Miss Everleigh encountered a stain."

He narrowed his eyes at her. "Yet you remain focused on your task here. How commendable."

By the way she averted her gaze, she understood the rebuke. But her shrug did not look properly chastened.

He turned to Catherine. "My abject apologies. It distresses me to think that you received anything other than the warmest and most, er, hygienic welcome. Rest assured that I have spoken with Mrs. Barnes. She has been given full liberty to hire new help."

After a moment, Catherine nodded. But her mouth pressed into a tight line.

He offered her a very sympathetic smile. "I do hope that you're not regretting your trip here."

"Oh. No." She blinked, looking startled by the notion. "This house is a treasure trove, of course. These books—some of them are quite rare indeed." She gestured toward a rickety table, upon which several volumes rested. "First printings. Newton, Donne. To say nothing of the French literature." Here her tone grew cold again, her glance toward her assistant peculiarly vehement. "None of which belong *stacked together*—"

"You gasped at the cover," Lilah said brightly. "The satyr, with no clothes on his bottom half. For your health, I thought it best disguised."

Christian coughed to cover his laugh. Evidently old Rupert had cultivated racy tastes in his reading. "Shall I—"

"She cannot read French." Catherine spoke in a high, tense voice. "Did you know that, Lord Palmer? Can you credit it? An assistant who knows no French!"

"I did believe us still in England," Lilah said to him. "But Miss Everleigh informs me *au contraire*."

"That is not how one uses the phrase!"

"A late lunch," he said hastily. "Perhaps? Anyone hungry?"

"Famished," said Lilah.

"Exhausted," Catherine snapped. "I will retire for an hour. One does hope that the staff can manage to scare up some clean water, so I may wipe off this grime."

Gathering her skirts, she stormed for the door. But at the threshold, she stopped quite abruptly and turned back. "Lord Palmer," she said.

"Miss Everleigh," he replied.

"Good afternoon to you."

He bowed.

The door slammed behind her, leaving him to wait silently beside Lilah as the sound of Catherine's footsteps faded. Seven, eight, nine, ten—

Both spoke at once.

"I instructed you to *befriend* her—"

"That woman is a witch; there's a reason she has no friends!"

"Well," he said, "and there's a reason you've no choice in the matter. You're a thief, and not a clever one. You got caught."

"I'm a very good one," she said bitterly. "Only I was out of practice."

"So you're a career thief, then! How fascinating. Tell me more."

She crossed her arms. "Why would I?"

"Why, to keep digging your grave, of course." He squatted down to pick up a handsome-looking volume. How fitting! With a laugh, he held it up to her. "*Crime and Punishment.* I don't suppose you've read Dostoevsky?"

"That depends. Does he write in French?"

With a sigh, he dropped the book. It was mildly aggravating to observe that she looked fetching coated with a layer of dust. She was dressed like a governess whose employer inclined to lechery, her black hair scraped into a tight chignon, a shapeless gray gown encasing her from chin to feet. But the drab pleats could not disguise the generous curve of her hips when she shifted her weight. Nor could her hair be tamed by pins. A dark lock had escaped, and unfurled along her throat like a suggestion: *touch me here.* Meanwhile, her pique made her eyes brighten to the shade of sapphires.

Touch her, indeed. One of her cheeks bore a smudge. He very much wished to remove it for her. With his tongue.

He turned away from her to make a frowning study of the stained glass. A seasoning of lust would make this grim wait more bearable, but he could not allow it to distract him.

Ludicrous proposition. She was a criminal, the object of his blackmail. He'd never lost his head over a woman who wasn't an equal. Wit and intelligence were what charmed him. A woman of spirit.

She fit that bill too closely.

Well, he would simply not allow her to become too charming. "More servility," he instructed as he turned back. "And far less cheek."

"There's no need for me to be servile," she retorted. "She already treats me as though I'm a street sweeper—or worse!"

"Enough," he bit out. "You are not here to argue—only to obey. Do you understand? You have a great deal to lose—your freedom, above all. Do you imagine I could not have you jailed by nightfall? If Peter Everleigh has not noticed the absence of those letters, a telegram will suffice to alert him. Then, perhaps, you will envy the street sweepers."

She did not so much as flinch. But all the life, the charm and fire, disappeared from her face. The smile she gave him was somehow disturbing. It was emptier than space.

"Of course, you're right," she said. "Forgive me, Lord Palmer. I don't know what I was thinking."

He gritted his teeth against the absurd urge to temper his harshness. Every commander knew the value of discipline in the ranks. "Good. Now start afresh with her. Go to her rooms; see if she has gotten clean water for her bath."

"I will, if you wish it. But she'll promptly rebuke me for confusing an assistant's duties with those of a maid. Better to let her rest for an hour, don't you think? She didn't sleep well last night, and you know how exhaustion wears on the temper."

He considered that. "Fine. After lunch, then, you will apologize. Once that's done—"

"Lord Palmer." Her smile now looked more genuine. "Forgive me if I venture that an Everleigh Girl knows how to placate and ingratiate herself better than you do."

He supposed that was true. With a grunt, he looked over the room again. What a peculiar mind had created this monstrous chimera of a house! The same mind, no doubt, had been responsible at one time for hanging that tattered banner in the corner. The shaggy lion looked half the size of the unicorn it was rearing to fight.

"This is the newest part of the house," she said, "if you can believe it."

"I can't, in fact."

"The eighth Baroness Hughley had a great admiration for the Gothic. The style, she felt, was a perfect representation of man's yearning for the heavens, and all the lofty aspirations thereby entailed."

He snorted. Florid and a bit vague. "What aspirations are those, pray tell?"

She spread her hands. "You ask the wrong woman. I'm quoting a book of family history. The highest I've aimed is a good salary and a bed of my own."

He smiled against his will. "I'm not sure I believe that."

She linked her hands at her waist. "Ah, well. You know us criminal sorts."

No, he thought. He was not sure that category began to capture the first thing about this woman.

Stop. He forcibly redirected his attention toward the books, resuming his prowl through the piles. Meanwhile, she sank to her knees, rooting through volumes. "One of these," she began, then trailed off. When she spoke again, she sounded frustrated. "So many in French!"

"It's an old library," he said. "Latin and French tended to rule the day."

"I didn't guess it was so important."

He glanced up and caught a strange look on her face, almost of despair. "Important for what?" he asked.

She sighed, then picked up a book and flipped through its pages. "For being a—" Something thudded onto the floor. "Proper lady," she finished absently. "Look at this!" She picked up the object, revealing it to be a small dagger with a curved blade.

He whistled. "Hand me that."

It was a very fine specimen, indeed. The crystal hilt

lent it surprising heft. He rubbed his thumb over the blade. An intricate geometric design had been engraved into the steel. "One of these Hughleys was a nabob," he recalled. "Stole vast fortunes from Indian princes."

"The seventh Baron Hughley, that was."

He looked up, surprised. "Clearly your conversations with Catherine haven't all been quarrelsome."

She shifted her weight, looking discomfited. "She did tell me a bit. And as I mentioned, I found a book last night—the Hughley history. Rather interesting what a family can achieve with pots of money at its disposal."

When she wrinkled her nose like that, she looked very young. Someone's daughter, he thought, oddly startled. Someone's sister? He flipped the dagger in his hands, causing her to gasp. "Where is your family?" he asked her, and then flipped the knife again, simply to enjoy her reaction.

"Slash your wrist," she said, "and there will be no wedding."

He flipped the knife into the air over his head, catching it again by the handle. "I was a soldier, Miss Marshall." Surely she remembered that. She had quoted the damned poem at him, hadn't she?

"Do soldiers play with knives?" she asked. "I thought only fools did. Fools who have yet to get cut."

He gave her a dangerous smile. "But you see my face. I've certainly been cut, in my time." He hurled the knife across the room.

Thunk. Impaled in the door, the blade quivered musically. Wide-eyed, she looked from his face to the blade, and back again.

"I'm on friendly terms with sharp objects," he told her.

She lifted her brows. "How very good to know."

Her dry tone caused an odd feeling to prickle over him. He recognized it, after a moment, as embarrassment.

Good God. Had he just been showing off for her? What in heaven's name ailed him? If he wanted admiration, he need only take a walk in public. Half the country still wanted his autograph. An astonishing number of women claimed to carry his likeness in their pockets, some blasted sketch they'd clipped out of a newspaper.

But not Lilah Marshall, he suspected. Nor Catherine Everleigh. Here was irony! He found himself closeted with the only two women in England who did not fawn on him.

Catherine saw him as a nuisance—a gatekeeper to untold collectibles. What did Lilah see? A bully, no doubt.

His pride disliked that. His *vanity* disliked it. He had grown rather accustomed to playing the hero. It so conveniently spared him the need to create another role for himself. But he had a feeling that whatever Lilah saw was far truer . . . and no cause for pride.

He waved her toward the door. "Go on, then." Seducing her was one thing. Caring for her opinion was far less acceptable. "If not to disturb Catherine, then to prepare your . . . placating."

"Yes, my lord." Picking up her skirts, she made for the exit—pausing by the door to look again at the knife. "It's a very fine dagger," she said. "Perhaps you shouldn't leave it embedded like this. It might damage the blade."

"The blade is steel," he said curtly. "Stronger than you can imagine." He would not be lectured by a woman on weaponry.

"Very well." But instead of leaving, she faced him again. "I did find out one thing that may prove useful. Miss Everleigh is lonely."

Clearly she thought him dull-witted. "Yes. You told me as much. Friendless, you say. Any other insights? If not, that will be all."

She acknowledged his sarcasm with a pull of her pretty mouth. "What I mean is, she wants a champion. Her brother disapproves of her participation in the business. He was furious when their father left her a full share. Everybody heard of his objections."

"You're right," he said. "Everybody heard of that."

"Listen," she said curtly, in a tone that said, *you dolt.* "She is enamored of the Hughley women—did you know that? They were scholars and artists, and wives and mothers to boot. But what she likes is how their husbands supported their interests. She longs for that kind of support." She paused expectantly.

Indeed, it was a useful piece of information. He gave a curt, grudging nod. "All right."

She smiled, looking far too satisfied with herself. And she still wore that damned smudge—a provocation in itself.

He heard himself say, "Of course she wishes for a husband who admires her. What woman doesn't? But I thank you for the obvious tidings."

Her eyes narrowed. "Forgive me. Of course you're right. We women are very predictable." Then, with a surprising show of strength, she yanked the dagger out of the door, hefted it once in her hand, and threw it.

The blade flashed by him. It came so close that he felt the flutter of air displaced by its passage.

Thunk.

Speechless, he turned. The knife now pinned the ancient tapestry to a mortared joint in the wall. It pinned the *eye of the lion* to the wall.

That was a happy accident. Surely.

"Oh, look," she said from the doorway. "It seems a woman can surprise you, after all!"

For the second time in a quarter hour, the door slammed soundly shut.

CHAPTER SIX

$\mathcal{D}$inner that evening started at the unconsciona-
bly early hour of half seven. "Country hours,"
the housekeeper had said. Lucky thing that Lilah had
brought *The Lady's Guide to Refined Deportment*, which
contained an entire passage on the curious schedule
kept at country estates. Otherwise, she would have had
no idea what to make of Mrs. Barnes's remark.

As she set out from her room, she took a wrong turn.
The house was larger than one realized when viewing its
facade. The two stories extended very deep, the result—
Lilah had learned from the volume of family history—
of an extension joined to the rear of the Tudor structure
by Baroness Hughley the fourth.

Alas, Baroness Hughley the fourth had grown up
during the English Civil War, an experience, Lilah gathered, that had left her with a fervent appreciation for
confusion and hidey-holes. Peculiar passages and odd,
twisting halls distinguished the rear extension, and it
was one of these passages that led Lilah not to the din-
ing room, but to a peculiar, secret half floor, more of a

short hallway really, where she found herself lingering in
startled delight.

Upstairs, the residential apartments opened onto a
corridor furnished with the typical suits of armor and
marble statuary. But this hall looked to have been borrowed wholesale from some eastern potentate's palace.
Turkish carpets blanketed the flagstones. Handsome
carved screens concealed the plaster walls.

The auction house had pretensions to grandeur. But
beyond the marbled public rooms, it was, after all, a
place of business, marked by bare floors and workaday
furniture. Never before had Lilah found herself in a
place that spoke so strongly of power and wealth—and
she was at full liberty to explore. How diverting!

Somebody was occupying the area, for the wall
sconces were lit. Checking her pocket watch (not strictly
appropriate for evening attire, but Lilah had not for-
gone all her old habits; every dress she owned contained
a hidden pocket or two), she discovered that enough
time remained before dinner to allow a brief prowl. If
discovered, she would simply claim that it was her duty,
as Miss Everleigh's assistant, to survey the area. These
screens, for instance, might fetch a very good price at
auction.

Four doors lined the short hall. Her hairpin opened
them easily. The first room was a small, attractive salon,
with dark wallpaper and large, handsome oil paintings
depicting a string of Hughley scions and their hounds.

The second room contained a billiards table, the
green baize visibly warped by time and the damp. A hint
of ancient pipe smoke lingered in the furniture.

The third room was a very fine water closet, done in
Moroccan tile.

The fourth room . . . ah! A fire burned low in the hearth, and on a low scrollwork table, a glass of wine sat, half-emptied.

She hesitated, one hand on the doorknob, unnerved by the depth of her curiosity. She was a practical woman. Pragmatism was a woman's best advantage in the world. Lord Palmer was her enemy. Her interest in him was only . . . practical. She must learn as much of him as possible, the better to protect herself.

She walked into the room. The desk was littered with a variety of letters, many of them bearing diplomatic insignia. A curious group of correspondents—all of them Russians, some of whom she knew from their patronage of the auction house. Obolensky was a special emissary of the czar, whom Susie had shown through the Slavic collection during the party last week.

She nudged aside the letters. Beneath them lay a large map of London, on which somebody had circled the location of the auction house. Other areas had also been notated—neighborhoods that an aristocrat typically avoided. Mile End, St. George's-in-the-East—these made up part of Nick's territory, poor areas whose local bigwigs paid monthly tributes to her uncle.

Mile End. Who was the bigwig in Mile End? A Russian, wasn't it?

She stepped away, frowning. What use had an English war hero for such interests? Were this a theatrical set, such props would have marked him as a spy . . . and not for England.

Dinner was predictably joyless. Palmer tried to lure Miss Everleigh to speak more of herself. She answered his attempts with enervated courtesy, not so much rebuffing his charm as presenting a mask of perfect indifference to it.

He turned the conversation toward Buckley Hall. Here, Miss Everleigh grew animated. As Lilah nursed a single glass of wine and forced down bites of overcooked venison, Miss Everleigh launched into a lecture on the furniture of the Sun King.

Lilah did not incline to paranoid fantasies. English viscounts did not trouble themselves with espionage, particularly not for Russians. Of course they didn't.

Palmer noted her silence. "And how fare you, Miss Marshall? You seem tired. Did you set yourself too exhausting an aim?"

She gathered that was a subtle reference to her dagger throwing. "No," she said brightly, "I was not taxed in the least. Is *your* arm sore, sir?"

It seemed there were two subjects, after all, on which Miss Everleigh would wax enthusiastic, the second being Lilah's manners. "You might refrain from mention of bodily parts at the table," she said icily. "I am surprised, Miss Marshall. I thought conversational politesse was the main talent for which my brother employed you."

Lilah delayed her reply with a long sip of the Bordeaux. "Forgive me," she said evenly. "It's true, I find myself somewhat fatigued. I have never kept country hours before."

These tidings sank into an astonished silence. "You have never been to the country?" Miss Everleigh asked at last, as though her ears might have deceived her.

"I've been to the seaside, miss. But only for the day."

"Then you're bound for pleasant surprises," Palmer said. "The quiet, for one."

"Yes, I noticed it last night." Along with the immense darkness outside, which had terrified her, and driven her to stay up till dawn with that book on the Hughley family.

As though he'd read her mind, Palmer said, "Miss Marshall made a study last night of my ancestors. Some ancient volume of family history, lying about in her rooms. Did you manage to finish it, Miss Marshall?"

She smiled at him. "First page to last."

"A pity," said Miss Everleigh. "Sleep might have equipped you to prove more useful. I trust you won't fritter away tonight."

Lilah bit her tongue. "No, miss. I expect I will sleep very well."

"Excellent. Though I hope you will stir from your rooms at an earlier hour than you managed this morning."

Lilah did not let her smile budge a fraction. She did, however, take the comfort of fondling her dinner knife. It was sharp, and there was satisfaction in knowing that if she chose, she could rid Miss Everleigh of that stray wisp of hair currently escaping her blond coiffure. It would hardly require the pause to take aim.

She felt Palmer's eyes on her. She glanced over. He dropped his gaze to the knife.

She pulled her hand back into her lap.

The dimple appeared in his cheek. He was fighting a laugh. Clearing his throat, he turned and addressed some bland question to Miss Everleigh. More discussion of the Sun King.

Lilah sighed. It was the most vexing development imaginable that she should feel, at odd moments, a real liking for him. He was a bully and a blackmailer—but that made him little different from many acquaintances of her youth. Once she'd realized he had a purpose in stealing those papers other than to torment her, she'd found her anger hard to hold on to. It was the way of the world, after all; one did what one must to thrive. And she *had* been clumsy—all but begging to be caught as she'd hidden beneath that desk.

No, moral indignation would not have furnished her the key to disliking him. Not when he, unlike most of his brethren, spoke to her as a real person. Not when he caught her little jokes and laughed, albeit reluctantly.

He did not want to find her charming, either. That was obvious. A fine pair they made, struggling to dislike each other despite having every good reason to do so.

But if he was some kind of underhanded plotter . . . well, *then* she could loathe him properly. Hypocrisy, after all, was her least favorite quality. A traitor disguising himself as a war hero? That was dirtier business than her uncle's.

She studied him as he flirted with Miss Everleigh. She could not square her suspicions with her gut feeling. Something was rotten, but she didn't sense he was dangerous—not in an underhanded way, at least. More in a . . . kissing kind of way.

Heaven help me. She looked down at her plate to hide her blush. Knowing him better would help her make up her mind about him. But time in his presence only seemed to erode her wits further.

The days settled into a predictable pattern. Lilah was not invited to dine downstairs again, which suited her perfectly. She took her suppers in her sitting room, then read until exhaustion overwhelmed her dislike of the dark. At dawn, she hurried—and failed—to beat Miss Everleigh to breakfast. Then, for the next twelve hours, she trailed her mistress like a sheepish dog, trying her best to learn more of the woman without appearing chatty or forward or inattentive to the tasks at hand.

Some days, Miss Everleigh lost patience with her, and sent her off to comb through rooms on her own, with the instruction to set aside and make note of objects that promised good value. These days felt positively magical. As a child, Lilah and her sister had often pretended to be explorers, hunting their household for buried treasure. Now she did the same—but instead of discovering the pennies her father had used to hide, she uncovered items that belonged in museums. Beneath a pile of yellowing canvas, she found a pair of silver candlesticks, intricately engraved with a variety of exotic beasts, elephants and tigers. She forced open a broken chest of drawers, and out spilled chess pieces carved from ivory and inlaid with precious jewels. Cobwebbed corners concealed figurines, china plates, and handsomely painted tiles, abandoned and forgotten by long-dead generations.

Meanwhile, out the window, she saw things that city life had never shown her. A sunset as red as blood, in a sky so wide that it was a wonder the clouds didn't get lost. Storms showed themselves on the horizon an hour before they arrived, so one could see rain slanting at a distance while sun still shone across the lawn. One day, a band of tinkers trundled up in a yellow caravan to sell their wares. Miss Everleigh would not let her go meet them, but she watched from the window as the housekeeper purchased pots and pans.

Fiona had nursed a dream of growing old in the countryside. Property in London was very dear, but careful savings might purchase a cottage in some village far from London, where nobody would ever discover a girl's past. She'd made a habit of memorizing poems about country lanes and babbling brooks and the like.

But you don't even know if we'll like the country, Lilah had told her once.

Well, one day we'll go and find out, won't we?

Now Lilah found herself in the middle of her sister's dream. But Miss Everleigh's punishing schedule left no opportunity for outdoor explorations . . . until one afternoon when she dispatched Lilah to the farthest corner of the house and forgot to summon her afterward. The sun still rode high in a clear sky as Lilah finished her work. At last she saw the chance to explore the charms of the pastoral.

But three steps down the lawn toward the wood, she discovered what Fiona had never guessed, and poets never bothered to mention: country air was poisonous! First her eyes began to water. Next, her nose caught an itch. At her third sneeze, she turned back for the house in a state of high alarm.

It was just her luck to run into Lord Palmer in the front hall. He was dressed for riding, in tall boots and a close-fitted hunting jacket. "Where is Miss Everleigh?" he said curtly. "Why are you not with her?"

She held up one finger. The next sneeze was coming.

"You have a single task here." He underlined his point by slapping his quirt against his thigh. "To assist—"

The sneeze exploded, knocking her back a pace. "It's dreadful out there!" she said. "Don't go!"

He blinked. She sneezed again. When the fit subsided, she saw a smile tugging at his lips "Spot of hay fever?"

"Is that what it is? Is it curable? Oh, I—" She sneezed again. "Drat it!"

He handed over a handkerchief, which she gratefully pressed to her runny nose. It smelled of him—soap and leather and clean male skin, with perhaps a hint of horse. "Avoid the greenery," he said, "and you'll recover."

"There seems to be a great deal of it here." Yet he looked aggravatingly hale, his bronzed skin suddenly suspect. He had been out in the sun very recently. "How do you not suffer?"

"Country raised," he said.

That sounded like a curse. "I must go lie down." But when she started past him, he caught her arm.

"You must go assist Miss Everleigh. You are not here on a holiday."

"She put me to my own work, and—" She pulled free in time to spare him her next sneeze. "She's not likely to welcome me in this state, is she?"

Looking at her, he sighed. "All right. Come with me." Turning on his heel, he started off down the hall.

She hurried after him. A brief, twisting, confounding route led them to a door that opened into the hallway she had discovered once before. She slowed, a nervous flutter distracting her from misery. He was leading her into his study! What would she say about the map? Would it be wiser to pretend not to notice it?

But it transpired that he had cleared away any incriminating documents. With the drapes pulled back and daylight spilling across the bright Turkish carpet, the room looked very different—a far less likely site for the conduction of treason. She felt foolish, suddenly.

Country air rotted her brain as well as her health. He was no traitor. There must be a very good reason for him to correspond with all those Russians.

But then why had he hidden their letters? One only hid things one needed to conceal.

He crossed to a handsome cabinet, pulling out a decanter. "Odd as it sounds, whisky is the quickest cure." He splashed a finger into the glass and carried it back to her. "I'll leave a portion in the kitchens for your use. Ring for another glass in the evening, along with a spoonful of honey. That always suffices for my mother."

"Oh, she also has hay fever? Was she raised in the city, too?" Perhaps his mother was a well-born Russian, which would explain his connection to luminaries from that nation.

"In Sussex." His eyes narrowed. A journalist had described their color as "the lambent shade of a summer sun." At the time, reading the description, Lilah had snorted. But she now grudgingly admitted that it was a very fine turn of phrase. She reserved judgment, however, on whether his golden hair really constituted a "magnificent mane of leonine splendor." "I can't imagine why it concerns you," he said.

She remembered his mood the night he had seen his sister in the street. His family, for some reason, troubled him. She offered an apologetic smile. "I merely wish to assemble a map—a list of places that are safe to visit, and won't kill me when I set foot outdoors."

A slight smile erased his severity. "The condition isn't so perilous. Inconvenient, I'll grant you. But not life threatening."

"Says one who doesn't suffer from it!" She took a sip of the whisky. "I can't believe one isn't warned before departing town. I tell you, it took one breeze, and suddenly I was suffocating." She spared an envious thought for all the people breathing freely right now of London's soot-stained air.

"I don't mean to be dismissive," he said. "I do know my mother suffers greatly at this time of year." He glanced out the window, which offered a fine view of oaks and shrubbery in blossom. *Poisonous* blossom. "But the whisky should help. How are you feeling now?"

She took a testing breath, and felt no urge to sneeze. "Yes," she said, "I think it's working." With enthusiasm, she finished the rest of the glass. "You could pour me a spot more, if you like."

He laughed. "I think a finger will suffice for you."

"I'll wager your mother would take my side." She hesitated. "Is she originally from Sussex?"

"Her family hails from Ireland." He sat down across from her. "And if I recall, she has never complained of hay fever when visiting her cousins. So, there you have it, Miss Marshall: Tipperary is your safest destination."

"Tipperary! But my own—" She stopped, horrified by her near slip.

"Your family is from Tipperary as well?" he asked pleasantly.

"No. Of course not. Surrey, in fact." *You dolt!* For four years, she'd been Lilah Marshall, daughter of a clerk who hailed from the bland, irreproachable Home Counties. And now, dazed by evil hay and a finger of whisky, she had almost undone the whole effort.

Head tipped, he was studying her. "Yet you do have the look of the Irish about you."

She bristled. "I certainly do not." Fiona had looked

Irish—Fiona of the auburn hair, eyes greener than grass. She'd taken after Da that way.

Lilah, on the other hand, took after their mother's side. Dark hair and blue eyes. *My little English bluebird*, Da had called her. *You'd not draw an eye in a crowd of High Churchers.*

He'd meant that as a compliment, of course. Being able to move unnoticed was a great asset in his line of work.

"No, I'm afraid I'm quite right." The dimple had popped out in Palmer's cheek, so she knew to prepare for teasing, "I definitely see a touch of the old country about you."

"Hardly, my lord. I'm a regular English wren."

He lifted his brows. "But that sounds quite plain. Whereas I was thinking instead of your . . ." He paused, looking arrested. "Why, you make yourself sound as plain as your name. 'Marshall.' As English, one might say, as a Sunday roast." A devilish sparkle entered his amber eyes. "So perfectly, unexceptionably unmemorable. Very convenient, for a thief."

Certainly he had Irish blood. No other race possessed the gift for second sight. "I'm an Everleigh Girl," she said. "That night in Mr. Everleigh's office was a singular occurence."

"But by your own admission," he said, "you are *out of practice.* Ergo, once upon a time, you thieved a great deal more often."

"Marshall is a fine name," she said stridently. "No plainer than Stratton, in my view."

"Indeed. One can't argue that. And your mother's name, may I ask?" He sat back, stretching his long legs before him, inadvertently—or perhaps deliberately— flaunting the pronounced musculature of his thighs.

Those breeches fit him like a glove. The effect was . . . distracting.

"My mother's name?" she repeated absently. Nobody had ever asked her about that. He had very powerful calves, didn't he? She hadn't realized calves could be handsome, but the close fit of his buckskin proved it. Strapped with muscle! Put those calves to auction, and all the ladies would bid. "Smith," she said. "Her name was Smith."

"Of course!" He gave a rich, resonant laugh. "Smith and Marshall. John Marshall, dare I guess? And Mary Smith."

She returned his look defiantly. "Sarah Smith." Now she must remember that, in case he tested her again later. "But how kind of you to take an interest in my genealogy, Lord Palmer."

"Oh, I'm finding you more interesting by the minute." He paused, frowning.

She wrestled against the urge to feel flattered. *Interesting* was not a compliment. The wealthy used that word for any number of trifling diversions. God's sake, far too frequently they used it to describe the weather.

More to the point, his curiosity might undo her. "I wish I deserved your interest," she said. "Alas, there's nothing so remarkable about a clerk falling in love with the daughter of his colleague. Your parents, on the other hand—what a grand romance it must have been, for an English viscount to fall in love with an Irishwoman."

"Half Irish," he said. "And not as rare as you'd think. So your father was a clerk, was he? At which place of employment, Miss Marshall?"

"How *did* your parents meet? I do adore a good love story."

"Yes, I'm gathering you're quite fond of any number of stories. Whereas I particularly like tales of misadventure." He leaned forward, bracing his weight against his thigh by one elbow. He'd rolled up his cuffs; his bronzed forearms looked hard as iron, dusted in gold. The veins stood out prominently. "Tell me, how did the daughter of a respectable, law-abiding clerk find herself equipped with the skills of a lockpick and thief?"

Heart skipping, she rose. "Well, I do feel much better now."

With a cat-in-the-cream smile, he came to his feet as well. "So glad to hear it. Will you tell me your true name sometime, Miss Marshall?"

She manufactured a laugh. He knew nothing other than what she led him to suspect. How she'd betrayed herself, she had no idea—and that in itself concerned her as nothing else did. First she'd let him catch her stealing. Now she was letting him see through her.

Or did he truly have the second sight? Now that she knew he was partly Irish, she could see signs of it everywhere—his brawny build; the squareness of his jaw; his noble height and the breadth of his shoulders. *No lad like a Tipperary lad*, as Cousin Sally used to sing. "How amusing you are, Lord Palmer. And how imaginative."

"And how intrigued," he said agreeably. "For it comes to me that a wise host should know his guests better than I do."

That sounded like a very pleasantly spoken threat. The last thing she required was for him to dispatch some investigator to learn more about her. What if somebody from Everleigh's caught wind of his interest? "But I'm not your guest," she said.

"No." His smile tipped into a menacing angle. "Not a guest at all, are you? But lovely, all the same."

She had been prepared for another jab—not a compliment. "Thank you."

"Don't." He reached out and laid a finger against her cheek. "At this rate," he said softly, "you will wish you were plainer, before long."

Only his fingertip touched her. But that small point of contact rooted her in place.

"Do you know," he said, "you wore a smudge at just this spot the day I arrived here."

Bewilderment delayed her reply. What an odd thing to remember! "Yes, I . . . didn't notice it till I was dressing for dinner." She'd had dust and dirt everywhere.

"I mourned its disappearance when you came to the table."

She blinked. "But . . . why?"

"I wanted to lick it off you."

The notion made her stomach feel curiously liquid. "How odd," she whispered.

"Oh, I can get odder." He leaned in and touched the tip of his tongue to her earlobe. He whispered into her ear: "I like how you taste."

"You . . ." She swallowed. "You sound as if you want to eat me."

"In small bites. Ask yourself if you would like it." He stepped back, his look hot and unwavering. "Will you go find Miss Everleigh? Or will you stay here with me?"

She snatched up her skirts and rushed out. It took the length of the hallway for her pace to slow. What bizarre agitation! A single brush of his fingertip, the tip of his tongue, and some husky words should not have caused such upheaval.

Halfway to the attic, she figured it out. Palmer had devised the perfect way to torture her. Each brushing, tasting touch of his—and worse, each show of restraint—lured her body into a collusion with him. He made her long to be reckless.

Why, he was a rake! A proper one, not the clumsy approximations that galumphed through Everleigh's ballroom. He aroused her curiosity as much as her appetite, all the while reiterating that the choice belonged to her.

And the routine worked! Her vulnerability to it amazed her. She had always considered herself wiser than the girls who traded kisses for perfume and jewelry. What possible appeal could material objects exert when their price might cost a girl's independence?

But Palmer didn't try to bribe her. All he offered was an awareness of her own hungers—and the invitation to explore them, if she liked. *Ask yourself. Small bites.*

He made erotic poetry of her right to choose. Oh, dangerous indeed!

In the attic, another surprise awaited her. Miss Everleigh knelt on the floor, surrounded by piles of cloth, her face bright and exultant. She looked up, her transparent joy making her breathtakingly beautiful. "Persian brocade." She held up a length of glimmering silk and, miracle of miracles, *laughed*. "Safavid dynasty! Can you believe it?"

Lilah tried to smile. If Palmer wanted her to focus on her task, he'd best stop touching her. Certain things she didn't need to know about herself—weaknesses better left unexplored.

"It's priceless," Miss Everleigh said. "Truly—did you ever imagine this house should contain anything so astounding?"

"No," Lilah said wistfully. "I did not."

CHAPTER SEVEN

Waiting did not suit Christian's temperament. Nor, for that matter, did Catherine Everleigh. She showed an admirable devotion to her work, and little interest in anything else. Their conversations at dinner flowed only when speaking of her discoveries. He would not persuade her to look on him as a friend, much less divulge confidential information about Russian clients.

Instead, he placed his hopes in his thief. In the mornings, he patrolled the edges of the property and debriefed the men he'd hired to stand guard there. Midday, he took his supper over parliamentary reports, catching up on years of debates that he would be expected to know, once he finally took his seat in the House of Lords. And in the afternoons . . .

In the afternoons, he met with his thief.

On his instruction, Lilah Marshall had taken to stealing into Catherine's rooms during dinner, to make copies of the lady's correspondence. Each afternoon at half four, when Catherine withdrew for her nap, Lilah delivered these copies to his study.

But if Catherine was Bolkhov's conspirator, she never wrote to him. Her letters largely concerned her brother's financial affairs. He was misappropriating company profits, and she seemed helpless to stop him. Solicitors, accountants, even the Everleighs' stockbrokers—none were spared Catherine's accusations.

It made for pathetic reading. Pointless, too. Yet he continued to require Lilah to copy the letters—and then, having delivered them, to sit for a while and keep him company.

It spoke ill of him, no doubt, that daily tête-à-têtes had become the highlight of his routine. He would do better to focus on the vast task of acquainting himself with the duties ahead—politics, and the stewardship of great estates, and the various other tiresome chores that fell to Lord Palmer to supervise. And he did apply himself . . . until half four.

Lilah appeared. She waited while he read the letters. And then he offered her tea and induced her to idle conversation, and let himself remember what he had once hoped for himself: the warmth and enfolding comfort of a peaceful life. Companionship. Easy affection.

That he should find a ghost of these old aims in the company of a thief seemed blackly amusing. But fitting, somehow.

Christian had no illusions about his future. Since his brother's death, he had wrapped himself in dreams of murder. Longing for blood as ardently as a suitor for his beloved, his dreams twisted beyond repair, he could no longer embrace his old hopes. He could not envision with any optimism a return to the kind of innocence that made it possible to limit one's dreams to a house full of hand-knitted doilies and gentle laughter. And even if he could . . . that was not the kind of life given to a peer of the realm.

And yet . . . at half past four, he cast off Lord Palmer and remembered Kit Stratton. A man without enemies. A lad who, at military academy, had been renowned for pranks, bunking classes, cheekiness to tutors, and all manner of flirtation with local girls.

Lilah liked this man. She did not recognize him for a ghost, an impostor in Lord Palmer's shoes. Every day, she entered Christian's study with studied stiffness. But she never left until she was flushed with laughter.

"Ask her about the British Museum," she told him one afternoon as they sat by the window sharing a strong pot of tea. "She was talking about the Oriental collection this morning. She has very passionate opinions about what's wrong with it."

"Of course she does." He had broken from form today, too restless to read; he had gone for a ride after his midday meal. The exercise had left him loose and relaxed, and he sprawled at his ease in a wing chair, his boots atop the window ledge, ankles crossed. "Finding faults is her main pastime." One could not say the same, thankfully, of his thief.

She shrugged. "It's required, I suppose. What is a curator who can't spot flaws?"

She looked very pretty today, in one of her less severe dresses—blue velvet with a square collar. The shade darkened her large round eyes to the hue of storm clouds. Her dark chignon had not yet escaped its pins, but he had faith; the hour was early, yet. "Oh, finding fault is a very valuable skill," he said. "And her application is very wide-ranging. Last night at dinner, she decided that the main problem with the British Army was our tendency to draw soldiers from the dregs."

"Goodness." At times, between her large eyes and that wide, pretty mouth, she put him in mind of a homunculus, designed purely for the telegraphing of emotion. At present, she radiated amused dismay. "What did you reply?"

He lifted his teacup, breathing deeply of the steam. "I told her that the dregs proved surprisingly stalwart in the face of cannon fire, while the crème de la crème seemed more content to critique from a safe distance."

"And her answer?"

He lifted his brows. "She asked if I referred to myself."

Her laughter was husky, a fantastically warm and rich sound, inherently too generous a reward. She could have convinced a dullard that he was the second coming of Beau Brummel, simply by giggling. "No easy rejoinder to that, I think!"

He laid down his cup. "Yes, a neat checkmate. Either I pointed out that I had been on the front lines, thus placing myself among the dregs—or I claimed otherwise, admitting to cowardice."

She tapped her spoon against the saucer. "Well, which did you choose?"

"I asked her if she'd like to see my medals." He winked.

"Let me guess: she took you to task for vanity, then."

"No, she said she had inspected a Victoria Cross before, and was sorry to learn that the medal was cast from common bronze." He smiled. As the Irish would put it, Catherine was a proper corker. "Then she added—'You would think they would use silver, at least.'"

Lilah gaped. "No human will impress her. Nobody alive, anyway. A pity you cannot pose as a carpet—or one of the late Barons Hughley."

"The ghost, perhaps? Shall I hunt up some chains to rattle outside her room?" He sighed and rolled his shoulders, then stood to stretch fully. Her gaze fell to his throat, where his collar lay open, before bouncing away toward the window.

He hid a smile as he sat back down. "I confess," he said wryly, "I'm finding it rather difficult to romance a woman whose conversation consists solely of complaints."

Lilah's mouth had gone dry. What a peculiar thing to make her breathless: the sight of a hard, muscled body stretching with the languorous grace of a lion.

He knew it, of course. As he sat back down, the dimple showed in his cheek.

She cleared her throat. "Why do you wish to marry her, anyway?"

"She's beautiful," he said. "An heiress. Why wouldn't I?"

She hesitated. Their afternoon conversations always devolved into idle talk. It was dangerous to converse with him so freely; she knew it. Her pulse still felt slightly unsteady, simply from one glimpse of the strong column of his throat, where his collar lay open.

But she never managed to heed wisdom, and walk away once she'd delivered Miss Everleigh's letters. That woman never made friendly conversation, and the rest of the staff labored under the mistaken apprehension that Lilah was too lofty to chat. She was lonely, perhaps. In London, she was always surrounded by people—her fellow Everleigh Girls, at work; and Susie Snow in the evenings, for they shared a room at a boardinghouse in Bloomsbury.

Besides, as long as Palmer didn't touch her, what harm was there in growing to know him? *Know thy enemy.* Wasn't that advice from the Bible? Or Shakespeare. Either way, it made a time-tested strategy. "I can think of many other, wealthier heiresses who might catch your fancy," she said. "Ladies, I might add, who are famed for their kindness as well as their looks. Miss Maudsley, for instance. She's famously nice."

He arched a blond brow. "Sweet young ladies like Miss Maudsley draw men like flies to honey. The competition would prove exhausting."

"And you don't imagine you could best them all?"

He smiled. "Are you about to compliment me, Miss Marshall?"

"No." She sniffed, to let him know that she was serious. "You know very well that your reputation makes you a very romantic figure for the debutante crowd. Even if you were ugly and charmless, they would sigh after you."

"Ah. You compliment me anyway," he said softly. "Perhaps you can't help yourself."

His charm was like a sticky, invisible web. She resisted its pull. "You don't even like Miss Everleigh."

"You sound so certain."

"Am I wrong?"

"Tell me how you reached your conclusion. Have I, in some way, misbehaved with her?"

She hesitated. "You couldn't possibly like her. She's . . ."

"Sharp-tongued," he said. "Prickly. Aloof. But put

yourself in her place, Miss Marshall. A woman of intellect, in a world that prefers women to be featherbrained. A woman of ambition, in a world that casts women only as mothers and wives. All those qualities that make her difficult to know—could they not be disguises for what makes her a fine choice for a man of discerning tastes?"

A very peculiar feeling rushed through her. To her horror, she recognized it as jealousy. Before she could check herself, she blurted, "A woman needn't be cold or rude to be intelligent."

"Is that so?" His hand came over hers, his palm heavy and callused, shockingly warm. "I suppose you're right. But it's the wiser course, I think you'll admit. A woman of such rare appeal, who fails to disguise it—she invites all sorts of troublesome attention."

His slight smile took her breath away. It seemed that he was not speaking of Miss Everleigh now.

Clinging to wisdom, she pulled her hand free. "Poor Lord Palmer. At last, you have met your Waterloo—a woman you can't charm."

"Alas," he said softly. "I do believe there are two of them in this house."

She bit her lip. She'd never favored fair-haired gentlemen. But she'd been cooped up, deprived of the sun too long now, to remain immune to a man who looked like a piece of sunlight, golden hair and eyes like whisky, and that easy smile, which offered no judgment. He presented a very fine argument for blonds.

"Well, that's your fault," she said. "If you returned those letters to me, I'd be charmed all around."

He gave a chiding click of the tongue. "Poor Miss Marshall. Forced to earn back through honest labor the fruits of your thieving."

"Is my labor honest? I thought it was spying."

"Whether it's successful is my main concern. New proposal: I'll pay you by installments. The moment Catherine laughs at one of my jokes, I'll hand you a letter."

"Is *that* all you want? Then make a joke about Paisley shawls. She was ranting against them yesterday—loathsome, cheap facsimiles of the Indian originals."

He retrieved his tea. "I'll take that under advisement. But it may exceed even my own powers, to draw humor from a shawl."

"And here I thought you could do anything. Why, to believe the newspapers, you're the Queen's white knight. You slay armies singlehandedly, and squeeze poetry from stones!"

"Cheeky imp." His glance trailed down her body. "Far more pleasant things to squeeze than stones."

"Stop flirting with me," she said severely. "It's poor strategy on your part. You'd do better to conserve your energy for Miss Everleigh." And Lilah would do better for it, too. She could feel herself blushing.

"But how boring that would be." He put down his tea and reclaimed her hand. His middle finger stroked down to her knuckle, causing her own fingers to curl inward, trapping a shiver. "Where would you look for entertainment, without me?"

She made a fist. "It isn't entertainment that brought me here."

"Quite right." He turned her hand in his, coaxing her fingers to open, one by one. "I'm sure your time here has been very onerous." He rubbed his thumb down her palm, the massaging pressure unbearably delicious.

She'd spent the morning prying open ancient jars

to empty them of beads—all glass, to her disappointment. She could not quite bear to pull her cramped hand away. But she could certainly move the conversation to safer territory. "You should ask her about the tapestries tonight." His fingers were wicked. She would have paid him to touch her like this. "We found a Flemish mappemonde that sent her into ecstasies. Why, a full hour passed before she found another reason to scold me."

"A map of the world?" He released her, sitting back. "My brother collected those."

Her hand felt bereft. How stupid. "Would you like to see it?" Lilah had discovered it lying in a crumpled heap behind a sideboard. She felt quite proud about that. "It's still in the—"

"No, that's quite all right. We've got a dozen rotting away at Susseby."

His indifference amazed her. "You don't even want to see these things before you sell them?"

He shrugged. "I'm a heathen, Miss Marshall. I don't put much store in collecting things. Don't tell Catherine that," he added with a rueful smile.

"Oh, she wouldn't be surprised. Half the clients at Everleigh's seem indifferent to what they purchase. They send brokers to place bids for them. Not on specific objects, mind you. They have lists—anything Assyrian. All the Turkish carpets. I'll wager they never bother to use half of it."

He shrugged. "One can only display so many carpets."

"Then why continue to collect them? What a funny world! The people with all the money seem least interested in what they buy."

"Human nature." He took a sip of tea. "We tend to most want what we can't have."

She sighed and poured more tea, then reached for the sugar. She'd been up since four thirty. Certainly she deserved another lump. "Perhaps that's why I want so much."

"Such as?"

"A million things," she said with a laugh. "I wouldn't know where to begin."

"Name one."

She smiled. "Money, so I can buy all the rest of them."

He smiled back. "Were I a genie with three wishes, I would commend you. But for the sake of conversation, you must be more specific."

"I'm not sure I can be," she said honestly. "I'm still learning. There's a whole universe of delightful things that most people don't know about. It's like some grand secret kept by the rich. Russian caviar, French cheeses . . . mappemondes!" She shrugged. "Perhaps it's better that way, though. What you don't know about, you can't long for."

"But you've come to know," he said quietly. "And so you long?"

She hesitated, growing aware of a sharp, fragile feeling. Why did he want to know her so well? And why did she wish to let him?

"I've never been poor," she said. "Don't mistake me." She had her uncle to thank for that, as much as it chafed.

"Of course not. The daughter of a clerk." He lifted his tea to her in acknowledgment.

"Yes," she said slowly. In truth, she'd grown up cheek by jowl with poverty. Half of London lived in the slums. Meanwhile, the other half seemed to find this quaint.

Sometimes they came through the East End on guided tours, gawking and gasping from their plush, cushioned vehicles. They didn't go slumming to expand their minds, nor to develop compassion, although that was their claim. They did it for entertainment. Poverty titillated them. The makeshift measures of the poor, the newspapers stuffed into broken windows and the rubbish burned for warmth, reconfirmed for them their own superiority.

She'd been raised in streets the rich would never dare to walk. She'd grown up speaking in the round vowels and dropped consonants of an East Ender. But her desires were not jokes. She would not share them for the entertainment of a viscount.

"Money doesn't make a person special," she said. "It doesn't breed taste or decency or character."

His gaze was steady, open. "I would never argue otherwise."

"Good," she said. "Because many do seem to think themselves better people for the fullness of their pockets. When what they are, in fact, is lucky. Money is luck. It gives you protection, and allows you to take chances that others can't. You can visit the British Museum on a weekday, when others must work—it's closed on the holidays, did you know that? You can study antiques, instead of worrying about next week's wages. You can develop good taste, if you like."

"Yet many fail to do so," he said. "And comfort, for all its perks, can stifle one's initiative. For instance, I doubt most clerks' daughters would dare to pursue a career."

There was a compliment in his remark. She hesitated before accepting it, knowing how easy it would be to give herself away. "Perhaps it's not the career I want. Perhaps I only want the wages."

"Nothing wrong with that." He offered her a wry smile. "On a soldier's pay, I did think longingly of the first-class compartment. Velvet cushions make far nicer seating than a wooden bench."

She snorted. "When did you ever travel on wooden benches? You were always the son of a viscount, even when a soldier."

"A second son," he said. "Raised in wealth, yes. But I always knew it would never be mine. I would make my own way—that was made clear to me as a boy."

The rich did things so oddly. In Whitechapel, a family shared what it had, no matter who was firstborn. "That seems unjust. Surely there was money to spare."

"But I didn't want it," he said. "That is . . . Naturally it sometimes chafed, seeing my brother take the lion's share of attention. But it was also a great blessing. I would have the freedom to make my own place in the world. A freedom that Geoff didn't have." He glanced into his teacup, then set it down. "Didn't want, either. Were life just, he would still be here. Overseeing the estates, adjudicating tenants' quarrels. Speechifying in Parliament, and whatnot."

Something complex and raw lurked beneath his light words. It had never occurred to her that he might feel ill suited to his position—that anyone would scruple at such an inheritance. "You don't want the title?"

"I want my brother back." His mouth compressed into a grim line. "All the rest is detail."

She remembered reading of his bereavement in the newspaper. He'd been a stranger, then—a distant figure, no more real to her than myth.

But now, as she looked at him, she recognized a kindred spirit. He'd lost somebody dear. That death had changed the entire course of his life.

Behind him, out the window, a flock of birds winged past, dark silhouettes against the lowering sun. The distant trees lifted their leaves to a passing breeze. Beautiful scene. Fiona would have liked the country, after all. Had she lived, *she* would have been here right now. The Everleigh Girl. And Lilah . . . a secretary. The instructors at the typing school had felt she had promise. With Fee's support, she would have finished the advanced course.

It would have made a more respectable path. Tedious, but safer. A secretary could age, and turn gray. An Everleigh Girl could not.

"You would still be a soldier," she said. "Had your brother lived."

He nodded.

"That's dangerous labor."

"True. The danger was the rotten bit." He gave her a fleeting smile, sharp with self-mockery. "But there was also a great sense of camaraderie, of course. A sense of joint effort, and true brotherhood. And it wasn't all violent. Rebuilding a destroyed village, shoring up the banks of a flooding river—we did a great deal of good in the world."

"I imagine a viscount can do so as well," she said hesitantly.

"Of course." He paused. "But it's a position best suited to an autocrat, I think." He cocked a brow. "Or a collector, or a sybarite. I was never very fond of the gilded cage."

A gilded cage sounded much nicer than a soldier's

barracks, or a windowless room at a boardinghouse. "You seem to inhabit it easily enough."

He acknowledged her cynical tone with a brief bow of his head. "Indeed. I'm an excellent fraud."

A thought struck her. They were both living lives that rightfully had belonged to their siblings. "Then so am I," she said.

He lifted a brow. "How are you a fraud?"

"Everleigh Girls aren't meant to pick pockets."

"Nor are viscounts," he said with a wolfish grin. "But I put one over on you, didn't I?"

She narrowed her eyes. "Luck."

"So you'll tell yourself."

"If you want to do good, why haven't you taken your seat in Parliament?"

"You *have* been reading about me." He sat back, eyeing her. "Do I intrigue you, Miss Marshall?"

Overmuch. "Know thy enemy," she said—a timely reminder to herself. *Enemy.*

"Are we enemies, then? It feels otherwise."

She caught her breath. He'd admitted to this odd rapport, brought it into the open. It thrilled and frightened her at once. He was studying her with his beautiful eyes, irises like honey, his gaze frank, challenging: *Be as brave. Admit it.*

"We should be enemies." God help her, that would be so much wiser.

"Or allies," he said. "Our goal, after all, is the same."

"You're my blackmailer."

"And you're a thief. But that hardly outweighs your other qualities. Intelligence. Wit. Self-possession. In the field, Miss Marshall, I would want you at my back."

She took a hard breath through her nose. "I thank you for the flattery—"

"That isn't flattery," he said. "Flattery is more poetic. If I wanted to flatter you, I would remark on your beauty. Your thick, dark hair. The slope of your shoulders. The color of your eyes. Last night at dusk, the sky reminded me of you." He gave her a half smile. "And now you look very wary. Do you imagine me a liar? Surely you've glanced in a mirror, once or twice."

She groped for good sense. "Miss Everleigh is far more beautiful."

"Miss Everleigh is many things," he said. "Lovely, intelligent, learned. You're all of those things. And you're fascinating."

She stood, tea sloshing over her fingers. "I don't think—"

"Have I frightened you?" He rose, towering over her. "That was hardly my intention. Merely to say—I can think of many grounds for friendship between us."

She spoke very faintly, staring at his chest. "It's not friendship you're discussing, though."

"It could be. Let me take you to bed. I'll show you there what I mean."

"Stop asking."

"All right." He took the cup from her hand. "I'll stop asking," he said gently, and bent to kiss her.

His kiss was just as devastating as she'd remembered. No—it was more. His mouth was warm, his tongue sure and insistent, and this time she did not hesitate before opening her mouth. He made a growling noise as he licked into her. Her hands closed around his coat, digging through the thick layers of fabric until she felt the flex of muscle in his back. He was built like an animal, a great strapping beast, brutal strength, a lion's proportions.

Small bites. She wanted to be eaten.

He lifted her by the waist, swallowing her gasp. The world tilted; he carried her down into the wing chair, so she sprawled across his lap, only the iron banding of his arms to support her.

And still he kissed her—a slow, deep tangle of tongues, frankly carnal, nothing polite. She grasped his face, felt across his cheek, the sharpness of his cheekbone, the hard bone of his jaw. His stubble scratched her palm; he smelled like starched cotton and soap. She tilted back her head so his lips could reach her throat.

With a growl, he licked down her neck, biting lightly. Hot pleasure pulsed through her. She liked his teeth. She caught his wrist and squeezed it.

His hand turned in hers. Caught her fingers and lifted them to his mouth. He kissed her palm, meeting her eyes over their interlinked fingers. His were a wild pale gold, the eyes of a night creature on the hunt. "Lift your skirts," he said hoarsely.

She stared at him. She was draped over him like a carpet. This was no position in which he could accomplish . . . regrettable things. Was it?

"Lift your skirts," he repeated very softly. He licked the full length of her palm, then lowered her hand and placed it firmly on her calf.

What did he intend? What was *she* doing? For her hand obeyed even while her mind still balked. She lifted the hem, inch by inch, and his breath hissed against her temple, an urgent encouragement as her calf came into view.

He took hold of her calf, nudging her own hand out of the way—higher. "Go on," he said.

She would stop now. In just a moment. Above her knee, she would stop. She pulled her hem higher, dazzled by the sight of her own slim calf, so ladylike in its embroidered stocking. His hand followed, trailing in a sure, firm stroke. His palm wrapped around her knee, a hot, solid warmth. She stared at this sight, the breadth of his large hand, tanned from the sun. These were her finest stockings, purchased on an extravagant whim; they looked all the more delicate beneath his grip. All the lovelier. So easily he might have ripped them. How tightly he held her!

"Higher," he whispered.

Caught in some spell, she obeyed. He made a noise deep in his throat as she revealed the ribbon that tied her stocking at her thigh.

He slipped one finger beneath the edge of this ribbon, a hot shocking touch against her bare skin. A breath escaped her. A strange little puff. The sight was . . . wholly, unbearably erotic. The hard, callused press of his hand against her tender skin. The place between her thighs began to ache. His hand seemed to claim her. *Mine,* it said.

"Higher," he growled.

She trembled, unable to take that final step.

His hand slipped upward, out of sight. Enveloped by her skirts. With his palm, he cupped her fully. He pressed hard, in that place where she ached, empty and needing.

A gasp tore from her. She laid her face in the crook of his shoulder.

He ground his palm against her. "Here," he rasped.

His hand made a solid pressure against her. Her quim pulsed, a greedy demand.

His lips came against her ear. "The things I would do to you," he said. "Give you what you need."

Her hips jerked. *Do it.*

"Say the word." He pressed harder. "Yes, that's it. Rock. Rub against me."

Ah, God—

"Say it." He was growling against her now. "Tell me you want this."

I want this.

"Tell me to take you."

Take me. The words rang so clearly in her head that they penetrated her fever. She pushed away from him.

"Stop!" She scrambled to her feet, knocking her skirts down. "Stop! It's my choice, you said."

"Yes." He loosed a long, hard breath. His blond hair was wild—from the clutch of her hands, she realized. *She* had done that to him. She had mussed him up, left him disheveled. Put her mark on him. *Mine.*

She stepped backward, away from that thought. Away from *him.* Away from her own stupidity.

Turning on her heel, she left before her mind could change.

CHAPTER EIGHT

W e're calling it the Martini-Enfield." Mr. William
Scott, of the Small Arms Factory at Enfield,
pulled the rifle from his carpetbag and laid it on Christian's desk. He was a portly, bald, bespectacled man,
with a shining, round head and a wide, strained smile.
He was wearing a sprig of oak leaves in his buttonhole,
which he fondled nervously.

He would not have been smiling at all, had he realized
the narrowness of his escape this morning. Christian had
eight men patrolling the grounds, who had not been fore-
warned to expect a guest. Had they lacked military back-
grounds, they might not have recognized the vehicle's
insignia of the Royal Small Arms—in which case, Mr.
Scott would never have reached the front door. Instead
he would have been shown to a shed, in gag and shackles.

"It's a handsome rifle," Christian said. Thinner than
previous models, with a barrel encased in fine-grained
wood. Whose opinion did Scott want? Palmer's, or
Major Stratton's? And whose opinion was *he* voicing
now? Only fools valued a gun for its beauty.

"Isn't it?" It seemed that Mr. Scott sensed the impropriety of his unannounced visit. He atoned with an excess of enthusiasm. "The most beautiful gun in the world, we like to say." With a flourish of his pudgy hand, he indicated the wood encasing. "No more singed hands. And a safety bolt, mind you. That will prevent any problems with her trigger."

Why was it that guns were always referred to as female? Perhaps, Christian thought, because men wished to handle them as much as they feared them. He picked up the rifle, lifting and sighting a spot out the window.

"Sighted to two thousand yards," said Mr. Scott helpfully.

"Indeed." He turned the rifle and found himself looking through the sights into a window of the east wing, which extended out from the body of the house like the foot of an *L*.

Lilah stood at a window, staring out toward the fields. Was she thinking of him? Of his hand between her legs, and the hot sounds he'd drawn from her . . .

He gritted his teeth. Mr. Scott might be hoping for his admiration, but he would not appreciate such a visceral demonstration of it.

As Christian schooled himself, he became riveted by the details revealed by the magnified power of the scope. He could make out the fine details of the buttons at Lilah's throat—gray, unadorned, she was wearing that wretched ash-colored dress again. Her lower lip looked full and tender, protuberant, as though she were pouting. The glossy dark tumble of her chignon was collapsing down her nape—a waste, when he was not nearby to run his fingers through it. She pressed the flat of her palm against the glass with great force, as though trying to push free.

She looked like a trapped woman. Glaring out at the countryside as though at distant salvation, denied to her.

How well he knew that feeling.

"How does it feel?" asked Mr. Scott.

Boredom and impatience and the uncertainty of his predicament probably accounted for most of his fascination with her. Animal lust explained the rest. So he told himself as he lowered the rifle.

"It's weighted differently than the Martini-Henry," he said. "Bit heavier."

"Only by a few ounces. A negligible difference, I assure you."

Christian turned back to eye the man's rotund figure. He'd wager that William Scott had never trudged uphill in a driving rain, toting a full pack and a tent along with his rifle. If so, he would have known that a few ounces could matter.

But Palmer would not point that out.

Mr. Scott lifted his brows hopefully. "Have you noted the bayonet?"

Christian tossed up the rifle and caught it by the stock. From the corner of his eye, he saw Scott flinch.

Inventors and their children. He returned the rifle to the table with a show of conciliatory care. "New placement for it," he noted. Formerly, the bayonet had been affixed to the side of the barrel, rather than beneath it.

"Precisely. Men complained that it got in the way when firing. Not that you had such trouble," Mr. Scott added quickly.

Got in the way. That was one way to put it. In the heat of battle, Christian had seen a man gored by one of his own panicking comrades. "Not so much trouble," he said dryly. He'd been drenched with blood before he'd managed to bandage Smaldon's wound.

The memory darkened his mood. His time in the army had never seemed particularly savage. But of late, when these memories resurfaced, he viewed them with startled eyes, amazed at how casually he'd borne the carnage.

No going back. Even his memories were holding him at a distance now.

"Well." He felt suddenly exhausted. Ashmore had written—but without news. Nor had Christian's men found any sign of Bolkhov, here or at Susseby. And so Christian waited, idle and useless as a decoy on hunt day. No wonder he felt rather hollow. "It's a fine gun. But I'm no longer in the service."

"My goodness, of course not." Mr. Scott nudged up his spectacles with the tip of his thumb. "But your endorsement, my lord, would mean a great deal."

"My endorsement." He spoke the words flatly, not wanting to understand them.

"Yes, indeed. We hope to outfit the entire military with this model. But you know how Parliament balks at authorizing any *useful* expenditures. The safety of our fighting men is nothing to them, not when weighed against all manner of useless fripperies. The beautification of parks, and the building of grand thoroughfares and whatnot—"

He interrupted Scott's fine, mounting sarcasm. "I am not political." He said it very levelly, because he did not fathom why the proposition should suddenly touch off such anger. He'd been saddled with this position, this yoke that he'd not been born or trained to bear. His brother had welcomed and wanted it, but now *he* must wear it, and it anchored him as solidly as iron. *My goodness,* of course he no longer served in the military. He was the Viscount bloody Palmer. He read parliamentary reports over lunch.

"Oh . . . yes," Mr. Scott said hesitantly. "Of course, my lord. Only . . . have I mentioned the cartridges? I do think you'll approve of them." He jammed his hands into his pockets, as though to physically check his excitement. "Mind you, the Martini-Henry has its place still. We'd not propose to scrap them entirely. They never jammed on a man who knew how to handle a cartridge properly. But all the reports of trouble from the Sudan *have* put a crimp in our side. So we came up with a new type of cartridge—quite clever, really. Uniform to a millimeter. They're interchangeable with a machine gun and a carbine to boot. Imagine the possibilities!"

"Marvelous," Christian said. "Some very bloody times ahead."

Mr. Scott blinked. "Indeed. But *we* shall do the bloodying. Our brave men will be safer, with this weapon at their disposal."

He nodded. He would never argue against a better weapon.

"So . . . what do you say? Would you recommend it?"

"As I said. I have not yet taken my seat in the Lords. Once I have done—"

"But you certainly have Parliament's ear," Mr. Scott said. "And that of the general public. The world at large! We're taking it on tour, you see—several military colleges in America have expressed an interest. An endorsement from the Hero of Bekhole would mean a great deal. We would be most grateful to have a letter from you, to excerpt in our advertisements." Scott offered what he no doubt considered to be a winning smile.

Christian nodded. The Hero of Bekhole, of course. He was not Geoff, and everybody knew it. Instead he would be cast as the smiling mannequin, whose hastily considered opinions might afford a prime quote for the sale of munitions. "I'd have to test it," he said. "But it looks to be a splendid weapon, yes."

"Yes! 'A splendid weapon,' exactly." Beaming, Scott patted down his jacket. "I don't suppose you've got a pen and paper handy? Or—would you prefer to send me a longer passage, with that bit included? And perhaps, if you permit it, we might include a sketch of you in our advertisements, an artistic rendering of the moment when you received the Victoria Cross?"

Now he was going to be turned into a bloody cartoon. "Why not?" And from there, soap boxes. Join the Everleigh Girls in hawking Pearson's. Why bloody not, indeed?

Mr. Scott looked delighted. As Christian walked him out, he waxed poetic about his vision for the campaign. "And if I might suggest it, you could make mention in your letter of the advantage of the new cartridges—perhaps, if you agree, an observation of how handy they might have proved at Bekhole."

Christian fought a bizarre urge to laugh. Seventy of his men had overcome three hundred of the enemy, soaking the vale with their blood—but yes, what a pity it hadn't been even bloodier. He was grateful, when they entered the entry hall, to cross paths with Lilah, whom he called over to be introduced. Mr. Scott, forced to make courtesies that did not allow for mention of his rifle, showed himself out posthaste.

"Why is everyone wearing oak leaves?" Lilah asked, when the door at last closed.

Christian loosed a long breath, calling his thoughts back from some black churning place. "It's Royal Oak Day."

"Oh. Of course."

She would not quite meet his eyes. A flush rode her cheeks, reminding him of pleasanter matters. What he'd done recently to make her blush like that.

"What is Royal Oak Day?" she asked.

He blinked. She couldn't be serious. "Mobbing Day," he said. "Patching Day. Shig-Shag Day, in some parts."

She nodded solemnly. "Gibberish Day, in others?"

"Come now. The celebration of King Charles the Second's escape from the Roundheads?"

She blinked. "Goodness. Time truly does stand still in the countryside."

He looked her over. "Are you certain you're English?"

She scowled. "I will not indulge in renewed speculation about my parentage."

The banter was lightening his mood, at least. "King Charles hid up an oak tree at Boscobel House, to escape the opposing army."

"How kingly."

He smiled. "Hence the leaves. All good subjects wear a sprig of Royal Oak on May 29, to demonstrate their loyalty to the Crown. Is it not so in Surrey?"

She shrugged. "I don't suppose anybody sees a need to demonstrate their loyalty in Surrey. It's guaranteed. What happens to those who refuse to wear the leaves?"

"Nothing good," he said. "Boys in these parts—in most parts, so I thought—will flay you with nettles if you don't wear the oak." He remembered his own childhood. "Or pelt you with rotten eggs. I used to pilfer a baker's dozen from the kitchens on May Day, just to ensure they stank properly come the end of the month."

"Goodness," she said. "A pity I don't have any oak leaves at hand. I rather like this gown."

She had recovered her composure, and her tartness was rapidly returning as well. He smiled at her to speed the process. "Yes, well, I think you're quite safe indoors." Though she'd been staring out that window earlier, as though she wished otherwise.

"I wouldn't count on it," she said. "The maids were muttering among themselves in a very dark tone earlier."

"Then let's fetch you a sprig."

"Oh . . ." She cast a wistful glance toward the door. "I don't know. I rather like breathing freely."

She'd not set foot outside since her wheezing attack, then. No wonder if she felt a touch fidgety. God knew he'd been battling the sensation for days, despite his morning patrols. He started for the door. "Give it a try," he said. "You may well have adjusted by now."

Hesitantly she followed. She stepped outside after him, pausing on the porch to tip her face toward the sun. "It's always so cold in the house."

"No sneezing," he observed. "Shall I give you a tour?"

Her eyes drifted shut. "Only if you promise not to touch me again."

If she didn't want him to touch her, she should know better than to close her eyes. Now, as he stared at her freely, all he could imagine was how she would look, exhausted from his attentions, tousled and flushed in his bed.

He had a broad window in his bedroom. The light

would fall across her in just this way, picking out the faint hints of freckles on the round crests of her cheeks. How far did those freckles extend? The blasted gray gown offered no hints, forcing his gaze upward again. She had a girlish fullness to her face, which made a provocative contrast to the self-possession of her bearing as she opened her eyes and smiled at him.

She'd known he was looking at her. She'd let the moment draw out, for some private feminine reason. The knowledge brushed over him like fingertips—stealing away his breath.

"Perhaps I've adjusted, after all," she murmured. She took a deep breath to test the notion, then released it with a growing smile. "Yes, quite clear. I wonder if I dare . . ."

"I've no doubt of it." He let go of the door, forcing her to make a split-second decision to leap clear of it. "Come along," he said. "Even a city mouse deserves a holiday." And her presence acted like a cure on the murky mood that had gripped him.

London still had wild places. In the north of the city, a great heath stretched for miles—once the hunting ground of highwaymen, now a holiday destination. Armed with a picnic basket, Lilah had once explored the heath with a group of Everleigh Girls, who had hoped for some wild adventure—perhaps to fight off a boar or two.

Alas, the only boars they'd encountered had been of the human variety, for crews of ill-bred mashers roved the fields—to say nothing of the endless stream of sheepish lovers, stumbling disheveled from the concealment of the trees. In the city, even the wilderness had a crowd.

But rural Kent was different. Lilah walked for a half hour at Palmer's side before sighting another human—a farmer driving his team of oxen through a far-off field of wheat. The sight drew her to a stop. Man and animals made a singular silhouette against the great open sky. So it might have looked centuries ago, on that day when King Charles had hidden in his oak tree.

Palmer leaned against the hedgerow, letting her look her fill as he shredded hawthorn leaves. The breeze lifted the pieces and carried them past her like confetti.

"The sky is so large here," she said. He was behaving himself with remarkable chivalry, making sparse conversation and touching her only to help her over difficult bits of ground.

She should be grateful for it. Instead, she rather itched for his attention. "I recall seeing hills on the train," she went on. "But it looks very flat now."

"Those hills are to the west and south," he said. "We're nestled in a broad valley here. Perfect target for invading armies."

She cast him an amused glance. "Do you expect one?"

He smiled. The sunlight glimmered off the stubble on his square jaw, and lit his long lashes to gold as he glanced beyond her. "No one ever does. But eighteen centuries ago, on a clear day, you could look to the hills and see the glint of Roman armor. They marched this way en route to London. Farmers in these parts are constantly plowing up artifacts from Caesar's troops."

"Really?" Delighted, she followed him catercorner across a pasture. They took a narrow footpath down into a stand of hazel trees, where light fell dappled through glossy green leaves, and yellow streamers of cat-kins hung low from the branches. Somewhere nearby, a yellowhammer sang his age-old song: *A little bit of bread and no cheese; a little bit of bread* . . .

An awful noise rent the air. The yellowhammer exploded into flight, and Lilah bumped into Palmer as he halted.

"What is that?" she asked when it came again. The shrill, wordless cry sounded agonized . . . and beastly.

"Sheep." He changed course, helping her hop over a shallow creek, then clamber up another bank to a stile, which he unlocked quickly. Across the rutted lane, a sheep thrashed in the grip of the mirroring stile.

"Poor thing!" It was fighting wildly against the bars that trapped its rear half. "Is she hurt?"

Palmer circled around the beast. "You're a proper Londoner, all right."

"I am not," she said.

He snorted, then shucked off his jacket. "Here, hold this."

The jacket came flying through the air. She shook it out, then folded it neatly over her arm. Meanwhile, the beast loosed another earsplitting complaint.

"I haven't sneezed once today," she said. "It only required an adjustment!"

He crouched down to inspect the sheep's predicament. "What's wrong with being a Londoner?"

She was a Londoner by birth. That hardly meant she wished to be defined by her origins. It seemed a short skip to her, from *knowing* one's place to being told to *stay* in it. "Would *you* like being called a Londoner?"

"I've never given it thought," he said absently. "But if you mean to change your stripes, you might start by learning the difference between a sheep and a ram. You can tell by his horns . . . Got himself into a proper fix, this one."

The ram slashed out a hoof, causing Palmer to spring back. "Careful!" Lilah threw a nervous glance down the lane. "It would make a long dash to Buckley Hall while you lay here clutching your innards."

He laughed. "He's not a tiger, Lilah." He rose, giving a firm stroke to the ram's matted wool. The ram gave a vicious shriek.

"I don't think he likes you," she said.

"Yes, he's quite a fierce one."

"My point exactly."

"Says the city mouse."

"Call me a mouse of the world," she said with dignity. "I have no proper place. The world is my home."

He laughed. "There's a philosophy. All right, lad." That, she hoped, was directed to the ram. "Calm down, now. You're among friends." He slid his hand beneath the ram's jaw and lifted it. As the ram's nose tipped skyward, it ceased to struggle.

"There you go. Better, isn't it? Yes, I thought so." Palmer's voice made a soothing spell as he leaned his full weight into the animal. "Just a moment more, then. You're almost free." He looped his other hand around the animal's body, seizing him beneath the belly. "Step back, Miss Marshall. I'll lift him clear."

That thing had to weigh fifteen stones! She folded her hands at her mouth, prepared to shriek for help. Palmer braced himself, thighs flexing visibly; then, with a full-bodied grunt, he lifted the beast free and dropped him in the lane.

"Oh, well done," she cried.

The ram shook itself smartly, then trotted off, brisk and purposeful as though late for an appointment.

"Ingrate," she called. Not even a backward look in thanks!

"Shall we follow?" Palmer asked as he dusted himself off.

She handed him his jacket, and they fell into step again. But at the first turn, a man appeared in the distance—a hunched, grizzled figure in a patched jacket of homespun cotton, who walked at the head of a churning, frolicking flock of sheep. "Maurice!" the shepherd bellowed—at the ram, it seemed, for the beast trundled up cheerfully, and was quickly absorbed by his milling brethren.

"Got caught up in a stile," Palmer called.

The shepherd pressed one finger to the floppy brim of his hat. "Thanking you kindly. Name's Jessup. I'm thinking you'll be the new lord?"

Palmer walked toward the man, but Lilah halted, alarmed by the flock's unruly gambol. Most kept near their shepherd, but a few forerunners, dirty and bleating and boisterous, came galloping toward her. She looked left and right. The hedgerows offered no escape.

"Palmer?" Her voice came out as a squeak. He was cutting with fearless disregard through the thickest part of the flock.

Lilah wrapped her arms very tightly around herself. The first sheep reached her. What a stink it made! Another trotted past, shoving and nipping at its leader.

She had no experience of sheep. Dogs, cats, and donkeys, yes; she'd briefly lived above a costermonger as a child, and on very cold nights, he'd refused to keep his beast in the backhouse, preferring to let her sleep by his bed. Unpleasant surprise, encountering a donkey on the

stairs. Her mother had not liked it. But at least the mon-
ger had kept his animal on a lead. These sheep seemed
to think they owned the road!

"Stop that," she snapped, as a beastly big one brushed
her skirts. Stepping aside, she recoiled from a soft object—then jumped at the shrill bleat. She'd stepped on a
lamb! The tiny creature toppled backward onto its spin-
dly haunches, goggling.

"Did I hurt you?" she gasped.

The lamb bleated.

"I'm so terribly sorry. Well, go on, then." She waved.
"Shoo!"

It made no move to rise, gazing at her with limpid
accusation. It had the long, dark lashes of a courtesan,
and a small, perfectly white nose.

"Pretty," she said softly. She glanced down the lane.
Palmer and the shepherd stood in the dip of the road,
making conversation about the state of the stiles. The
bulk of the flock still lingered around them.

On a bolt of daring, she reached out to touch the
lamb's head. So soft!

The lamb butted its small skull into her grip. Why, it
wanted to be petted. It leaned into her like a cat.

She swallowed a giggle as she scratched its ears. She'd
had a tabby as a girl. He had liked to lean into her in
just this fashion. He'd liked to be scratched beneath his
chin, too.

So did the lamb!

Palmer's laughter rang out. She looked up, expecting mockery, but he was absorbed in his conversation.
The shepherd, too, was grinning, his posture straight
and proud, a fine contrast with his earlier slouch. He'd
cast off his shyness.

She frowned as she fingered the lamb's velvet-soft ear. Palmer had a gift for putting people at ease. It was an inborn quality, she suspected, nothing to do with his money or station. He radiated a bone-deep comfort, never uncertain of himself or at a loss with anybody. Whatever the situation, he seemed to belong.

That was a fine skill. Pity it was wasted on a viscount, who would have belonged wherever he liked, even if he'd had the personality of a Gorgon.

On a plaintive bleat, the lamb shoved its entire body against her. Its nuzzling made a fine remedy for this unsettling feeling inside her. It had troubled her all day, strengthening every time Miss Everleigh had snapped at her for doing something wrong.

Wouldn't it be nice to feel certain of one's place in the world? To be able to cease striving, and expect only welcome.

She gathered the baby into her arms. It did not object. Slowly she stood. Londoner, indeed—look at her now! She was holding a lamb like a proper country girl!

"Now, look there," said Jessup to Christian. "She's made a friend."

Christian turned. Lilah stood at the crest of the rutted dirt lane, laughing at the squirming bundle in her arms.

How delighted she looked. He felt himself smile. Behind her the bright sky stretched out, scudding clouds forming fantastical castles. The breeze carried the scents of wildflowers and sunbaked grass.

It would have made a fine painting. *Joy in the Spring.*

"Pretty lady," Jessup said shyly.

He nodded. An odd feeling whispered through him—another, in a day of moods. It felt more like a memory than anything else. A very old, rusted sense of wonder, belonging to childhood. Something in her unselfconscious enjoyment . . .

He'd felt that kind of joy, no doubt. He'd been a happy child. Dreaming of noble adventures, of becoming a hero. But what a great distance lay between boyish ideals and the bloody reality. Kill a dozen men, barehanded. Win a medal. Become a cartoon, advertising guns.

Boys grew up. Wonder faded. But he remembered it as he looked at her now—that feeling of faith in infinite possibilities. How much life had promised: adventure, magic, dragons to be slain. A princess to be won.

One thing he'd gotten right as a boy: he'd dreamed of a dark-haired woman. The specifics were lost, but surely his princess had looked exactly as Lilah did now. Laughing, her long black streamers of hair lifting on the wind, pleats and flounces fluttering at her bodice and wrists and skirts, so every inch of her appeared vibrantly alive. Like an extension of the elements, the wind and sun and endless sky behind her.

She noticed him watching her, and her laughter faded. She set the lamb back onto the road, and he saw in her studied movements that she sensed the precise nature of his attention, too. Well. He was no longer a boy. There was a darker, more complex pleasure in watching her childish delight yield to womanly awareness.

She came toward him slowly. He bid farewell to the shepherd, who gathered his flock and turned into the wood. Lilah sidestepped a few stragglers, smiling faintly at their bleats. As she reached him, a cloud passed over the sun, casting the lane into dimness. Oddly theatrical effect. It invested the moment before she spoke with a dramatic quality, quite accidental.

"Where do we go next?" she asked.

Anywhere that would make her laugh again.

"Back," he said. "I suppose you've gotten your fill of the country."

"I'm not sure I have done." The moody light lent her smile a mysterious edge, which disappeared instantly as the sun reemerged. "I wonder if that shepherd would sell a lamb to me, to keep as a pet?"

"Lambs grow up," he said. "Best to keep them in the country."

She shrugged. "Perhaps I could train it to leash. Were I wealthy, it would be a fabulous eccentricity, to walk my sheep through the park every afternoon."

He smiled. "I don't doubt—"

A gunshot cracked through the air. Dirt kicked up in the road.

Christian lunged—nerves and instinct seizing her by the waist, carrying her down beneath him into the dirt. Hooves thundered by—the last of Jessup's sheep, startled into flight. He gathered her more tightly beneath him, making his body a shield as frightened animals pounded past. The ground shook—not from hooves, he realized, but from the thunder of his pulse.

Finally. The waiting was over.

Her breath beat a hot tattoo against the base of his throat. He seized her arms and hauled her to her feet. She came without protest, allowing him to pull her against the hedgerow, heeding silently as he shoved her through the stile and down the short slope into the stand of concealing trees.

Christian pulled out his pistol. "From the east," she said breathlessly. "Did you see it strike in the road? The bullet, I mean."

"Yes." He stared narrowly up the bank. The shot had come from the high ground. He must leave her to pursue. He had one aim here. *Bolkhov.* Christ God, but the bastard had done it. Followed him here. At last, he had a chance—

"Go, then." She had produced a knife from her pocket. Stood with it unsheathed, resting easy in her right hand. A throwing dagger. "I'll be fine."

For the briefest moment, he was startled—and then, just as quickly, he wasn't. She'd already proved she knew how to wield a knife. Naturally she would carry one— even here. Naturally she would offer to wait alone, with a gunman on the loose. She had seen that bullet kick up dirt. Yet she offered to wait, alone.

Instinct hardened into truth as he gazed back at her, composed despite her ragged breathing, alert and ready to defend herself. She was no ordinary woman. The mystery she posed was not a product of his boredom. She deserved his fascination.

"A hunter." The words came reluctantly, but there was no choice. He could not leave her alone with a gunman nearby. Not while she waited, fearless and armed, prepared to defend herself from a threat that should never have touched her.

He pulled her into a slow retreat down the slope.

Her steps dragged. "Won't you go look?" she asked.

"As I said. A hunter must have strayed onto the estate. The boundaries aren't marked."

"Of course," she said after a hesitation.

Perhaps she was Londoner enough to believe the

lie. But men did not poach during daylight hours. Any country mouse would know that.

He took hold of her arm to hurry her along. "Come," he said. "Quietly. We'll make our way back to the house."

"But . . ." Her voice shook slightly as she let him pull her into a trot. "This . . . hunter. He's on your lands. With . . . very clumsy aim."

Her knife, he saw, was still out, held at an angle poised to launch. She was scanning the trees with a fierce, narrow-eyed sobriety. What a cool head she had—not for a woman, but for anyone. For a soldier, even. Any man would do well to make her his ally.

"I'll get you back to the house first," he said.

They did not speak again until they had reached Buckley Hall. He ushered her safely inside, then went to the stables. Minutes later, as he rode out with two of his men, he caught sight of her at an upstairs window, looking out.

The sight touched off that strange feeling again. Boyish dreams. A woman waiting in the tower, keeping watch.

Or a siren. Myths, after all, did not only speak of princesses. The siren always appeared in the traveler's path, waiting to distract him from his destination. The myths never spoke of where the siren took him, though.

Perhaps she took him somewhere better. He could believe it. A woman like Lilah, strong and composed and unshakable in danger, could be a destination in herself—not for Lord Palmer, of course. But for some other man . . . a fortunate man, free to choose his own path. A man whom a viscount could envy.

CHAPTER NINE

"I hope you've finished your own preparations," Catherine Everleigh said. She was pacing her sitting room as the maids packed her clothing. "I intend to leave at daybreak, not a minute later. You will not make me miss the first train."

Lilah looked over the assorted luggage. So many clothes! A housemaid was folding away a fine silver gown that Lilah had never seen. Perhaps Miss Everleigh meant to wear it in London.

The trip came at a very fine time. Lilah still wasn't sure what to think of the gunshot yesterday. A hunter, Palmer had said. A very clumsy one. But his manner had suggested otherwise. He'd hustled her back to the house in a grim silence that had caused gooseflesh to rise on her skin. For hours afterward, she had paced by the window, not relaxing until she saw him return.

Of course it had been a hunter. The countryside held no particular dangers. Stray rams—but Palmer had shown himself well able to wrestle with them. And why should she worry for him anyway?

London would clear her head, she hoped. "I'm already packed," she told Miss Everleigh. They did not even intend to stay overnight. What did she need, but her reticule and hat and pocket money?

"Good." Catherine smoothed down her lace cuffs. It seemed the telegram from her brother had pulled her from bed. She wore a ruffled silk bed robe in shades of sherbet and marigold, an oddly sunny choice for a woman made of ice. "I can't imagine what Peter is thinking. To let that idiot take his enamels from the warehouse! I don't care if he brought an entire army with him. They are the *center* of the Russian collection. Without them, we'll have to cancel the auction—and never once, in fifty years, have we done so. It shan't be some Slavic princeling who breaks that record!"

"I'm sure you'll manage to reason with him, miss." Lilah pitied the poor client who thought to cross her.

"Reason!" Miss Everleigh snorted. "These foreign princes have no grasp of logic. He signed a contract with us! Does he think English law will bend to suit his whims? The threat of a lawsuit will teach him better."

The maids exchanged a speaking look. Lilah gathered that Miss Everleigh had been fuming for some time. She offered them an apologetic grimace.

Miss Everleigh caught it. "And *you*. Feeling cheeky, I see!"

"No, miss, never."

"I hope you're not expecting a holiday in town. While I meet with this rube, *you* will deliver the tapestries to Mr. Batten. Demand a full accounting of what it will take to restore them."

Lilah could not imagine having to demand anything of Batten. A stooped little gnome who haunted the workshop in Everleigh's basement, he was infamous for chattering. A girl had to devise desperate excuses to break away from him. "I will bring you a most thorough report, miss."

"Good." Miss Everleigh bent down and buckled a bag shut with barely leashed violence. "Well, to your bed, then. No dillydallying! We've a long day ahead—I mean to return on the evening train."

Lilah bid her a properly chastened farewell, but once in the hallway, her spirit rose like clouds. An entire day in London! She would catch up with her fellow hostesses, learn what mischief the girls had gotten up to. The business with Mr. Batten wouldn't take more than half the day. Afterward she would stroll through Covent Garden market, taking in the sights, and remembering what it meant to go where she pleased, without Catherine Everleigh hanging over her shoulder.

As she passed the stairs, a dim, strange noise caught her attention—a shrieking scrape, abruptly cut off. Intrigued, she took hold of the banister and listened more intently. Could it be the ghost? The maids had told her about him. They claimed to hear him every night, rattling a saber down some secret route through the west wing.

With her mood so lively, a ghost hunt seemed more appealing than attempting to sleep. She started down the stairs, heading for the noise.

The sound led her through the empty, glass-walled orangerie. A light flickered ahead. She heard the murmur of low voices, masculine, hushed and tense. She stepped around the corner, into a small room where five men sat sharpening knives and cleaning guns. Good heavens!

She retreated immediately, but it was too late—the largest brute had spotted her. She heard him say something. Palmer appeared from around the corner.

"Can't sleep?" he asked, his pleasant tone a jarring counterpoint to the giant knife in his hand. In his other hand he held a strop—a heavy length of leather that would make a weapon in its own right.

"I thought I heard . . ." *A ghost?* He would laugh at her. "Never mind. I'll leave you to it."

"Wait. If you can't sleep, you might as well help."

As she turned back, she noticed how her candle shook. She gripped it harder. Surely there was some unremarkable explanation for this scene. Something other than where her mind led. *A hunter, indeed.* This looked like a hunting party of its own. "Help with what?" she asked.

He combed his free hand through his shaggy hair. He looked very piratical in those shirtsleeves. "I assume you know how to sharpen a knife, as well as to throw it?"

"Yes, but . . ." Thoughts of the Russian correspondence had not troubled her in days. But now it came to mind. Wedded to the stray gunshot, it sent a shiver through her. "I would not like to disturb you."

"Disturb us in what?" He glanced back toward the assembly. "You've met the assayers, haven't you?" He gestured her to follow him back around the corner.

"No, I haven't met them," she said faintly. They had risen to their feet, the better to display their assembled muscle. Their nods and bows looked suspiciously unpracticed.

"Ah. Well, that's my oversight." Palmer sounded quite amiable for a man laboring over weaponry at half past eleven. "Here are Mr. Jones, Mr. Stowe, Mr. Potter, and Mr. Penn. Gentlemen—Miss Marshall." To Lilah he said, "Now you've taken note of them, you'll no doubt see them prowling about the estate, canvassing for improvements. The land is next to go, once I've cleared the house of junk."

"Junk, is it? Don't use that word with Miss Everleigh." And for her own part, she would believe these were assayers when pigs started to fly. Two of them sported the oversized knuckles found on brawlers. She recognized them—they had ridden out with Palmer yesterday, after he had brought her back to the house.

"One of several things I don't intend to use with her," he said. "But you, Lilah . . ." He offered her a lopsided smile, and held out his knife.

No point in fleeing. If this was indeed something nefarious, she'd already seen it in full. She set down her candle and took the dagger by its hilt. "Have you a whetstone?"

"Several." He pulled out a chair at the small table. The other men excused themselves with polite mumbles. They took their weapons with them, she noted.

She dragged the whetstone closer, then set the blade against it. They'd been working for some time; the air smelled burned, sharp with fresh metal shavings, and . . . was that a hint of black powder?

Palmer was surveying the gun rack. No jacket tonight. No waistcoat, either. She'd never imagined that shirtsleeves and suspenders could complement a man so well. Generally it took a drunkard to go abroad without his clothing. But Palmer did not sport a drunkard's belly. His shirt clung lovingly to a flat abdomen and lean waist. His trousers, thus cinched, cupped his round, high bottom. A very *muscular* bottom. When he crouched to retrieve a screwdriver, she could almost detect the flex of his—

As he rose, she yanked her attention to the blade in her hand. He straddled the stool across from her and began to disassemble the rifle. "Fine technique you have," he said.

She'd learned it on her father's knee. *Lily* had learned it there. Lilah Marshall should not have known the first thing about it. "A curious tale. I learned the skill quite by accident—"

"Can you clean a rifle, too?"

She hesitated. "No, I've never handled one."

He laid a screw on the table, then set to untwisting another. "I'd teach you to shoot," he said, "but not on a Martini-Henry. The cartridge tends to jam." He frowned. "And I've seen the recoil break a boy's shoulder, come to think of it."

"Heavens."

"Service rifle," he said with a shrug.

"I suppose that explains it." The assayers had military bearings.

He looked up, brow lifting. "Explains what?"

Good Lord. "Nothing."

His lips quirked. "You're blushing. Now I'll insist on the answer."

She shook her head and scraped the whetstone harder. "Your assayers look very . . ."

"Competent?"

"Large," she said carefully. "Do they usually operate in gangs?"

"You'll have to ask them. I've little grasp of the profession."

There was a fine evasion. She shot him a challenging

look. In reply, she got a wide smile that told her nothing. He lifted his rifle by the buttstock and began to break it into pieces, his movements quick and confident.

Yes, he'd certainly been a soldier. But now he was a viscount. And viscounts did not usually assemble troops in their country homes.

For several minutes, she pondered this mystery at leisure, the only sounds the complaint of metal against stone, and the scraping of Palmer's brush along the pieces of his rifle. Because her task required no special concentration, she began to count the weapons hanging from the rack. Some were hunting rifles. But the pistols were not for sport.

He noticed her survey. "I take it you haven't been in the gun room before."

"No, not yet. But Miss Everleigh will certainly want to look over the weaponry."

"No point," he said. "It's mine, not the estate's."

"So you are a collector, after all."

"But not a hoarder. I use the guns."

"All of them?"

He sat back, flipping the gun by its stock. "Some of the rifles I used in the war. The pistols—the two nearest are also from my time in service."

"And the rest?"

He gave her a crooked smile. "Perhaps I do hoard, after all." His glance dropped to her work. "Looks about right."

"Yes, I think so." She held it out. "Have you another for me?"

He held the blade up to the light, angling it to inspect her handiwork. "Not a throwing dagger, this one."

"No," she said softly. "I believe they call that a machete." Nick sometimes carried one, when his task—in his own words—*required persuasion*.

Palmer gave her a surprised glance. "Have you handled one?"

She scowled. "Of course not! What do you take me for?" And then, because she couldn't resist: "I'd prefer a cutlass, anyway. A proper handle can be useful."

His smile was slow and delighted. "You'd make an excellent strategist in Her Majesty's ranks."

She knew it was a compliment, but she wasn't in the mood to be admired. "To say nothing of the assayers. I had no idea that they went armed to the teeth."

"Yes, and Buckley Hall so short of undergrowth to chop. Why are you wandering the halls so late? Aren't you bound for town on the morrow?"

A neat change of topic. "On the very first train."

He took up a rag and polished the muzzle of the gun. "You'll stick by her during your trip, of course."

"Of course."

"At every step."

She bit her lip. "*Every* step won't be possible. She plans to meet with a client."

"Then you'll wait outside the door. Eavesdrop, see what you can learn."

She snorted. "*That* would make a fine scene. You needn't fear competition—he's trying to pull his property from the Russian auction. She's out for his blood."

His long lashes dropped, veiling his expression. "Nevertheless," he said, rubbing hard at a spot on the muzzle. "They'll be alone, and I don't like that. See what you overhear."

He took a curious interest in Miss Everleigh's business, didn't he? Frowning, she studied him. The lamp behind him limned his shaggy blond hair, creating the illusion of a halo. Had it not been for his scar, he might well have posed as an angel. An avenging angel, yes. He had the coloring for it, and the cheekbones, and the tall, powerful build.

The notion suddenly struck her as a black joke. He was the last thing from angelic. He was a liar—she knew it in her gut. He'd been lying to her from the start. "Unless your aim is to start a rival auction house, I can't imagine why you'd care about her dealings with a client." Or her business correspondence, on which Lilah reported so diligently each day.

"I'm a jealous man," he said mildly.

"Perhaps. Yet I don't think you've any real interest in her—not romantically, at least."

He looked up, knocking a lock of blond hair from his eyes. "Is that so?" he said coolly.

"If you did, why would you spend so much time flirting with me?"

He laid down the gun. "I haven't flirted with you," he said evenly. "At one point, I was going to make you come, but then you ran out. Is that why your temper's so sour? Come around the table, and I'll fix it for you."

She flushed. Men did not use such language with decent women. "Do you mistake me for a whore as well as a fool?"

A muscle flexed in his jaw. "Both would be more convenient."

She stood. Let them have it out, then. "But I already offered to become your whore. My body for the letters—and you turned me down, if you recall. You said I would get them back when she agreed to marry you. But that won't ever happen, will it?"

He was very still. "That depends," he said. "If you do as I instructed—"

"No." She was tired of this deceit. "You want something else from her. I thought for a time I didn't need to know what that was. Didn't *want* to know. But now it seems I have no choice—for I *need those letters*. So tell me what you need to happen in order to give them to me. Be honest, and perhaps I can help you get it."

"Fine," he said quietly. "A new bargain." He rose and came around the table. Only when his hand closed on hers did she realize that she had picked up the machete. He loosened it from her grip and set it aside, but did not let go of her hand. He yanked her fist to his chest, pressing it there so she felt the vibrations as he spoke. "We'll renegotiate, shall we? *Honesty.* You start. Tell me who you are, Lilah Marshall. Where you learned to throw and sharpen a knife. What your true name is. And who keeps you so afraid that you would sell your body for three slips of paper."

His gaze was merciless, drilling. She looked away. "There must be some other—"

"No. We start there: what happens if you don't get back the letters. That, I would very much like to know. Tell me that. Tell me *who*. And in reply, I'll be honest as well."

"You ask for the one thing," she said very softly, "that you know I will not give."

"No. I merely demand honesty. Do the terms suit you?" He paused. "No, I didn't think so."

Frustration made her tremble. He seemed to sense it. His grip gentled. He lifted her hand to his mouth. "I can speak to one thing," he murmured against her knuckles. "You're no whore." He kissed her pinky, then her ring finger. "If you were truly for sale, I would have bought you a hundred times by now. And I still would not be done with you."

A shuddering breath slipped from her. Even now, at this moment, he could unsettle her so simply. Send her slipping sideways from fury into desire. "My secrets are boring," she said. "Don't you see? You've no need to know them! I'm a common thief, who answers to a very ordinary master. There is nothing—"

"No." His grip suddenly crushed her. "That is where you're wrong. You answer to *me*. And God help you, Lilah, but I am coming to enjoy it. Remember that, next time you want to ask me questions. I have as many for you. And I want the answers just as badly as you do."

A cleared throat broke them apart. One of the assayers hesitated in the doorway, his glance politely averted. "Must speak to you a moment, m'lord."

"Go," Palmer said to her. "I will see you tomorrow evening, for your report."

Everleigh's Auction Rooms occupied the corner of a wide street not far from the market at Covent Garden. Its broad stone face gazed with curtained dignity upon the constant stream of traffic—which, at this afternoon hour, consisted mainly of farmers driving emptied carts led by oxen. At the top of the carpeted steps, two footmen lounged against the brass rail, idly watching the throng of quarrelsome young men who were sporting down the pavement.

"There will be other footmen posted during the auction," Ashmore said. He stood beside Christian on the roof of a neighboring building, inspecting the scene through a battered field glass.

"Four at most." Christian had taken careful note during the ball. "Two to handle the carriages, two at the door. What of the other entrances?"

"The footpath to the east is used by the employees. Not guarded, as far as I can tell. There's also the alley in the rear, where cargo is received."

"They'll close that down. The czar is sending a proxy to bid—his people will insist on the closure, for security."

"You know this for a fact?"

"Yes." Since the appearance of the damned candelabrum, he had been in steady communication with the Russian embassy. Obolensky seemed skeptical that Bolkhov yet lived; the possibility indicated a failure of intelligence among his own men, spies throughout London who kept tabs on Russians.

Still, he had agreed to investigate. Capturing Bolkhov would be a great boon to his career. The general had absconded from his post, taking half his troops with him. Mutinies were not the kind of insult the Russian government forgot or forgave.

"A risky ploy," said Ashmore soberly. "If they catch him first, we'll never know it."

"That won't happen." To remain forever uncertain of Bolkhov's fate would be tantamount to a curse designed to drive Christian mad.

"Look. Here comes Catherine Everleigh." Ashmore handed him the field glass.

Catherine's traveling cloak billowed as she swept down the front steps. At her heels hurried Lilah, looking harried and cross. He could make a good guess about what had put that expression on her face.

"Something amuse you?"

Christian realized he'd begun to smile. "That woman has a natural gift for unpleasantness."

"Is that your spy trailing her?"

He nodded.

"Brilliant strategy," Ashmore said, "employing hostesses for an auction house. My wife is considering the same for her perfumeries. Says she could cut the product in half and sell twice as much, as long as the salesgirls were pretty."

For some reason, the remark rubbed him wrong. "She's got a brain," he said. "Lilah, I mean."

"Oh? I'm sorry to hear it."

Christian snorted. "I'd imagine your wife would object to that remark." Blindfolded and drunk, Mina Granville could have outwitted a chess master. Her company spanned the Atlantic, supplying perfumes and lotions to every debutante from Philadelphia to Warsaw.

Ashmore cut him an odd look. "So she would. But we're not speaking of wives."

Christian checked the impulse to argue. "You're right," he said. A stupid woman would have served him better.

But her company would not have been nearly so satisfying. Without Lilah at Buckley Hall, he'd have lost his mind by now.

She was not merely a distraction. It had begun to trouble him deeply that he had involved her in this game. She deserved better. She deserved . . . a tower. Some profoundly safe place, where she could watch from the window, well above the messy fray, and want for nothing.

Ashmore was still watching him. "Time must drag in

the country," he drawled. "It occurs to me to wonder—
however are you keeping yourself occupied?"

Christian snorted. He would need to be deaf to miss
the ribbing note in the other man's words. "I take regular walks."

"Not alone, I hope?"

"Indeed. Marvelous for the constitution."

"Mm. Do you know what else profits a man's constitution? Or shall I spare your bachelor sensibilities?"

"Stuff it." He ignored Ashmore's delighted smile and
turned his glass toward Catherine Everleigh. *There* was
his proper concern, damn it.

Catherine was turning a tight circle on the pavement,
evidently searching for a carriage that should have been
waiting. She drew her hands out of her muff, jabbing
the air for emphasis as she spoke up to the footmen.

The men rushed down the steps to her. One bowed
low; the other bounded down the street, hunting between parked vehicles.

"Coachman gone missing," Ashmore observed.

"God help him." Christian handed back the field
glasses. "I should follow."

"Who? They're splitting up."

Christian wheeled back. Catherine was stalking
down the pavement toward the footman, who had located coach and driver. Lilah, meanwhile, had turned
on her heel in the opposite direction.

He swore. "She's meant to follow Catherine. She
knows this. *All times,* I said."

Ashmore shoved the glasses back into the case. "You
go with Catherine. I'll follow the other one."

"Lilah." He caught Ashmore's look. "That's her
name."

Ashmore cocked a brow. "I'll remember that. Are you certain you have your lovely Lilah managed? For she appears to be hailing a cab."

Christian resisted a black urge to laugh. *Managed* was not how he would describe it. He shoved aside the memory of how she sounded when she moaned, instead thinking of a more recent moment.

She was very good with a knife. For a clerk's daughter, she was too good, and too calm under pressure, by far. And for a thief . . . she chose to steal objects of no use to her whatsoever. For her *ordinary master,* she said.

Christ. He cursed through lips that had gone numb. Could he have been such a fool?

"You follow Catherine," he bit out. "I'll make sure I haven't pulled an adder into the nest."

Neddie's tavern was windowless, the air thick with smoke, most of it wafting from her uncle's cigar. Lilah waved it away. "Can't you put that out? Since when did you favor tobacco?"

"Gentleman's habit." He sucked the tip into a fire-bright glow. "Getting soft," he added when she coughed. "Must be that country air rotting your lungs. Where did you say you've been?"

She hadn't told him. A good thing, too. Otherwise he might have written her at Buckley Hall. As it was, she'd nearly choked when Susie Snow had handed over his letter this morning. "You can't write to me," she told him now. "It's too risky."

Nick's silver eyes narrowed as he tapped his cigar, casting ash onto the floor. The ground was already thick with discarded shells, sticky with spilled beer. "Fear I'll sully your postbox?"

She sighed. With other people, Nick plainly traded on his fearsome reputation. But with her, he got prickly about it. "I don't lodge alone," she said. "The other girl I share my room with—she also works at Everleigh's, and she's the greatest gossip alive. It's a wonder she didn't steam open the envelope."

Certainly Susie had been glad to speculate. *A gentleman admirer?* she had cooed. *You've been busy in the country! You must tell us all about it.*

Fortunately, the other girls had been more interested in what Lilah could tell them about Lord Palmer. She had come up with some ridiculous story about the fine figure he cut on horseback. Miss Everleigh's appearance had spared her the need to embroider further. She'd never been so grateful to be summoned for a scolding—this time, for forgetting her new position.

If you wish to return to hostessing, you need only say the word, Miss Everleigh had snapped, before dismissing her for the afternoon to see to her own business before they reunited at Paddington Station.

"All I'm saying," Lilah told Nick, "is that until this business is done, you can't write to me at all."

Her uncle shrugged. "She wouldn't have found any interest in that note, unless she knows how to crack code—in which case, send her my way. I've got a project or two I could use a hand with."

Good Lord. She could just imagine what he'd do with Susie. Like a cat handed a limping mouse, he'd grow bored and shred her in five seconds. "It doesn't matter. I've blended in at Everleigh's. I do nothing to draw notice; otherwise I'd never have made it so far. I don't want anyone getting *curious* about me."

Old Neddie came over with a pint and a basket of fried oysters. Nick thanked him with a fat coin, far too generous; he owned this place, after all, and could have eaten for free. But it was his strategy to keep his old friends thickly buttered.

He rolled his cigar in his fingers, studying her. "You've got a lot of fear in you, Lily. I don't remember you being so timid."

By old habit, the words stung. She reminded herself that she wasn't a part of this world anymore. In her new life, timidity wasn't a weakness. It was ladylike. "I've got something to lose now. But I shouldn't have to tell *you* that." He was a fine hypocrite, making her feel guilty about turning her back on her kin, when *he* was trading on threats to manipulate her. "You're counting on me wanting to keep my position. Otherwise your threats wouldn't work, and you'd have no hope of getting back those letters."

"I've made no threats today," he said. "But I thank you for the reminder. You got the letters with you?"

She'd been dreading this question since she'd deciphered his demand for a meeting. "Not yet. But soon."

He made no reply. He didn't need to. His silence, and the slight cruel smile that curved his full lips, spoke the threat for him.

"You always stood by your word before," she said. "Has that changed? The last week of June, you said."

He sighed, then lifted one finger to signal the barman. "You'll wet your lips before you go."

"Why do you need the letters, anyway? None of those men is rich enough to be worth your time. They're mere vestrymen, not a fat cat among them."

He glanced back at her, his dark face thoughtful. "Why would you need to know?"

When she'd worked for him, she'd been too young to share fully in his confidences. But he'd trusted her. He'd sometimes even asked her advice. She felt the loss of that now, a funny little pang. It wasn't only she who'd turned her back here. "Never mind," she said.

Neddie brought over a mug, slammed it down in front of her, and then stalked off in his usual cheerful way. "You drink it," she told Nick. "Miss—I can't go back to work with liquor on my breath."

"Miss Everleigh wouldn't like it?" Nick purred.

She caught her breath. There was no way he could know she was working for Miss Everleigh, unless . . .

Cold purled down her spine. "You've a spy," she said. "At the auction house?"

He offered her a gentle smile. "Apart from my dear niece? Why, what a suspicious man it would make me, if I thought you weren't sufficient." He picked up the mug, forced it into her hand. "We'll toast your successes," he said. "My Lily's moved up in the world. Assistant to the pretty owner." He lifted his own drink. "*Sláinte*."

She barely tasted the ale. "Why? Why would you care what happens at Everleigh's?"

"You're there," he said. "Why wouldn't I care?"

She didn't believe for a moment that he worried for her. Not as a habit. Had he been so inclined, he never would have trained her into a thief, and set her on her first job at thirteen years of age. "You've no cause to fear for me."

"No?" He eyed her. "Crossing swords with viscounts, and cozening pretty rich girls . . . you've set yourself up for a mighty grand fall, I think."

"But you'd be glad to see me fall," she said softly. He'd said it often enough. "My comeuppance. You've been waiting for it, haven't you?"

He sighed. "I'd be glad to see you back where you belong, Lily. So much talent going to waste, while you lick those swells' boots." He paused. "Of course, you've not been licking boots recently. What kept you away these last few weeks?"

She knew him too well to miss the silken note in his voice. This was the voice he used when interrogating a man, before he turned to force. "You can't . . . you can't doubt *me*?"

He ran his finger around the rim of his tankard, considering. "Tell me where you've been, and I'll think on my answer."

God above. She'd had nightmares about this moment. She didn't know everything about his business, but she still knew enough. That he'd let her make her own way was something of a miracle—but then, she was his niece. Blood must mean something!

Blood *did* mean something. "I knew you thought me low. But to betray you? Why, you must think me some new form of dirt."

"Calm yourself." He took a long sip. "I never accused you."

"Oh? What did you mean to say, then? Speaking to me as though I'm a—" She could not think of an insult low enough. "A *McGowan*—"

"Here now," he said curtly. "Lots of money flows through those auction rooms. Would have caught my interest, with or without you. But when you disappear from town without so much as a word, I'm bound to wonder where you went."

"Well, stop wondering." She realized she had a stranglehold on her mug, and set it down with a thump. "I was at Lord Palmer's estate." No point in lying, when the truth would serve her better. "The man who caught me—he's the one who got me the position with Miss Everleigh. I'm helping her ready his estate for auction."

Nick's expression didn't alter a whit. "Curious of him," he said. "Inviting a known thief under his roof."

"And into his bed, if he has his way."

Her uncle's face darkened. "That's how you're getting back those notes?"

She felt a spiteful pleasure in his reaction. *This* was what he had driven her to. His own niece. "Maybe so."

His jaw flexed. He loosed a harsh breath, then growled, "Are you willing?"

She wouldn't push her revenge further. If Nick thought Palmer meant to force her, he'd go after him, rank be damned. Nick would probably enjoy it the more, for the fact that Palmer was a lord.

But the truth was hard to speak, even so. "Yes," she muttered. "God help me. I'm too willing."

He grimaced. "Ah." He bolted the rest of his drink, wiped his mouth with the back of his hand. "Well, then. That's a different brand of foolishness."

"Idiocy," she whispered. "I know it."

He looked at her narrowly. "You watch out for yourself, Lily. These toffs aren't like us. Don't see us as people. He'll use and discard you without losing a night of sleep."

"I know it." She was on her feet, though she didn't remember how. Relief had brought wings with it; she could see in Nick's face that he was no longer doubting her. Instead he felt . . . pity.

He stood to walk her out. "You know the way of it, I hope." He cleared his throat. "To avoid complications, I mean."

His gruffness made her turn red. Good heavens. He was asking if she knew how to avoid pregnancy. "Yes, yes, of course."

At the door he paused, one palm pressed flat against the wood. "I mean it," he said. "I can arrange for you to speak with someone. Peg Mulry would help."

Peg Mulry had used to watch her when she was small. Now Peg made her living at a high-class brothel. "Please don't," she said in a strangled voice, and shoved open the door.

The sudden bright sunlight made Nick squint. "No use in prettiness," he said curtly. "If it's a career you want, a child would be the end of it."

"I know that." She edged into the open lane. "But thanks so much, Uncle, it's very kind of you to think of me."

He laughed at her. "Kind, is it? And now you're fixing to run away, hands clapped to your ears. Is that how these nobs like their women? Empty-brained dolts?" He fluttered his lashes. "*What's a cock, m'lord? I've never heard of it.*"

"You're awful!" She turned to stalk toward the high road, catching only at the last instant the way his face hardened.

Too late for warning. A hand closed around her elbow. "What in God's name," Palmer bit out, "are you doing here?"

CHAPTER TEN

$\mathcal{F}$or a single terrible moment, she felt certain that Nick would force a confrontation. His gaze pointed murderously at Palmer's grip on her arm. "Lord Palmer!" she said loudly. "What a pleasant surprise!"

Nick's gaze lifted to hers. *Turn away*, she begged him silently. *Just go.*

He went back into the tavern, slamming the door.

"Friend of yours?" Palmer asked.

She tried to pull free, but his grip was like iron. God save her! The streets here were full of eyes. The last thing she needed was a savior coming to intercede on her behalf, and calling her by a name Palmer would not recognize.

She laid her hand atop his, leaning into him in a welcoming manner. "Were you following me?" she asked with a smile.

His lion's eyes narrowed on her. "Obviously."

"Then you'll drive me to Paddington Station?"

A muscle ticked in his jaw. He glanced back toward the pub. "Perhaps I should introduce myself first."

No. Neddie's was Nick's home turf. No matter the cause, he would not cede an inch of ground in that place. If Palmer went inside and confronted him, matters would turn ugly in an instant.

"Please," she said. But he looked mutinous. Changing tactics, she spoke to him as a soldier, quickly. "You'd need men at your back to go into that place. And there's no call for it, anyway. I can explain."

After a moment, his posture loosened the slightest degree. "I'm sure you can. Whether you can be truthful is my concern." But he turned her toward the high road.

At their next step, a piercing cry split the air. A little boy bounced to his feet from a nearby stoop. "It's Kit!" he cried. "You're Kit, aren't you! Look, it's Kit!"

A ball came bouncing out from an alley. Lilah braced herself. That alley was where the urchins liked to hide from Nick, who would force them to school if he caught them.

Sure enough, in the next moment, a band of children swarmed into the road, surrounding them. "Good God," Palmer muttered, for they were at the center of a scrum, surrounded by small tugging hands and babbling demands for handshakes, autographs, a spare coin—

This last request occasioned a shocked pause, followed by a flurry of high-pitched accusations. Somebody delivered a knock to the offender's shoulder that sent him sprawling into the dirt. "Don't ask him for money," yelled a little girl. "You dolt, it's our Kit! He's a hero!"

"No hitting," Palmer boomed. The edict cast a spell of silence over the little crowd; a dozen grubby faces turned upward, amazed that their hero would talk to them.

Lilah tried to ease away. Palmer's grip tightened on her elbow. "Not an inch," he said softly to her. Then, clearing his throat, he looked over the ragtag crew. "I will be glad to shake your hands. But first you will line up like proper soldiers."

The band broke into a mad, shoving scramble, cursing at each other in language that caused Palmer's eyes to widen. What a ludicrous situation! Lilah swallowed her laugh. Overhead, shutters were banging open left and right, men and women hanging out into the street to watch, calling out encouragements. One man added his own hooting cheer for Palmer's bravery. "Britannia! Britannia!"

The little girl stamped her foot. "Quiet, now," she told the crew. Then, with a sweet smile at Palmer: "Will that suit, sir?"

The band had managed to arrange themselves in a crooked row. "Excellent," Palmer said. "Hands out, now. Ready, soldiers?"

Lilah recognized some of the onlookers' faces above. She found herself holding her breath, praying for their discretion as she was dragged down the line by virtue of Palmer's grip on her elbow. With his free hand, he dispensed handshakes. "Excellent posture," he told one freckle-faced admirer. "Chin up, that's it, that's very fine," he said to another.

The last and smallest boy offered him a trembling salute. He returned it crisply. "Satisfactory?"

The little boy nodded. "Yes, sir."

Palmer loosed an odd snort. She realized he was fighting a laugh. "Excellent. All of you march bravely on to school, then."

A dozen jaws dropped. Then, in a flurry of giggles,

the children dispersed in every direction, grabbing balls and discarded toys as they went.

"Pleased that someone finds this amusing," he muttered as he hauled Lilah toward the high road.

"Yes, school's the best joke going in these parts. Let go," she added through her teeth. "You're about to break my arm."

His grip eased. "It's your throat you should be worried for. Do you know where you are? This is no place for an afternoon stroll."

She peered up at him in amazement. "Afraid of the children, are you?"

He turned his attention to the road ahead, his mouth pressing into a tight line. "What were you doing here, Lilah? Who was that man?"

The lie came to her in a burst of divine inspiration. "He's my fence."

"Your fence."

"Yes. I come here to fence the goods I've stolen."

He released her elbow as though it burned. She had only the briefest moment to register the stupid hurt she felt. He looked at her as though she were a leper.

Then his hand found the small of her back, pressing firmly to encourage her to keep pace. "And what," he said tightly, "did you come to sell today? Something from Buckley Hall, I expect?"

Heaven help her. She did not want him to think she had stolen from him. But as excuses went, it was the best she could manage. "Just a candlestick," she said weakly. "Miss Everleigh didn't think it so valuable."

His coach was waiting on the high street. The footman on the step looked pale and as jumpy as a rabbit.

When he spotted Palmer, he heaved a visible sigh and pulled open the door so eagerly that Lilah expected it to pop off its springs.

Palmer all but threw her inside. He pulled shut the door behind him, and the coach launched into motion. By the suddenness of it, no doubt even the coachman imagined he'd escaped some dreadful fate.

"It's just a neighborhood," she said in amazement. "People live here. Most of them aren't even criminals."

"Present company excepted," he bit out.

"Why are you so angry?" She smoothed down her skirts. "You knew what I was from the first night you met me."

"And to spare yourself the consequences, you agreed to a bargain. You were not to let Catherine out of your sight."

There was the rub. Now she must paint herself not only an unrepentant criminal, but a welsher to boot. "She was going to a bookshop." Lilah tried for a careless shrug. "She wasn't in the mood to confide secrets to me."

His jaw flexed. He was grinding his teeth as he looked away. Slowly and methodically, he drew the shades—blocking out the left window, then the right. In the dimness, he faced her. "What am I to do with you?"

Nerves fluttered through her stomach. "You want me to follow her everywhere? I'll only annoy her. Then she'll tell me nothing at all."

His gaze pinned her against the bench. "I should burn those notes. Teach you the cost of disobedience."

A pity he hadn't met Nick after all. They would rub along very well, being cut from the same tyrannical cloth. "Is it your job to school me?"

"God knows you need an education," he growled. "If you are so reckless with your life as to traipse into East End taverns to consort with scum—"

Scum! She was suddenly angry. Neddie was decent people, and many of his patrons were old friends. "Scum? Like those little children, you mean? I admit they have poor taste in heroes, but you can't blame them for it. They believe what's printed in the newspapers. Why, they probably think *me* semidivine, simply for having stood in your shadow."

She heard his sharp breath. "Will they speak of it?"

"Of having met you?" She laughed blackly. "They'll tell the story to their grandchildren, no doubt."

She didn't understand the look on his face. "And you at my side," he said in a strange, bitter tone.

"Forgive me," she said stiffly. "How awful that your name should be sullied by connection to mine."

"Oh, it's not me who stands to suffer."

The remark baffled her, as did his black expression as he sat back and rapped his knuckles against the bench. *Thump. Thump. Thump.*

"If I were decent," he said, "I would leave you on the next corner."

Frowning, she watched him. But his dark face yielded no clues. She edged aside the shade. The traffic circus was jammed. "If you leave me, I'll never make the train in time."

He blinked, as though summoning his thoughts from distant places. "I'll give you a ride to Paddington."

Then he meant to keep her on? Relief flooded her, light as a laugh. She locked her hands together to trap the urge to thank him. "I won't steal again. I promise you that."

"Why bother?" But he spoke without heat. "Tell me this. You said you were out of practice. Why have you returned to thieving?"

She bit her lip. His intent, sober look seemed to undo something inside her—an inward scaffolding that she needed, to hold herself away from him. "I don't know."

"You do," he said. "And I want the answer. You have talents, true intelligence . . . This position with Catherine could be a real opportunity for you. Why would you risk it?"

She shook her head, hesitant. It felt wrong to embroider her lie, to deepen the deception, when he looked at her with such . . .

"Whatever drives you," he said, "it puts you into danger. Of course there are decent men in Whitechapel. But your *fence* isn't one of them."

Concern. He looked at her with concern. In his face, in his voice . . . concern for *her*.

How long had it been since she'd felt cared for? And how foul, what a black joke, that *he* should be the one to do it! "Don't worry for me." She spoke roughly, defiantly, as she looked into her lap. "I can't . . ." *Defend myself against it.* "It's boring."

"Yes." She could feel his gaze on her. He had not looked away for a moment. "I see how much it bores you. It brings tears to your eyes."

She flinched, mortified by his acuity. She would have covered her face if it wouldn't have exposed her further, in a way. "Stop it."

"Gladly. I don't need these distractions. But apparently someone must worry for you, since you're too much a fool to do it yourself. Where are your people, Lilah? They should look after you better than this."

Her people? The only people who had ever worried for her were dead. Her uncle would not fit the role Palmer required. Nick was the reason she was trapped in this mess, pinned under the magnifying glass of a rich man who should have better ways to entertain himself than the dissection of her soul. "I can look after myself."

"I'm certain you can. I've seen you with a knife." He was silent a moment. "Something I learned in the war, though: survival comes down to luck. And when you push your luck far enough, it always turns rotten. Yours, I think, is running out."

She lifted her face. "Yes. That started the night I met *you*."

His eyes narrowed. "Is that what you tell yourself? Whereas I've begun to think I'm the best friend you have."

"Why? Because you didn't hand me over to the police? If you truly cared for my safety, you'd give me back those letters." She felt her mouth twist. "You want me out of danger? Then give them to me right now, and let me go."

"Perhaps I would, if I believed for a single moment that you wouldn't take them straight to Whitechapel." His smile was sudden and sharp. "Or maybe I wouldn't. Maybe the real problem is your confusion on whom to fear."

She caught her breath as he moved onto her bench.

"Perhaps," he said, "I've been too easy on you." He laid his hand on her throat, stroking his thumb over her jugular as he watched her with lambent gold eyes. A predator's eyes. His hair was slicked back today; he saved dishevelment for the country. The strong bones of his face, the flawless elegance of his wardrobe, the heavy wool coat tailored precisely to the brutal muscle of his body—he radiated wealth, confidence. He looked like someone only a fool would cross.

She tried to avert her face. He gripped her chin, holding her in place. "I should be less kind to you," he murmured. "That's where I've gone wrong. A devil wants those notes? He's a gutter rat with a gun, Lilah. A squadron of police could take him down. Whereas I . . ." He slid his hand into her hair, hooking it hard. "I have better cause to be a villain than that gutter rat could dream. And the police cannot touch me. I am a bloody goddamned hero. I could put you in prison without lifting a finger. I could drag you through the streets, and people would applaud."

She drew a strangled breath. "Are you trying to frighten me?"

He pulled her forehead to his. "*Yes.*" The word brushed against her lips like a kiss. "Be afraid. Fear *me*. It would be wiser. And far more pleasant for you. Think of it: no more running into the slums. No more answering to thugs." His fingers loosened from her hair; he brushed his knuckles down her cheek. "No more lies," he said. "No more thieving. Simply . . . submission."

God help her. She stared at him, riveted despite herself. He did not frighten her. But his talk of power—it was the most erotic speech she'd ever heard.

She touched him very lightly. Laid the flat of her palm against his chest. He was powerful, yes. But here was her power over him.

A muscle flexed in his jaw. And then he lunged at her.

His kiss was deep and carnal, and she fell into it wholly—his tongue in her mouth, hers in his; demanding, seizing, taking. He came over her as she sagged, gripping her face, opening her mouth wider. *Yes.* This was what she wanted. *Take me.*

He pushed her flat onto the bench and came down atop her, so his torso crushed into hers. She wrapped her arms around him and he knocked up her skirts, hooked her leg behind the knee. Had they been quarreling? Now they understood each other perfectly. He squeezed and stroked her thigh as she bared her neck to him; instantly he accepted the invitation, licking his way down her throat. As she squirmed, he repositioned himself so the bulge of his erection pressed against the juncture of her thighs. He rolled his hips, a silent promise: he was well able to satisfy her.

Her eyes rolled back in her head, perhaps. Later she would wonder why her memory of this moment, this feverish eternity, consisted only of sensations and sounds. The ripping of fabric—his palm, so hot through the flimsy cambric of her drawers, searing her inner thigh— the bite of his teeth at the top of her shoulder. She saw nothing.

And then she felt the bold, skillful prying of his fingers through the slit in her drawers. She gasped and arched. All the stories the girls told made sense to her suddenly. He opened her like a flower. He found the spot that made her pulse. What she had always dismissed in other women as recklessness, as a risk not worth taking, proved to be the finest decision she'd made—to open her legs and let him touch her. Her body reassembled itself. It became an instrument of pleasure, strummed expertly by the insistent firm stroke of his hand.

She wanted more. She gripped his waist, feeling through layers of cloth the hard flex of his back. She wanted the bluntness of his erection to replace the teasing promises of his hand. She groaned a demand, and his teeth closed on her lower lip in warning. Below, his fingers breached her, a slight burning, delicious pressure as he parted and opened and widened her.

"Quiet," he rasped, and she froze, and he pressed very hard, and she convulsed—once, then again, around his fingers.

She opened her eyes, dazed. He stared down at her, his face dark and wild, his hair mussed, his lips wet from hers.

"In this matter, you're obedient," he said. "Perhaps I should fuck you properly."

The words sent a thrill through her—hot and liquid, and then, as the pleasure faded, horrible. Cold.

She pushed his shoulders, wanting him off her, away. For all the effect it had, she might as well have pushed a mountain. He slowly eased apart from her. With conspicuously unhurried movements, he ran his palms down her legs and grasped her ankles. He swung her feet off the bench, settling them on the floor, and then brushed her skirts down over her thighs. He sat back, then, studying her with merciless intensity.

A strong premonition of distress overwhelmed her. The world was sinking back into clarity, cold reason in its black-and-white palette. She had erred here. She had revealed something better kept secret.

"Shall I, then?" he asked.

The raggedness in his voice struck her. He was far from unmoved, himself.

That realization made a balm for her abraded dignity—and fueled her sudden anger. "No." She cleared her throat. "You won't. You aren't quite the villain you aspire to be."

His eyes glittered. "Take heart. One of these days, I will surprise you."

"You already have." She took a deep breath for bravery. "I only wish I didn't like it so much."

A muscle flexed in his jaw as he moved back to his bench. But he did not reply. After all, what answer could he possibly make to that admission? She knew better than he what a fool it made her.

The coach slowed. They were pulling into the queue alongside the curb at Paddington. She wanted to cry out, or pound her fist. Instead she put it against her lips, which trembled. How had he gained this much power over her? It had nothing to do with his blackmail.

"On the other matter," he said with frightening calm. "The gutter rat. I will destroy him for you. That can be my payment. We can dispense with the letters altogether."

She had never heard that savage note in his voice. It succeeded where his threats had not; at last, she felt fear.

She did not want him to go to war with Nick. She could not say who would win. She could not say . . . whom she would want to win.

"No," she said. "I want our original agreement. That's all."

"A pity," he said after a moment. "I would have enjoyed it."

"It could be the work of poachers." Howard Stowe had served under Christian in Afghanistan; more recently, he had put his scouting skills to keeping watch of comings and goings on the perimeter of Buckley Hall. He led Christian now into a stand of oak trees, where bright-winged butterflies and songbirds flitted to and fro beneath the boughs.

"Very stupid poachers," Christian said. The temper in his own voice gave him pause. He'd returned to London very late last night, and had chosen to closet himself with a bottle of whisky rather than risk his restraint by summoning Lilah for a more thorough debriefing. He no longer trusted himself around her. His judgment was corrupted. And he needed, God's sake, to be able to trust himself. For his family, he needed to be steady.

"Aye," said Stowe, "it's a poor place to set a trap, right on the path. And I've never seen rabbits caught by such an effort."

Christian knelt at the edge of the pit, knocking aside the woven mat of branches that had disguised it. He bit back an oath. The bottom of the pit was lined with six sharpened spikes. A bit much for a rabbit, indeed. "How deep is that? Six feet?"

"Deep enough to catch a man." Stowe squatted beside him. "Would have taken some muscle to dig it."

"Or sheer lunacy." Christian scanned the vicinity. "There." He rose and walked into the brush. Seven paces from the pit, concealed amid the trees, stood the pile of earth that had been excavated.

Howe whistled. "Took some effort to move it all."

And time. And murderous determination. Christian looked back the way they had come. The turrets of Buckley Hall were visible over the crest of the hill. The house stood very close, not five minutes' walk away.

He turned back, scanning the glen, breathing hard to channel his rage. A very lucky thing that Catherine Everleigh showed such dedication to her work. She had not once stirred outdoors. And her assistant . . .

His jaw clenched. Lilah had been setting out for a stroll alone that day he'd found her sneezing in the hall. Had an allergy not beset her, she might well have come this way. It was the clearest path into the woodland.

"We must assume there will be others," he said. "Put Potter on the search." Another member of the old regiment, Potter had an uncanny sense for where the enemy might lay an ambush.

"Will do. And if you'll allow it, I'll go down to the village pub tonight, pass word around that the poaching won't fly no more." Stowe spat a long stream of tobacco juice. "This ain't the only trap I've found. Handful of snares elsewhere on the property. Don't want nobody stealing up at night to collect rabbits, and find themselves at the bottom of one of these."

"Or at the wrong end of a rifle," Christian said. "You go anywhere, you go armed."

"Yes, sir."

He realized that Stowe was standing at stiff attention, waiting for orders or dismissal. Old habits died hard. "Drop a word of warning," Christian said. "But keep the cause vague. If the magistrate gets wind of this, he'll want to know who did it. I don't want some local lad rotting in jail for someone else's crime."

He caught the twitch of Stowe's hand—an aborted impulse to salute. Stowe saw him remark it, and offered a sheepish grin, flashing the wad of tobacco stuffed into his cheek.

Christian began to roll up his shirtsleeves. "Let's dismantle this."

"Oh, no call for your help, sir."

Christian shook his head. He could not walk away before the foul thing was disarmed. "Go ask Mrs.

Barnes where you might find a shovel. I'll start with the stakes."

As Stowe started up the rise, he lowered himself carefully into the pit. He ripped the first spike out of the ground, then held it up to the light. The oaken spike had been carved into a point that would pierce straight through muscle and tendon.

Bile churned up his throat. Lilah had never been to the country before. What a welcome this would have given her. How long would she have lain here, bleeding, calling out with no reply, until she died?

A vision came to him, a nightmare as clear as the spike in his hands. Her cry for help. The sound of leaves crunching underfoot. Her face lifting toward the daylight. A shadow falling over her. Bolkhov's face filling her vision.

A thousand times since his brother's death, he had seen such nightmares. But for the first time, it was not his mother or sister who suffered. Stay out of *Whitechapel*, he'd told Lilah. But Buckley Hall was hardly safer—and he, no less dangerous than any East End thug. He'd brought her into the crosshairs of a madman.

He tossed the stake over the edge of the pit. If the discovery of this trap proved anything, it was that he could not afford distractions. Bolkhov did not want to kill him. Otherwise it would only take a bullet. What the lunatic intended was to terrorize and torture him. Nobody in Christian's proximity was safe.

In light of that, what did his inward turmoil matter? He had imagined himself on a bed of nails last night— or a rack, stretched unbearably by incongruous compulsions: fury at her recklessness and lies; anger at his own brutal treatment of her; and worst of all, desire. Desire to touch her again. Desire, God forgive him, to know her beyond touching. Beyond fucking or fighting. Beyond anything so simple.

There was his true sin. This gruesome trap showed him so clearly. For what could he achieve by drawing her closer but the temporary satisfaction of his lust, and far darker and more lasting possibilities besides? He had no tower for her. Instead, he could be her death.

The hell of it was, if he respected her less—if she were less intelligent, less accomplished, and even, perhaps, less gloriously, infuriatingly deceitful—he would never have wanted to know her. And he would have endangered her now without a thought.

For he *was* a bastard. He cared for nobody but his own. *Catherine's* fate hardly troubled him. He didn't lie awake worrying for her.

And people called him a hero.

In grim silence, he yanked out the rest of the spikes. When Stowe returned, he claimed the shovel and sent the other man off. But the labor of refilling the hole made a poor penance. Both women at Buckley Hall deserved far, far better.

CHAPTER ELEVEN

$\mathcal{N}$ ot entirely awful."

Not entirely awful! Had a more satisfying verdict ever been spoken? Hiding an amazed smile, Lilah began to replace the teacups into their crates. Her judge turned away to consider the rest of the dusty room. *Tap-tap-tap* went Miss Everleigh's pencil against the notebook she carried.

"This will be our staging space," she said, her voice echoing off the bare walls. "We'll begin with the most breakable items—porcelain, crystal, all the delicate wares. You have the list still?"

"Right here, miss." That she was entrusted with it seemed encouraging, too. Now that they had finished their canvass and begun the more detailed work of appraisal, Miss Everleigh's temper had mellowed. Her mood, Lilah had observed, followed her work exactly; if it was proceeding at a satisfactory pace, she sometimes even managed a smile.

"Your job is simple enough," Miss Everleigh said. Her attention fell to the vase Lilah was wrapping. "Careful, there. Don't swaddle too tightly."

"Yes, miss." Lilah tucked the loose end of linen into the lip, then carefully placed it into a crate filled with wood shavings. That was the last of the hard-paste porcelain, for which she was thankful. Handling such valuable objects made her anxious of her grip.

Together they looked over the china still to be cataloged, a minefield of dishes littered across the floor. "You'll take the English plate," Miss Everleigh said. "Bone china only. I'll start with the soft paste. Once you've labeled an item, you'll write a brief description. Focus on distinctions that might increase a piece's value—and imperfections that might lower it. For instance, that vase you just put away. What did you observe before wrapping it?"

"A small scratch in the glaze along the rim," Lilah said instantly. "Barely noticeable."

"Highly noticeable," Miss Everleigh corrected, "to the clients who will be bidding on it. What else?"

Reluctantly, Lilah started to peel back the linen wrapping.

"No," Miss Everleigh said. "From memory, if you please."

Was this a test? Lilah hoped so. A test meant that Miss Everleigh saw a chance for her to prove herself. "The stones are agate and jade. The underglaze is very vibrant."

"What color?"

"Red."

"Red as a brick? Red as blood? Red as a rooster's—"

"As copper," Lilah said.

"Yes, precisely. It's a classic example of Jihong porcelain." Miss Everleigh eyed the crate. "One of two dozen in existence, if that."

Lilah goggled. "And you let me wrap it?"

"Your hands seem steady." She shrugged. "Keep your notes in plain language. The more florid descriptions are the job of the catalog editors. They know best how to stir the public's interest."

Breathless, Lilah waited. This was all very interesting information, nothing she'd ever learned as an Everleigh Girl.

But her instruction was over. "Proceed," Miss Everleigh said, and gathered up a porcelain figure, carrying it to her seat at the table. With elegant economy, she turned the figurine with one hand, while with the other, she began to take notes.

Lilah turned to her own business. For the first few minutes, as she worked through the cups and saucers, she remained acutely aware of her employer's scrutiny. But when a half hour had passed without scolding, her nerves settled, and she began to make good time with her share of the china.

She was unprepared, then, for Miss Everleigh's sudden remark. "Lord Palmer takes an interest in you, I observe."

She nearly dropped a saucer. Inwardly cursing, she made a great frowning show of concentrating on her next notation: *C-F-44. Minor imperfection of pattern: one branch of leaves is in different shade of paint.* "Why should you say so, miss? I rarely see him about the house." In fact, she'd not seen him since leaving town, yesterday.

"You meet with him regularly, don't you? In the afternoons." Miss Everleigh wrinkled her nose. "These maids cannot keep from gossiping."

"He—" Drat the gossips! "I don't—sometimes he does invite me to take tea with him, but I—"

"Tea, is it?" Miss Everleigh's voice was perfectly neutral, though her next words revealed her opinion. "I'm not surprised. All you girls are very good at making impressions on gentlemen."

There was no wise reply to *that*. On a steadying breath, Lilah turned over the saucer. It felt as smooth as a baby's bottom. *See, miss, how industriously I work.*

"Curious name, 'Everleigh Girls.'" Miss Everleigh loosed a brittle laugh. "I wonder what my grandfather would have said, had he guessed that his auction rooms would become the byword for women who advertise tooth powder on the sides of omnibuses."

"I can't imagine," Lilah said carefully. Their truce, she gathered, was approaching its conclusion. "I have never been called to advertise anything myself."

With an unpleasant smile, Miss Everleigh looked her over. "No, I suppose you haven't."

Lilah laughed. She did not mean to do it, and Miss Everleigh looked startled. "You find that amusing? I am given to understand that you girls jostle and compete for such . . . opportunities."

"Some of us do." The girls who wished to call themselves to the attention of wealthy patrons did indeed dream of such fame. "I had always hoped for different."

Miss Everleigh's jaw ticked, as though she were chewing on what she would say next. "Such as?"

Lilah spotted a way back into their accord. "It would be my fondest dream to be a professional woman, such as yourself. To do work that depended on my knowledge, rather than my . . . conversational politesse, as you once put it. I was very happy, miss, when I learned I was to assist you here."

Miss Everleigh visibly flinched. Then she reached

for a new miniature, turning it over and over in her hands—searching for what was wrong with it.

But it seemed the little figure, of a shepherdess playing a pipe, bore no imperfections. Frowning, Miss Everleigh laid it down. "It isn't done," she said, staring at the shepherdess, "for a woman to be called professional. The very idea sounds . . ."

Had Lilah offended her? "Perhaps that's the wrong word. Forgive me, I didn't—"

"No." Miss Everleigh looked up, her expression adamant. "That is precisely the right word, Miss Marshall."

"Well." Fighting a foolish smile, Lilah swaddled her cup and took up another.

"But it would take far more than the work of a single estate to provide you the requisite training," Miss Everleigh continued stiffly. "I learned this trade from birth, you know. As a little girl on my father's knee, I began my education."

"Yes, miss. Of course. I would not dream—"

"And the price is steep, to nurse such ambitions. You are pretty enough, Miss Marshall, in your own way; perhaps the advertisers won't have you, but some decent man might. Certainly that would be the safer path—provided his offer was satisfactory."

Bold words, from a sheltered heiress! In amazement, Lilah looked up.

Miss Everleigh lifted one slim shoulder in a shrug. "I am not naïve," she said. "Nor do I endorse immoral practices. I am certain you could find an honest man, a butcher or a . . ." It seemed her knowledge of the middling professions was not great; for a moment, she faltered. "A bank clerk," she said finally. "To marry, I mean."

Between a butcher and a clerk was a great ground to cover. But Lilah doubted that Miss Everleigh was looking to be tutored on the difference. Mutely she nodded.

"It is not exciting," Miss Everleigh said, "to think of security. But you strike me as a practical woman—surely too wise to fall prey to the perils of romantic nonsense. Should your position feel tenuous, you will think wisely and at leisure on how to provide for yourself. The appeal of a man like Lord Palmer is far outstripped by the peril."

With amazement, Lilah finally understood what was happening. Miss Everleigh was warning her not to be seduced.

Why, it was a kindness. The girl was not quite as icy as she appeared. "I understand," Lilah said. "And I thank you for the advice, miss." She mustered up the will to seize this opportunity. Her own feelings for Palmer could not be allowed to interfere, foolish and useless as they were. "If I dare say so, I believe you have it wrong. The times I've spoken with his lordship, it has always been in reference to you. I do believe he has an . . . affection for you, miss."

That sound that came from Miss Everleigh could not possibly have been a snort. Her expression, alas, was hidden now in study of the shepherdess. "Any number of gentlemen express any number of sentiments," she said in a muffled voice. "Whether one credits those sentiments is a different matter."

An intuition stalled Lilah's reply. Was it possible that this beautiful girl did not believe her admirers' compliments to be genuine? Surely she must know that she was a most eligible young woman. Not blue-blooded, of course, but between her beauty and the great whacking dowry she'd bring, any number of aristocrats would gladly take her in marriage. "It's true, gentlemen are prone to say what sounds best. But I vow to you, miss, his lordship's interest strikes me as genuine. Moreover, his ardent admiration for your work—"

"That's enough." The cold words sliced like a blade across her speech. "I need no lectures on that matter from *you*."

Lilah silently accepted the rebuff. After bundling up the last cup, she stood and said, "I can help with the Sèvres, if you—"

"The ability to see what is there"—Miss Everleigh's fierce tone stopped her in her tracks—"to see what is *plainly* before you, instead of what you wish to see— that is the key to a proper appraisal."

Lilah sat down slowly. "Yes, miss."

"Palmer does not require money." A flush stained Miss Everleigh's smooth cheeks. "It is indelicate to speak of, but the truth is oft indelicate. Palmer does not require my fortune, and if beauty were his aim, there are a dozen eligible beauties on the market who would flirt and smile far more readily than I."

How bizarre this conversation was! She must defend a woman she disliked to the very woman herself. "None of them can boast of your accomplishments, miss. None of them would know the first thing about Jihong porcelain or Persian brocades, or how to take an estate to auction."

"True. Do you believe the clients of Everleigh's who call you beautiful?"

Lilah's instincts prickled. "Miss? I don't—"

"The ones who flatter you, Miss Marshall. Who beg your hand for the waltz, only to whisper in your ear of a house in St. John's Wood . . ." Miss Everleigh made a curious little grimace, as though choking back the urge to be sick. "Promising a pile of priceless jewels, along with their undying love and affection. Do you believe those men?"

She wet her lips. "No, miss. I do not."

"Yet you would counsel me to believe a man who claims to love me for my *skills*. Who could have his pick of pretty debutantes, but prefers the woman who would rather be alone with cold ceramics?"

This cynicism would have been shocking, had it not been so familiar. Lilah saw now the main impediment to Palmer's suit: Miss Everleigh was as much a pragmatist as Lilah.

Yet there was no choice but to persevere. She needed those letters. Moreover, she needed to get away from Palmer. He was ruining her already. Destroying her peace. It wouldn't take her uncle to leave her in pieces, ere long.

Thus, she needed Miss Everleigh to accept Palmer's suit. "Miss, I do believe his claim to admire you." Lies, bold lies. She didn't sound convincing even to herself. "Not all men are so shallow as you suggest." That was true. "Viscount Palmer is a man of rare tastes." She believed that. What other lord would have spoken to her like a friend—and then kissed her like a ravening beast? "Perhaps it's his time in the military that has set him apart." Chasing her down to Whitechapel. Then, despite his foul mood, taking the time to humor a ragtag band of children. The memory of his kindness warmed her. "Why, he's probably the most extraordinary—"

"Does he pay you?"

Lilah gaped. "Miss? I don't underst—"

"He has enlisted his sister to aid his courtship, so why not you as well? Indeed, I can think of no other reason for your impassioned championship of the viscount." Miss Everleigh spoke very rapidly now. "Or—if not he, then I could see my brother being desperate enough to put you to it; heaven knows he has tried any number of other ways to get rid of me. Why not marriage to Palmer?" She issued a cutting laugh. "Of course, there is a third possibility, nearly too sad to contemplate. For how pathetic would it be for you to imagine, even for a second, that you stood to gain from flattering me? How deluded, how woefully ignorant of your own station and possibilities, to think I might actually come to like you, to feel fond enough of you, to support your ambitions! For you overreach yourself sorely if you imagine that you would ever win a position like mine. Why, it is so far above your station it might as well be a princedom. For to be a curator, Miss Marshall, one must first be a person in possession of breeding and *taste*."

Well, that did it. Lilah put her hands on the table and shoved herself to her feet. "It would indeed be pathetic," she said, "to attempt to rouse any emotion in your heart warmer than indifference! I should count myself lucky only to be spared your contempt. But I do agree, most pathetic of all would be to hope for any outcome similar to yours—for you are unkind, Miss Everleigh, and cold, and above all the unhappiest woman I've ever known, despite having every advantage in the world!"

Miss Everleigh rose, her posture magnificently stiff. "You are through here," she said. "Through at Buckley Hall, and through"—she swayed, catching herself on

the table—"at the auction rooms. Go pack your things."
She panted. "I want you on the train by nightfall."

"No." Lilah put a hand over her mouth, horrified.
What have I done? "No, please, I'm so sorry, so very—"

Miss Everleigh collapsed to the floor, china shattering around her.

"My best guess is adulterated foodstuff."

The doctor's pronouncement came clearly from
around the corner. Mrs. Barnes, who had come out
of Miss Everleigh's room to eavesdrop, clapped her
hands to her mouth. "Can't be," she whispered to
Lilah.

Something had made Miss Everleigh very sick. She
had vomited several times, yet her fever kept building.
Dr. Hardwick had sat with her all day, but his medicines
showed little sign of assuaging her misery.

"Is the rest of the household at risk?" came Lord
Palmer's quiet voice.

Lilah exchanged an alarmed look with Mrs. Barnes.
The older woman laid a hand on her own forehead as
though to test herself.

"That was my concern earlier," the doctor allowed.
"But I understand that no one else has sickened. That
is an encouraging sign. It further persuades me that the
culprit is some contaminated food, ingested solely by
the young lady."

"What could it have been?" Palmer wanted to know.

"Nothing from my kitchen," Mrs. Barnes muttered.
Lilah waved at her to hush.

"The most common toxin is contaminated milk,"
the doctor said. "But Buckley Hall has always had its

dairy from the Elders' farm, and I trust their sanitation implicitly. Personally? My suspicion fixes on the chocolates that Miss Everleigh kept by her bed. She had eaten several of them today."

"I see." Palmer paused. "Well, I do thank you——"

"And rest assured, my lord—I shan't breathe a word of this. Your sister need not worry on that count."

"My . . . sister?"

"Oh, don't mistake me! I'm quite certain that Miss Stratton procured the chocolates from the finest purveyor. But I would nevertheless recommend that you warn her, in case she also purchased a box for herself."

"I don't follow you," Palmer said sharply. "My sister has not been here."

The doctor sputtered. "I—perhaps I'm mistaken. But the note was from Miss Stratton. She invited Miss Everleigh to share the truffles with you——"

"What note?"

Dr. Hardwick sounded increasingly panicked. "I never meant to pry! I examined it only to see if it yielded clues to the chocolates' provenance. I am sure Miss Stratton intended them as a—a very pleasant gift! But travel by post, you know—it exposes foodstuffs to all manner of contaminants . . ."

Palmer came storming around the corner. Lilah and Mrs. Barnes barely had time to jump out of his way. He disappeared inside Miss Everleigh's suite.

The doctor came rushing after, clutching his bag to his chest. He drew up beside Mrs. Barnes. "I did not mean to distress him!"

"No," Mrs. Barnes said faintly.

The three of them waited in a breathless silence until Palmer emerged again, two maids trailing him in a panic. "Where is this note?" he bit out, as the maids took shelter behind the housekeeper.

"I—" Dr. Hardwick looked to Mrs. Barnes, who spread her hands, looking helpless. "I suppose it was thrown out with the sweets."

"But it was signed?" Palmer demanded.

"By Miss Melanie Stratton," Hardwick said haltingly. "Was I mistaken? I simply assumed by her surname . . ."

"And the note was addressed here." A muscle ticked in Palmer's jaw. "To Buckley Hall?" His questions were assuming a clipped, military precision. "It implied that I would be present to share the gift?"

"I confess I did not look at the direction. It never occurred to me—"

"Yes." Mrs. Barnes squared her shoulders. With the dignity of a martyr before the firing squad, she stepped into Palmer's line of sight. "I saw the envelope. I tossed it into the fire along with the chocolates. Forgive me, my lord. I simply wanted the nasty things gone."

Palmer took an audible breath. In the next moment, with an unnerving completeness, he mastered himself, becoming once again the picture of polite composure. "Thank you, Mrs. Barnes. That is very good to know." To the doctor, he directed a nod. "Until tomorrow, sir."

His departure left a stunned silence, which the doctor leapt to fill. "Someone must sit with her at all hours. I would prefer someone literate, for I have left very specific instructions for the medicines." He handed a sheet of paper to Mrs. Barnes, who looked it over and passed it onward to Lilah.

Was *she* to play the nursemaid? The woman on the sickbed had sacked her this morning.

Absently she trailed Mrs. Barnes back into the sickroom. "Call into question *my* kitchen," the woman was muttering. "Why, I've never served spoilt food in all my sixty-six years."

Miss Everleigh lay insensate amid a pile of pillows, her unbound hair a pale tangled cloud around her slack face. Mrs. Barnes laid a hand on her brow, frowning at what she felt. "I'll take first watch," she said to Lilah. "Come fetch me at half four. And leave those instructions."

"Yes, ma'am." All sickrooms smelled the same. It was impossible not to think of Fiona. Gratefully, Lilah started to retreat.

A faint call from the bed made her turn. Miss Everleigh was squinting in her direction. "Is that . . . Miss Marshall?"

Mrs. Barnes clucked. "Yes, that's right." She stroked Miss Everleigh's hair from her face. "Quite a scare you gave us, miss."

"Tell her . . . stay."

"What?" Lilah approached, panicked. "She can't mean it," she told Mrs. Barnes. She could not bear this stuffy little room. "You have far more experience in a sickroom than I!"

"Mean it," Miss Everleigh rasped. "Miss . . . Marshall. Stay."

But they loathed each other! In disbelief, Lilah stared down at the girl. It was madness, of course, to imagine that Miss Everleigh intended to punish her by this request. Selfish, paranoid madness. But what a talent the girl had for hitting a sore spot!

"Seems she wants you," Mrs. Barnes said. "Did you take heed while the doctor was explaining the dosage? Here, read it again."

Lilah took the paper with a trembling hand. *Turn down all the lights.* That was the very first line the doctor had written. *Nothing must disturb her.*

"Are *you* all right?" Mrs. Barnes asked.

Heat burned in Lilah's cheeks. No doubt she looked a fine coward. *She* was not the one whose life was at stake. "Yes. I'm fine." Girding herself, she settled on the little stool. Miss Everleigh's eyes had closed again. She looked as waxen as a corpse. "Leave the medicine on the table."

She waited until the door had shut. Then, with a shaking hand, she turned down the lamp.

There. Darkness was not so bad. Miss Everleigh's pallor made her dimly visible. The smell of sickness, sour and pungent, hung sharp in the air.

Miss Everleigh dragged in a rattling breath. Her hand twitched once on the counterpane.

A memory came to Lilah. How desperately she had longed, that faraway night, for Uncle Nick to reach her. To pull her to safety, or simply . . . to grip her hand, so she would not feel so alone.

She laid her hand over Miss Everleigh's. "I am with you," she whispered. "I won't go just yet."

Minutes might have been hours. A crack in the curtains showed her the moon for a little while. Then it passed out of view, and time crawled.

Each random creak, each whisper of wind against the windows, made Lilah flinch and remember tales of the ghost who haunted the halls. But no specter appeared to disrupt the darkness. Gradually, as Lilah listened to Miss Everleigh's pained breaths, she found herself wishing otherwise. She would welcome the appearance of a spirit—even a demon, slobbering blood. Proof of Satan's wickedness would not frighten her. If his evil was real, then so, too, was God. If some souls were cursed after death to roam the earth, then others surely were lifted into heaven.

She hadn't abandoned Fiona. She had done her best; she wouldn't blame herself for what had happened. But it would be so much easier to bear if she felt certain that her sister had not died afraid—or that afterward she'd woken from fear into God's arms.

Bring on the ghost, then. She prayed for it. *Show us we can hope for better in the hereafter. Show me that you mean to save her, if you let her die.*

But this heretic philosophy went unnoticed by the heavens. Meanwhile, four times Miss Everleigh choked in her sleep, requiring Lilah to lift her onto her side so she might expel noxious fluids. "It's all right," Lilah murmured. "I'm here."

Once, Miss Everleigh opened her eyes and spoke. "Poisoned," she rasped. She tried to lift her head before collapsing back into the pillows.

"Shh, don't sit up, now. You're sick, but you'll be all right."

"He isn't . . . here. Is he? Please check! So . . . dark."

Lilah turned up the lamp. "Nobody's here but me, miss."

The girl's bright, feverish eyes made a sweep of the shadowed room. "Yes," she said. "Alone. Don't . . . let him in."

"Lord Palmer, do you mean?"

"My . . . brother. He'll . . . kill me."

"He's not here," Lilah said slowly. "I won't let him in."

The girl's eyelids dropped shut. Her face grew slack again.

Fever could produce delusions, of course. But Lilah still felt chilled an hour later, when Mrs. Barnes came tapping at the door. Everyone knew Peter Everleigh resented the terms of his father's will. She had never seen him exchange a warm word with his sister. Who knew how he treated her behind closed doors?

As she stepped into the hallway, she felt as though she were waking from a nightmare. Palmer rose from a nearby chair, a burned candle at his feet. "How is she?" he asked.

She rubbed her eyes and leaned back against the wall. "She's better, I think. Awake, on and off."

"Speaking?"

She opened her mouth, then thought better of it. Catherine's sickbed rambling was not hers to share. "Only nonsense. She's feverish, still."

Palmer gripped the back of the chair. Veins stood out on his broad hand; his knuckles looked white. "She'll make it through," he said flatly.

"Yes, of course." His mood seemed as bleak as her own. God above . . . had she figured him wrong? Did he truly care for Catherine after all?

She had no energy to wrestle with her stupid, shameful jealousy. "Step in and have a look, if you like."

"No, I'll stay here. You should get some sleep."

A strange laugh slipped from her. She felt edgy and haunted, the last thing from fatigued. "A drink would suit me better."

He studied her a moment. "All right," he said. "I could use one as well."

CHAPTER TWELVE

*L*ilah huddled on a loveseat by the fire, watching Palmer move around his study—shifting papers from chair to table; procuring glasses from the cabinet; uncorking a bottle. It was soothing to watch him. His body spoke of competence, power. He moved with economical grace, loose and easy, a man trained to fight.

"Here you go." He offered her a toast glass. "Brandy, neat."

She rolled the glass by its stem, feeling the sharpness of the cut edges. The beveled crystal captured the firelight and splintered it into dancing points. "You were waiting in the hallway all night?"

He prowled over to the window. Lifted aside the curtain to look out. "Couldn't sleep."

That jacket fit him a shade more loosely than his normal suits. The left pocket hung a fraction of an inch lower than the right. In Whitechapel, she would have noticed that telltale sign immediately.

He was armed.

"I never sleep very well here," she said softly. Nor, she was coming to suspect, did he.

"Why is that?"

She looked into the depths of her brandy and shrugged.

"Ah. The lady rebuffs me." His tone was gentle. When she glanced up, he offered her a slight smile. "Another secret for me to pursue."

She thanked God he could not guess her most troubling secret: how difficult it was to look away from him. Standing against the dark curtains, with firelight gilding his leonine hair and drawing shadows beneath his cheekbones and full lower lip, he looked like a mythic figure. Some medieval tapestry: the hero who had been bloodied, his long scar left by a dragon's claw.

To prove she could look away, Lilah turned toward the fire. "It's not a secret why I can't sleep. It's too dark. In the city, there's always light somewhere, isn't there? Even in the rankest rookery, you'll find a lamp burning in a window, or a public house shedding light across the lane. But here, once everybody is asleep, there's only darkness."

"Some count that a blessing."

Not he. He traveled armed in his own house. "Who?"

His footsteps were soundless. A hunter's prowl. He sat in the chair opposite. "People who want quiet," he said. "People who value peace."

She remembered the interview in the newspaper in which he'd claimed to be one of those people. But he'd lied. "Were you merely waiting tonight? Or were you standing guard?"

"Both."

His honesty startled her. She remembered Miss

Everleigh's fears about her brother. "Are you here to . . . protect her?"

He sat back in his chair, pulling his face into shadows. "Wouldn't that be noble?"

She considered the question. Were her suspicions correct, he was playing some deep game that involved spying on Catherine Everleigh—to say nothing of the "assayers" who prowled the estate with knives and guns. That endeavor could not be upright. Yet he had given her just as much evidence to consider him decent, and to like him, against all odds.

Like did not quite capture it.

The table between them was littered with papers that might have helped her decide about his motives. But she did not care to look at them. Her mind, she realized, was already made up.

He lifted his glass to the light before he drank, admiring the effect as she had. "They're Irish eau-de-vie glasses," she told him. "Very rare. Well over a hundred years old." She had wrapped up an identical glass, yesterday. "You should probably fetch me something else to drink from. It would take a year of my salary to repay you if I dropped it."

He tossed back half the glass, then wiped his mouth. "Break it, if it makes you feel better. I don't give a damn."

From another man, that would have sounded like a boast of wealth. Instead, it seemed a comfort. *Your feelings are worth more than the cost.*

She set down her glass. "Whom were you guarding against tonight?"

"Back to interrogation, are we?" He offered her an unpleasant smile. "Very well, let's play. Why are you afraid of the dark?"

"I'm not! Of course I'm not." She felt embarrassed that he had guessed it.

"A pity," he said after a pause. "I prefer fears like that. Simple fears, that can be cured."

"Your fears aren't so simple, I take it."

He shrugged. "Do heroes have fears?"

"I imagine they have enemies. Is that why you're armed?"

His surprise showed only in the slight hesitation as he lowered his glass. "Am I?"

"Your left pocket. A pistol, by the weight of it."

Holding her eyes, he rose and stripped a knife from his boot, which he laid across the nearby desk. With a roll of his shoulders, he shucked off his jacket, tossing it beside the knife. Then he turned to his waistcoat, holding her eyes as he flipped open the buttons.

She had never seen a man undress. It was a different process, more aggressive, than a lady's careful unlacing. He yanked open the buttons. Shrugged out of the waistcoat and tossed it aside. His wife, one day, would watch him undress. She would admire how his shirt clung to the heavy bulk of his shoulders, the leanness of his waist.

"Do you like what you see?" he asked softly.

"Yes."

He'd not expected bravery. His head tilted a fraction. A line formed between his brows. "Are you all right?"

Her mood was indeed strange. So many hours spent reliving what had happened to Fiona—and what it meant to be alone, helpless, in the face of death. The sickroom clung like a pall to her. "You know," she said on a breath, "I've come to like this house." She glanced around, taking in the scrolled woodwork that trimmed the ceiling—the Turkish carpet—the handsome wooden screen in the corner. "Six generations born and died here. There's history in the walls."

"And skeletons, no doubt." Palmer settled into his chair again. "The ghost, still pounding to escape."

No. There were no ghosts, to her sorrow. "I doubt it. The Hughleys loved this house. They explored the world so they could bring back treasures to fill the halls. It strikes me as very . . . ."

"Morbid?" He was watching the fire, his mouth a grim line. "All their treasures bound now for auction. All their adventures, forgotten."

She frowned. "Comforting, in fact." Why . . . perhaps Miss Everleigh wasn't alone in her wish for a place to belong—somewhere she might always be welcomed, not for her skills and accomplishments, but simply for the person she was. "No matter how far they traveled, they always had this house to welcome them home."

"True. Did you ever wonder why they altered it so often?"

"Miss Everleigh says they were innovators. Visionaries."

He glanced at her, the firelight shadowing his face. "They kept knocking down the walls. Expanding them, making new routes for egress. Not much innovation in that. As visions go, it's the dream of claustrophobics."

The notion unsettled her. "What do you mean to say?"

"I mean, they traveled to escape this place." He reached for the bottle, splashed more liquor into his glass. Set down the bottle and stared at it. "Came back very reluctantly, already itching to leave again."

She did not like that idea. "It was their home. They were a famously loving family—"

"It's a house," he said. "That doesn't make it a home. And family—yes, family is important. But it can trap you more neatly than four walls and a locked door."

Her chest tightened. She knew that truth too well. She would not have imagined hearing it from *him*. "I like my version better." She needed that inspiration. "Imagining them free and bold, wandering the world with this place waiting like a beacon."

"Maybe you're right," he said at last. "It's a romantic idea, Lilah."

Lilah. Sometimes she was still Miss Marshall to him. She did not understand the logic that governed his use of her name. She only knew that when he addressed her familiarly, her stomach dipped, and for a brief moment, she grew soft and foolish.

Foolish, indeed. The last time they had conversed at length, he had instructed her to fear him. Then he had offered to kill her uncle.

That she believed he could do it was . . . deeply attractive. Nick had no power over him—not even the power to intimidate. How could she not be drawn to such immunity, such perfect freedom?

She cleared her throat. "I'm no romantic." Far from it. She was a cold-blooded woman indeed, if she could desire a man for his ability to kill.

"There's nothing wrong with romanticism, of course."

"No, of course not. It's quite ladylike." She directed a black smile into her glass. "Of course, Miss Everleigh reminded me recently that I do not enjoy a lady's privileges. She suggested I find a butcher to marry." She glanced up, shrugging. "Perhaps I will."

He blinked. "Any butcher in particular?"

"A decent one. The problem, of course, is that decent men want decent wives—even the butchers."

His smile looked peculiar. As though he were hearing an unpleasant joke. "And you think you aren't decent."

"We both know it. I'm a common thief."

He looked away. "No call for the butcher to find out."

"Yes, I'll have to hide my history from him. More than enough for him to accept that I once was an Everleigh Girl."

In profile, his jaw looked hard as flint. "If he were fool enough to condemn you for that, he would not deserve your honesty anyway."

"And my virginity?"

Slowly he faced her. "What of it?"

"Surely I would owe him that, at least. In exchange for his protection."

"Is that what you want?" he asked very quietly. "Protection?"

"Oh, who knows?" This man had shown her that she knew herself far less well than she'd imagined. "I thought what I wanted was simple—to be a lady." Her laughter felt false. "It was my sister's plan, actually. We would remake ourselves. Our accents, our deportment. For gentlemen never tell a lady—a proper lady, like Miss Everleigh—to *take it on the chin*. It's their duty to shelter her from harshness. And that seems quite pleasant, never to be expected to endure. To be free to pursue better things, like . . . beauty and honesty and honor. So we—I—set out to become that kind of woman. A woman whom men seek to protect."

What a strange look he wore. "Then you've succeeded."

"No, not yet. But I'll know it when I do. He will treat me as if . . ." As if her sensibilities were spun of priceless glass.

"As if you're cherished," he murmured.

"Yes." She had his attention now. But like some wicked drug, a small taste wasn't enough for her. "It won't be the butcher who gives me that, though. He'll be too suspicious of me at first. His friends will have warned him about Everleigh Girls, the rumors that we're whores in disguise. He'll need to overcome his doubts before he loves me. Of course, once he discovers I'm a virgin, he'll feel quite smug. He'll try to cherish me then. But it will require false pretenses. He'll never learn about my past. He'll never even ask, for fear of what he might find out. And if somehow he does learn my secrets . . . why, he'll recoil."

He had not looked away. "You've given this some thought."

She nodded. "Generally on the nights after you've touched me. I lie awake, thinking about it. There are ways to fake virginity. Some count it a great deceit. But I think, piled on top of all the other lies I mean to tell, it won't make much difference. Whereas if I had cause to hate this butcher—to resent that I had saved myself for him, this happy fool who would condemn me if he knew the truth about me—well, that would be far worse. One shouldn't hate one's husband. Don't you think?"

He laid down his glass. "Lilah . . ."

A strange exhilaration coursed through her, fear and excitement at once. He understood what she was about now. His focus was so hot and intense that it brought a rush of blood to her face. "Ask me something," she said.

For she would tolerate no false pretenses tonight. "Ask me something I never told you."

He slowly rose. She moved aside, making room for him on the settee. He sat down, but he did not touch her. "What is your sister's name?"

"Was. Fiona is dead."

The compassion in his face caused her chest to tighten. She had so much more practice in hiding truths than revealing them. "How?"

She cleared her throat. "Appendicitis. The doctor came too late. She'd been hiding the pain for days."

"It's difficult, isn't it?" His mouth twisted. "Difficult, *hell.* I try not to think on Geoff. Otherwise it becomes . . . unbearable, at times."

Unbearable. She recognized that single word, the naked honesty within it, as the greatest intimacy he'd ever shared with her. And like a gin addict given a sip of the poison, it awakened a terrible desire in her. With all her heart, she wanted to crack his mystery. To make *him* spill his secrets, speak of everything he'd kept hidden.

Yet at the same time, with a fierce panicked desperation, she also recognized how impossible, how unlikely, what a miracle that would be. All she could do was bare herself, and hope he did the same in reply.

"I have an uncle," she said. "But he is not really family."

He caught her hand and lifted it to his mouth, kissed her fingers with a strange formality. "Why is that?"

"He took care of us—Fiona and me—when both our parents were gone. But he was . . ." She hesitated. "Too young, I think, to know how to care for us properly. He felt . . ." Ah, what a strange word to use to describe Nick, but she knew it was true: "Honor-bound," she said. "He felt honor-bound to try. My mother—his older sister—had been very dear to him. But perhaps we would have done better in the poorhouse." She winced. "No, of course I don't mean that. But he . . ."

He was watching her. Listening. The gentleness in his face would break her heart.

"He took over my father's trade," she said. "And it changed him."

He placed her hand in her lap, then touched her face very lightly, tucking a curl behind her ear. "He became a clerk?"

"No, of course not." Her smile felt real now. "My father was no clerk, and you know it."

He traced the slope of her neck, his touch whisper soft. "Then what?"

"Nothing too awful. My father wasn't violent by nature." How breathless she sounded. She felt giddy, drunk on her own confessions. "But he did anything you might imagine that could make money and get a man jailed, if caught at it. My uncle, on the other hand . . . he's a crack shot."

He gazed at her for a long, steady moment. She felt color rise to her face. It wasn't shame that made her blush. Her entire life, she had been a criminal's daughter, a criminal's niece. But she'd always wished to be more. To be *seen* as more—and never as much as by this man, God save her.

He leaned forward and kissed her mouth. His lips felt gentle, questing, as though they searched for an answer to some question that could not be put into words. When he drew back, he said, "You've come very far. It's a testament to you. Your wit and your courage."

What a miraculous interpretation. She bit her lip to

stop a smile. Then she reached for his necktie, fumbling with the knot.

She sensed his gaze on her face, but she could not meet it. She concentrated instead on the knot, acutely aware of how her fingers trembled.

The knot yielded. Silk whispered across cotton as she pulled the tie free. She opened his collar, baring his throat, then leaned forward and kissed the corded muscle.

He hissed out a breath. She looked up into his eyes. "A hero called me courageous," she said. "It seems he was right."

"Ah. A hero." He reached for her hand, laid it on his thigh. Slowly he set to unbuttoning her sleeve. "Is that what you see in me?"

"No. When I think of a hero, I think of some distant figure from the newspapers—some upright stranger who gives boring speeches."

He smiled faintly, his attention on his work. "Then you have it right. He's a stranger to me, too, this idiot from the poem." He rubbed his thumb across the tender skin of her inner wrist, then lifted it to his face, inhaling deeply. "That charge at Bekhole," he murmured against her wrist. "It was a desperate gamble. Not a choice, not an act of courage, nothing borne of ideals. My aim was to live. I hoped we would kill more of them than they killed of us. And so we did. Turn around," he added softly.

Butterflies fluttered in her stomach. She resettled herself. "That isn't fair to you."

His mouth touched her bare nape. Her eyes drifted shut. His fingers skimmed down her back; her gown began to loosen. "What difference does it make?" he asked. "I have an entire country to applaud me, if I need it." His hands worked now at the laces of her corset. "Peculiar, though." His voice was growing husky. "The admirers all ask the same questions. *Was it very horrible? Do you think on it often?*" Cold air whispered against the top of her spine. His lips found the spot, a teasing kiss far too brief for her liking. "I know what they want to hear. I tell them: *No. Not so very bad. I don't think on it much at all.* And they call it a brave face, and applaud me again. But there's no bravery involved there, either. I'm only speaking the truth."

"But that's a blessing," she said. "To be able to forget." One that she envied. The darkness would not frighten her, if only she could forget what it meant to be trapped in it, alone.

The corset loosened quite suddenly. His knuckles brushed the length of her exposed spine, pausing to massage her lower back. "But I don't forget," he said. "I remember Bekhole very well. The blood and the fear. The way I had to steady my voice during my instructions to the men. My envy . . ." His hand stilled. "My envy for a stray tree, its leaves shaking in the wind. The only tree on that field. That it could stand amid so much slaughter without fear . . . I longed to *be* that tree. Or to protect it, for nobody else would."

Clutching the gown to her chest, she twisted back. She caught the quirk of his lips before he shook his head. "The scrubbiest little tree," he said. "But I felt the oddest anxiety that it should not be destroyed."

"And was it?"

"Of course." He caught her hand, gently tugging it loose. The neckline sagged. He made a low sound in his throat, unmistakable approval. "Leveled by cannon shot."

She shivered.

"You're cold? Come here." He drew her into his side, his arm around her shoulders. Her cheek pressed against his chest. For a moment, as he idly stroked her arm, they sat in a companionable silence, the fall of her gown arrested only by the pressure of their bodies pressed together. "No," he said at length, "the tree didn't make it. But when I do dream of the war . . . I dream only of that tree. Of my failure to save it. It had grown there for decades, untouched. Perhaps it bore fruit. Its world, its concerns, had no bearing on ours. It was innocent. But we destroyed it, regardless."

"You . . . grieve for the tree?"

"Yes, well." He angled a crooked smile down at her. "I never said it made sense."

She reached up to touch his face. That wicked scar that came so close to his beautiful eye. "How did you get this?"

She felt his jaw tighten. "A man gave it to me."

"I didn't imagine it was self-inflicted."

"Lilah." He pulled away. "I tell you what I can. Where I'm silent, it's for your sake. *You* are the one I'm protecting here."

His words shot a powerful current through her, more elemental than even desire. *Protect me, yes.* "So you know my worst secret, but I'm to be spared yours?"

"Your worst secret." She could not read his expression. "Was that all?"

Stung, she pulled up her neckline. He diminished the effort it had taken her to tell him. "Do you require all the bloody details? How low must I paint myself?"

"You think you've painted yourself low? Because you've stolen, now and then. Because you were born to a family you would not have chosen."

She opened her mouth, then shut it. His question felt like a trap. "Do you mean to say you don't think me so very bad?"

He made a noise of amusement, low and husky. It startled her. And then, in conjunction with his slight, growing smile, it seemed to brush across her skin like fingertips, stirring a thrill that made her stomach dip.

"Well," she said, barely audible, "I am a thief, you know."

"Very bad," he murmured. "Irredeemably wicked." He leaned forward, brushing a strand of hair from her cheek. "*J'accuse.* You say I am hard on myself. But you're no different in that, Lilah."

Her brain was broken. It interpreted his expression as tender and affectionate. The way he looked at her made her chest heavy and full, so she could not breathe.

"If you think me better than a thief," she whispered, "then you really have no cause to blackmail me, you know."

"So I don't. Look where you laid my tie. Those are for you."

She had ignored the documents. But now, as she stood and nudged aside the neckcloth, she recognized the shape of the papers. She flipped them over, then looked back at him, amazed. "But I haven't . . ."

He rose. "You'll take them back to London," he said quietly. "Tomorrow. Your obligations here are done."

Back to London. What a curious sensation, to have such a great weight removed so suddenly, without warning. Her troubles with Nick were over. She would be free of this nightmare. And . . . free of Palmer, too. Her blackmailer. The only man who would ever know her truly—who would recognize her as the girl who had climbed out of Whitechapel into the marbled halls of Everleigh's.

A testament, he had called that.

She did not want to leave him just yet. "You go too easy on me," she said softly. "Won't you demand anything else before I go?"

His fingertips settled against her cheek, five points of infinitely light contact, which seemed to electrify her whole body. "Yes. I think I will."

"Then take it."

His eyes narrowed. That was all the warning he gave her before he pounced. His hands at her waist, strong and commanding, lifted her; he carried her across the room.

By the window sat a low daybed, fashioned in a much earlier age, when women's panniers had spread six feet across. He laid her down there. Stripped off her dress with quick, sure movements. She made no sound. Simply watched him. She had made her choice.

He reached across her, toward the knife he'd laid down earlier when he'd disarmed himself. It felt right to turn for him, to let him cut her free of her underlinens. If he asked, she would bare her throat for him tonight. He knew her. He could do as he pleased.

The blade clattered as it landed in some distant corner. He looked her over, his nostrils flaring. She recognized his expression. Desire and fury were not so different. Both burned. She reached for him, but he shook his head, a small, precise tic.

"I'll look, first." His words were rough. He caught her arms and laid them above her. Then, with the back of his hand, he traced down her body. The base of her throat. The swell of her naked breasts. He took an audible breath as he passed over her nipples, which peaked for him. She shifted, restless beneath his devouring gaze, and saw how it affected him; the tensing of his jaw, the ruthlessness that came into his face.

"For weeks now," he said, his voice almost soundless, "I have made love to you in my mind. But I did not . . ." He placed his thumb in her navel, his mouth a hard line. "I did not do your body justice." His hand skated down to her hipbone; he gripped her there as he leaned down to take her nipple in his mouth.

No gentleness. She wanted none. His lips closed around her, a hard, sucking pressure. Her body replied, clamoring in pulsing throbs as he laved her. His other hand charted the fullness of her hip, massaged the back of her thigh.

Her hands found their own mind. They landed on his hard waist, clutching at the fabric that kept his skin from hers. "Take this off." That was her voice. "Do it." She would have her fill of him. No posturing, no disguises.

He retreated, straddling her with his knees as he ripped off the offending layers. She understood then why he'd castigated his own fantasies. She'd dreamed of his body—she had imagined she knew its shape. But laid bare, his chest was broader, more powerfully developed than she'd guessed. She reached up to touch it, smoothing her palms over the sparse blond hair, then lower, to the animal flex of muscle in his abdomen. She hooked her fingers in the waistband of his trousers. The front was now tented so prominently that she hesitated, a moment's fear fracturing her desire.

His hand caught hers. "Go ahead," he said very softly. "Take what you want."

Yes. *She* wanted this. The buttons looked complicated. But there was no lock, no fastening she could not coax open. She fumbled once, then figured out the way of it. The first button yielded. Then the second. The heel of her hand brushed the head of his cock, and he hissed out some unintelligible sound, a spell perhaps, for it triggered a wash of heat through her. She quickened her work. Now the third button. The fourth, ah, God, he was large; the trousers yielded and she pressed her palms to his lean flanks, smoothing over the hot muscled density of his hips as she shoved off the trousers.

His thighs were brawny, strapped with muscle. And what lay between them . . .

She laid her hand against his cock. The thick, solid length of him.

He groaned. Caught her hand and pulled it free. He laid his large body down onto her, a heavy hard weight that trapped her with his cock pressed between them, an inch shy of where she needed it. She squirmed, trying to twist herself into position, but he breathed, "No." Then his hand slid through her hair. Hooking it in a strong grip, he pulled her head back, so he looked into her eyes.

"Tell me your name," he said.

She stared up at him, panting. "Please."

He adjusted his hips, so the head of his cock pressed solidly against the opening of her quim. "Your name."

Yes. *Yes,* that was where she'd wanted him. "Lilah," she gasped.

His hand tightened in her hair. It should have pained her. But in this terrible state, strung on the edge of need, it registered only as another kind of pleasure, fierce and sweet. "Your real name," he ground out.

Lily. The syllables formed in her mouth. What did it

matter now if she spoke them? He saw her. He knew her in every way that counted.

But one shred of sanity remained to her. It was the rule of Whitechapel, the rule of survival: never surrender everything.

She jerked her hips. He hissed out a gasp. She'd found her mark. The tip of him pressed into her, a blunt, burning pressure.

His grip loosened; his hips moved. He pushed, slowly opening a place she'd not known existed. Not like this. For a frightened beat, it was too much. He was too large. Or she too small. She tried to draw back—squirm away.

But he was done with hesitations. His hands closed around her hips. Pinned her in place, his eyes as fierce as suns. He thrust, a hard sharp move that brought his hipbones into hers. Filling her. Full beyond measure. She could not breathe. She . . .

He retreated. Penetrated her again. Leaned down and filled her mouth with his tongue, allowing no retreat, brooking no resistance. Her hands found his buttocks, closing around them, a merciless muscular flex, rhythmic now as he fucked her. *Fuck.* That word had never made sense . . . a man's word, unbearably dirty.

But he was fucking her now. And her body welcomed it. The discomfort was gone. She could take him forever. *Never stop.* The rhythm was leading somewhere. *Keep me here.* His strong, hard body was pounding into her, his hips slapping into hers, his gaze locked so fiercely on her face, *make me yours,* she was so hot, soft, melting beneath him. She would take him forever and ever, until . . .

He was whispering in her ear. She could not make sense of it. She was only sensations, a building crisis. He eased away to reach between them, to the spot where they joined, and through her fever she registered this sight, the hard muscled plane of his belly, the sight of his cock moving deeply within her, his muscular thighs flexing as he thrust, as his thumb slipped over her quim and touched that spot—

She cried out. *There. That.* She caught his hips, dragged him against her as she convulsed around him. His teeth closed on her shoulder. He went very still, locked inside her, rigid as stone as the pleasure ebbed away.

And then he moved once more, one deep thrust that caused her to contract again, on a startled gasp, no, there could not be more, but there was—

He pulled out of her. Spilled his seed across her thigh as he kissed her mouth, her cheeks, her throat and shoulders. Yes, it was what she deserved. She closed her eyes and felt a smile drift across her mouth. He kissed that, too, as he came back over her. His fingertips, so light, skated across her mouth.

"Yes?" he said roughly.

Oh, yes.

That poor butcher.

CHAPTER THIRTEEN

One of the maids dragged Lilah out of bed just before noon. "Begging your apologies," Holly said, "but Miss Everleigh wishes to speak with you."

Groggy, Lilah stumbled to her feet. Her corset lay discarded on the floor, the laces loosened to their ends. If Holly wondered at the cause, she did not ask as she set to tightening them again.

But the sight brought Lilah to full alertness. She blushed as the maid helped her dress. Her body felt . . . different. More sensitive. The corset seemed to crush her breasts. And when she stepped into her gown, she felt a soreness between her legs, a twinge that triggered a deeper quickening.

She'd not slept much. Before she had left Palmer, she'd made him try to coax her name from her again. And then again . . .

Holly was speaking. ". . . much recovered. The doctor is with her now. She'll be on her feet by tomorrow."

But Lilah would not be here to see it. She'd been sacked. Among other things. Smiling to herself, she followed Holly out into the sitting room.

"Oh." Holly picked up an envelope from the tea table. "His lordship sent this before he left."

"Left?" Lilah opened the envelope. Enclosed was a train ticket, and a brief note.

"To Sussex," Holly said. "A telegram came this morning. Some trouble with his family."

You'll be in London by nightfall. But you will not deliver those notes by hand. The penny post works. —P.

She smiled at the edict—then faltered beneath a premonition of oncoming foolishness. She was not going to weep on the train, was she? She'd gotten exactly what she wanted. Regrets would be idiotic. What did she imagine—that he would offer marriage? Of course not.

But to be given only a single night with him . . .

From the doorway, Holly cleared her throat. "Miss Everleigh was *most* anxious to see you, miss."

Yes, most eager to remind her she'd been sacked, no doubt. Lifting her skirts, Lilah hurried after the maid.

In Miss Everleigh's bedroom, the doctor was packing up his bag as his patient lounged among a dozen pillows. She looked pale and fatigued, but her hair was neatly plaited. The open windows had aired the room of any lingering reek. "Miss Marshall," she said, her voice slightly hoarse. "The maids said you were shut up in your rooms. Why is that?"

No thanks for having nursed her, but Lilah expected none. "I could not leave before I saw you well." She hesitated, realizing that if she wished to keep her position as a hostess, she had no choice but to grovel. "I do hope you will forgive me for the other day. My behavior was—"

"No." Catherine struggled to sit upright. "I mean, why aren't you at work?" She knocked her plait behind her shoulder. "This ridiculous man tells me I must remain bedridden until tomorrow, but that's no reason for *you* to dawdle."

Dr. Hardwick inched toward the door. Lilah stepped aside to let him pass, taking the opportunity to ponder her best reply. Had the sickness given Miss Everleigh amnesia? "I . . . before, you said—"

"Enough of what I said!" Miss Everleigh shot an odd, panicked glance toward the doctor. "Sir. Will you shut the door behind you?"

Dr. Hardwick bowed, then pulled the door shut with a thump that smacked of relief.

"Now." Miss Everleigh cleared her throat. "I believe you were making an apology. And I certainly deserve one."

Lilah folded her hands at her waist and did her best to look meek. "I am cursed with a rash temper, miss. There is no cause or excuse for it."

"Is that your claim?" Miss Everleigh blew out a breath. "Well. I suppose . . . there are two shrews in this household, then."

Had she just made a . . . joke? At her own expense? "Termagant," Lilah said tentatively, "is the term I prefer."

The barest smile touched Miss Everleigh's mouth. "Why not harpy? Or vixen? There's a very long list to choose from, when one speaks of sharp-tongued women. All of them invented by men, I expect." She paused. "I thank you," she said stiffly. "For last night."

How long ago that seemed! So much had followed. "It was my duty, miss."

"Yes, of course." But Miss Everleigh sounded oddly uncertain. "At any rate . . . I propose a bargain. In my illness, I may have made an . . . odd remark."

So she remembered her fears of her brother. That did not bode well. Feverish delusions would not have lingered with her. "No, miss. I recall no such thing."

"I see." With one finger, Miss Everleigh outlined the embroidery in her quilt. "Well, I can admire discretion. In exchange for it, I will reserve my own speculations. And I will allow you to learn what you can from me." She looked up, frowning slightly. "If that is still your wish."

Amazed again, Lilah curtseyed. How easily she'd slipped out of her troubles! "Does this mean I'm to stay?"

"Have you not heard a word I've said? I can't manage this estate on my own. Of course I *could* have done, had it not been for that trip to town—and this pathetic bout of illness. Chocolates! Who would have imagined? I cannot blame Miss Stratton, but I will certainly have a word with the confectioners at Armand's—"

What would Palmer say to this news? More to the point, how long would he be gone? For Lilah had until the last week of June to do as she liked. Until then, her uncle would not look for the notes. And she could think of many uses for her time here. Last night could mark the start of her education, rather than the entirety—as long as Palmer proved willing.

She remembered his hoarse words, in the hour before dawn. *You have talents,* he'd said, *you do not even understand.*

No, she did not foresee any objections to continuing her tutelage.

"Don't look so cheerful," Miss Everleigh snapped. "I stand by my previous opinion. Your ambitions outstrip your abilities—and your potential as well. I encourage you to aim lower. Far lower, in fact."

Lilah swallowed a snort. "You do indeed seem much recovered."

Miss Everleigh flipped her hand toward the door. "Go on, then," she said. "To your work. And come back before dinner, to make a report of what you've done."

Where had Palmer gone? Days passed without sign of him. Miss Everleigh, entirely recovered now, paid no notice to his absence. With no call to break for a formal dinner, she kept Lilah working till ten thirty in the evenings. At last, Lilah's fatigue outweighed her fear of the dark; once in bed, she fell asleep immediately.

Thankfully, Miss Everleigh's illness seemed to have burned away the sharpest edges of her tongue. She showed flashes of patience, and a grudging gift for instruction. With painstaking care she taught Lilah the small differences between mundane objects and priceless ones. For instance, a lovely, patterned vase might be worth nothing—or, thanks to a single small mark, hidden amid its flowery print, it might be the rarest and most valuable of enamelware.

"Always keep your eyes open," Miss Everleigh told her. "It never fails that your last look turns up the greatest finds."

Lilah took the advice to heart. She kept her eyes open at all hours, looking out the window for Palmer's return. But her watch only ever rewarded her with a different and more disturbing sight. The strapping assayers prowled through the trees at all hours, singly and in pairs. Sometimes they conferred on horseback. Their jackets fit very loosely over their military-straight backs.

She made herself look away whenever she saw them. The force of her curiosity unsettled her—as did her dreams. Palmer had awakened a hunger in her that she'd never suspected. Her dreams each night left her sweaty and breathless. But that premonition of future grief lingered, giving her a constant warning. If she awaited his return, it was only for the satisfaction of his body. Now that she had the letters, his problems did not concern her.

Five days passed like this. Miss Everleigh commented only once on her distraction. "If you drop any of the crystal, you will pay for what you break."

After asking how much the dish in question was worth, Lilah took pains to ring for coffee at the top of every hour.

On the sixth day, Miss Everleigh declared their work with the breakables was done. They moved now to the more exhausting task of appraising the furniture. This was physical work, which normally—so Miss Everleigh said sourly—was performed with the aid of footmen. But Mrs. Barnes had yet to find men worthy of that position at Buckley Hall.

The stable hands were fetched inside to assist, but their smell quickly outstripped their utility. Miss Everleigh dismissed them. "We can manage it ourselves," she told Lilah. "You seem made of strong fiber, and I am no fragile flower."

Wasn't she, then? Lilah found herself increasingly surprised by her employer—and more skeptical of Miss Everleigh's claim that men would not admire her for her skills. For the icy heiress never seemed more charming than when, with gritted teeth, she insisted she *could* turn over a table on her own, thank you very much—and then laughed in delight at having managed it.

By the evening, having upended countless chairs and settees to look for flaws and carpenters' marks, both women were sweaty and covered with grime. But they had made better time than anticipated, having nearly completed their catalog of the furniture in the west wing. Only one chest remained, which they had not managed to unlock. Miss Everleigh could find no match for it on the rusted ring of keys the housekeeper had provided.

The dust was making Lilah sneeze. "Let me have a try." And then she could go bathe this grime away.

"I tell you, I tried every key twice."

"Sometimes it takes a bit of coaxing, is all. But I'm sure you're right." On the sly, Lilah slipped a hairpin from her coiffure. "Why don't you ring down, see if Mrs. Barnes has any other strays lying about?"

On a huff, Miss Everleigh thrust the key ring at her and stomped over to the bellpull. "One would think a *proper* housekeeper might take an interest—"

"Done!" Lilah flipped open the latch and lifted the lid of the trunk.

"How on earth?" Miss Everleigh hurried back over, then clapped a hand to her mouth. "No! Oh, no!" Nearly keening, she reached into the trunk to retrieve a dusty bottle, which she wiped on her skirt with no regard for the dirty streak it made. "This is awful!"

Lilah picked up a bottle. Naturally, it was in French. "Château." She knew that word, at least.

"Château Lafite Gilet." Miss Everleigh stamped a

foot. "Oh, but it hasn't been stored properly!" She let the bottle sag in her grip. "I feel ill."

"It's very rare, then?" All wine seemed much the same in Lilah's eyes—mutton dressed as lamb. Watching the drunken antics at Everleigh's, she'd supposed it the preference of those who liked their poison to come packaged more respectably than gin.

"This vintage, yes. It might have fetched a prince's ransom, if only it had been kept properly. And drunk in time!"

Lilah shifted the bottles aside, counting silently. "Twelve bottles."

"Such a waste."

"Are you certain it's gone bad?" They had visited the wine cellars earlier in the week. Remembering Miss Everleigh's discourse, Lilah felt the inside of the trunk. "It's been kept out of the sunlight. The wood is not warped, so it hasn't been damp."

"It will have turned by now, regardless. The yokel who put them here—" Miss Everleigh made an ill-tempered grunt. "Wine is meant to be aged, not buried!"

"But if it hadn't turned? You could still set the lot."

"There's no way to tell," Miss Everleigh said dismissively.

Lilah almost laughed. Amid all these high-flying rules about valuation, it seemed typical of Miss Everleigh to overlook the simplest technique. "Needn't one only taste it to judge the quality?" She reached into her pocket and pulled out her knife. "We could uncork a bottle."

Miss Everleigh's eyes narrowed in a familiar look of disapproval. "That would hardly be proper, Miss Marshall. These bottles belong to the estate."

It was too late in the day to perform her chastened routine. "So we're to throw out the whole lot on a guess? If it's still good, you could fetch a profit from it. How could Lord Palmer object?" Besides, in order to object, he would first have to return to Buckley Hall. How long could one remain in Sussex, anyway?

Miss Everleigh had lifted the bottle to inspect it more closely. "This year was rumored to be sublime."

"I don't think I've ever tasted a wine that was sublime."

Miss Everleigh glanced up. "You've no idea what you're missing."

Lilah repressed a snort. She had a very good idea that she was missing a great lot of things in life. Fewer, though, of late.

She checked herself before she looked again out the window, toward the ever-empty drive. "If you've had it before, you'll know how it's meant to taste. Isn't that right?"

Miss Everleigh gave a single, small nod. Then she pressed her lips together. "It's not done." But a smile escaped. She quickly trammeled it. "This is terrible," she said severely. "Not in the least professional."

"Forgive me," Lilah said, "but it seems very professional, to make sure the wine isn't swill before you toss it."

Miss Everleigh glanced toward the bellpull. "If we rang for glasses, they'd want to know why."

"In some parts, people drink straight from a bottle, did you know?"

Miss Everleigh wrinkled her nose. "A very peculiar practice."

"Or convenient." Lilah took the bottle and set her blade to the seal. "Well?"

Miss Everleigh huffed out a breath. "I can't . . ."

Not one to incline to tippling, Lilah nevertheless felt egged on by a devil. "For the sake of professionalism, miss."

Miss Everleigh picked up her skirts and hurried to close the door. "Just one sip," she said as she turned back. "To confirm it has turned."

Lilah sliced the seal, then speared the cork and yanked it out. "That smells delicious," she said, surprised.

"I cannot believe I'm doing this," came Miss Everleigh's faint reply.

Lilah held out the bottle. "You're conducting a very thorough appraisal of the estate, miss. Sacrifices must be made."

Taking the bottle, Miss Everleigh hesitated once more. "I am setting a very poor example for you." But she required no further encouragement before tipping back the bottle. Swishing the wine about her mouth, she grimaced. "It's not what it once was," she said after swallowing. Then she sighed, looking glumly over the trunk's contents. "We could not, in good conscience, auction this lot."

"Sad," Lilah said. "That something could go from wondrous to wretched, for want of proper storage."

"Oh, it's not *wretched*." Miss Everleigh bit her lip. Then she thrust out the bottle. "Here. Try it." At Lilah's transparent surprise, she shrugged. "It's the ghost of greatness. But if you've never tasted greatness, why, then you may well admire it."

Lilah took the bottle. The smell truly was divine— sharp and robust, with the faint hint of blackberries. She tilted back the bottle for a taste.

Cherries and cream, thinning out into anise. The bitter finish made her wrinkle her nose. "Coffee."

"Very good, Miss Marshall!" Miss Everleigh brought her hands together. "You have a nose. Who would have thought?"

Lilah gathered that the compliment was not to her actual anatomy. She handed the bottle back. Miss Everleigh took another swallow without even wiping the rim. "Tannins," she pronounced, blinking rapidly. "They would not be so pronounced, were this still 1867." She laughed at her own joke, then gave the bottle back to Lilah.

"Another?" Lilah asked, just to be certain.

"I can't drink all of it myself."

This was how, an hour later, with the room cast into twilight darkness, they still sat amid the dusty work of their day, the bottle between them, while Miss Everleigh recounted Young Pete's boyish misadventures with a bottle of stolen port.

"He couldn't even make it to the water closet?" Lilah felt appalled and amused at once. The poor maids!

"Not in time. But he certainly stayed there the rest of the night!" Miss Everleigh loosed a snorting laugh. "My father took to calling him Peter Porter after that. Oh, he *loathed* the name." Her laughter faded. "He still does." She gave a pull of her mouth. "No quicker way to needle him than to call him Porter."

Sensing the downward dive of her mood, Lilah held out the bottle. "Last sip."

"I couldn't." Miss Everleigh brushed down her rumpled skirts. "I'm already lightheaded. And look at me. Dinner will be laid in an hour."

The thought of going back to her own rooms, with only the silence and her thoughts for company, made Lilah push harder. "Here, do take it. We must dispose of the evidence."

Miss Everleigh lifted her brows. "That sounds like the advice of a criminal."

That gave Lilah a bad start—until she saw the faint smile on her employer's mouth, quickly disguised as Miss Everleigh lifted the bottle and polished it off. "Do you know," she said as she returned the bottle to the floor with a thump, "I rather like forgoing a glass. It makes one feel very . . . carefree. Where did you say that people favored that practice?"

"The East End, miss."

"Oh." In the shadowed dimness, Miss Everleigh looked at her closely. "Is that where you're from? You don't sound it."

Mindful of what she had claimed in her interview for the position of hostess, Lilah hedged. "I did rent lodgings there, when I was studying for my typing certificate."

"You can type!" Miss Everleigh retrieved the bottle, picking at the label. "I didn't know that. I've always wanted to learn. My hand cramps so awfully when I write." She shook it out, by way of illustration.

Lilah hid a smile. Miss Everleigh's love of wine clearly outstripped her tolerance for it. "I would be glad to teach you, miss."

"Would you? I'd like that." Miss Everleigh set down the bottle again, gazing at the trunk. "It really isn't fit to be sold," she said. "But perhaps Lord Palmer would like to drink some." She grimaced and waved. "No, no. He's very discerning with his wines. He . . ." Her eyes narrowed. "I expect he'll throw them all into the rubbish."

"I can't imagine how marvelous it must taste," Lilah said, "when it's in its proper state. It's quite delicious already."

"Yes. So it is." Miss Everleigh nodded. "Go on, then."

"Go on, what?"

"Open another." She waved toward the trunk, saying with magnificent, slightly slurred arrogance, "I am in the mood to celebrate."

"Celebrate?"

"Why, yes. Don't you realize?" On a broad smile, she clambered to her feet and threw out her arms. "The treasures we've discovered! Jihong porcelain. Mappe-mondes! Our auction shall outstrip any of Peter Porter's by far."

Lilah burst into giggles.

"I am serious," Miss Everleigh insisted. "My brother is . . . *insufferable*. Convinced that women have not a brain in their skulls. He would *never* have given me Buckley Hall had he imagined . . . oh." She blinked. "Peter Porter? Is that it?"

Lips pressed together, Lilah nodded.

"Peter *Puker* is more apt. You should have smelled his bedroom! The maids scrubbed and scrubbed the carpet, but the reek lingered for days . . ." She fell into giggles as she flipped her hand toward the trunk. "Hurry up," she said. "Open another!"

In the middle of the night, Lilah woke from a dream about water—a great pool of it, clear and quenching as it rose past her waist. Her eyes opened into darkness. Her head pounded. Her mouth was dust dry.

She stumbled to her feet. Oh, good Lord. She hadn't drunk so deeply since the first time Fiona had stolen a bottle of brandy from Nick. She grimaced and fumbled her way toward the pitcher of water on her dresser.

The pieces of the evening reassembled. She had taken her dinner in Miss Everleigh's rooms. No wonder gentlemen enjoyed their cups! It had been very pleasant to trade laughter and gossip. Miss Everleigh had wanted to know Lilah's most awful tales about the rogues who patronized the auction house. How did the hostesses bear their flirtations?

At some point, Miss Everleigh had decided to educate her in proper wine tasting. She had rung for three more bottles—including a sweet, white Hungarian that Lilah had liked far too well. Having withdrawn to seats by the fire to nurse their last glasses (but they hadn't *nursed* them, precisely), Lilah had asked Miss Everleigh about the old days at the auction house, when her father had governed. Miss Everleigh had been full of touching anecdotes. Why, she had teared up, once or twice. She had seemed particularly moved by the revelation that the hostesses—

Oh dear. With her hands around the pitcher, Lilah froze. She had admitted the girls' nickname for Peter Everleigh. Why, his sister had been delighted by this disrespectful moniker. " 'Young Pete,' indeed. He will never take my father's place," she had told Lilah in a fierce slur.

Forget it. She won't remember in the morning, either. Lilah lifted the water jug to her mouth.

It was empty.

She lowered it with a groan. If she didn't find some water, she'd die.

She grabbed her knife, retied her robe, and made her way downstairs. In the cold, silent kitchen, she split the wax seal on a bottle of well water and drank it straight down. Opening another for the journey, she started back up the stairs—but a noise from above made her hesitate. What had she been thinking, coming down in only her robe? Were those voices?

She crept up to the landing.

"—cannot endure this," Miss Everleigh said vehemently.

Why on earth was she still awake?

"I understand your disappointment. I share it myself." That was Palmer's voice! Palmer was back! Lilah shifted to peek up around the corner. The door to the drawing room stood ajar, casting a wedge of light across the floorboards.

Had Miss Everleigh known he was planning to return tonight? Had she stayed up to wait for him?

Lilah tightened her grip around the bottle, disliking that thought immensely.

"Yes, I know," Miss Everleigh said in reply to some murmured remark. "I must say, you have been very kind." She paused then for what seemed like forever. "Yes," she said at last, her voice much softer. "That's quite true. Thank you, my lord."

Now came another quiet remark. After nearly a week, the timber of his voice worked some kind of spell on Lilah. She found herself breathless, desperate to make out his conversation.

But it was Miss Everleigh's reply that came clearly. "Quite right. Thank you, *Christian*." Her slow laugh announced the lingering effect of the liquor. "And I suppose you must call me Catherine, then. It's only fitting."

Water sloshed into Lilah's chest. It trickled like ice down her skin, but she barely felt it. Her jealousy burned too hot.

The wedge of light widened. Above, soft footsteps—Miss Everleigh's, Lilah guessed—mounted the stairs.

Had she imagined that she might like the woman after all? No. Always trust the first instinct. *Witch*.

Now came a heavier tread. She spared the rest of her loathing for him, this rotted, deceitful man who would seduce an employee while courting the mistress—

But he hadn't seduced her. *Oh, God*. She closed her eyes, wishing desperately that she could forget her own role in it. Her stupid babble about the butcher. Her breathy question, so transparently desperate: *Won't you demand anything else?*

Her loathing swelled. It felt fiercest for herself. What a pathetic fool she was!

The footsteps faded. They had both gone upstairs. Perhaps they were together now in Palmer's rooms.

She grimaced violently. Even in a drunken stupor, Catherine Everleigh was a *real* lady. She would not join Palmer in bed until they married. Then she would murmur to him all night long. *Christian, Christian . . .* Bah—a ridiculous name for such a hypocrite. *Kit*. Even more absurd! That stupid poem. He said he was no hero, and he was right. Little did England's pious patriots know they had memorized an ode to a smooth, handsome *blackguard*.

Christian. He had never asked Lilah to call him by his name—not even when he'd demanded to know hers.

She was glad she had not told him. Fiercely proud of her restraint.

The footsteps were returning. God in heaven, she couldn't face him now, not when humiliation blazed as brightly as a flag on her face. She gathered herself, ready to dash all the way back to the kitchens and hide in the pantry—

But these footsteps were *mounting* the stairs. They were following the path the others had taken.

Foreboding prickled over her. She frowned up into the darkness. That could not be Palmer. Someone else—a third person—was stealing quietly up the stairs. It was not a woman. That scuffing sound was made by the tread of a hard-soled shoe.

The new footmen weren't due till next week. There were no indoor servants who were male.

Lilah slowly set down the bottle. She reached into her pocket and took hold of her knife.

This isn't your business. Hide in the pantry. He doesn't deserve your care.

Too true. What a dolt she was! Gathering her skirts, she stole up the stairs after the intruder.

CHAPTER FOURTEEN

*L*ilah paused in the shadows of the upper landing, listening intently. The intruder had moved off the stone stairway into the upper hall, his weight raising a creak from the floorboards. Now silence. Now several creaks, then silence again.

He was varying the pace of his steps, the better to avoid the telltale rhythm of footfall. That was a common trick among burglars. He knew what he was about.

Lilah crept to the top of the stairs. To the left lay her rooms and Miss Everleigh's. The man hesitated, then turned right, toward Lord Palmer's apartment and the passage to the west wing.

Lilah inched around the corner into the shelter of a tall suit of armor. She was lighter than the burglar, and by dint of old habit, had taken note of which sections of the floor were noisiest. These advantages allowed her to dart across the hall soundlessly. She ducked into the servant's passage and groped forward.

The lamps were out. If the design mirrored the passage adjoining her apartments, there would be a door soon enough to the right. It would open into Palmer's washroom, allowing staff to fetch up warm water for his baths.

A doorknob came into her grip. She opened it, surprising Palmer at the washbasin. He lunged immediately out of sight—then pivoted, a pistol in his hand. *Good.* She lifted her knife to point beyond him to the door to his bedroom.

He did not follow her gesture. His face showed plain astonishment. "What in God's name—"

"Someone's coming," she said softly.

He pivoted just as the door swung open. The stranger swore—genuine surprise, distress—and yanked the door closed. "Stay where you are," Palmer bit out, and shouldered through the door, disappearing from sight.

She leaned out of the servants' passage, listening hard. She heard a scuffle in the hallway. Perhaps a muffled groan. But no gunshot.

Silence settled. Heart pounding, she stepped fully into the washroom—then jumped as Palmer reappeared in the doorway, breathing hard. "Go to Miss Everleigh," he said. "Lock her doors and barricade them." He did not wait for agreement before turning on his heel.

A fine idea. She slipped back into the servants' passage and groped her way through the darkness. The next door to the left opened into the hall; she did not want that.

The door after it belonged to Miss Everleigh. But it was locked.

Cursing, she retraced her steps and cracked open the door to the hall. Dead silence. Squinting left and right, she edged out along the wall. The knife felt like a friend in her sweaty grip. If somebody grabbed her, she'd stick him.

Bloody hell. Miss Everleigh had locked the outer door as well. Holding her breath, Lilah dared a light knock.

No reply.

She knocked harder, then rattled the doorknob.

Nothing.

She remembered the sound of Miss Everleigh's slurred laugh. What a night to fall into a liquor-logged sleep!

She reached into her coiffure for a pin with which to pick the lock, and only then realized that in her own drunken stupor, she *had* managed one thing—she had taken down her hair and plaited it for bed.

Swallowing a curse, she started for her own room. But suddenly a commotion rose from below—a hoarse shout, a thud, and the sound of something shattering. *Why* did Palmer not use his pistol? She thought with wild black humor of what her uncle would say. A gun was only useful when one was willing to *fire* it.

The disturbance ceased. She caught the faint rhythm of Palmer's voice. Relieved, she flew down the stairs.

Palmer was standing in the entry hall. A body lay across the threshold, booted feet just visible. As she stepped off the staircase, Palmer crouched down by the body.

A figure emerged from the cloakroom. A man with a knife.

"Palmer!" she cried. The figure turned and sprinted toward her. She wheeled for the stairs and a hand closed around her throat. She stabbed her knife into it. Her blade rebounded off bone.

She pulled free but he caught her and dragged her against him; snatched her wrist and twisted it behind her back. Writhing, intending to bite, she saw a stranger's face, snarling, murderous. He squeezed her wrist, forcing the knife from her nerveless grip.

A great weight knocked into them. She dragged herself free, then scrambled to hands and knees. Palmer was on top of the man. Grappling with him. They rolled, a brawling vicious tangle; the man rose over Palmer, his knife glinting—

Palmer seized his wrist. They struggled now in silence for control of the blade, their breathing harsh, the silence otherwise profound, terrible—

Palmer broke the man's grip, the knife clattering to the floor. The man howled and grabbed at Palmer's throat—but Palmer moved faster, hooking his arm around the other man's neck, dragging him to his feet as he thrashed, seizing his head and jerking sharply—

The crack was sickening. Palmer opened his arms, and the man's body dropped lifeless to the floor.

She had never seen a man killed like that.

Palmer turned on her, his face a mask of rage. "You were meant to go to London!"

She crawled backward, finding her feet and lurching up. "Who—what—"

He shoved his hand through his hair. "Jesus God." He looked down at the body, then knelt, hunting roughly for a pulse.

"He's dead," she said. No doubt.

He looked up, his eyes blazing. "What were you *thinking*?"

"I—I wasn't." She'd seen the knife. Instinct had taken over.

Men appeared in the doorway. She jumped back—then recognized them. The assayers. Two men half carried, half dragged a third inside. The one who had collapsed in the doorway. He looked dazed, but she saw no blood.

Something flashed by her, causing her to flinch. It clattered onto the ground in a distant corner: the stranger's knife. Palmer had tossed it away. He had also taken note of her jumpiness. He was staring at her, a black, flat stare. "Take this one," he said.

For a moment, she thought he was speaking to her. Then the assayers leaned their wounded friend against the wall and came over to pick up the corpse, slinging it between them.

"All men to the house." Palmer spoke in sharp syllables, chips of ice. "Forget the property lines. Every side, defended."

"Yes, sir."

Defended against what? "Is there more than one of them?" Lilah looked wildly around. This house made an awful defense. Too many doorways. Too many windows. She spotted her knife, and bent to pick it up.

Quick as a striking snake, Palmer caught her arm. "You're hit."

"What?" A bolt of fear coursed through her. She looked down. One of her sleeves was ripped. Flimsy fabric. Blood on her forearm.

She scrubbed it off with the intact sleeve. "A nick." A strange laugh escaped her. "I'm all right."

"Lilah." His expression was unrecognizable. Chillingly cold. "Did you alert Miss Everleigh?"

"No, she didn't answer me—"

"Good." Without warning, he swept her into his arms and started up the stairs.

*   *   *

Sometimes the better part of wisdom lay in silence. Lilah held her tongue as Palmer shouldered through the door into his apartments. He walked straight into his bedchamber and dumped her on the bed. "Stay there." He turned on his heel, leaving her in silence.

The night's chill gradually registered. Why, that was right; she was wearing her robe. Barely dressed. She yanked the hem over her ankles and drew a shaking breath. The room was handsome, full of dark, heavy furniture. None of it for sale. She'd never been into his suite before.

She ran a hand over the coverlet. Soft, expensive fabric. Silk, dyed the shade of dried blood.

She recoiled. Pulled her hand back into her lap. Looked at her wrist, which had stopped bleeding.

Somebody had sneaked into the house. Palmer had broken his neck. Strong enough to lift a ram; strong enough to snap a spine. Why be surprised?

Her thoughts felt disjointed. Unnerving. She locked her hands tightly together, and counted the roses in the border of the carpet.

The door opened, giving her a bad start. "Make a noise!"

Palmer exhaled, a rough sharp sound. "Forgive me," he said curtly.

He laid a small bottle onto the nightstand, a water pitcher beside it. From his pocket he took a roll of gauze, unwinding it in short, violent jerks. "I booked you passage. I gave you the letters." The words drilled like bullets. "What else do you require to be gone?"

She'd fluttered and sighed, anticipating their reunion. But he looked at her now with fury. Nothing made sense. She groped for words, and found instead the first prickle of anger, sharpening on her tongue like needles. "I answer to Miss Everleigh now. Not you."

A humorless smile curved his mouth. "Of course." He pulled a handkerchief from his pocket and sat down on the edge of the bed. Wetted the cloth in the pitcher. "Give me your arm."

In his cold voice, that sounded like a threat. "No."

A muscle ticked in his jaw. "I am trying," he said, "not to *throttle* you."

"Why? What did I do?"

His hand closed into a fist. Veins springing up, knuckles whitening. "What in God's name were you *thinking*? Running downstairs?"

She scowled. "You should be grateful. He was coming for you."

"What of it?" he snapped. "Do I strike you as weak?"

She bit her lip. That was the very last word she would have chosen. The crack of her assailant's neck would haunt her. "You were distracted," she said very softly.

"Yes." His mouth twisted. "It's a problem, isn't it?" He did not wait for her to puzzle that out before seizing her wrist. His fingers felt very warm. He laid the cloth to her arm.

His hand was trembling.

"Palmer?" His blond head bowed, concealing her view of his face. "Are you—"

"I should have driven you to the station myself." He spoke very low. "Tied you onto that train. You were not meant to be here."

She understood nothing. Or . . . perhaps she did. "You expected him? You knew he was coming?"

He looked up, his mouth twisting. "Of course not."

Bewilderment swam through her. A thousand baffled questions, none of which seemed to fit neatly into words. Something horrible in his face, as he stared at her—something she had never wanted to see. *Fear.* For her?

She tried to pull back. He did not let her. Scowling, she focused on his grip. She preferred him colder. Furious. What made him so afraid? She wanted to take a knife to it—a large one. A machete.

"You are leaving on the first train." He reached over and took up the vial. Splashed its contents onto the handkerchief, which he laid back against her arm.

She sucked in a breath. "That stings."

"Yes." He watched his own work, the gentle pressure he exerted against the cut. "The bleeding has stopped."

"I can't go. Miss Everleigh won't let me."

"She goes with you. Her brother has called her back to town."

"But . . ." She shook her head. "The estate?"

"Peter will manage it."

"How convenient," she whispered.

"No." He looked sharply into her eyes. "It was my doing. I met him in town, on my way back from Sussex." His mouth flattened. "I did wonder why he hadn't mentioned your return."

A chill wracked her. Understanding, at last. This wasn't over. "You expect more trouble."

"I expect nothing else."

She hesitated. "Not a burglar, then?"

He shook his head.

"But he . . ." For an assassin, the man had been clumsy. "He didn't even attack you. Here, when he found you."

"He went to the wrong room. He was looking for someone else."

"Who?" Not her. Why would anyone come after her? "*Catherine?*"

"Anyone," he said. "Anyone close to me."

She felt cold again, a violent shivering wave. With her free hand, she tried to draw the robe tighter, but it was a flimsy affair, not meant to provide warmth.

His gaze sharpened. "What is it? Something else? Did your head—"

"No, I'm fine." She took a steadying breath. She was no sheltered lady, to be overcome by vapors. But . . . "I'm out of practice with . . . that."

He whispered something too low for her to make out. Then he leaned forward, pressing his mouth to her forehead, breathing deeply. It was not a kiss. It was more basic. Skin to skin. "May you always be out of practice," he said. "Always."

Her eyes closed. Now, she was warm. With his lips pressed against her, his strong hand bracing her shoulder, she would not shake.

She felt him sigh. He eased away and retrieved the gauze. Thrice he wrapped her wrist, then knotted it soundly. "Too tight?"

She shook her head. "It's nothing."

He laid her hand back in her lap, the movement oddly formal. "It is not nothing." He nudged her chin up, so their eyes met. "You will not mention my name in London. Do you understand?"

His knuckles felt rough. His cheek was bruising. These small observations seemed important: the lock of blond hair curling over his ear. The length of his lashes, the way they curled. She wanted to touch him; to stroke the grimness from his face. He was about to explain things. She could feel the truth gathering between them like darkness. In another moment, she would make herself ask for it. But not yet.

"Why did you leave for so long?" she asked.

A brief, fraught pause. She realized that question wasn't safe, either. "I was at Susseby." He sat back, letting go of a long breath. "It . . . The house is gone."

"Gone?" She shook her head once. "What do you mean?"

"Burned to the foundations. There's nothing . . ." His gaze wandered the room before returning to her. He, too, seemed to be struggling with his focus. "There's nothing left but ashes."

God above! What a run of ill luck! She reached for his hand where it lay on the counterpane. His skin felt cold to the touch now. She gripped his fingers, rubbed them to bring back the warmth. "Is your family all right?"

"Yes. I've sent them . . . elsewhere."

"But what happened?"

His gaze locked on hers, square and unblinking, and she knew the answer before he spoke. "It's all of one piece," he said. "Tonight, and Susseby."

She went still. Arson, then? "The man you killed?"

"Some hireling." He looked down at their joined hands. Turned his palm into hers, threading their fingers together. "He was sent by a man named Bolkhov. The man who gave me this." With his free hand, he touched the scar that ran so closely to his eye. "A general in the Russian army. Deposed, absconded from his post. His troops ransacked the Afghan countryside after the war. I was tasked to hunt him down. He held me responsible for those we killed. Among them, he claimed, were his wives and children. And so he vowed to take revenge. Susseby," he said. "And tonight. And . . . all the rest."

The gunshot. The assayers with their weapons. *The wrong room,* he'd said. "He wants to hurt Miss Everleigh?"

"He knows her." He pulled his hand free, laid it on the coverlet, stretched his fingers. His knuckles were swollen from the brawl. "Under a different name, he contributed several pieces to the auction she's curating. He enjoys his taunts," he said quietly. "One of the pieces, he knew I would recognize. Until I saw it, I had no notion of how to find him."

Comprehension swept through her. "You're using her to hunt him."

"That was the idea." His smile looked black. "Instead, I gave him new prey."

"She has no idea of the danger," Lilah whispered.

"She does now. We spoke earlier. But other dangers concern her more greatly." He shrugged. "Her brother is looting the auction house—fixing the books, embezzling from the accounts. By the terms of her father's will, she has no authority to interfere until she is married. She proposed a trade: my help in containing Peter, for hers with luring out Bolkhov. It's hardly fair, to my mind. But she was insistent."

Lilah's thoughts had turned to more selfish concerns. "You're not really courting her, then?" God forgive her for her relief.

But he saw it, his face darkening. "Lilah. This is no game. If it took a marriage to trap him, I would do it. Bolkhov means to kill everyone close to me. He has already managed it once."

God above. "Your . . . surely not your brother?"

He looked away. "A telegram arrived last week. Geoff's grave had been disturbed. That was what drew me to Susseby. By the time I arrived . . ." He knocked a piece of lint from the bed, then stared at his hand, the fist it made. "It's a wonder no one was killed. The fire spread quickly. Strong wind, that night. The ashes carried all the way to the village."

She did not know what to say. It was an unspeakably maniacal thing, to persecute a man by targeting his loved ones. Even her uncle would have recoiled at such evil.

"It was only a house, of course." He spoke flatly. "But that is the last loss I will incur." He glanced back at her, his face remote. "You are leaving Buckley Hall. And in London, you will not know me. We are strangers, from here forward. For your sake."

"Strangers." The idea seemed impossible. Foul and offensive. But for weeks, she had felt out of her depths here. Only now did she realize that there might be a greater price to pay than the loss of her position, her dignity . . . and her heart.

Agonized, she studied him. *Strangers.* Her father and uncle had never agreed on anything but a single principle: no matter the cost, survival came first. Becoming a stranger would be wise, sensible, safe. His face was impenetrable to her now, beautiful and severe, as though she were indeed a stranger, her feelings immaterial.

But his eyes spoke differently. He watched her as closely as she watched him. She saw the mirror of her own feelings in his eyes.

He was trying to protect her. How dare he imagine that she would not do the same for him?

"Once, in your study, I saw a map." She spoke softly, choosing her words with care. "My uncle, whom I told you about—he knows those areas you circled. He knows them very well. Do you think this Bolkhov might be hiding in one of them? If so, my uncle could help you."

"Lilah. My God." He rose to his feet. "Have you heard a single word I've said? I want you *out* of this."

She scrambled to her feet. "But I am in it! There is no getting out. I work for Miss Everleigh, don't you see? And my uncle is no ordinary—"

"Forget your uncle," he snarled. "Forget Catherine. She knows a bargain when she sees one: she means to use me as I use her. She is *useful*. But you, Lilah . . . you're a goddamned weakness. And if you care so little for your own life that you would risk it on me, you're a fool."

She caught her breath. Those fierce words burned away the last vestige of her numbness. He cared for her. He could not hide it. She would not let him. "Then I'm a fool." But not a coward. "I can help you, though. I *can*." Nick could. She would find a way to make him do it.

He dug his hands through his hair, then spun and stalked to the door. "We will not have this conversation." Yanking the door open, he said, "Get out."

"Don't you want to know my name, before I go?"

That caught him. He turned on her, furious. "*No.* I wish to know nothing about you. Are you deaf? Listen once more: I have put everyone I love in danger. *Everyone.*" He stepped toward her, a violent movement, arrested abruptly. "I have buried my brother's body. His death—my doing. Susseby—my doing. I have robbed my sister and mother of their home. I have exiled them. And tonight, I killed a man, and then I wiped away your blood. You have no care for yourself. Fine. But *I* care. I care and I will not risk you. I will be *dead* before I take your help. Is that clear to you?"

Everything was clear. This snarling speech, his terror—for *her*—was the most dreadful, beautiful ode she'd ever heard.

"My name is Lily Monroe," she said. "Niece to Nicholas O'Shea. *That* is the man you need now."

He sneered. "Fine." He seized the doorknob again, pulling so hard that the wood cracked as the door lurched open. "You've said it. Now go."

He wasn't hearing her. "You know my uncle. They call him Saint Nick. King of Diamonds, the Lord of the East End." Was he listening? "He controls half the city. The *darker* half." She watched his profile, the stony set of his jaw, the rigid line of his shoulders. His silent, physical rejection. "All those areas you circled on the map—they are his. He *owns* the people there. With the letters, I can propose a new trade—"

He turned, his expression black. "And does he own you? He's the one whom you fear, isn't he? The bastard who blackmailed you." An ugly smile twisted his mouth. "The other bastard, that is."

What irrelevant nonsense was this? "It makes no difference." In the face of this danger, it didn't matter. "He could help. I could *make* him help."

"It matters." He stared at her. "I will not give him cause to blackmail you again."

"But there would be no need! I have the—"

"You're right. There's no need." A muscle flexed in his jaw. "The Russian auction will be held in a fortnight. I've made arrangements to lure out Bolkhov. This travesty ends then . . . if not beforehand."

"But what if it doesn't? Why not use all the weapons at your—"

"I had hoped you esteemed me better," he cut in.

"Foolish, I know. What cause have I given you for esteem? But if you think I'll send you back to the bastard who put you into this mess—to beg for his *favors*, by God—then you think me some species far lower than a coward."

Her lips shaped the words several times before she got them out. In that brief pause, anger sparked. "I think you a *bastard*," she said. "An arrogant ass! For it takes a bastard to turn up his nose at a friend! If *I'm* willing to do it, then why can't—"

"We are not friends."

He spoke so coldly that it took the breath from her lungs. "You're a liar," she whispered.

"And now you bore me." He bent to strip the knife from his boot. Laid it solidly on the table before turning back to her. "Still here?" The derisive curl of his mouth smashed into her like a fist. "I used you, Lilah. You were useful, for a time. But now you're not. I do see why you were so cool under pressure—the niece of Saint Nick; why, you're the aristocracy of the underbelly. But I don't mix with filth on regular occasions. I do thank you for the offer, though."

The pain twisted, making her reckless. She knew he meant not a word of his speech. He was trying to drive her off. But he certainly knew the proper way to do it. His words laid open her chest and bowed an ugly song across her heartstrings. "You'll take filth into your bed, but friendship is a step too far, is it? Friendship is for women like Miss Everleigh. You'll take *her* help, but not mine."

He shrugged and leaned back against the wall, the lounging posture of an idle masher, bored of low entertainments. "She sells her help for a price. You have nothing left that I wish to purchase."

She ignored the sting. "You told her to call you Christian. Was *that* necessary? Was your Russian lunatic listening then?"

A strange look came over him. "God above. Is that all it requires? Go ahead, then. Call me Christian. What does it matter?"

It mattered. He tried to pretend otherwise, but she knew the truth. "Christian." She stepped toward him. "Let me help you. Please. I—"

He caught her hand before she could touch him. Forced it back to her side. "I am done with this argument," he said very slowly, as though she were a child in a tantrum.

"But I'm not." She glared at him as his fingers tightened. "Hurting me won't end it, either."

He dropped her hand as though it burned. Setting his fist to his mouth, he stared at her, his expression bleak.

The silence felt brittle and sharp, as though the wrong word might fracture it into cutting shards. She did not know what to say next. The heaviness of defeat stole over her.

"Christian," she whispered. "Please. Don't be a fool."

Something fraught tightened the skin around his eyes. When it passed, his gaze had softened. He lowered his fist and breathed out. "Do you care for me, Lily?"

Her throat felt so full. A thousand words would not encompass the proper response. All she could manage was a nod.

"Then you'll trust me," he said. "You'll trust my plan. If the auction doesn't bear out . . . then, perhaps, we will speak of your uncle."

It was a compromise. Unsatisfactory, horribly insufficient. She wrapped her arms around herself, miserable.

"Lily," he said softly. "What a lovely name for you. Lily, you should go."

Was that all she would have from him? A compliment to her name. A flimsy bargain to talk again, in two weeks' time. At which point he might be dead already, when she might have saved him.

She deserved more than that.

She dropped her arms and squared her shoulders. "I will go in the morning," she said quietly. "But not tonight. I'll have something else before I leave."

Lily. The name fit her perfectly. She should not have told it to him. In this darkness his life had become, she remained the sole piece of light. But each secret she shared pulled her closer to him, to this stain he had become on the lives of those he loved.

Her bastard uncle could not have helped. Not when the full force of British intelligence had failed to locate Bolkhov. But she would have gambled herself on the chance. Endangering herself for his sake.

Surviving a war had taught him to recognize true mettle. An ally whom he could trust with his life. She was that, and far more. He would not risk her. This war was different from the other. His survival now was not worth the cost, if it meant losing her.

He touched her face. Standing before him, an exquisite vulnerability in the defiant tilt of her chin, she was his punishment. What he most wanted: what he could not have.

"You will not interfere," he said quietly, stroking her satin-smooth cheek. "I'll have your word before you go."

Otherwise he would make the decision for her. There was room for another woman in that remote cottage where his sister and mother now waited.

But he would not take her there unless necessary, for placing her with his family would compound the danger to her. Bolkhov had no way, yet, to know what she had become to him. Once he put her with his mother and sister, there could be no doubt. She would be just as vulnerable as they were.

She still had not replied. He grasped her by the shoulders, not caring if he frightened her now. "Give me your goddamned word."

"You have it," she said, almost soundless. "But first . . ."

A strange laugh escaped him. Did she imagine she would have to force him to it? "Lily," he said. A flower whose bulb nestled deep in the ground, where one never thought to look for it. Of course that was her name. She had taken him by surprise. He had never expected this.

He hooked his hand in her hair, pulled up her face, and looked into her pale, fearless beauty before he kissed her.

In the morning, she would be gone from his life. But in the meantime, God help him, he would pretend that she was his. That he had seen her waiting at a window in some tower, and slayed dragons to win her, and claimed her by right, and made that tower his home.

He picked her up and carried her to the bed. The light from the hearth painted her in rippling tones of fire. The smooth slope of her shoulder. The wide blue pools of her eyes. The fullness of her lips, which she pressed together to hide how they trembled.

There was no cause to hide that from him. He leaned

down to kiss her lips apart, to lick and suck them. "Tremble," he murmured. "As much as you like."

Her small sigh seemed flavored by relief. Her arms came eagerly around his shoulders as she drew him atop her. He felt the fleeting urge to smile. Did she imagine he would retreat now? He kissed her deeply, hard, to show her his intentions.

She took his tongue, drew it deeper into her mouth. Her hands slipped to his waist, her grip tightening.

The thin robe translated every swell and curve of her. Her slim waist, the delicate point of her elbow. The bloody bastard had grabbed her there—

He gritted his teeth and sat back, away from that thought, as he ripped off his clothing. He caught her hands when she tried to pull him toward her, holding them firmly. "Shh," he said. Then he picked her up by the waist. Her weight—the lightness of it—briefly disconcerted him. Her rich low voice, the ferocity of her spirit—it should have made her as solid and heavy as an anchor.

He laid her down again, on a cushion of pillows, bracing himself on an elbow above her. The picture of her, passive and tousled beneath him, a slight amazed smile flirting bashfully with her lips, deserved trumpets—the adulation of crowds.

But she was his. Only for his eyes. His, alone.

For now.

"Touch me," she whispered. Innocent. Mistaking his pause for uncertainty, rather than an inward battle against this savage possessiveness.

"I will," he said very quietly. But he would portion that pleasure out in small bits. Otherwise he would devour her without care or regard.

He started with her hair, running his fingertips lightly down the braid that spilled over her shoulder and swung off the bed. A single ribbon secured it. He pulled one end, and watched her hair slowly untwist.

He ran his fingers through it, drawing the thick locks over her breast. Her eyes fluttered shut. She liked this.

He threaded his fingers through her hair at her scalp, massing, tugging, and then spreading the strands out in all directions. She groaned beneath his strokes. Arched upward, like a cat being petted. His eyes fixed on the point where her robe caught on the twin peaks of her stiffened nipples.

He slipped one hand beneath her back, feeling his way down to the sash, slipping it free. She made a delighted noise and rolled toward him. The robe slipped off her, revealing small but perfectly shaped breasts, nipples pink and proudly pebbled. Her beauty pierced him like strong sunlight, burning him clean.

He cupped her breast in his hand. Tested its weight. She shivered. "Clever hands," she whispered. "You would have made a fine thief."

Did she not know he was thieving right now? Taking what did not belong to him. He wanted . . . not only her body but the future she would forge for herself, with the same wit and fearless initiative she had shown him so many times. He wanted her at his side. At his back. To love a woman and to depend on her courage were two different things. But she would offer them both, to the man she married.

To hell with the goddamned butcher.

It was a dark thought, ugly as bloodlust. He did not want to dwell on it when he might dwell on her. He leaned down and sucked her nipple into his mouth.

She gasped, wrapping his head in her arms, pulling him against her. Her shudders strengthened as he suckled her, ebbed as he drew away to blow lightly on her skin.

He pinned her arms over her head as he kissed her deeply. She had thrown herself in danger's path for him. That was his sin to bear. She should never have needed to carry a knife, at his side. Harm would never come to her again on his count. Everything he did henceforth would ensure it.

He kissed her wrists, then reached down to knock free the last clasp of the robe at her hips. She could guard herself from the world, but she never need do so with him. He pushed apart her legs, so she lay splayed and bare before him.

She made an awkward noise—a protest, swallowed. He wrenched his gaze to her face, and found her blushing and unable to meet his eyes.

"You are beautiful," he said. He bent to kiss her plump inner thigh. He licked the salt from the crease of her leg.

She squeaked. "This is . . . French."

"Not yet." He breathed deeply of her, musk and ambrosia and every secret note that no aphrodisiac had yet managed to capture. With his tongue he trailed a path down to her knee. It was dimpled, a realization that unseated something inside him. So much left to discover, and no time. Ambition and panic twisted inside him. No time to waste. He could revisit her knees later.

He licked back up her thighs and then, giving her no warning, parted her quim with his thumbs.

Her hips jerked. Shy, she tried to close her legs. He moved his knee, holding her thighs apart. She would not hide from him.

Her eyes found his, wide and dazed. He offered her a fierce smile, then lowered his head and licked her.

Her stifled cry felt like a hand tightening on his cock. *Yes.* He tasted her, licked into her, penetrated her with his tongue. Prepared her for his fingers, which he slid into her with great care as he kissed upward to her clitoris, that small throbbing knot that he teased and sucked as he felt her channel grow wet.

He had dreamed of this. Had dreamed of the noises she would make when he made love to her with his mouth. But the reality—her twitching, thrashing, murmuring pleasure, her scent, the softness of her restless thighs as they closed around his head—was beyond . . . anything.

Lust, rage, hunger, all the primitive desires were not so different from each other. *Conquer.* He sucked harder. Caught hold of her hips and pinned her down when she tried to resist her own pleasure. "Too much," she gasped. Which was exactly right. He laved her again and again. *Accept this.*

He felt the spasms take her. She tightened around his fingers, a fierce clutching rhythm that made him swallow in triumph. Her hips jerked in his grip. He reached down to grasp himself. Paused over her, wrestling with his restraint.

Her hand closed on his cock. "Now," she whispered.

His need was red and dark and merciless. He fitted his cock to her opening, tight, moist, hot, soft— ah, God; he caught her stifled gasp in his mouth as he slowly pushed into her.

The shock went bone deep as he looked into her eyes. *Mine.*

No. He closed his eyes, his mind, to the word, and

began to rock into her; God in heaven he would not rush this, he would bring her to her peak again, he would—

Her hips moved against his tentatively; then with some moaning murmur she caught the way of it, her hands digging into his sides, scraping down to his buttocks. She pulled him into the hilt, and he gasped.

"Yes," she said into his ear. "Yes, yes, yes."

"Lily." That was all he could manage. And then, on a groan, on a wave of pleasure so intense that sparks formed in the darkness behind his eyes, he was lost. He ripped himself away from her, spilling his seed safely.

Lost.

Her arms came around him, drawing him back.

He was not lost yet. Not until she let him go.

The next morning at half ten, the stable hands loaded the last of the luggage atop the hired carriage. Inside, as Lilah took her seat across from Miss Everleigh, she allowed herself a final look at the house. Once she had thought it monstrous. Now it seemed mythical, the scene of a fairy tale.

She had learned a great deal in that house. And she had lost something there that could never be recovered. She was glad of it, fiercely. Regretless.

Only . . . what if she could not help him? What if Nick refused her offer? What if this madman murdered him? What if—

She could not bear to look at the house a moment longer. She would start searching the windows for a glimpse of him. "We should go," she said to Miss Everleigh. Overhead, the clouds were gathering into a great bruised knot. A robin winged by, breast as red as a warning as he fled from the storm.

"Yes, quite right." The lingering effects of the wine made Miss Everleigh look sallow and ill. But she, too, seemed entranced by the house, gazing out with shadowed eyes until the carriage turned into the trees and took them out of view.

When they joined the main road, the jostling made Miss Everleigh groan and clutch her head. Lilah held out a flask that Mrs. Barnes had filled with tea. "It will help."

Miss Everleigh waved it away. "Nothing will help," she said bitterly, "unless it's poison for my brother. This is the last time he will interfere with me. I promise you that."

Lilah sat back against the cushions. It felt relieving, somehow, to be presented with such clear-cut rage. She herself was an inward stew of murky, churning emotion; anger was far easier to manage. "You can't reason with men," she said. "The bulk of them think us puppets, who dance for their amusement. And even when they do care for us, they think of us as fragile dolls, best kept on a high shelf lest we somehow get broken."

Miss Everleigh looked at her so queerly that for a moment she thought she'd overstepped, and braced herself for a scolding.

But it seemed that their drunken camaraderie had wrought a change. "I don't intend to reason with him." Miss Everleigh opened her reticule to retrieve a vial of powder. "Give me that flask. I'm fixing my head."

"What is that?"

"Powdered willow bark. Doesn't your head ache?" She dumped the powder into the flask, shook it vigorously, and then pinched her nose as she took a long swallow. "I will never drink again."

Lilah allowed herself a smile. "Not until you're offered a good bottle of Château Lafeet."

"Lafite Gilet." Miss Everleigh made a chiding *tsk*. "We must find you a proper French tutor. You will not advance without a grasp of the language—or at the very least, a knowledge of the pronunciation." She offered a wry smile.

Lilah did not know whether to take her seriously. "I would adore to learn it."

"We will call it an exchange of services, then. You will teach me to type. I will procure you a tutor."

"Truly?"

The other woman arched a brow. "Do you not find it a fair bargain? Shall I revise it?"

"I find it quite splendid!" The only good news she'd had today. She caught herself as she glanced out the window. There was nothing to see through the oaks.

"Of course, at this late age, it will be a hard road," said Miss Everleigh. "Languages are best learned as a child. You cannot afford distractions."

"I mean to entertain none," Lilah said in puzzlement. Was she being accused, in advance, of dillydallying? "If you fear that the lessons would interfere with my duties at the auction rooms—"

"No. You misunderstand." Miss Everleigh sighed. "You see, I don't intend to reason with my brother. It's pointless; I see that now. Instead, I mean to give him exactly what he wants."

Jarred by the change in topic, Lilah proceeded cautiously. "How is that, miss?"

"First tell me this. Do you love him?"

For a stupid moment, Lilah thought that she referred to Young Pete. And then her horror intensified as the truth dawned on her. "*No.*"

"You do not love the viscount. I wish to be very clear on the matter."

Flustered, Lilah took the defensive stance. "I can't imagine why you'd ask!"

To her shock, Miss Everleigh blushed. "I do not make a practice of speculation. But at times, when I caught you looking at him—and sometimes the way you spoke of him had an air of . . ." She cleared her throat. "Well. It's a simple question, no need to make it complicated. You love him or you don't. Which is it?"

Lilah felt her own face warming, a strange mix of panic and misery curdling her veins. Love? *No.* She did not even allow herself to think the word. "It would make me the greatest fool alive," she said, "to reach so far above my station."

"Countless women have been fools of that kind." Miss Everleigh did her the kindness of looking away to study the view. "I cannot claim to understand it. But I do gather it is a common weakness, and not worthy of . . . condemnation."

This was even greater generosity than the offer of a French tutor. It penetrated Lilah's stormy mood like a struggling ray of light. Had they truly become friends? She could think of no other motive for this kindness. Miss Everleigh offered a salve for her pride, and a tacit promise not to judge her.

"I will work very hard at French," she said quietly. "I promise you, miss." No matter what else happened, she would cling to the prospect of a true profession. It was her raft in the storm to come.

"Good," said Miss Everleigh. "I am glad to hear it, for your sake." She stripped off her gloves, then held out the flask. "Straight from the bottle," she said.

Lilah took a deep breath. "Cheers," she replied, and took a swig.

CHAPTER FIFTEEN

$\mathcal{H}$elp that bastard?" Nick gave her a disbelieving look. "Did you lose your mind, out in the country?"

Lilah sighed. They were standing on the balcony at the House of Diamonds, Nick's gambling club. She never liked to visit here. Below, at numerous tables scattered across the thick red carpet, men were throwing money away with an abandon that sickened her.

But she'd written to Nick for five days in a row with no reply, and she'd had no luck ambushing him at Neddie's, either. When he'd finally written to propose a meeting here, she'd been too relieved to quibble over details.

"Just hear me out," she said. "I'll make it worth your while."

"Can't think how," he said. "Not unless you've got the crown jewels in your pocket."

She hadn't expected this to be easy. Nick was the most stubborn man she'd ever met. He would not throw water on himself to put out a fire, if it meant following somebody else's plan for him. "I know you don't like him. And I know you've no cause to do favors for me. But I've come anyway. Please hear me out."

He frowned, then gave her a long, encompassing glance, his gray eyes sharp. "You look right tired, Lily. You feeling all right?"

She shrugged. "It's just the lighting." The glare of the electric chandeliers made everybody look sallow.

"Modernity isn't pretty," he said. "Adds some glamor, though."

She nodded. In truth, she was exhausted; she'd barely slept since returning to London. But she knew better than to admit to Nick that she'd been tossing and turning with worry for a toff. "Can we speak somewhere private? It's very loud in here." The crowd below wore evening finery, but disported themselves as raucously as brawlers at a gin palace.

"Sweet music of the dice," Nick said. But he pushed himself off the railing, leading her with springing steps down the balcony to an unmarked door.

He had redecorated his office since her last visit. Dark, striped paper covered the walls. The tasteful Smyrna carpet would have won Miss Everleigh's approval.

She took a seat in the wing chair that faced the desk. The grain of the leather slid like butter beneath her fingers. "You're doing very well." Nick disliked being instructed, but he wasn't immune to flattery.

He dropped into the seat opposite, grinning as he shoved aside a ledger. "Can't complain. You see the archbishop down there, at the poker table?" He snorted. "Calls himself Thomas Duckle at the door, as if we've never seen a bloody newspaper."

That door—the famous red door, which admitted wealthy ne'er-do-wells at all hours—stood open thanks to Nick's generous bribes. Gambling had been declared illegal, but he had the police in his pocket, and several politicians, too. The only group he did not bother to placate were the moralists, whose furious editorials had offered the House of Diamonds a great deal of free advertising over the past few years.

"Congratulations," she murmured. "Perhaps Mr. Duckle will sell you a place in heaven."

"Oh, I've got better uses for my coin than that," he said with a wink. He folded his hands together atop the desk, flexing his wrists so his rings rapped the wood. "You bring those letters? Or is Palmer still lording them over you?"

"He gave them to me for nothing."

He frowned. "Right he did."

That cynical tone made her sit straighter. "It's true," she said fiercely. "He asked nothing for them. He gave them to me from kindness." *To get me free of you,* she did not add.

He sat back, smiling faintly. The gambling house had a strict dress code, which Nick always followed when resident. In his formal black suit and crisply starched cravat, he looked almost lordly. "Sounds about right, then. It's a fool who'll give away what he could name a price for."

She would not be drawn into pointless argument. "He's looking for someone. A Russian. A very dangerous character. The man probably hides among his own people. There are several Russian communities in your territory, aren't there?"

"They make no trouble," Nick said evenly. "So it's none of my concern."

"It concerns *me*."

"No, Lily. It doesn't."

"This Russian, he's after Palmer's family—"

"The Strattons, is that right?"

His thoughtful tone confused her. Then it gave her a fledgling flutter of hope. "Yes. His mother and sister—"

"Seventh viscount in his line," Nick went on. He pulled apart his hands, took hold of one of his rings and turned it idly around his finger. A ruby cabochon the size of a marble. "Second cousin to a couple of dukes. Hell, he's even related to the Queen. Ancestors came over with old Willy the Conqueror, don't you know."

"You've been reading up on him."

"Thought it wise." He tipped his head, dark hair falling across one eye. Fine suit, yes. But the shaggy hair of a ruffian. "How much Irish you reckon you'll find in a family like that?"

"His mother," she said triumphantly. "She hails from Tipperary."

He burst into a laugh. "Is that what he told you? Aye, no doubt they ventured beyond the Pale once or twice. Seized some land from law-abiding Catholics. Don't make them Irish, though."

She bit her tongue. She must stay focused on her aim. "I don't have any interest in defending his ancestors. It's him that I . . ."

"You what?" Nick leaned forward. "What is it, exactly, that brings you to my doorstep to do his begging for him?"

"I'm not doing it for him. He doesn't even know I'm here."

"Sure he doesn't," he said smoothly.

"It's true." The next words came out clumsily, for they effectively bared her throat to Nick. "I care for him."

He surprised her by sighing. "Oh, Lily." He sat back, raked a hand through his black hair, then shook his head. "Well, it's an old story. But I thought I taught you better. Fiona, now—she was softhearted. Took after her da. But you? I thought you were smarter."

She was foolish, to be sure. No use in disputing it. "You don't know him," she said softly. "I can't hope to persuade you that he's far better, far kinder, far worthier than you think. Not like the rest of them. Of course you won't believe that. But if you have any faith in me— then *I* will beg you. I beg you to trust my judgment, for once."

His gaze dropped, his long dark lashes veiling his eyes. He nudged the ledger book straight, squared its edges with the corner of the desk. "All right, then let's hear it. What are your hopes from him?"

"My hopes?" She frowned. "What do you mean? My hope is to find this Russian—"

"Your hopes for *you*." He looked up sharply. "I don't give a damn for Palmer. Let's speak of what does matter. You want me to help this toff. Find the Russian who would hurt him. What's in it for you? Think he'll marry you for it?"

She flinched. "Of course not."

He studied her a long moment, in which his steady gaze made her feel increasingly exposed, awkward and flushed and miserable.

"Oh, but you do hope, don't you?" He spoke very gently, which somehow made it worse. "And why not? You walk around that auction house dressed like a lady, talking like a lady. And the swells bow to you, just as they

would to a lady—but you'll never be one of them, Lily.
It's not that you don't deserve it—God knows you've
done a tip-top job, remaking yourself. Had I known you
had the talent for it, I never would have wasted you on
thieving. You'd have made the finest swindler London
ever saw."

She could not hold his gaze. "But?"

"But the swindle ends, darling, when they ask who
your father was. And your grandfather, and his father
before him. Old William the Conqueror, he's not in
our line. His son killed our kind for sport, back in the
day."

"I know it." She spat the words. "You needn't tell me
this."

"I didn't think I did. But then you came here to beg
for one of them. And unless you give me a solid reason
why, I'll be thinking you—with love, Lily; always with
love—the greatest damned fool in the city."

"Here's a reason." She raised her head and glared at
him. "You won't have those letters unless you help me
find the Russian."

"Ah." He steepled his fingertips against his mouth as
he considered her. "Threats, is it?" he asked softly. "That
wise, Lily?"

"No." The syllable was threadbare. She cleared her
throat and found her voice again. "But if your life were
on the line, I would make threats to save it. And I'll do
it for him, too. Punish me as you like."

"As I *like*." He whipped his hands down against the
desktop, the crack making her jump. "What I *like* has
nothing to do with it. You'll never make a lady—but
you could've been a fine, powerful woman. Stayed here,
run an empire with me. But no." He stood with violent

force, and she leapt to her feet, scrambling around the chair to bolt through the door.

But he didn't come after her. He stared at her, scowling, and her hand, after a moment, slipped off the doorknob. She gathered herself to her full height. "The letters," she said. "For the Russian's location. That is the offer."

"No," he said flatly.

With the collapse of her hopes, fear seemed to leave her, too. She felt, above all, exhausted. "Very well." She pulled open the door.

"I've a different bargain," he said. "Nonnegotiable."

She wheeled back.

"You're family," he said evenly. "But this is the last time I'll do anything to serve Palmer. Understood?"

"Yes. *Yes.* Thank you—"

"Not yet," he bit out. "God's sake, Lily, have you forgotten everything? Hear the price first. Sit back down."

Something was afoot at Everleigh's. Lilah knew it the moment she alighted from the cab. The footmen were not at their posts on the front steps. Concern overrode the anxiety still lingering from her conversation with her uncle. She paid the driver and hurried around to the back entry.

The hall was empty. The counting room was locked. Even Mr. Chisholm, that permanent fixture in the contracts office, had deserted his desk. Rattled, Lilah pushed through the green baize doors into the public corridor. Lavender Ames and Maisy Lowell were hurrying up the grand staircase.

"Vinnie!" she called. "What's going on?"

Lavender looked back but didn't slow. "Quickly," she said. "There's a meeting called in the auction room."

Lifting her skirts, Lilah took the stairs by twos. As she reached Vinnie's side, she found herself at the edge of a crowd. The entire staff of Everleigh's was funneling through the double doors into the oak-paneled hall where auctions were conducted.

Young Pete stood at the rostrum, his sister at his side. Just below them, the senior employees had assembled: the company solicitors; Young Pete's secretary; and Mr. Hastings, who officially was Peter's assistant, but in practice led most of the lesser auctions in Peter's place. They were clustered in a tight, obsequious circle around a tall man, exquisitely dressed in dove gray, whose back was to the crowd.

She recognized the breadth of his shoulders, the way his blond hair curled against his collar. His military-straight posture.

As though he sensed her attention, he turned. Their eyes met across the crowd. He did not smile.

An elbow prodded her, making her flinch. "Hey now," Vinnie said. "Isn't that Lord Palmer?"

Her heart gave a queer thump. Like a thousand pricks from a needle, this wave of foreboding. She nodded.

"Why do you suppose he's here?"

"I've no idea." She cleared her throat. "Perhaps . . . to announce the date of the auction of Buckley Hall?"

But even as she spoke, she knew the idea was absurd. Vinnie confirmed it: "I can't imagine they'd assemble us for such an announcement. Perhaps for a royal estate, but you said Buckley Hall was not so very rich."

"It was rich." Richer than any estate she could imagine. "But not grand enough for this."

Vinnie gave her a sharp look. "Are you all right?"

"Quiet now," Young Pete called. He rapped the gavel against the rostrum, causing the assistant auctioneer below to give a proprietary wince.

Maisy Lowell snorted. "Look at how Hastings fondles the thing!" For he had reached out to pat the rostrum as one might soothe an addled horse.

"He's in love," Vinnie cracked.

Lilah felt her lips curl in an automatic smile. But she barely registered the joke. Palmer had looked away from her almost instantly, and from this distance—which suddenly felt so much larger than the width of the room, with him surrounded by fawning lackeys—he seemed every inch the stranger he had asked her to make him. Not the man she had lain with until dawn six nights ago. Not the man who had feared for her, and then called her his weakness.

No, the man across the room looked incapable of weakness. He wore a look of bored amusement that she remembered from the first days at Buckley Hall. The look, she had thought back then, of an arrogant, bullying ass.

"All right now, *quiet*," Young Pete called, far more loudly than needed; the room had been designed to carry voices as clearly as an opera house, and everybody had already hushed anyway. Into the tense and excited silence, he continued: "Over five years ago, now, we mourned my father's passing. I know we mourned together, for my father always considered you all to be as dear to him as family, and your grief was a testament to your fellow feeling. At every moment, since then, I have striven to do his legacy justice."

"You'd imagine his sister had done nothing," Vinnie muttered in Lilah's left ear, while in her right, Maisy whispered, "She looks as sour as vinegar, doesn't she?"

"It is in honor of that legacy," Young Pete went on, "that I have called you here today. For as family, you deserve to share in our joys as much as our sorrows." He lifted his hand, beckoning his sister nearer to him.

And then he motioned also to Palmer.

Vinnie gasped. "Do you think—"

"No," Lilah said. *No.* She crossed her arms and gripped them very tightly. She must be mistaken. They had not been in London a week. She had met with Miss Everleigh every afternoon, for lessons in typing that also served to organize their notes on Buckley Hall. By no sign or odd mood had Miss Everleigh indicated that she had news of a private and unusual nature.

Yet Peter was still speaking. "It is my great good fortune to announce the betrothal of my sister to Viscount Palmer. Lord Palmer, as you may know—"

Her ears shut out the words. They buzzed senselessly around her: Pete's speech, Palmer's words of thanks, Vinnie's excited babbling. The roar in her ears made it all unintelligible. She could not remove her eyes from Palmer. *Christian.* Could not look away, though it seemed to burn her very vision when he lifted Catherine Everleigh's hand and kissed it.

Miss Everleigh smiled.

The astonished applause threw her back into herself. She would be sick, surely. She felt cold and jittery, as though she had drunk too much coffee, and then gone on a whirligig after.

"You never let on," Vinnie was saying to her. "How did it happen? How did he win her?"

And Maisy, too, was demanding details: "When did they fall in love? Did you guess it right away?"

"I . . ." She could not do this. No amount of thieving could have prepared her to put on this kind of performance, tell these kinds of lies. What filled her throat, her mind, was only the truth: *No, they did not fall in love at Buckley Hall. We fell in love. I fell in love with him. And I swear to you, until this moment, I was certain that he did as well.*

But that wasn't right. He'd never spoken of love. And she had explicitly denied it. Was she in love? She had promised herself she wasn't.

Oh, God. She had lied.

"Excuse me," she said, and pushed through the women. Thank heavens the double doors had been left ajar; otherwise, heavy as they were, she might have been forced to throw herself at them, again and again, battering herself until they opened, or she fell apart . . .

She fled through the empty hall, down the slippery echoing staircase, past the deserted salons where she had laughed and flirted and traded quips with a hundred gentlemen whose names she no longer remembered.

The butcher! She burst out through the doors, emerging into a light rain, coming to a stop at the top of the stairs, barely cognizant of the marveling looks from passersby on the pavement. *Think of the butcher. Or your career.*

But this ache was swelling, an unbearable pressure in her chest. Once it cracked, she'd be done for.

He'd never spoken of love. He'd only warned her. *Become a stranger. It is safer.* He had all but told her he would be her downfall. But he'd imagined the danger outward. How much easier, were that so! For neither he nor anybody in the world could save her from herself.

Stupid, stupid. She started to walk, blindly pushing past her fellow pedestrians. A vendor of hot oysters called out a warning; he ducked out of her path, grease splattering her wrist. She wasn't wearing gloves. She'd left them inside.

Fiona, we made no plan for this.

When she finally halted, she found herself at the bustling edge of the marketplace. A hundred carts, vegetables and fruit, livestock lowing, women bawling their wares. By dint of long habit, her hand closed over her pocket to protect her purse. She felt the hilt of her knife. The sensation gave her an odd jolt, a sick thudding sense of sinking back into herself.

The world looked unchanged. She dashed away her tears—when had *that* happened?—and became immediately unremarkable. The next lot of passersby didn't even look at her. Even in her fine gown, she fit right in with a common crowd.

She took a long breath, then sidestepped out of the way of a slow-moving oxcart. By a cart selling hot pies, a bearded man was about to clip the strings of a housewife's purse, for she had turned away for a moment, forgetful, to see to her fussing children.

The knife was still in Lilah's hand. She lifted it and watched it go.

The thief squawked in surprise, his sleeve pinned against the cart. The housewife shrieked and grabbed back her purse; the vendor bellowed for the police.

Lilah stepped up and retrieved her blade. Thief, housewife, and baker gawped at her.

She was still good for something. Good for a lot

of things, in fact. She bobbed a brief curtsy and then turned away, quickening her pace when she spotted the approaching bobbies. Ladies did not throw knives.

Nick was right, after all. She would never be a lady in truth, but she did make a powerful woman.

At the corner, she made herself turn back toward Everleigh's. The engagement changed nothing. It did not alter *her*. She remained the same: a woman who fought for the people she loved. She'd never been a coward.

She'd never been a figure of pity, either. Before the day's end, she would write two notes of congratulation to the newly betrothed.

The fire in the hearth had caused the windows to fog. These cold rains had not ceased in a week, sparing no part of the home counties. They had soaked the ruined bones of what remained of Susseby, raising a strange reek that had permeated Christian's skin. He'd walked through the property again three days ago. But he could smell the ash even now, battling with the stale, cologne-clogged air of Peter Everleigh's office.

Catherine signed the last page of the contract, then handed it to her family's lawyer, a rotund, balding man who treated her as though she were no older than ten. He flipped through the pages, checking each with officious care.

"I was thorough," she said to him.

He gave her an indulgent smile. "Of course you were, dear." He handed the contract across the desk to Christian's lawyer. "Lord Palmer must cosign acknowledgment of each clause. I assume you'll wish to review them first."

"Thoroughly." Dyson slipped the documents into his briefcase. "Shall we reconvene in a week?"

"So long?" Catherine sat forward, ignoring her brother's restraining hand. "I'd hoped to have it settled before the engagement party." She grimaced. "If we truly must have one."

"We must," her brother said tightly. "I will not have it said that this marriage was done in haste. Let them think we've been planning it for some time."

Catherine wanted her independence posthaste. The contract, once signed, would guarantee it. It laid out the terms of a marriage that would function, as far as Christian could tell, in the same regimented fashion as any business partnership.

"A week is perfectly satisfactory," said Catherine's lawyer.

"Quite right," Peter snapped when Catherine looked ripe to protest again. "You will give us all cause to wonder at your hurry."

Her mouth thinned as she glanced toward Christian. The meeting had not gone smoothly; Peter had seemed surprised by a number of Catherine's conditions— above all, the clause that required her future husband to allow her fifty hours a week to pursue her professional obligations.

"You can't intend to stay on here," Peter had spluttered. "Why—Palmer, do you mean to allow this? Your wife to *work*?"

Christian had felt curiously anesthetized since his last walk through the ruins of Susseby. But Peter Everleigh's distress was mildly diverting. "We can review it tomorrow," he said now to Dyson. "Will that suit you, Catherine?"

She shrugged off her brother's grip as she rose. "Very well, thank you. Lord Palmer, will you escort me to my office?"

"Later," said Peter. "I need a private word with his lordship."

"Yes," Christian told her. "I'd be glad to do so."

They walked in silence through the bustling public hallway. Once they had mounted the stairs, Catherine gestured him inside her office and pulled shut the door. "Thank you," she said.

"For what?"

"For being so cold to my brother." She waved him into a chair. "I hope you will always prove so cold to him."

He smiled faintly. He was coming to understand her better now. A brother like that would have driven him to become a misanthrope, too. "You understand there are more private terms to discuss. Terms we cannot put into writing."

"Yes. I hoped we might speak of them now." She pulled open the drapes. The cloudy light fell across her, making her skin opalescent.

Her beauty was truly remarkable. He admired it as he might a sculpture in a museum: worthy of praise, but nothing to do with him. "Did you ask Peter about the discrepancies in the accounts?"

"He claims ignorance. Accused me of misunder-standing the finances." She sat down, clasping her hands tightly atop her neatly cleared desktop. For a moment, she frowned, clearly wrestling with some private emo-tion. "Perhaps the accountant was wrong. I believe Peter would embezzle from the company profits—he never loved this place as I do. His dream is a career in politics, not art. But to falsify our clients' accounts . . . it's plain thievery. He doesn't just put our company at risk by stealing from them; he risks his friendships in society, and those mean everything to him."

"You say no one else has access to the client accounts. No trustees of any kind."

"No," she said softly. "Everleigh's has always been a family affair. No shareholders. And by the terms of our father's will, Peter retains sole directorship until I marry."

"Then no one else could be responsible," Christian said. "And the evidence is plain. He's been at this game for two years at least."

She blew out a breath. Then a bitter smile twisted her mouth. "He lies so freely." She ripped apart her hands, clenching the edge of the desktop. "The moment we wed, Palmer—I am suing for control of the finances."

He nodded. "And I will support you in every way." That was their bargain. "Just as soon as this other matter is resolved. It won't be long now."

She sat back, studying him gravely. "Are you certain? Demidov—or Bolkhov; whatever his real name is—declined the invitation to the party." She opened a drawer, handed him the note.

Christian recognized the handwriting. That illiterate scrawl. He'd seen it only once before, on the note that had sent him rushing to York, too late to save his brother.

"I don't understand such men," she said. "Revenge is such a waste of energy. Has he nothing else to occupy him?"

Christian gave her a measuring look. She knew the danger now. He had explained it very clearly, the night they had agreed to marry. But her composure seemed genuine. No fear. None of the anger she rightfully should have felt upon discovering herself at the center of a web designed to snare a lunatic.

But perhaps she felt trapped in that web herself. She needed help if she meant to protect the auction rooms from her brother.

He wished he were a different man. Able to reassure her. Able to apologize, or feel regret for the position in which he'd placed her. Instead, he said, "He mentions a gift in this note."

"Yes." She offered a thin smile. "It is the custom among Russians to felicitate the newly engaged with a present." She reached into her drawer again, handing over a small object, gleaming. A ring.

His jaw clenched. The gold was as bright as the day it had been forged. The bastard had polished it.

"You recognize it."

Go with my blessing. Never forget that I am proud of you. "Yes," he said. Bolkhov had stripped it from his hand four years ago, in that cave in the Hindu Kush.

The graveyard at Susseby currently overlooked a set of chimneys rising from rubble. After he rebuilt the house, he would bury this ring with his father, to whom it had belonged.

"He proposed it as a wedding ring, did you see? Had you not told me the whole of it already, I would have found that quite odd." She cleared her throat. "Better than chocolates, though, I suppose."

There was the regret he'd been searching for. "I'm sorry," he said quietly. "I have put you into a fine mess here."

"But you will get me out of another one." She

straightened a pen lying next to the inkwell. "I would eat a dozen more of those chocolates, if that's what it took to save this company from ruin."

He didn't doubt it. At odd moments, she reminded him a little of Lilah. Both women had steel at their core, and the grit to endure any number of vicissitudes, as long as it guaranteed their aims.

It seems quite pleasant, never to be expected to endure. Lilah had told him that once. And he had wanted nothing more in that moment than to guarantee she never endured another injustice in her life.

Lilah's secrets were not his to share. Catherine, ignorant, had decided to keep her on as an assistant, which was . . . inconvenient. *Infuriating.* It held Lilah too close to the eye of this storm.

But Christian had bitten his tongue bloody against the urge to suggest that Catherine reconsider, demote her back to a hostess. If he could not offer Lilah a future, then he would not sabotage her chance at something better than the butcher.

The smell of Susseby was back in the air now. He pushed it out of his lungs as he rose.

Catherine stood as well. "Do you know, it's a pity Demidov—Bolkhov—turned out to be rotten. His wares will fetch a very handsome profit for us. That candelabrum alone will go for a hundred pounds."

"All the better for you," he said flatly. "He won't be alive to take his share." He slipped the ring into his pocket. "Your hand is too fine for such a heavy band. What is your taste? Diamonds? Emeralds?"

"Either."

He angled a black smile at her. Never had a betrothed couple been so well matched in their transparent lack of enthusiasm. "Perhaps you should choose the ring your-self. I expect you know jewels better than I do."

A light knock came at the door. "Come," called Catherine. "No," she said to him, as light footsteps halted behind him. "My brother handles all the gemstones. But I hardly want his advice on the matter. Miss Marshall, you seemed to have a fine eye for jewels. Have you any suggestions?"

He held himself very still.

"Diamonds," came her low, husky reply, "would be the usual choice. But amethyst would complement your eyes quite well, Miss Everleigh. Lord Palmer, allow me to congratulate you now in person."

He rose and turned, offering a slight bow. She looked fatigued. Deeper shadows under her eyes than he'd ever seen, though she was back in town now, where there was light even in the small hours of the morning.

She could not hold his gaze. "I'm interrupting," she said. "I'll come back later."

"Was there something that needed my attention?" Catherine asked.

He knew he should leave. But he could not look away from her. She sensed his attention. He could tell by her rising color. "Mr. Batten has finished the restoration of the tapestries. Will you have a look?"

"I'll be down shortly. Apprise Lord Palmer as you walk him out. I didn't get a chance to tell him of the repairs."

"Yes, miss." Very stiffly, she led Christian out the door.

"You've no interest in the tapestries," Lilah said to him in the hall.

"No, not really."

"I'll let you go, then."

Stupid, that the words could catch in his chest like that. That the proof of her wrecked sleep should disturb him so deeply. It was a far milder toll than what he sought to spare her. He would go. At once.

But he heard himself say, "No. I'll see the mappemonde now."

In silence she led him down two flights of stairs, into an empty laboratory whose tables were littered with antiques in disrepair. Two tapestries stood stretched against the walls. He walked over to the mappemonde, gazing on it for a long moment. To imagine that this was how men had once envisioned the world: small expanses of fertile land surrounded by vast, dragon-riddled seas—and the darker, unknown terra incognita. How had the uncertainty not driven them mad?

But perhaps, in a world lit only by candles, they had felt better acquainted, more comfortable with such darkness.

He glanced at Lilah, who was staring fixedly away, toward a small window that showed no view but brick wall. "I imagine you don't like this map," he said.

"No," she said immediately. "I much prefer the other one."

The tapestry to the left, he'd never seen before. "Was this also at the estate?"

"Yes. Last century, French. But Miss Everleigh thinks it valuable in its own right. You don't often see fairy tales as the subject of such pieces." Lilah frowned at it. "She says it's a fairy tale, anyway. It's not one I've ever heard."

He studied it. In the foreground, two young knights bowed—or groveled—at the foot of a king. In the upper left quadrant, Christian located their swords, abandoned in a distant mountain range, atop which sat a fearsome-looking dwarf. In the upper right quadrant, a grand castle stood in a verdant valley, overlooked by a third knight and a crowned queen. "It's the tale of the Water of Life." He glanced back to the king. "See the goblet? The king falls ill, and his three sons go out into the world, one by one, to find the cure."

"Let me guess: the firstborn is evil, and the second is stupid, and only the youngest has the courage to outwit the monster."

"No bravery in this tale. Only diplomacy. The first two sons are too vain and proud to reply to the greeting of the dwarf who guards the pass. But the third is courteous, for which the dwarf befriends him. He offers the young prince advice, and a few tools that save the day. The king is healed, and the prince ends up winning a foreign princess and a kingdom of his own."

"That's not a tale about diplomacy," she said. "The moral is never to be too proud for friendship." She slid him a brief, pointed look. "You never know when that friend might come in handy. So never turn up your nose at an offer of help."

He let that rebuke pass in silence, for the argument was settled. "I always thought the moral of these tales was to know your place."

Her laugh was unpleasantly sharp. "Yes, that sounds right, too."

Did she imagine he had lied to her? That her past, her upbringing, mattered a damn? "The third born is humble due to his station," he said evenly. "He acts selflessly. Whereas the firstborn fails because he acts from greed—wanting only his inheritance, without any sense of the duties that should properly drive him. And the second born, who should be noble, waging battle for his ideals, wants only the glory, and none of the blood."

"So he wants to be a hero."

"Yes."

"Fitting for you, as a second born."

He shrugged. "You know what I think on that subject." And she should know, too, that he was the last man on earth who would attach importance to what others would think of her, should they learn of her history. Public perception meant nothing.

"Why?" she asked, her expression wan. "You *are* a hero in every way that counts. It's gotten you the hand of a princess, hasn't it?"

He sighed. She'd sent him a note of congratulation on his engagement. He had wondered—he wondered now—if she knew how deeply her courtesy sliced. How well she had mastered manners, which were, after all, only another weapon to those fluent in them. "In fairy tales," he said, "the princess is almost always in disguise."

Her smile was as sharp as her laughter had been. "And so was Miss Everleigh, until now. Everybody's talking of it. How calm she seems. Why, she even smiles at the hostesses."

"She smiled at you long before she returned to London. You'd melted her quite thoroughly, though you didn't know it." He gave her a real smile, genuinely amused by the thought. "In the fairy tales, you would be the hero who slayed the dragon."

She crossed her arms. "Fat chance of that. I'm far from selfless."

"You'd be the second born," he said. "In the rare tales where that one wins. Fighting for your ideals."

"Ideals!" She turned away, looking over the treasures on the tables. "Money, maybe. I would fight for that."

"'Better things,'" he quoted softly. "'Beauty and honesty and honor.'"

She recognized her own words. Her face darkened as she turned back.

He did not like her reaction. The memory of the night she had spoken those words in his study, and then asked him to demand something of her . . . it lived in him like a piece of light. That it should bring such misery to her face was one of the more disquieting sights he'd ever seen, and God knew he had many to choose from.

He took a breath, thinking again of Susseby—the great grave where the house had stood. But the air smelled pure here. Clean, clear. Scented with that perfume that was not Pearson's soap, but simply her skin, and nothing else.

She was staring at him, mouth trembling. "If you see me that way, then how . . ."

"It's because I see you that way." She had shown him how to be a hero. For her alone, he could be one. "I should go," he said reluctantly.

She looked back to the tapestry, her frown less a scowl than a fight for composure. "Yes. You know the way out, Lord Palmer."

CHAPTER SIXTEEN

The night was unseasonably cold. As Lilah wrenched open the door to the back passage, she shivered. Her evening gown was cut low across her bosom and left her arms entirely bare. When she had ordered this scarlet silk, and paid dearly for the seamstress to line the skirt's brocade panels with iridescent beading, she had envisioned the liveliness of the night she would wear it—the attention she would gather, gentlemen admiring her.

She had not envisioned skulking in wait of Nick.

"Hurry," she said as he appeared in the alley. "There are guards posted."

Nick stepped inside, kicking the door shut with one polished shoe. In silence, she helped him strip off, hanging his coat and scarf on a nearby hook, tucking his hat out of sight behind a pile of umbrellas.

The pile tipped. She caught them before they could clatter to the floor.

"Steady, now," he murmured.

"Yes." She took a deep breath. Dim strains of music

filtered through the ceiling, the party well under way now. She picked up a brush and handed it to Nick. "Quickly."

People who came through the front door employed footmen to knock the dust from their hems. The rest of the world did it for themselves. Nick brushed down his sleeves, then his trouser cuffs. "Aye?"

She looked him over in the dim light. The dark dress coat was cut expertly; he used a first-rate tailor. He'd stripped off his rings, confining his glitter to gold sleeve links and a gold watch chain that snaked, gleaming, over his black waistcoat. "Yes," she said. Nobody upstairs would look twice at him. Or—no, certainly they would look. He cut a handsome figure even when rumpled, and formal wear suited him. He'd even cut his hair.

She could not resist one last attempt to change his mind. "Are you certain there's nothing else you want of me? Something—"

"Certain as the sunrise." He took her arm in a firm, steadying grip. "Lead on, Lily."

She balked. "Miss Marshall. You cannot slip up here, Nick."

His glittering gray eyes narrowed. "Mind whom you speak to. Miss Marshall."

She took another deep breath. "Right." Her uncle did not make mistakes. She could count on him for that.

She led him up the servant's stair, taking care to keep her sweeping train out of his path. What he hoped to gain by mixing with the crowd, she had no idea. But he'd wanted introductions to certain clients of the auction rooms—one of the men whose letters she'd stolen, and a few others, besides. She'd had no idea how to arrange it until this party had been announced.

As they crested the stair, the music grew distinct. Young Pete had hired a full orchestra to regale the crowd—three hundred of London's brightest lights assembled in record haste to celebrate the engagement of the year. She opened a door concealed by an arras, and Nick slipped past her.

She waited a minute longer before stepping out. He'd already disappeared, a wolf loose in the henhouse. Amazing that a trail of feathers and blood did not mark his passage.

"Lilah!" Lavender Ames swept up, grabbing her elbow. "There you are. I was looking everywhere. What kept you?"

Vinnie was too shrewd for Lilah's comfort. She'd sensed something amiss over these last few days. It was only friendly concern that motivated her. "Too much champagne while dressing," Lilah answered. "I'm a bit dizzy."

"Well, you know the cure for that—another glass!" Laughing, Vinnie pulled her down the hall, into the refreshment room. A grand banquet would be laid at one o'clock; until then, guests grazed on platters of oranges and cakes, tiny French bonbons, and shrimp on ice. The staff had worked overtime, planning in days what usually required weeks.

Lilah accepted a glass of wine and then drifted away from Vinnie to the archway that opened into the ballroom. The scene looked familiar from a dozen other parties at Everleigh's: the men in uniform black; the blondes in pastel tulle and lace, the brunettes in richer, vivid hues. If only she could remember how *she* usually felt at such events—how she comported herself; how she smiled. She felt as wooden as a puppet tonight.

It took a minute to spot Catherine Everleigh. She stood at the top of the room beside her new fiancé, resplendent in an emerald gown, receiving compliments from the dozen guests encircling them.

Naturally, Palmer lifted his eyes just as Lilah allowed her glance to shift to him.

Her heart constricted as they stared at each other. Could he divine, by her face, the tumult battling through her? In its physical force, unhappiness was not so different than desire. But it weighed far more heavily, a leaden pressure in her chest. Of late, breathing seemed the trick to master—to say nothing of getting out of bed in the morning, knowing she must report to Miss Everleigh, who seemed unusually peaceful and gentle-tempered.

Everyone had remarked on the change—even Susie Snow, whom Miss Everleigh had greeted in passing yesterday. "Love is truly a power," Susie had said last night, rolling her eyes as she flopped into bed.

So it was. It blinded everyone else in this ballroom, Lilah prayed, to the long look she shared with Palmer now. His expression revealed nothing. But the force and directness of his gaze, as it moved slowly down her, made her suddenly hot, and far too miserable to remain here.

She turned away—and smacked directly into her uncle, who steadied her with a hand at the small of her back.

"Just what he expects," Nick said gently. "You think he'll thank you for helping him? We're servants to his kind, whether or not we draw a wage."

She sidestepped to be free of his touch. "It doesn't matter. You offered a bargain. I've kept my end of it."

"Of course you did. *We* don't welsh," he said. "You can't say the same for them."

She had heard this speech already. Her naïveté was a sore disappointment to him. He'd not raised her to be the kind of girl to lose her head. "Did you find your men?"

"Aimsley isn't here."

"I slipped his name into the invitations. He intended to come." She forced herself to resume her survey of the ballroom, forbidding herself to look in Palmer's direction. But of course, Aimsley made that impossible. "There—top of the room, by the . . . couple." Catherine Everleigh was glowing.

"Where?"

"By the orchestra screen." Mr. Aimsley, a member of the Municipal Board of Works, had a shock of gray hair, and a reputation among young girls. "He's got a debutante on his arm."

Nick's slow smile looked very satisfied. "Amy's got him around her little finger, doesn't she?"

"Amy?" Lilah studied the young woman, a pretty redhead. "You know her?"

"Very well," he said.

Amy wore the white muslin and the bashful, head-ducking smile of a girl raised in Mayfair. "She's good."

Nick cast her an odd look. "I don't waste my time on anything less." He touched her elbow lightly. "You remember that, Lily."

Why, he was trying to encourage her. She managed a faint smile. Better than wallowing in misery. "What do you want of Aimsley, anyway?"

"Oh, this and that." He returned his attention to his prey, the slight smile on his lips a fine facsimile of well-bred boredom. "It's a wonder, Lily, what laws these fools cook up. Put a cramp in an honest man's plans, I tell you."

She snorted. "Then I can't imagine they trouble you at all."

He offered her a wry grin. "Aye, well." He tossed back his champagne as though it were plain ale. "I might surprise you yet."

"There you are!" Susie Snow pushed squarely into their conversation, her color high as she sketched Nick a pretty curtsy—canting low enough to show her décolletage to full advantage. As she rose, she offered him a flirtatious smile. "Introduce us, Miss Marshall."

Susie never had been able to resist a handsome face. "Mr. Nicholas Shay, of Manchester. Mr. Shay is in textiles. Mr. Shay, may I present one of our hostesses—"

"Miss Sue-Ellen Snow," said Susie, simpering. "But I promise, I'm not frosty in the least."

"What a pity," Nick said, sliding effortlessly into an upper-crust drawl. He'd required no tutor to learn it; he had a natural ear for accents, which Lilah had always envied. "I rather like getting nipped."

Susie's eyes widened in delight. Lilah spoke into Nick's ear. "Don't approach Aimsley until he's away from Palmer." Then she walked away, leaving him to amuse himself with Susie. Blood and feathers, indeed.

Throngs gathered around the dance floor, chatting idly. "Tremendous match for her," Lilah heard a woman remark. "Palmer, of all men!"

A gentleman replied, his envy plain. "Oh, I would say the bargain is fair. I've never seen the Ice Queen smile before. Quite fetching."

"Yes, you've already pointed that out. But why the rush? You don't think—"

"Bother that. I only want to know, how the devil did he manage it? Even the Prince of Wales couldn't—"

"It is called *charm*, Stanley. Pity you don't have an ounce of it."

Miss Everleigh had warned her once against eavesdropping. Lilah would have been glad to retire to some quiet room to wait out the party, but with Nick on the loose, it felt too risky. Fear thrummed quietly through her, a low, unsettling fever. He could still undo her, if he wished. It would only take a few words—to Susie, perhaps.

"Beautiful couple," someone else said in passing.

"Isn't she lovely? I never thought—"

Lilah was standing by one of the small salons. The door stood closed, for the Russian wares had been removed in preparation for auction, and the curators had yet to arrange the exhibition to follow.

"Just look at them, I imagine they'll be the toast of the—"

She opened the door and stepped inside. Shut the door soundly and exhaled. "Burned toast," she muttered.

The empty room amplified the sound of her voice. She allowed herself a slight smile. A pity, indeed— Stanley had no charm, and she had no wit.

Take hold of yourself. Nick was right; she'd been raised to do better than this. To have more *pride* than this. She crossed her arms, pacing a small circle in the echoing room. Why should she be the only one to suffer? She would go outside, find a man to flirt with. She would show Christian that his fiancée was not the only woman in the room who—

The door opened. She wheeled. Christian stepped inside. "What the hell is he doing here?"

She stared at him. His impassivity had fractured in recent minutes. He looked furious, flint-jawed, vibrating with rage. He looked *beautiful*. That evening suit fit him like a glove. "Who do you mean?"

"Do not play the idiot. Your *fence*."

"Keep your voice down," she said quickly. "That door doesn't lock."

He cast a glowering glance around the room, then took her by the arm and dragged her into the same curtained alcove where she had once, so long ago, lectured an incompetent pickpocket. "Why is he here? You were done with that business!"

She laid her hand over his, her intention to push him away. But the shock of his skin, the warmth of his hand, riveted her. "Is that any of your concern?"

His glance fell to where she touched him. His nostrils flared. "You have a talent for trouble, don't you? I should have packed you off. Let you stew with my mother."

Her heart skipped a beat. Had he truly entertained that possibility? "But why? I'm a stranger to you." She stroked her thumb over his knuckles, and was rewarded by the way his mouth tightened as he looked down into her eyes.

"Get him out of here," he said very softly.

"You no longer command me."

He grabbed her chin. "Will you gamble on that?"

Delight coursed through her. Yes, *this* was what she'd needed—his attention, his undivided focus.

She shrugged, letting him see how immune she was to intimidation. "Call for the guards, then. Have him thrown out yourself."

"Yes." He released her and pushed aside the curtain. "I think I will."

"But—" She waited for him to turn back. "That's my uncle."

"Your . . ." He stared at her as though weighing whether or not to believe her. Nobody ever expected Saint Nick to be so young.

"Yes, that's right," she said. "My uncle. And if you called the guards down on him, he might be forced to say how he got inside. That would be very inconvenient, since I was the one who admitted him."

His eyes narrowed. Such a dangerous look. "What are you about, Lily?"

"Lilah," she corrected. "Better yet, *Miss Marshall.* We are strangers, are we not? Indeed, what do you care for my convenience? Go ahead; summon the guards."

He let the curtain drop shut. "I told you," he said. "I told you I did not want him involved. I told you to keep yourself out of this!"

"And I am." She shrugged. "I will not tell you that Nick has already turned up three solid leads in Bethnal Green. Is your Russian graying? Built like Napoleon?"

He swore, then pressed his hands together against his mouth. Diamonds as small as pinpricks glittered in his crisply starched cuffs. "You have a taste for death," he said. "Is that it?"

"I have a taste for you."

He stepped toward her, crowding her against the wall. She lifted her chin, drinking in every detail of him—the glimmer of his oncoming stubble. The shadow in the bow of his upper lip, where it joined his sharp philtrum. The amber striations in his honey-colored eyes.

"I expected better of you," he said very softly. "You are wiser than this."

She was disappointing men left and right, it seemed. "Yes, I'm quite a dolt. I would like to help you stay alive." She offered him a half smile. "Very indecent of me, really, taking such an interest in another woman's betrothed."

"You think this is a game?"

"No." She looked him over. "Were it a game, you would look far less imposed upon. Or is it indifference?"

He stepped into her. The full pressure and weight of his body crushed her into the wall; she was forced to turn her head aside.

"Do you feel that?" he asked softly in her ear.

She did. Through the layers of cotton and silk, wool and cashmere, he was hardening.

"That is not indifference," he growled.

The success of her ploy thrilled her on some primal level. Her body wanted to loosen, to part, to yield—here, behind a curtain, in an unlocked room adjoining the crowd. "That's lust," she managed. "Hardly rarer than indifference. Why, errant fiancés are the lifeblood of this place. Why else do all the men buy jewelry, but to apologize?"

His mouth touched her ear. "Is that what you want? For me to fuck you, right here?"

The thought swam through her like the finest vintage Château Lafite Gilet had ever produced. "Would you?"

"Yes." He pulled her face around to his. "And then, Lily, I might as well put a half-emptied gun to your head, and spin the chamber before I fired. It would be one and the same."

"I know that game," she said. "Funny enough, I believe it's Russian."

He cursed and shoved away from her. "You are worth more than this. Whatever it took to persuade your uncle—" He paused, spearing her with a blazing look. "What was it? What was his price?"

"Not so much."

He took her face in his hands, gripping hard. "Whatever it was, you are worth more. More than his sorry hide, and certainly worth more than—"

"You?" She laid her hands over his, holding them there. "Maybe so. Maybe you're the fool here. Where I come from, we know better than to scorn a friend's help."

"You are not my goddamned friend."

"Then what am I?"

His kiss was savage. Deep, furious, a claiming that she welcomed with lips and tongue and teeth. He slammed her against the wall, and she hooked her arms around his shoulders to hold him there, kissing him back, the beading on her gown digging into her flesh, silk rustling between them. He cursed and ripped free of her.

"This is done," he bit out. "Done, do you hear me? If you won't see reason, then that bastard will." He turned on his heel and stalked out.

God in heaven. Did he mean to confront Nick? She loosed a shaking breath, then knocked her skirts into place and hurried after him.

Christian's long legs outpaced hers. Heads turned as she flew past, trying to catch up with him. From the corner of her eye, she saw Miss Everleigh take notice, but she could not afford to slow. She must catch him before he found her uncle.

In the hall, she cast off all regard for witnesses and lunged to grab his elbow. "Please, you—"

He shrugged her off. He had spotted Nick ahead, turning away from one of the men on the list. That man, Mr. Morris, looked pale and distressed, and made a quick exit down the grand staircase for the lobby.

That left Nick alone in the hall. He saw them coming. He faced Christian squarely, and smiled.

"Why, if it isn't Lord Palmer! Fancy meeting you here." His glance flicked to Lilah, who frantically shook her head and waved for him to follow Morris down the stairs.

He ignored her. Of course he did. He had never backed away from anybody.

"You do not belong here," Christian bit out.

"Not in public!" She wrested a pin from her hair and picked the lock on the nearest door—a small room stocked with odds and ends, chairs and crates of candles. "If you must—"

Nick waved toward the door with a mocking flourish. "If the good Lord Palmer wishes it." He walked through the door. Christian stalked after him.

She followed, pulling the door shut. "This isn't necessary," she said. "Christian, I tell you, he means only to help!"

"Go, Lilah." Christian kept his eyes locked on her uncle, who hooked his thumbs in his pockets and fell into a slouching posture, his half smile speaking a taunt. "You needn't be here."

"Such concern for her." Nick *tsked*. "One would almost imagine you cared."

"I'll be damned if you manipulate her again."

"Pot preaching to the kettle, I think." Nick tilted his head toward Lilah. "Remind me, Lily, how you earned back my letters?"

"I told you—"

"The letters you blackmailed her to steal?" Christian spoke very coldly. "Great care you take with your kin, O'Shea."

Nick laughed. "Aye, and you lot talk a fine game, no doubt about it. Much lip service to high ideals. Meanwhile you're rolling in it. Easy to judge, from on high."

Christian made a noise of disgust. He pulled open the door. "Get out, or I'll have you thrown out."

She braced herself, for she knew that reckless look on Nick's face. He was done suffering disrespect. "Now, that you won't do," he said in a soft, controlled voice. "That is . . . unless you want me to take Lily along."

"I'll go," Lilah said quickly. "If that's what it takes—"

"I would sooner send her to hell."

Nick's brows lifted. "This is the bloke you want me to help, Lily? Quite grateful he seems."

"Nick." Had these men been dogs, their hackles would have been raised. "Please. You have a cooler head than this." She turned to Christian, whose murderous gaze still fixed on Nick. "Someone will hear. Is that what you want? For us to be discovered here, together? Nick—" She swallowed. "Just go. Please."

"Not yet." Nick sidestepped around her, his eyes locked on Christian. "I've still got a few people to see in that ballroom. In an hour, maybe."

Christian shut the door with ominous care. "You have no friends here."

"Oh, I've got one or two. But I'm not sure what to make of my niece right now. She's clearly got some poor taste, lifting her skirts for the likes of *you*—"

Christian backhanded him. The cracking blow sent Nick sprawling into the crates. Lilah cried out and scrambled forward to help her uncle up. "Please," she said, though she knew it was useless; he would not listen now. "*Think*—"

He stepped around her and drove his fist into Christian's face.

They went down in a brawling heap. As they rolled, she leapt clear, her hands at her mouth to trap a hysterical sound.

They were well matched. Too much so. Grappling, they staggered together to their feet, neither gaining purchase. They would kill each other before this was over. Nick drew back his fist—

The door flew open. It slammed into Nick and sent him staggering sideways.

Miss Everleigh gasped, then stepped inside and closed the door. "What is going on here?"

Panting, Nick wiped his mouth with the back of his wrist. The sight of blood on his cuff seemed to amuse him. He shoved himself slowly up the wall to his full height, a showy, provocative move that made Miss Everleigh take one startled step away from him.

He made a low, amused noise. A click of his tongue. "Easy, darling. I won't bite *you*."

She shot an alarmed look at Lilah. "I am calling the guards." She turned for the door, but Nick slammed his palm against it.

"Your assistant won't like that," he said.

Christian growled. Lilah caught his elbow. "Stop it," she hissed. "Both of you."

"Well, Miss Marshall?" Nick was smiling at her employer. "Won't you introduce us? I've long wanted to meet this pretty thing."

Miss Everleigh drew herself to her full height. "Who is this man?"

"Nobody," Lilah said miserably. "He's leaving."

Nick cast her a sharp glance. "I'm not done here yet."

"You're bloody." She touched her mouth to show him where. "You can't go back into the ballroom."

"You have five seconds," Christian said coolly.

Nick turned to face him, looking amused. "Says who?"

"No," Lilah snapped into the gathering weight of their silence. "Yes, Nick, you must go—or *I* will call the guards!"

He glanced toward her. "Breaking the bargain, then?"

She took a deep, miserable breath. "Yes."

"Oh ho," he said. "Very well. Gives me the chance I'd been wanting." He turned for the door—but instead seized Miss Everleigh's hand. With a flourish he bowed over it, kissing her knuckles as she gaped at him. "Nicholas O'Shea at your service, miss. Admirer of your fine good looks, and uncle to your deeply confused assistant, Lily Monroe, who once assisted *me*. Despite her current bafflement, she's a girl of great wit, I think you'll agree. For certain, I can't think of another impostor clever enough to worm into your service." He chucked her chin to close her slack jaw, then offered her a wink. "God knows many will have tried."

Lilah sagged back against a crate. A hand closed over her arm, a steadying grip. Christian's. She could not look into his face. She could not look at Miss Everleigh, either.

"The devil take you," she said to her uncle.

He shook his head. "The devil prefers lies, Lily. And if this lot dislikes your truth so much, they're not worth the bother. You come home where you belong. Not a person in Whitechapel won't welcome you."

He let himself out. The sound of the latch seemed to echo. Small click. Sound of a guillotine dropping.

She squared her shoulders and made herself look at her employer. Miss Everleigh was staring elsewhere—at Christian's hand on her arm.

Lilah jerked away.

A line formed between the woman's pale brows. "You will meet me in my office, Miss Marshall." She turned on her heel and left.

Silence settled, pure and deep—the hush after a terrible accident. Or before one.

She rounded on Palmer. "There," she said. "Now you've done it. No better than Nick!"

"Lily," he said gently, but she shoved him away when he stepped toward her.

"You're not the only one who knows how to fight." She spat the words. "Will serve me well, when I'm back in Whitechapel."

"That won't happen," he said flatly.

Some toxic stew was bubbling up inside, anger and panic and disbelief intermixed. Nick had done it now. Christian had ensured it. "You said we weren't friends? I guess you meant it. You didn't care for a moment what your brawling would cost *me*."

"He has no power over you now," he said sharply. "The truth is out. You're free of him."

"Was that your plan?" Her laughter sawed, jagged pieces in her throat. Nick had been right about him, in a way. He stood before her, tall and beautiful in a suit that would cost a working man a year's wages, arrogantly oblivious to the wreckage he and her uncle had just made of her life. "You can't solve anything."

"Lily—"

She started for the door, but he grabbed her elbow. She didn't fight this time. All the fight had left her. "Call me Lilah, then." Her voice sounded funny. Rough. "I might as well enjoy it one last time."

"Enjoy it?" He paused a long moment. "Do you prefer that name?"

What a strange question. She stared at the door. "I did. I thought it more elegant."

"Whereas I rather prefer Lily." She felt his hand brush her face. The touch was tender. Soothing. The way one might stroke the face of a feverish child.

She turned her head away. "I must go speak with her."

"And then we'll leave," he said. "I'm taking you to my family."

The room grew blurry. She blinked very rapidly, till it came back into focus. She would not cry. That would be childish indeed. "What point? I'll be safe enough." She blew out a breath. "Besides, how would you explain me to your mother? You're engaged to someone else."

"It doesn't matter," he said.

She turned to him on a deep breath. "But I won't go. Because you *are* marrying Catherine Everleigh. Aren't you?"

He gave her a long, inscrutable look. "I could take the choice out of your hands."

"Yes. You could be just like Nick, if you wanted. You've already made a fine start tonight."

His face darkened. "Very well. Then she'll keep you on. I'll make certain of it."

If he meant that to comfort her, then he was an even greater fool than she. "Don't bully your future wife for my sake," she said, and had the satisfaction of seeing him flinch before she left.

*   *   *

Lilah had braced herself for a torrent of accusations. But as she stepped into the office, she was startled by Miss Everleigh's first words.

"I asked you." The woman paced in a tight circle, causing layers of taffeta to froth and crunch. "I asked you if you loved him. You said *no*. Did you not?"

Lilah nodded.

"So I will not take the blame for this mess. I will not undo it. I require a husband. He promised not to interfere with my business. And my brother won't dare cross me. Not as Palmer's wife."

Thrown off guard, Lilah said softly, "I imagine not."

"So I won't break this engagement." Miss Everleigh pivoted to face her. "I will marry him."

"Yes."

"But . . ." Miss Everleigh's mouth twisted. "You do love him. Don't you?"

"It makes no difference."

"No. It doesn't. Not now." A pause. "Oh, why didn't you tell me *then*?"

Lilah smiled, though she felt no humor. "You said it yourself, once. The butcher or the clerk—those are my choices. I must not aim above my station."

"There would be no *aiming* required on your part!" Miss Everleigh pressed a hand to her mouth. "I heard what he said! I saw how he—" She shook her head, then fell into the chair behind her desk. "No. You're right, of course. It would be a terrible mésalliance on his part."

"No doubt."

"Yet would it matter?" She yanked her shawl from her shoulders, kneaded it furiously. "Palmer could get away with murder, if he liked. The public worships him! Why, he could marry an East End factory girl, and they would only . . ."

Lilah saw her register her mistake. "A girl of my background, do you mean?"

She had never witnessed her employer at a loss for words. But suddenly Miss Everleigh could not meet her eyes. "Is it true, then? What he said? That dreadful man? I think . . . I think I recognized his name."

Lilah sighed. "Yes. From the newspapers, no doubt. Nick O'Shea is my uncle."

"Your uncle!" She pulled her shawl to her chest in a convulsive recoil. "Why, he was so . . . So pert! So forward! A more ill-bred man I've never met!"

"Probably not," Lilah agreed. "If it's any consolation, I think he meant his compliments to you."

Miss Everleigh blushed. "Very odd compliments, if so." She hesitated, looking at Lilah in open bewilderment. "Nicholas O'Shea. Doesn't he run some . . . illegal house of cards?"

"Among other things."

"And you . . . worked for him there?"

"No." Lilah sat down across from her. "But everything he said was true." She would give her uncle the credit: he'd chosen his words very carefully. His brand of honor was not, perhaps, the kind that Miss Everleigh would recognize, but in his own twisted way, he adhered to a code. "I did assist him, though. The activities were often illegal."

"Well." Frowning, Miss Everleigh smoothed the shawl across the desktop. For a moment she appeared lost in the pattern it presented. "That is very . . . But you don't *still* break the law?"

"No." Lilah cleared her throat. "Not recently, miss." As long as one was very conservative in one's definition of *recently*.

Miss Everleigh spoke to the shawl. "I should sack you, of course. That is the . . . proper thing to do."

"I expect nothing else."

Miss Everleigh took an audible breath. "Have you ever lied to me about other things? Things aside from your name?"

"Yes," Lilah said. "I told you I did not answer to the viscount. But I did then. He knew of my past. He had caught me in a compromising situation. And he used me to pry into your business."

"Because of the Russian man."

"Yes."

Miss Everleigh nodded slowly. "What did Palmer use to persuade you?"

"I took something from your brother. Letters from his associates on the Municipal Board of Works." She added in a rush, "It was the only time I have broken the law since I joined Everleigh's. But my uncle threatened to expose me if I didn't get the letters for him."

"You stole from Peter?" Miss Everleigh struggled to contain her smile, but failed. "Really?"

Lilah nodded.

"But . . . only once?"

"Yes."

"And you did it to . . . keep your uncle happy."

"I knew I could not keep my position here if he told you the truth about my past."

Miss Everleigh picked at the fringe on her shawl. "It's really so important to you, to work at Everleigh's?"

Lilah spoke honestly. "It was always my dream to live

decently. As for how I did it . . . I was happier as your assistant than as a hostess. I truly did aim to make a career for myself. But either position would have been preferable to working for my uncle again." She sighed. "And I knew that would be the only choice remaining to me, if I were exposed by him."

"But how awful," Miss Everleigh murmured. "What a wretched predicament."

The sympathy surprised Lilah. But she knew better than to hope. She merely shrugged.

Miss Everleigh shoved her shawl aside. "So. Does he mean to help, your uncle? With this Russian idiot?"

"No idiot, I think. More's the pity. He's a danger to you, miss."

"So Palmer says. But a man like your uncle . . ." Miss Everleigh cleared her throat. "He must have a good deal of experience in dealing with brutes."

"Palmer will not take his help."

Miss Everleigh sputtered. "Palmer is mad! What does *he* know of such matters?"

Lilah bit her tongue. But this show of ignorance grated unbearably. "Lord Palmer is hardly clawless."

"No, no, of course not. But honorable men, raised decently, can hardly begin to understand the criminal . . ." Miss Everleigh colored. "The criminal mind. Not your kind of mind. But the true, hardened, criminal mind."

This conversation suddenly struck her as blackly humorous. "You needn't spare my feelings. It's all right. I won't be offended."

"But perhaps it's time someone did spare you." Miss Everleigh scowled. "Bullied by your uncle, extorted by Palmer . . . I am very sorry for it, Lilah."

Lilah sat back, astonished. "I . . . thank you."

But Miss Everleigh was not finished. "You have a fine mind. It seems a waste to cast you back into the criminal world. I fear you would excel too well there. You would become as hardened as your uncle." She offered a crooked smile. "Who knows? Perhaps you would even come to take over his business. What a sad end that would be! I think we must spare you that." On a brisk nod, she rose. "I see no reason for your uncle's revelations to travel further than they have already spread—provided, of course, that you are ready to swear off any lingering obligations to him."

Lilah's chest suddenly felt very full. Her throat as well. She barely managed to get the words out. "I feel none. I assure you. And I . . . I cannot tell you, Miss Everleigh, how much I—"

"Catherine. In private, we can be informal, can we not?" She took Lilah's hands, pulling her to her feet. "Will you do me one favor, though? I would like to speak with your uncle privately."

Lilah recoiled. "I don't think that's wise. He's—"

"I only wish to entreat his help," Catherine said blandly, "in this matter of defeating the Russian. Palmer need never know of it."

Was she mad? "You saw the words they exchanged. He won't lift a finger to help the viscount."

"Then perhaps he will help me." Catherine smoothed down her skirts. "If Lord Palmer is to be believed, I'm in as much danger as anyone."

"You don't know my uncle. He's not sentimental. That you're a woman won't matter in the slightest."

Catherine gave her a small, hard smile. "Good. I'm not sentimental, either. But I am wealthy. I think your uncle and I can reach an understanding. I can afford it."

Nick certainly appreciated a rich payday. But he'd turned down money before, when disrespect had attached to it. And Christian had certainly insulted him tonight. "I don't know if he'll listen," she said. "But . . . I suppose I can speak to him."

"No. I will deal with him directly."

Lilah recognized that stubborn look. "He can't come here. I would take you to him, but—"

"No. Give me his direction, and I will arrange a tête-à-tête. There, another lesson for you: that is French, for a private meeting involving two people." She cast Lilah a speaking glance. "And only two."

"I don't think . . ."

"Having you there would only muddle matters." Catherine snapped her shawl open; a delicate scent filled the air as the cashmere settled around her shoulders. "Or do you fear for my safety? Would he molest me, do you think?"

"No," Lilah said slowly. Then, recalling the scene in the storeroom, she revised her opinion. "Not unless you . . . requested it."

It was a night of spectacles. Catherine Everleigh blushed and ducked her head, but could not quite hide her smile.

CHAPTER SEVENTEEN

here was a small wedge of grass, barely a proper park, that sat diagonal from Everleigh's, bounded off from the pavement by a black iron fence. The property had, for several decades, been the subject of an ongoing lawsuit, its rightful possession disputed by the owners of lots to left and right. At one time, in a spiteful gesture, one of these disputants had installed a bench on the grass, and a plaque inviting passersby to sit and dwell at leisure on the fruits of injustice.

It was from this bench that Lilah watched the carriages queue at the curb, disgorging well-heeled men and women in receipt of invitations to the auction of "A Collection of Russian Antiquities and Treasures, Including Rare Coins, Enamels, Prints, Metalwork, and Diverse Other Curiosities."

She had not been invited. All of the Everleigh Girls had been given a holiday, much to their amazement. Vinnie and Maisy had asked Lilah to join them on a tour of the zoo, to be followed by a late luncheon at Mott's, with champagne and oysters. By now, they were probably half-sozzled, and surrounded by gentlemen willing to fund their way to drunk.

A small part of her regretted having declined their company. She might be sitting with them now, laughing as she drowned her cares in wine.

But the laughter would have been false. And it would take more wine than the world possessed to douse these cares that churned through her as she watched the footmen—strangers, replacements for Everleigh's ordinary staff—pull closed the heavy double doors after the last of the guests.

She could not imagine what Catherine had told her brother, to account for the upheaval in the usual routine. The presence of the czar's man, perhaps, had persuaded him that extra measures of security were fitting. It was all speculation: she knew nothing. Catherine and Christian had come up with some plan together, for all she knew. She prayed the precautions would suffice, sealing the auction rooms into an impenetrable fortress that Bolkhov could not penetrate without being discovered. When the doors opened again in two hours, she would rise to her feet in relief, and walk away grateful.

And then, only then, would she allow herself to burn as she dwelled on this image of Catherine and Christian conferring, making plans to which she would never again be privy, speaking in the hushed, intimate tones of a man and his future wife.

A passerby tipped his hat, then looked startled. She realized she was scowling, her fingers shredding the stray leaf she'd plucked up from the bench. She glared at him, causing him to step a little more quickly down the pavement. It was not her job today to please gentlemen. She was on holiday.

All of London was on holiday, it seemed. The sun shone with great, balmy force on the families traipsing by, laden with baskets from market. Young ladies of that enviably middling rank—with enough coin to spare for shopping, but no great station that required a chaperone's guard—strolled arm in arm. Their laughter sounded happy, and the sound drove her to her feet, restless and miserable.

From that vantage, she finally saw the smoke. It curled in a thin dark ribbon from the building that neighbored Everleigh's.

The weather was too fine to build a fire. And she had never seen chimney smoke so concentrated and dark—not even on the coldest days of winter.

Her feet carried her across the road. Fear was usually a cold hand on her spine, nudging her away from danger. But now it prodded her forward. Friends did not abandon each other. She must find some way to help.

There was no hope achieving entry through the guards at the front. But there was a high window that looked out onto the back alley, to provide light to the receiving room. Six feet off the ground—but there was always a carriage block nearby. The window was kept locked, but what lock had ever kept her out?

The auction room was crushed. No chairs, no room for reckless elbows or a misplaced cough. Men jostled into the paintings hanging from the walls, calling out their bids with reckless abandon. As the price mounted, so did the clamor, though it was assuming a quarrelsome edge near the doorway, where a servant in livery was shouldering his way into the crowd.

Christian met him halfway, angling his head to allow for a private word.

"Smoke outside," the man said into his ear. "Next building. No other sign of trouble."

Catherine was suddenly at his elbow. "What is it?"

He took a deep breath. The air was clean. The view out the window showed blue sky. "Ashmore's on it?"

"Yes, sir."

Catherine pulled his elbow. "What's going on?"

"Nothing yet." Christian watched the window. The first drift of smoke now edged into view. Not so thick; a clogged flue might disgorge that dark cloud.

But whatever had started to burn suddenly found new impetus. A sizable cloud of smoke spread upward. And then—

An explosion rocked the room.

Screams. A sparkling shower of glass. The great window had shattered inward. Bidders shoved and pushed out of their seats, shedding shards. He pulled Catherine against the wall, turning his body to make a shield for hers as bidders shoved past. She fought his grip. "Let them pass!" he yelled into her ear. Shoulders and fists pummeled him as men scrambled for the exit.

She subsided, permitting him to twist and look toward the door. Men were trampling each other, stepping on their fellows to escape. Somebody wrestled the other door open—he glimpsed Ashmore's face before the crush forced him out of view. The crowd, given new egress, began to thin.

Catherine ripped out of his grip, running to stand beneath the great drapes. Firelight washed over her pale hair, glittered over the shards littering the carpet. The neighboring building belched flames.

"God's sake!" Peter Everleigh was yelling from his position at the rostrum. "Shut the curtains! Block it out!"

Embers were raining into the room, great burning chunks of paper carried over by the breeze. They floated through the shattered window, landing to smolder on the carpets.

One ember caught in Catherine's skirts. Christian slapped it free. The blow broke her daze; she dropped the drapes and lifted her hem high, stamping on scattered embers. "Help me! Peter! Put it out!"

But her brother had ducked out of the room.

"Come!" Christian grabbed her arm. "You can't stay here."

"Not until I've put them out!"

Patches of the carpet were smoking. He ground one beneath his heel as she hurried from spot to spot, stamping out the others. But more were falling by the moment. These efforts were useless.

He seized her by the waist and bodily carried her into the hall. From below came great shouts and thumps, the crowd forcing its way out. "Listen!" he said, as she fought to free herself. "Do you hear the bells?"

She froze. "The Fire Brigade."

"Yes. They're coming. You can't help now." He dragged her into a quick walk down the corridor. Scattered along the floor were handkerchiefs, pens, small slips of paper, catalogs advertising the wares. Bolkhov must still be next door. That explosion had been dynamite, which required a man to light the fuse.

"They must save it," she muttered. "I will not let it burn!"

"They will. Keep walking."

"Let go." She hauled her skirts well clear of her ankles. "The building is stone. We've sand and axes stationed on every floor. A direct connection to the main water line. Do your men know—"

"Yes," he said. "They do. They have the plans."

This answer seemed to satisfy her. They hurried in silence to the stairs. At the landing, he caught sight through the window of movement in the next building. He paused to count the floors. When he turned again toward Catherine, she was gone.

Lilah cursed. She was stuck halfway through the window, her torso resting atop a crate that stood against the wall. She had to pull herself up onto it. *You can do this.* The smell of smoke was growing stronger. *You must.* On a great groaning effort, she stretched out and caught the far edge of the crate. *Yes.* Slowly she dragged herself upward. Dratted bustle caught on the window frame, and then—

Free. She hoisted herself onto hands and knees, pausing to find her balance. The ground was eight feet below now.

The door flew open. Catherine dashed by, ash smeared across her cheek, her eyes wild. She went straight to the gate, fumbling a key into the padlock that held the bar shut.

"Catherine! Help me down!"

Catherine encompassed her predicament in one frantic glance over her shoulder. "It's on fire," she said. "The fire brigade is coming. I have to open the gate for them!" The padlock yielded. She threw down the keys, then put her shoulder beneath the bar, lifting it aside. As she pulled open the wide door, bright sunlight fell in squares across her, segmented by the iron grate that must be raised.

Catherine seized the bars, straining to lift them. The bells sounded very loud now. The brigade was turning into the lane, Lilah thought. "Let me help!"

With an enraged grunt, Catherine let go. "It's too heavy." She turned, sweeping a narrow glance across the room.

"That smaller crate." Lilah pointed. "Shove it over." She could make the leap in stages.

Catherine threw herself against it, moving it by inching degrees toward Lilah. "It—can't—burn," she panted.

"Stop there." A foot away. She could make that jump. She gathered her skirts in great handfuls as she shifted onto her feet. "Stand back." Deep breath. *Go.*

She landed heavily on the crate, splinters piercing her palms. Five feet to drop now.

"Hurry," Catherine said.

Lilah lowered herself onto her belly and wriggled her legs clear of the crate. Then, on another breath, she dropped to the ground.

Catherine steadied her, then pulled her over to the grate. "Together," she said, as Lilah took hold of a bar. "One, two—"

Three.

The grate scraped upward. A foot of clearance. Another foot. "Stop," Catherine said, and got down on her hands and knees, wriggling her way out into the lane. Lilah clambered after her.

"You!" Catherine was running down the rutted lane toward a steam engine. Too late—the last of the battalion disappeared into the other building. "Wait! Come back!"

A man stepped out from behind the steam engine. Another battalion—Lilah could just make out the second vehicle. She put her fingers in her mouth and whistled. "Oi! We need your help!"

He shoved his helmet back, then broke into a run toward them. Catherine's steps slowed. "There's fire," she yelled. "Fire in the—"

He reached into his heavy jacket and pulled out a truncheon.

No. *A pistol.*

Catherine jumped backward—too late. He caught her around the throat, spinning her so the pistol pressed to her temple. "You," he said to Lilah. "Come here. Or she dies."

"Are you awake? Lilah!"

Catherine's voice drew her out of darkness. She opened her eyes, disoriented. Her jaw throbbed. Dizzy. A single shaft of light spilled from a small window somewhere behind her. Wooden wall, five inches from her face. Bags to her right, mounded along the wall— hay, by the itch in her nose. Rough floorboards, splinters digging through her skirts.

She took a sharp breath, then nearly gagged at the stench. Wet animal.

"Please," Catherine whispered. "Say something, if you're awake."

She couldn't move. They were roped waist to waist, Catherine's back pressed against hers. "I'm awake."

"Oh, thank God!"

"Premature," Lilah muttered. Premature to be feeling grateful. "Where are we?"

"Spitalfields, I think. I spotted the church as we passed."

She'd seen more than Lilah had. Bolkhov had bound their wrists, then roped them to each other. Put them on the floor of some kind of vehicle, covered them with a blanket, and driven them . . . here. "What is this place?" The walls pressed so close. She didn't like tight spaces, but at least there was light.

"I don't know. A shed?"

"Right." A shed might be anywhere. She wished she'd gotten a glimpse of their surroundings. But when the carriage had stopped, Bolkhov had come inside with a cloth reeking of some drug.

"I'm so . . . *very* glad you're awake. You were . . . it's been an hour at least."

An hour? That couldn't be right. Seemed like only moments had passed since Bolkhov had opened the door of the coach. Lilah had thrown herself at him, hoping to fall out of the vehicle. To spill into the road where some passerby might spot them.

But tied up with Catherine, she'd not managed to move fast enough. He'd grabbed her by the hair and smashed her face against the bench. And then . . .

A sweet sickly smell. Blankness.

An hour. The absence of it touched off a deep, primal fear. Death would be like that. Just . . . nothing.

Her shiver was contagious. She felt it pass into Catherine, at her back. They both were going to die here.

No. She yanked against the ropes, and Catherine squeaked in protest. "Sorry," she muttered. "But we've got to get free. Have you got any give?"

"None. I—stop that!"

She scowled and ignored the order. "He'll hurt us worse."

Catherine's head knocked into the crown of Lilah's skull, making her wince. "I know, but . . ."

"Careful with your head." She swallowed bile. "Please." Her head seemed to be pounding worse and worse. "That drug," she said. She felt strange. So woozy. Couldn't just be the blow. "What was it?"

"Ether. Or chloroform? I don't know. He didn't use it on me. He . . ." Catherine cleared her throat. "He said he would keep me lively for the night ahead."

How steadily she spoke that awful promise. Not a single note of fear. Lilah wouldn't let herself be outclassed. "We won't be here tonight." One way or another. "Did he say where he was going?" It would be good to know how long they had till his return.

"To find Palmer." She heard Catherine swallow. "Perhaps it would be best if he caught him. Three of us could overpower him. Maybe."

"He won't bring Christian back here." She knew it in her bones. "He doesn't mean to hurt him." Not physically. Not until everyone else was dead.

She yanked against the bonds, ignoring Catherine's hiss. This was no way to die. Bound like an animal, trapped like a rat . . .

The thought triggered a strange wave of déjà vu. Her chest tightened. It wasn't dark. But the walls, pressing as close as a coffin . . . She'd been trapped like this before.

If only she'd managed to break out of the carriage! But without the use of her hands, there'd never been a hope—

Her hands. "Catherine." She spoke with her heart in her throat. "Did he take my knife?"

A brief silence. Then: "You carry a *knife*?"

She grinned, to hell with how it hurt. "I'm not as much the lady as I look. Can you reach my pocket? See if you feel it?"

The ropes tightened. Burned, then began to cut. She gritted her teeth against the pain, understanding a little better why Catherine had objected.

"Yes! Oh God above, Lilah, I can feel it—"

"Can you *reach* it?"

"I . . ." Catherine twisted hard, and the rope tightened like a vise around Lilah's ribs. Squeezed the breath from her. She fought the urge to protest—inhaling would only hamper Catherine's reach.

"I have it." Catherine spoke very flatly. "Stay still. I'm . . . pulling it . . ."

Sparks at her vision. She dared not breathe. The sparks turned red, then black. Great blots swarmed over her vision—

She dragged in a breath, and Catherine gasped. Tears came to Lilah's eyes. She'd cost them their chance. "I'm so sorry—"

"It's in my hand." Catherine was breathless, too. "I can't—can you take it? I can't unsheathe it from this angle."

Lilah sent up a silent prayer. How long had it been since she'd sat by this girl's sickbed and despaired of God? She regretted it now; she willed him to forgive her as she stretched out her fingers, grasping blindly, flexing and twisting as Catherine grunted against the crush of the ropes—

"*There*." She felt the engraved sheath. She knew this knife better than the back of her own hand. Better than her face in the mirror. "Don't move. Hold steady."

"Hurry," Catherine said softly. "The ropes . . ."

"I know." Her grip was sweaty. She pushed her thumb along the sheath. *Come free.* This knife was an old friend. *Show some love.* A gift from her father, the week before he'd died. *You're old enough now,* he'd said. *Respect this blade, and it will never do you wrong.*

The sheath yielded. "All right," she whispered. "All right. It's unsheathed. But I can't get a grip on the hilt. Can you . . . do you feel all right, trying to cut the rope?"

"*No.*" Now Catherine's voice shook. "I'll cut you."

"Do it! Just—" She froze. "Do you hear that?"

Footsteps. A cheerful whistle, drawing nearer.

"It's him," Catherine said in a low voice of dread. "We're done."

"Do it," Lilah gasped. "Catherine, cut the—"

The door shuddered. No time left. Bolkhov was opening the lock.

"Don't let him see the knife," she hissed. "And whatever you do—*don't drop it.*"

The door swung open. It was barely a door—the height of a child. Bolkhov shoved himself through in slow increments, head then shoulders, wriggling. The sight was agonizing. Were Lilah on her feet—were her hands free—it would not have taken a knife to disable him. A solid kick to his head would have done it.

He clambered to his feet. He looked like somebody's doting grandfather. Short and solid, a mane of white hair and a rosy, full face, dressed in pinstripes, with a gold watch chain snaking across his waistcoat. He ignored Lilah, pacing around her to speak to Catherine.

"Where is he?"

Heavy Russian accent. Lilah could feel Catherine

shaking. *The knife, Catherine. Don't let go.* "I don't know."

A thud. A sharp crack. Catherine cried out, toppling sideways. Lilah was dragged down with her, her shoulder striking the floor. The knife—Catherine had fumbled it. It was sliding away. Lilah scrabbled—

Her fingers closed on the blade. She choked on the stabbing pain, wrestling against instinct, fighting not to let go.

"I don't know, I don't know," Catherine shrieked. "If he's not at Everleigh's—"

They had no time for this. She was going to drop the blade. "I know," Lilah spat. "You bastard. I know where he is."

Boots thudded into her line of vision. A hand hooked in her hair, ripping at her scalp as he hauled her back to a sitting position—and Catherine along with her. But she didn't let go, damn him.

His dark eyes burned into hers, black and burning like coal. "Where?" he said.

"The House of Diamonds. Whitechapel."

He grabbed her chin. Yanked it high as he looked into her face. "You are lying."

"A stupid lie," she managed, her voice strained by the awkward angle of her throat. Her hand would be mangled. Cut clean through. "If I was going to lie, I'd make it . . . a better one. He's got a secret office. Second floor. That's where he goes."

He glared at her. "You are nothing," he said. "Nobody. You might yet live. But not if you are lying. If you are lying, I will loop your entrails from the rooftops."

"It's the truth." God help her, if her uncle was not there . . . He took note of every man who entered his gambling club, but if he did not understand what a visit from a strange Russian meant . . . "The House of Diamonds. But you'll never get inside. He has guards."

He sneered. "We will see." He raised his hand. She had just enough time to brace herself before he struck her. Bright light. *Pain.* But the bastard didn't topple her. She still had hold of the blade, a searing coal embedded in her palm, agony spearing into her bones.

He turned for the door. She spat blood in his direction as he wiggled out.

Catherine was breathing heavily. "Do you—"

"Hush," she hissed. She was waiting—straining to listen—

There came the thunk of the padlock. "We've got about thirty minutes," she said. If they were in Spitalfields, the House of Diamonds couldn't be far. "I need you to hold still."

"You still have the knife?" Catherine's voice sounded very small.

"Yes." She squeezed her eyes shut, concentrating on the delicate maneuver of inching the blade through her fingers. Pinching it between her knuckles. Sliding it as far as it would go. Starting over again. Pain didn't matter. Only the blade.

The hilt came into her palm. But dexterity was a distant dream at this awkward angle. And her blood made the grip so slippery. "I might cut you."

"Do it," Catherine said fiercely.

She groped for the space between their torsos, flicking out the blade once—twice—hit something solid, and heard Catherine's sharp breath. "Sorry," she whispered, and tried again. If not that angle, then *this* one. If not this one, then—

"Got it." She could only make twitching motions. But it was enough. The scrape of steel against rope was the sweetest music she'd ever heard. But hard going. Her wrist cramped. Blood was slipping down her fingers, befouling her grip. But the rope was giving. She felt one thread yield, then another. Then—

The rope snapped. She turned on her knees, holding out the knife with her bound hands. Catherine's face looked bad. Blood all over her mouth. This room wasn't bigger than a wardrobe. Raw wood, the floor scattered with hay. "Cut me free."

Catherine seized the knife and sawed at the ropes at Lilah's wrist—laughing exultantly as they split and fell away.

Lilah returned the favor in three short, sharp slices. Then she turned immediately for the little door through which Bolkhov had crawled.

No hinges. Padlock on the outside. She threw herself against the door. Then kicked it, as she clutched her bleeding hand.

"Together," said Catherine, hauling up her skirts. They slammed their feet in unison.

No luck.

"God above!" Catherine turned full circle. "There must be some way out of here! That window . . ."

Lilah sagged back against the wall. That window was too small. A dog wouldn't squeeze out of it.

"It's done then," Catherine whispered. "We're going to die here."

You'd need men at your back, to go into that place. So Lilah had warned him of the Whitechapel tavern. Christian understood now what she'd meant. Someone had run to fetch O'Shea. As Christian waited, the tense silence took no language to translate. Each of these men around him, nursing their drinks and never removing their eyes from him, had the look of a brawler.

The door opened, O'Shea's lanky form making a silhouette in the doorway. As he stepped inside, the dim light revealed his slow survey of the assembled gathering, then his smirk as he located Christian in the far corner.

"Slumming," he said, in a clear, carrying voice, "has caught on like wildfire, I see."

Never be too proud for friendship. Never turn up your nose. It was the hardest advice he'd ever taken. But Christian rose now, and bowed.

The audience wasn't accustomed to such courtesies. They misinterpreted it. A dozen chairs shifted. Metal scraped. Someone stepped up behind him.

"Go easy there," O'Shea said pleasantly. He walked to the bar, pausing to confer with the mute giant who'd patted Christian down to check for weaponry. The man had found none; Christian was no fool.

Slowly Christian turned toward the man behind him. *I'd prefer a cutlass. A proper handle can be useful.* But Lilah would have had difficulty lifting the cutlass this man held. Nor would she mistake it as a friendly gesture. "Step away," he said softly.

A bruised, bulbous face. An ugly smile. Over Christian's shoulder, the man must have seen some signal, for he eased off, retaking his seat.

O'Shea came strolling over, a foaming pint in his hand. Very casual, all good humor. Each of his idle footsteps on the sloping floor struck like flint against Christian's banked rage. "Fine day to pay a call," O'Shea said. "Come to beg my help?"

He took a hard breath. "Yes."

Surprise briefly showed on the man's face. Then he turned to the room at large. "Oh ho!" He extended his arms, turning right and left as though to gather his audience's attention closer. "Did you catch that, boys? The grand Viscount Palmer wishes a spot of assistance!"

The snickers sounded forced. Uneasy. Even in this part of town, even with O'Shea's protection assured them, these men understood the danger in threatening a peer of the realm.

Let him grandstand. Let him do whatever he liked. Pride, principle did not factor. "Lily said you had three leads. Was she right?"

"Ah, well." O'Shea fell into a seat, rocking it back onto its hind legs. "I thought I'd made myself clear. My time isn't for—"

"He may have Lily."

The chair landed with a thump. "What?"

Suddenly Christian was looking at a different man. No humor now. Only cold, hard focus. "She was outside the auction rooms earlier. Now Catherine Everleigh is missing. And there's no sign of Lily, either."

"Goddamned—" O'Shea rose. "A fine job you've done! Let him sweep them right from under you!"

"All in Bethnal Green, the three leads. That's what she said. Which quadrant?"

O'Shea hissed and wheeled away. "Fetch the boys," he said to the brute at the bar. "Full arms." Then he cast a sharp look over the room at large. "No harm to this one. He'll see his sorry hide out." He started for the door.

Jesus. Christian caught his breath. "You know where he is?"

O'Shea's lip curled as he turned back. "It's nowhere in Bethnal Green. Slink on home, Palmer, and let the real men—"

Time elapsed. A flipbook, pages skipped. Somehow he had O'Shea pinned against the table. A knife at his jugular. The goon at the door had not thought to check the folds of his neckcloth. Goons did not wear them.

Cold steel pressed into his own nape. Whoever was holding it barely registered. "We have no time for quarreling. Do you agree?"

O'Shea studied his face. Then gave a grim smile. "Aye. That I do."

Christian lifted away the blade. O'Shea's pale eyes flicked beyond him. "Step off, lad."

The steel retreated. O'Shea sprang to his feet. Caught up with Christian halfway to the door.

"Your Russian just dropped by my club. I sent him scurrying away." O'Shea shouldered open the door, then hooked two fingers into his mouth to sound a piercing whistle that carried down the street, turning heads. "That'll bring us mounts."

"No need. Twenty men wait on the high street. Already saddled."

"Reinforcements?" O'Shea *tsked*. "A disappointment. Next time you visit, be sure to come alone."

"Where is his base?"

"Spitalfields. Mind you, I'd no cause to care before. Hadn't given *me* any trouble. Paid his rent on time, too." As they walked, O'Shea was feeling down his jacket, opening and closing hidden pockets to catalog the weapons he carried, some of which Christian only recognized from foreign armies: throwing stars. A small stiletto. A garrote, Christ God.

"But he's crossed a line, now," O'Shea said coolly. He glanced over his shoulder, nodding in acknowledgment to the handful of men who joined their number, keeping pace a length behind.

"Your men are not to interfere," Christian said.

"Oh, I—" O'Shea paused as they turned the corner and the high road came into view. He whistled again, this time in undisguised admiration of the phalanx of men waiting, saddled and ready, their weapons openly displayed. An astonished goggle of pedestrians had retreated to the other side of the road to gawk. "Aye," he said slowly. "Won't interfere unless it's called for. No use wasting my own."

Christian lifted his hand, extending two fingers.

A brief conference. Ashmore gestured. Two riders broke from the pack, galloping up and dismounting to hand over the reins.

O'Shea put one foot in the stirrup, then paused. "*I'll* be interfering, though. Nobody messes with mine."

"*Mine*." The word ripped from Christian. "Do you understand? Yours no longer."

O'Shea lifted a black brow. "Remains to be seen. But I like the show of spirit."

That the ass could joke, even in this moment, enraged him. "Where do we go?" he bit out.

O'Shea settled into the saddle. "No name to the street." He nudged his horse out onto the road. "Follow close now."

Lilah had savaged her palm. Could barely bend her fingers. Probably wouldn't have healed properly. She'd have lived out her life with only five working fingers. Throwing hand, ruined. Oh well.

A ripping sound. Catherine had torn off a piece of her petticoats. "Let me bandage it."

Lilah held out her palm. Catherine bound it and tied a knot too tight for comfort. But comfort didn't matter much now, did it?

Catherine joined her in leaning against the wall, her mournful gaze fixed on the window. She looked slack faced, like Bolkhov had smacked the spirit out of her. Her cheek was purpling.

There was still a faint hope, though. "The House of Diamonds belongs to my uncle," Lilah said. "Maybe he'll be there. If Bolkhov draws his attention, Nick might follow him back."

"Do you think?" Catherine turned, her eyes huge in her bloodied face.

"It's possible."

Not convincing. Catherine's glance strayed toward the window again. At length, she said, "Do you suppose Everleigh's burned?"

Wasn't that just like her, to be worrying about the auction house when the prospect of her own death might have afforded sufficient concern.

But Lilah liked her for it. That stubborn focus—it wasn't ladylike. She and Catherine had more in common than she'd once imagined. "Didn't burn," she said as a kindness. What did she know? "The fire brigade was there. Everleigh's will be fine."

"Of course." Catherine frowned. Then she turned and kicked again at the door. "This place! What *is* it? That window. This strange door. What stupid architecture!"

Strange feeling, to smile in the midst of this disaster. "Even now, you're finding flaws."

Catherine blinked, then offered a faltering smile. "Architecture *is* an art, you know."

"Architecture implies a plan," Lilah said. "Buildings in these parts just get slapped up." But they always did serve a purpose.

A prickling feeling touched her. She frowned around the little shed. Focused on the bags mounded along the far wall. "Hay." She'd seen bags like that a thousand times, hauled home on the back of a costermonger's donkey.

Catherine snorted. "For what? A pig? This awful reek—"

"A goat." She looked up at the small window. Nothing to see but a brick wall bound by crumbling mortar. This structure had been shoved straight up against the tenement building.

"It's a backhouse," she realized. Had to be. That reek of goat—"Kept a donkey here." Donkeys got lonely without company. Goats were the usual choice.

"A donkey couldn't fit through that door," said Catherine.

She was right. Maybe a goat could wiggle through it. But not a donkey. Which meant . . .

Lilah slammed her palms against the wall. Slowly walked the perimeter, feeling for cracks. "A horse walk."

"What?"

"A tunnel from the tenement, to bring in the donkey." Common in crowded slums. No spare space aboveground. She swept her hands wide. "Look for a door, Catherine." But she saw none. "There has to be a passage for the donkey. It couldn't . . ."

"*The hay,*" they said in unison, and sprang forward to haul the bags away from the wall.

There it was. A door. An unlocked door! Catherine hauled it open on a happy cry.

The passage was a maw of darkness. Cold breathed out. A musty sigh of death. No donkey had been down that tunnel in ages. It was narrow as a coffin. And Catherine was stepping into it. "Come on," she said.

Oh, God.

"What is it?" Catherine turned back, scowling. "Are you mad? What are you waiting for?"

"I can't." She heard her own words, registered their absurdity. But this understanding felt very distant. Her limbs locked tight. *Move,* she told them. But her brain had broken from her body.

"What do you mean?" Catherine caught her good hand and pulled. "Lilah, he's coming back!"

Of course. She would go. She took a step—and the cold flowed over her, and the door swung shut.

Blackness.

Her breath fluttered like a panicked creature in her throat. Impossible to catch. She had to walk. It was this tunnel, or death.

But death lay ahead as well. Better to die in light than in darkness. She'd already escaped death once in a place like this. She wouldn't be so lucky again. "I can't."

"Lilah. You *must.*"

A searing pain—Catherine had grabbed her bad hand, and was squeezing.

With a guttural moan, she ripped free. The tunnel closed around her, tighter and tighter.

A fist dug into her back. Catherine shoved her forward. "Walk. Now!"

The walls scraped Lilah's shoulders. She choked on a sob.

The fist dug harder into her spine. "Keep going," Catherine muttered.

Blind. "I can't . . . see."

"You don't need to see. *I* can see. Just go."

She took another halting step, then reached back, fumbling, and found Catherine's wrist. Warm and alive.

Catherine's hand slipped into hers. "I'm here." Firm grip. Strong, for a lady. "We're getting out. We're saved. Just walk."

If they died down here, nobody would find them for weeks. Her knees quaked like aspic, each step shakier. She couldn't breathe.

"Where will we go?" Catherine's calm sounded impossible. Eerie. So normal, her voice. "Once we're out, we'll have to hide."

"Yes." Her lips felt numb. The air was poison. So cold and still. A tomb.

"Everleigh's isn't safe. And we don't know where Palmer is. Do you know a safe place?"

She had to try twice to find her voice. "I do."

"Is it nearby?"

Very near. The warm glow of the lamps, the smell of fried oysters. Every last patron loyal to Nick, and willing to fight—for Nick's niece, yes, they would. They had watched her grow up. They would defend Lily Monroe. "The safest place in the world," she whispered.

"Then keep walking," Catherine said. "Let's get there."

*   *   *

Ashmore came strolling down the street, his steps un-hurried. He tipped his hat to Christian as he passed.

That was the signal. Christian took a long breath, his eyes fixed on the turn in the road. They had cleared the street. O'Shea had that kind of power here. Curtains drawn across all the windows. No onlookers. Inside, Bolkhov's flat stood empty, no sign of the women. They had to take him alive, get the truth out of him. *No one shoots. No one.* He prayed that Ashmore's men had heeded him, and kept their fingers off their triggers.

Beside him, O'Shea tensed. "Here he comes."

A white-haired devil in pinstripes came strolling around the corner. Hands in pockets, scowling slightly, as though cataloging the items he'd forgotten to buy at market.

The sight of Bolkhov passed through Christian like a shock. Disorienting. Electric. Four years since he'd seen Bolkhov in the flesh, but it might have been a minute. At last, this rabid dog was going to be put down. Pray God it was not too late—

He closed his mind to that avenue. To every extraneous detail save Bolkhov, who marched up the steps to the tenement across the road, then pulled a key from his pocket to unlock the front door, calm as a banker returning home from the city.

"Now," Christian said.

O'Shea split off, swinging wide across the street. The plan was to flank Bolkhov on either side of the stair. But Bolkhov had fumbled his key ring, dropped it on the ground. His curse as he retrieved it came dimly through the roar in Christian's ears. Later, perhaps, he would wonder at this bizarre moment—the pedestrian nature of a madman's struggle to fit a key into a lock.

But it offered a distraction he'd not anticipated. On instinct, he abandoned the plan.

Five bounding steps. Time slowed; gravity released him. He was flying. Bolkhov was turning, but Christian descended faster. Bolkhov's throat, so ordinary. So easy to catch in a chokehold. So easy to crush.

"Not yet!" That was Ashmore. He approached, gun drawn. Bolkhov gave a full-bodied jerk, the overture to struggle—then abruptly fell still. Other men now emerged from concealment, brandishing weapons.

"Where are they?" Christian spat.

Bolkhov's laugh sounded rusty. "A surprise from you, at last."

Christian tightened his grip, and had the satisfaction of hearing the bastard wheeze. "I will choke you to death right here." *Yes.* "Or you can answer."

Men carefully stepped past Christian. "Search again, flat by flat," Ashmore told them.

"Wait!" O'Shea had stepped aside to speak with someone—a man leaning out of a nearby window. "We'll try this," he said as he bounded onto the stairs. "Seems the Russian's been messing about in the backhouse."

Bolkhov stiffened. That was all the confirmation Christian required. "Take him," he growled at Ashmore, and shoved the Russian into the barrel of Ashmore's revolver before following O'Shea inside.

No words passed between them as they strode down the hallway. O'Shea led him through a doorway into a lightless passage, cold and moist. Damp earth sank beneath their boots.

Some silent prayer was making itself known. Let there be light for her. She did not like the dark. Let there be light ahead.

A sliver of illumination. A cracked door. O'Shea shoved it open.

The backroom stank of wet hide and rotted hay. Empty. God damn it, where was she?

Shreds of rope lay scattered across the floor. Christian stooped. Piece of woven hemp, frayed and split. He felt numb. This could not be. He would not bury her.

"Christ," O'Shea whispered. He lifted a hand away from the floor. His fingertips were red with blood.

The blood seemed to expand in a violent wave, hazing over Christian's vision. When a sound came from behind, he wheeled.

"Easy," said Ashmore. He was prodding Bolkhov at gunpoint into the tight quarters.

"Stand aside." He could see only Bolkhov now. Hear only the roar. He would make Bolkhov weep before he died.

Ashmore kicked shut the door and shoved Bolkhov into the middle of the room. The Russian turned full circle, his black gaze moving from gun to gun.

"Your last chance." These words came from him. Distant, echoing, as though in a dream. "Where are the women?"

A curious smile hooked up the corner of Bolkhov's mouth. "Gone. Very clever. Too bad for you."

Christian cocked his pistol. Bolkhov lifted his chin. He had a chipped tooth, bared now in a maniacal smile.

Someone was speaking. "This rope was sawed," O'Shea was saying. "Palmer. Lily carries a knife. You follow?"

Bolkhov's smile widened. "I cut out that one's entrails," he said. "Then I chewed on her bones."

"Bloody lunatic," O'Shea muttered. "I'll leave you to it. I'm going to look—"

"Hold." Christian spoke softly. He was nothing now but murder, a moment away from blood. "This won't take a moment."

"There's no call for this." Ashmore edged into his vision. "Kit, listen to me. I'll see he rots in the darkest pit this kingdom has to offer."

Bolkhov chuckled. "He is a killer. Like me. He knows the way."

"You don't know what it does to a man," Ashmore said, very low. "To kill in cold blood."

Cold blood? He was burning up. He would take Bolkhov with him. That grin would incinerate. But first, Bolkhov would confess what he had done to Geoff, and to Lily.

Lily.

She carries a knife.

The red haze thinned. Fine details returned to him: dust floating in the light. The wrinkled sag of Bolkhov's eyelids. The looseness beneath his chin. Even madmen aged.

He'd envisioned this moment for so long. An obsession and a mantra: the words he would speak before he killed this man. The curse he would leave ringing in Bolkhov's ears before he dispatched him to hell. The fear he would put in the bastard's face, the agony of oncoming death—

But Bolkhov was still grinning. And it signified nothing. Whether he feared, whether he repented, did not matter. Only one thing mattered.

Wordless, Christian pulled the trigger.

If the gunshot made a noise, he did not hear it. He heard nothing, but saw each detail: the blood blossoming between Bolkhov's eyes. The gory spat-ter raining against the wall. The sudden slackness in Bolkhov's face. He fell to his knees, then collapsed onto the floor.

Christian turned away. O'Shea was waiting. "Let's find her," Christian said.

CHAPTER EIGHTEEN

"I quite like this public house," said Catherine.

Lilah pulled her eyes from the door. She was doing her best not to keep watch. But it was tearing at her, not knowing where Christian was. Neddie said he'd lit out with Nick shortly before she and Catherine turned up. Had they found Bolkhov? Her nerves were strung tighter than a street-musician's harp.

Catherine looked far more relaxed. Chin propped on one fist, she slouched on the bench across from Lilah, a plate of fried oysters and two half-drunk tankards before her.

The sight was sufficient to inspire brief amusement. "I think this pub likes you back," Lilah said. Had anybody told her six months ago that she'd be visiting Neddie's with Miss Everleigh, she would have laughed in their faces and then directed them to an asylum.

But once Catherine had cleaned herself up in Neddie's washroom, she hadn't wanted to go. Lilah had asked a man to ride around the auction rooms, and he'd reported back quickly: the building was dark, but he saw no damage from fire. That had set Catherine's mind at ease. She'd decided to keep Lilah company.

"It's safe here," she'd said. "And I can't bear to face my brother just yet. He'll be full of questions . . . I'll wait with you until Palmer and Mr. O'Shea come back."

Shortly thereafter, some cheeky group had sent over two tankards of ale. Catherine had grimaced awfully at her first sip, which had inspired a great round of laughter. Now the entire pub had taken it upon themselves to send fresh rounds on the regular, just to see if she'd screw up her face again.

Catherine was toying with a fried oyster, inspecting it as though in search of flaws. "This establishment seems quite successful."

Of course it was. "Nick owns it."

She raised the oyster and gave it a dubious sniff. "Is he unmarried, your uncle?"

"Nick?" The thought was ludicrous. "Some husband he'd make."

"Indeed? He's of age, and he seems well established. How many properties does he own in London?" Catherine popped the oyster into her mouth, then made an enthusiastic noise and widened her eyes.

"I know," Lilah said by way of agreement. "Nobody fries them like old Neddie. As for Nick, this public house was the first place he bought." He'd needed some place to invest his ill-gotten money. The banks would have no truck with him, back in the early days. "Used to spend all his free time here, before he opened the House of Diamonds."

"He's almost—" Catherine put a hand over her mouth, evidently startled by her own poor manners; she had not yet finished chewing. She swallowed the oyster before continuing. "He's almost a proper businessman, then."

Lilah glanced again toward the door. Neddie said Nick had known where to look for Bolkhov. It was a hop and a skip away. They should have been back by now. "Proper? No. Businessman . . . I suppose so. Among other things."

"Criminal things," Catherine said solemnly.

"Well . . ." Lilah hesitated. Nick had long since passed the point of petty crimes; the profits were too trifling for him, now. "He doesn't let the law stop him, that's for certain."

"I imagine he doesn't let anyone stop him," Catherine said. "Saint Nicholas. The King of Diamonds. A very dangerous man."

Lilah frowned. "He never crossed anybody that didn't deserve it. And he's mostly a landlord these days. Owns every building for ten streets around us."

"Really?"

Catherine's amazement touched off an uneasy realization. *Stars above. I'm defending my uncle.*

Well, but it was true, wasn't it? Nick was turning a fine profit now aboveboard, though certainly he still kept a hand in the below. And wasn't there something gratifying about putting that look on Catherine's face? Lilah's kin might not be decent folk, but nobody would ever call Nick stupid. He had more power, in his way, than the mayor.

The aristocracy of the underbelly. So Christian had once put it when trying to drive her away. "Where are they?" she muttered. "It shouldn't be taking this long."

"Trust your uncle," Catherine said serenely.

Lilah snorted. "If I've got one piece of advice, it's to mistrust him with all you're worth."

"Oh, naturally. But . . ." Catherine looked into her tankard, delicately flicking at the foam. "You said he was honorable in his own way."

"In his own way. Give Nick a plan, and he'll turn it inside out, stand it on its head, fold it in half, and leave you so dizzy that you'll end up convinced the plan was *his* idea in the first place."

Catherine's brows drew together. "So he's a skilled negotiator, then."

Lilah suddenly remembered that conversation in Catherine's office, what seemed like ages ago. She'd asked for a meeting with Nick—to do with Bolkhov, she'd claimed.

But this line of questioning didn't touch on the Russian. "Why are you so interested in my uncle?" she asked slowly.

Catherine's lashes dropped. "Well . . . I'm not going to marry Lord Palmer, Lilah."

Her throat tightened. "Is that so?"

"Yes," Catherine said serenely.

She didn't know what to say. "Can you change your mind so easily? It's bound to cause a scandal."

"In polite circles, certainly. But . . ." Catherine shrugged. "I've never had any use for mixing with fashionable society. And even if I did, I could hardly marry Palmer. He's in love with someone else, you see."

Lilah folded her lips, bit them hard. "Do you think so?"

Catherine snorted. "I shan't dignify that with a response."

Lilah tried for a smile, but it slipped right off her lips. This conversation was tempting fate. "Where *are* they?"

Catherine opened her mouth, but Neddie forestalled

her, materializing beside them to plonk another round onto the table. "From the Hooleys," he muttered, before stalking off.

Despondent, Lilah lifted her mug and took a deep breath. Catherine, who had caught on three pints ago, hurried to hoist her own tankard.

"To the Hooleys!" Lilah yelled, and the boys in the far corner grinned and took their bows.

Catherine cleared her throat. "As for your uncle—I need somebody to manage my brother, you see. He'll drive our company into the ground otherwise. And I can't trust the courts. They always favor men when it comes to matters of business."

"Is that so?" Lilah didn't feel much like talking about business. If she hadn't known that Nick would come back here first, she would have been alone right now, clutching herself and praying. She buried her nose in the foam for a sip.

The door flew open.

"So I've been contemplating another solution," she thought she heard Catherine say, but she was on her feet, staring, breathless, nothing left in her but yearning, desperate hope—

One of Nick's men came in—and there was Nick! She slammed the tankard onto the table and started toward him.

Now came a wolfish-looking man, tall and dark, whom she didn't recognize. But where was Christian? Fear crystallized like an ice blossom in her chest. Her uncle spotted her, threw out his arms, and flashed a bright grin.

"Shot the bastard dead," he said. "I might like him, after all."

She pushed past him—and the breath left her. There, in the doorway—filling it completely, tall and broad-shouldered, whole, in one piece. Hale and handsome and wild-eyed—until his gaze found her.

She put her hand to her mouth. He was safe. *Shot dead*. It was over.

"—the hell you went," Nick said.

"We saved ourselves," came Catherine's clear voice in reply. "Nobody else seemed likely to do it."

His laugh rang out. "Pints for everybody then! To women who save themselves."

Christian started for her. She sidestepped around the wolfish man, who said, "I'll take something stronger than a pint, if you've got it."

The next moment, Christian was before her. Gripping her. "Are you all right?" He lifted her bandaged hand. "You're hurt."

"No, no." With her good hand, she caught his, gripping hard, thrilled by the strength with which he squeezed her back. "I'm fine now." The words sailed out as smoothly as a spring breeze. She was fine, indeed. His face told her so. He looked lighter, unburdened, *free*.

He pulled her into an embrace. Fierce, tight hug. She closed her eyes and wrapped her arms around him.

Hoots from the far corner. The Hooley brothers, sassing as usual.

His lips moved against her ear. "I'm taking you home."

She breathed deeply of him. Gunpowder and sweat. Beneath it, always, his essence. Magic to her. "Where is that?"

He pulled away to look into her face. "My home," he

said—and then smiled slightly, as the Hooleys shrilled again. "Our home. Do you mean to argue?"

It was too delicious a moment. Launched so suddenly from fear into joy, she felt as though she were floating, giddy, already drunk. "Maybe," she said, because in Whitechapel, a girl knew her own worth. She made a man work to earn her favor.

He laughed, a beautiful rich sound, and then bent and grabbed her by the waist. Hoisted her over his shoulder.

The Hooleys went wild. She craned around Palmer's body to look. All across the room, tankards shot skyward in approval. Even Nick was smiling, while Catherine, by his side, cupped her cheeks to cover a blush.

"Ashmore," Christian said. The wolfish man turned. "See Miss Everleigh home, will you?"

"Of course."

"Not for a while yet," Catherine said brightly. "Good night, Lilah! Lord Palmer!"

Lilah lifted her hand to wave farewell. Christian caught it and kissed her wrist. As he carried her out into the night, she started to laugh.

CHAPTER NINETEEN

*L*ilah woke from a nightmare of darkness into a world of blazing light. For a disoriented moment, she thought the room was on fire. Then her vision focused. Heavy walnut furniture, varnished by age. Cream wallpaper threaded with gold. Lamps everywhere. Sconces glowing along the walls. Candelabra flickering. Candlelight everywhere.

Somebody came off a nearby chair. Christian.

He sat down on the edge of the bed, reaching for her hand with great care. Earlier, he had ordered a bath for her. Left a dressing gown that enveloped her head to toe. Then he'd rebandaged her hand while he told her of what had transpired with Bolkhov.

He'd recited the tale calmly, while taking such tender care with her wound. She'd felt sure that he would join her in bed afterward. But the day had caught up to her, or the drug. When she'd yawned, he had insisted she rest for a while—alone.

And then he had come back to watch her while she slept.

She felt strangely tongue-tied as he stroked her wrist. How unlike her. A glance at the grandfather clock showed it to be half past two. "Do you think Catherine got home?" That was a safe avenue into conversation, she thought.

He laid her hand down atop the counterpane, smoothing the fabric around it as though to clear a safe perimeter. "Ashmore—he's a friend of mine; you saw him tonight. He'll have taken her home long ago."

Ashmore. That was the Earl of Ashmore, she guessed. She had read his name in the newspapers. "I hope so," she said. "She was asking very odd questions about my uncle. Almost as though . . ." She frowned. "Well, I don't think I imagined it. She means to ask Nick for help."

He frowned as well. "That is odd." Then the frown faded into a half smile. "But who knows? You make a fine argument for looking to Whitechapel for any number of things. Help, hope, love . . ."

Her tongue felt suddenly clumsy. It took a moment to wrap around the words. "Do you think so?"

"I know so." He reached past her to adjust the pillows. "Lie back again, Lily."

That was the last thing she wished to do. Her heart was suddenly racing. "I'm not tired."

"I know. But to see you here . . ." He cupped her face, stroking her cheek with his thumb. "There's a comfort you cannot begin to imagine, seeing you here in my bed. Safe, with me. Where you belong."

How could a girl resist that blandishment? She sank back onto the pillows, beneath the warmth of the heavy quilts. "Then here I'll stay," she said softly.

He smiled. Smoothed back her hair, then leaned down to kiss her temple. Very lightly, he touched the corner of her eye. The crest of her cheek. The slope of her jaw. Brushes as light as a breath.

They tickled. She wrinkled her nose. "What are you doing?"

"Counting your freckles," he said. "You usually hide them beneath powder, don't you?"

If he would only keep touching her like this . . . she would stay here forever. "Freckles aren't ladylike."

He laughed under his breath. "Oh, I beg to differ. Everything about you is ladylike, Lily."

Her smile felt too wide for her mouth to contain. So much light in this room! She rolled over to see the full extent. Ten candelabra. A dozen more candlesticks besides. "Did you fetch all these candles?"

"You don't like the dark."

She looked back at him. "You shouldn't humor me in that. It's childish." Why, it had almost gotten her killed today. A shiver moved through her.

Perhaps he saw it. The bed sagged; he lay down next to her, putting his arm around her waist and gathering her against him. "Be childish." He spoke into her hair, his breath warming her nape. "You're done with fear, Lily. I'll light as many candles as the world can supply, if that's what it takes."

She relaxed, eyes closing. Was this love, then? To be so easily accepted. Cherished even for weaknesses. "It was never just the dark, you know. It was being trapped in it, alone."

"I will never leave you alone in it again," he said.

A lump clogged her throat. Such a proposition. It would take courage for a woman to accept such an offer, for she would come to depend on it, and if it was ever withdrawn . . . what would be left of her? Only broken pieces. "I want that promise," she whispered. "But if you make it, you'd best mean to keep it. In the eyes of the law, even."

For a moment, he did not reply. She waited, biting her lip hard. She wouldn't take back those words. She was no lady, but she'd not settle for being treated as less than one. She wouldn't live with him in sin.

His mouth touched her nape. The softest kiss. "Do you remember the dream I told you about? The dream of the tree, which I could not protect?"

"Yes," she managed. "Of course."

"That was all I wanted," he said. "Never to be the hero. Not the title, not the applause. But something of my own. Something to protect and defend. And perhaps . . ." She felt the deep breath he drew against her skin. "More than that. When I ended him today . . . it could have kept going. That rage . . . it was burning me from the inside. Darkening the world. A bullet would not have ended it. Nothing I could have done to him would have ended it. But in that room today, as I aimed the gun . . . you were there with me. And there was no rage left, suddenly. No darkness. Only thoughts of you.

"So you're not simply the woman I want to protect," he said softly. "You protect *me*. I walked out of that room free, because of you. And when I told you I wanted to bring you here, tonight . . . I called this place my home. But it only feels so when you're here with me."

She opened her eyes to stare at a branch of candles. The flames blurred. "I would always protect you," she said, very low. "That's what I do, for me and mine."

"Yes," he said. "What a great good fortune it is, to be yours."

"Even though I'm . . . who I am?" She wouldn't speak

low of herself. There was no shame in being from White-chapel. Maybe not even shame in being Nick's niece. That look of admiration on Catherine's face tonight—what a pity that she'd had to see it in somebody else before acknowledging it in herself. "The niece of the King of Diamonds. For I don't mean to cut him off, Christian. I won't do his bidding any longer, but he'll always be family. I won't turn away from him, that way."

"I would not ask you to," he said after a pause. "I'll be damned if he uses you again. But he took you in as a child. I wasn't there to protect you then. But he was. And he played a role in making the woman you've become. The woman I want at my back, for as long as I live. I will never ask you to deny him."

Her eyes closed. There was too much beauty in the world. She'd never realized that. It could overwhelm a person, once she knew.

"May I speak to you of a future together?" he asked slowly. "Or would you prefer that I wait?"

"Are you mad?" She turned so quickly that he laughed and caught her by the shoulders.

"Mind your hand," he said.

She tucked it between her breasts for safekeeping. How her heart was pounding. "Speak," she said. "Go ahead."

Smiling, he smoothed her hair from her eyes. "Susseby will be rebuilt. From the ground up. Now, I confess, I've no notion of what it will require, or how long it will take. But I've an idea for a specific room—mirrored in glass. The countryside gets so dark, you see. But in this room, the light of a single candle will illuminate the whole. A music room, I think—always filled with light, no matter the hour."

Wonder prickled over her. She sat up, and he pushed himself up on one elbow, smiling at her. In the wash of light he'd created for her, he looked dipped in gold: his hair, his eyes, his bronzed skin.

Indeed, he looked very cocksure now. "Tell me," she said, unable to resist poking him, "who would want a room so gaudy?"

The dimple appeared in his cheek. "The woman who designs the rest of it. I warn you, she has odd taste in houses. If she can admire a pile like Buckley Hall, then God knows what she'll make of Susseby. But however it turns out, it will be hers." Very gently he stroked her hair. "And, one hopes, her children's, and her children's children, and the seven or eight or hundred generations to follow."

She tried to smile, but her lips were trembling too hard to hold the shape. "You told me once that you were a rogue. Remember?"

He blinked—and then laughed, a startled puff of air. "The first night we met. In that hallway at Everleigh's."

"Yes." She smirked. "Looks like I've ruined you."

He kissed her forehead hard. "So you have. My days of roving may be over. Of course, that depends on your answer."

She caught her breath. "To what?"

He threaded his fingers through her hair. "I love you, Lily Monroe. Will you be my wife? Or will you risk England's wrath by spurning a war hero?"

"No!" Then, just to be clear, she put it differently: "Yes! That is—I'll marry you. God save your soul, you poor toff."

Such radiance in his grin. He leaned forward to kiss her. But they had skipped something, which made her hold him off with one finger laid over his mouth. "Don't you wish to know if *I* love you? Perhaps I only mean to con you into marriage, then rob you blind."

He took her finger between his teeth. Curled his tongue down the fleshy pad, then sucked it deeper, raising a quickening pulse in her belly. How hot his gaze was. "It sounds a fair bargain," he said huskily, "for how busy I mean to keep you."

She wet her lips. "A good thing I do love you, then."

His lids dropped. She saw his nostrils flare. "Once your hand is healed—"

She bit down on her smile. "Distraction is the best medicine for pain. The French are very good at it, I hear." Then, letting her smile bloom, she sank back down into the sheets.

He came over her, grinning like a tiger as he took her hand and placed it carefully above her. "As a patriot and a hero, I cannot allow that insult to stand."

She laughed up at him. "Show me how the English Irish do it, then."

He pounced, devouring her mouth. But after a moment, she started laughing. This joy had to be let out. "Kit's charge," she said. "I've just seen it for myself."

He smiled against her lips. "Let the battle begin."

She gripped his face, to keep him just where she wanted. "The war is over, love. We won."

Keep reading for a sneak peek of

LUCK BE A LADY

The next installment in Meredith Duran's
Rules for the Reckless series

Coming out summer 2015 from Pocket Books!

CHAPTER ONE

London, August 1886

His name is William Pilcher," said Catherine's brother. "And it's no wonder if he stares. He has proposed to marry you."

Catherine choked on her champagne. From her vantage point across the crowded room, William Pilcher made a very poor picture. It was not his looks to which she objected; he had a blandly handsome face, square and straight-boned, and a full head of brown hair. But he hunched in his seat with the gangly laxity of a scarecrow leaking its stuffing.

No doubt that posture was intended to telegraph a fashionable insouciance. But it looked distinctly foolish on a man in his forties. Indeed, his confidence annoyed her. At the beginning of the musicale, she had noticed how fixedly he gazed at her. That was not unusual; men often stared. But by the third aria, Mr. Pilcher's look had grown lecherous. Realizing now that he had finally caught her eye, he offered her a thin, twisting smile. He was congratulating himself, no doubt, on encouraging a spinster's dreams.

Catherine snorted and turned to her brother. At last, she understood his mood tonight—the high color on his face, the poorly restrained excitement. "Peter." She spoke in an undertone, as the soprano launched into Verdi's "O Patria Mia." "For the final time. *You* will not choose my husband."

It was a matter of private regret that she resembled her brother so closely. The cross look that came into his face, and the temper that narrowed his lavender eyes, mirrored her own. "You make no effort to find one. And Mr. Pilcher is a fine prospect. Assistant chairman in the Saint Luke's vestry, with no small prospects. Besides, he has agreed to your terms."

Astonished, she opened her mouth—then thought better of it as the soprano descended into a low, soft note that provided no cover for arguments. Instead, she clutched her program very tightly and glared at the small type: "An Evening of Musical Delights from Italy."

For weeks now, ever since her broken engagement

to Lord Palmer, Peter had been harassing her to find a new suitor. He claimed to think of her happiness. She was nearly twenty-seven, he pointed out. If she did not marry this year, she would remain a spinster. *By the terms of Father's will, you cannot assume equal governance in the company until you are wed. Isn't that your wish?*

But her happiness did not truly concern him—much less the power she might gain once she married and became his full partner at Everleigh's. What he wanted was to marry her to some man who would forbid her to work at all. Then, Peter would have free rein to loot the place. He was already embezzling from the company to fund his political ambitions. He imagined she didn't notice, that her attention was swallowed wholesale by her duties. But he was wrong.

And now he'd solicited a stranger to accept *her terms*? He could only mean the marriage contract she had drawn up with Lord Palmer. But that had been the product of a different moment: Palmer had needed her aid in drawing out a villain, and she, having just discovered Peter's embezzlement, had felt desperate for a powerful ally who might force her brother into line.

In the end, fate had saved her from the rash plan to marry. Palmer had fallen in love with her assistant, Lilah. Their elopement had left Catherine feeling nothing but relief. She did not want a loveless marriage—or any marriage at all. It was not in her nature to be a wife: to subordinate her own desires and needs to a man's, knitting patiently by the fire in expectation of his return from the office. She had her own office, her own work, and a gentleman would never allow that. Better to muddle on independently, then, and find some other way to stem Peter's thieving.

But how? Unless she married, she had no authority to challenge him.

The aria soared to a crescendo. Peter took the opportunity to speak into her ear. "Only say the word. The contract is signed; the license easily acquired."

She snorted. "Lovely. I wish him the best of luck in finding a bride."

"Catherine—"

The sharpness of his voice drew looks from those nearby. Pasting a smile on her lips, she rose and walked out of the salon.

In the hallway, Peter caught up to her, his hand closing on her arm. She pulled away and faced him, still careful to smile, mindful of the guests chatting in an adjoining drawing room. "This isn't the place to discuss this."

He raked his fingers through his blond hair, then winced and smoothed it down again. Always the peacock, ever mindful of his appearance. "At least *meet* him."

"No." She should have known something was awry when he pleaded so sweetly for her to accompany him tonight. Like husbands, polite society had little use for women who worked. Nor was this crowd known to her from the auction house, for it represented the second tier of political and social lights in London—those who aspired to bid at Everleigh's but lacked the funds to merit an invitation. The truly rich were summering now in their country homes, in preparation for hunting season in the north.

Peter, on the other hand, had every reason to associate with this lot. He nursed dreams of a political career. He had managed to gain a seat on the Municipal Board of Works, but such power meant nothing outside London. Among these minor MPs and political cronies, he hoped to lay the groundwork for his future.

The family business had never held his interest. He was looting it in service of his true ambitions. But for her, Everleigh's was *everything*. Their father's legacy. Her sacred birthright. Everleigh's made her who she was—which was not merely a spinster, the "Ice Queen" that rude wits had dubbed her. She was a person of business. An expert in the field of arts and antiquities. A learned professional, regardless of her sex.

And she was done looking for common ground with her brother. "I am leaving," she told him. "Fetch my coat, please."

"You *will* meet him."

She started toward the cloakroom. He caught her wrist, his grip bruising now. "Listen carefully, Catherine. I have practiced patience with you. But you have mistaken it for indulgence. I have given my word to Mr. Pilcher that you will—"

"It will not help your prospects to be seen abusing me."

Peter's hand fell away. Far better to quarrel with him in public than in private, in this regard.

"*You* have given your word," she said in a fierce undertone. "Not me. When he asks where I have gone, simply explain to him the arrogance of your presumption—if indeed you *can* explain it. For it is perfectly incredible."

Peter took a breath through clenched teeth. "If you won't think of yourself, then think of Everleigh's. Don't you wish for children to carry forward the company? What is the future of the auction rooms, if not—"

"Stop it." Anger buzzed through her, her thoughts scattering like a swarm of livid bees. If Peter had his way, there would be no auction house for her fictional children to inherit. He was trying to tap into the principal now. Did he truly think Mr. Wattier, their chief accountant, would not have informed her of that attempt?

But she could not confront him before she had devised a way to check him. She had sworn Mr. Wattier to secrecy, for surprise was the only advantage she possessed. "Think of your own children. Find *yourself* a spouse. But you will leave me be."

"I think of your welfare," he said flatly. "If you do not wish to find yourself homeless and penniless one day, you must marry."

Now he was speaking nonsense. "I am far from penniless. I will remind you that half of Everleigh's belongs to *me*."

His smile made her uneasy, for it smacked of some secret satisfaction. "But you are not a partner in its directorship," he said. "Not until you are married."

That fact never failed to burn her. No doubt Papa had anticipated that she would marry long before the age of twenty-six. But he should have foreseen that Peter would abuse the authority granted to him in the interim.

What she needed, Catherine thought bitterly, was a puppet husband—somebody she could control, or somebody so indifferent that he permitted her to do as she pleased. But Mr. Pilcher would not suit. He was Peter's creature. What she needed was a creature all her own. "Regardless," she said. "Your threats hold no water."

"I have made no threats," Peter said softly. "But I will tell you a fact. If you do not marry, you leave me no choice but to safeguard your future through other means."

She stared at him. "What means that, precisely?"

He shrugged. "I have been thinking of selling the auction rooms."

The breath escaped her in a hoarse gasp.

"Naturally," he went on, "half the profits would go to you."

Had he struck her, here in public, he could not have stunned her more completely. "You . . . you're lying. This is a ruse to make me entertain Mr. Pilcher."

As though her words had summoned him, the scarecrow came into the hall. "Ah!" Pilcher manufactured a look of surprise. "Mr. Everleigh, how good to find you here tonight. And this lovely lady must be—"

"I fear I am no one to you, sir." Catherine kept her eyes on her brother, who *must* be bluffing. But he looked so pleased with himself. Rage roughened her voice. "My brother, however, has an apology to make." She inclined her head the slightest degree to Pilcher—

the only courtesy she could bring herself to pay him—then turned on her heel for the cloakroom.

Peter's voice reached her as she rounded the corner. "She is shy," he said. "Only give me a little time to persuade her."

"For such a vision," said the scarecrow, "I will gladly grant as much time as it requires."

A chill went through her, followed by a surge of panic. She needed a method to deter Peter from this mad course. There was no time to waste.

An idea seized her. Perfect madness—but what other recourse did she have? She knew just the man to bring Peter to heel. All it would require of her was a great deal of money . . . and a reckless disregard for decency and the law.

CHAPTER TWO

Dear Mr. O'Shea,

Your niece, Lilah, Lady Palmer, speaks highly
of your business acumen. I have a proposition
that promises to profit you handsomely. Please
reply at your earliest convenience.

Catherine Everleigh

———— ⚘ ————

Dear Mr. O'Shea,

Your silence suggests that I have given
offense. I would ask you to forgive my

forwardness in writing to you without the precedent of a formal introduction. I had anticipated that we would be introduced at the wedding of your niece to Lord Palmer. In consequence of their elopement, I chose instead to contact you directly. It was an egregious breach of etiquette, for which I apologize.

If you would be so good as to overlook my presumption, I would very much appreciate the chance to speak with you about a prospect that promises a handsome revenue for you. Your niece has assured me that you are a man of fine business sense. I trust you will not dismiss an opportunity for profit without first learning of the details.

Kind regards,
Miss Catherine Everleigh
Proprietor, Everleigh's Auction House

— ◈ —

Dear Mr. O'Shea,

As a particular friend to your niece, Viscountess Palmer (whom you once knew as Lily Monroe but who served in my employ at Everleigh's under the name of "Lilah Marshall," for reasons that <u>you</u> will not require a reminder of), I feel compelled to inquire after your well-being.

As you may know, your niece has embarked on an extended honeymoon abroad. It occurs to me that in her absence, you might have entered into some difficulty that prevents you from replying to the letters of her dear friends.

For her sake, my concern mounts each day that I do not receive a reply from you. Accordingly, I intend to request the police to pay a call tomorrow on the public house in Whitechapel known as Neddie's, where I am given to understand that your whereabouts would be known, were you still at liberty to discourse upon them. I hope very much to receive happy news from the constables of your continued health.

Again, allow me to extend my apologies for the forwardness of presuming an acquaintance that has yet to be formally effected.

Sincerely,
Miss Catherine Everleigh

Catherine,

I can only assume you've taken a hard knock to your head since we last saw each other. Then again, you and Lily were feeling a mite frisky after escaping that Russian bastard, and you were chugging Neddie's ale by the bucketful—so perhaps the night has slipped right from your mind.

But sure and certain you seemed sober enough the time before that, when I knocked Lord Palmer on his well-bred arse at one of your auction-house parties. Perhaps it was my mistake to kiss your hand that night, rather than your sweet little mouth—otherwise you would have remembered our meeting. Alas, that's the gentleman's way, more's the pity.

At any rate, I consider us thoroughly introduced. Put your mind at ease on that front.

As for visiting, don't bother to come if it's business that brings you. I've no interest in the sale of glittery bits, or whatever it is that lures toffs to your auction house like chickens toward a cliff.

However, if you'd like another taste of Whitechapel's finest, the door always stands open to a friend of Lily's—particularly a girl who can put away so many pints. This time, however, I won't be picking up the bill for you—for I am, as you point out, a man of fine business sense, and I know a potential profit when I see one. (Six pints, did you drink? So Neddie swears. But there's a legend gathering steam that says you drank ten.)

Cheers,
Nick O'Shea

P.S. I reckon you'll have remarked that this note was delivered by the superintendent of the Whitechapel Division of the Metropolitan Police. Kind of him, innit? Peelers in Whitechapel are tremendously friendly fellows. I reckon it's because I respect them so. I make sure Neddie never charges them a single penny. But that's business sense for you!

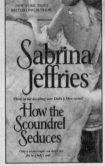